DEDICATION

Throughout the writing and editing of this book I have been supported by numerous encouraging people. But the book itself is dedicated to all the thinkers, doubters and encouragers among us without whom we would be the poorer.

PREFACE

This book contains a hidden meaning. You can take it at face value - a fast-moving adventure story about three children and the way in which they are caught up in a battle between two creatures; the Eagle and the Magpie.

Or you can also read it for hidden meanings. By this I mean the books are an allegory for the spiritual journey that takes place in all human beings as they seek to connect with God. In a loose sense the books trace the fall from that relationship, as shown by the behaviour of Jacob and Rebekkah in the nest, to the mending of the relationship. As the story develops the protagonists are caught up in a battle for hearts and minds between the Eagle and the Magpie. The accounts of human trafficking are used to illustrate the evil to which humans can stoop and is a subject close to my own heart. It is my hope that the books will make you think and possibly generate some discussion about theology, philosophy of religion and injustice.

ACKNOWLEDGMENTS

This book would not have been possible without the encouragement of many friends and family. Thank you for reading it and encouraging me to keep going.

1 THE TAYLOR FAMILY

Rebekkah Taylor was flying high above the human world on the back of a majestic golden eagle. She peered over the pulsating wing and observed the fields below, a huge patchwork quilt came to mind as she floated dreamily above them. Silvery rivers meandered like huge snakes with neither head nor tail. The comparison made her shiver although she was not afraid. As she surveyed the landscape, she was surprised to see the shadow of another bird reflected in the metallic water. Involuntarily, she tightened her grip on the neck of the raptor and turned to look over her shoulder. Squinting into the sun she couldn't see, but she had a strong sense that they were being followed by a malevolent force.

The dream ended abruptly when her brother crashed into her room.

"Rebekkah, have you seen my shoes?" He stood at her door scowling.

She looked at him with distaste. His red hair stood up angrily, and he was getting fatter she noticed, instinctively she swept her

1

fair hair back into a ponytail as she sat up in her bed. "No, I haven't and get out of my room!" She hunted around for a missile which she could throw at him. Her eyes settled on her school reading book, a tedious, dull story that deserved its fate. She picked it up and threw it at him, missed, and it landed pages open, splayed out on the bedroom floor.

Jacob stepped over the book and strode into her space. He stopped at the wardrobe, head pushed forward, glaring at her with large green eyes that reminded her of an elf. A fat elf. Furious, Rebekkah leapt out of bed and pushed her hand against the door. Grabbing her hand and pulling her backwards he then shoved her, causing her to stumble. Deliberately, she lay on the floor and screamed her loudest, most piercing scream. Ignoring her, Jacob wrenched open the wardrobe door and began throwing things into the room.

"Jacob!" his father's voice boomed from the doorway. "Stop that right now! And Rebekkah, stop making that awful noise!"

Jacob stood up, his face was as red as his hair, and he was panting.

The older version of Jacob grabbed at his son, and shook him, "Why do you do these things? What's wrong with you? Go and get ready for school. I haven't got time for this." He spat out the words as he pushed Jacob towards the door.

Jacob turned and smirked at his sister who howled at him.

"I hate you! Look at the mess you've made! Dad, aren't you going to make him tidy it up?"

Mr Taylor paused at the doorway, "I need to get to work! Get dressed Rebekkah, or you'll be late for school. Jacob, you are grounded for the rest of the week!" With that he was gone.

Jacob's room smelt. Not that he cared, but his mother did. The smell came from his shoes, so she had moved them to the cupboard under the stairs. She informed him of this fact when he emerged and sat down at the breakfast table.

Greedily he grabbed the cereal box and poured an excess of chocolate cereal into his bowl, leaving little room for milk. Oblivious, he added the liquid anyway, and most leaked onto the table forming a pool of light brown liquid. The cloth was plastic for ease of cleaning, so the liquid kept moving. His mother concentrating on her tablet was unaware of the chocolate stream trickling across the table towards her mug of black coffee. On reaching the drink, it was quickly encircled. Absent-mindedly, she picked it up and a large drop of milk plopped onto her newly ironed skirt. Sensing the invasion, she looked down to see the milky stain spreading on the thin material. Springing to her feet, she began yelling at Jacob, whilst dabbing furiously at her skirt with a dishcloth.

Rebekkah entered the kitchen, neat and petite in her blazer and striped shirt. She looked anxiously at her mother, who could be vicious once riled. Right on cue a dishcloth was thrown at Jacob with the instruction to clean up the mess he had made. It wrapped itself around Jacob's head and flopped over his nose.

"Oh, gross! That really stinks!" shouted Jacob, unwinding the cloth from his face.

Rebekkah suppressed a giggle, it served Jacob right. She grabbed yoghurt from the fridge and tore off the top.

Their father joined them and helped himself to coffee from the machine. He was grumpy, had been for days.

His wife looked at her watch, "It's time to go. Hurry up you two!"

Jacob grabbed his shoes and jammed his feet into them without loosening the laces. Rebekkah picked up her bag and made her way to the car. As they left, Rebekkah turned her head to look out of the window. High above her she could see a beautiful bird of prey gliding on the thermals. It recalled her dream and calmed her.

2 JACOB AT SCHOOL

Jacob was bored by school. At 13 he considered himself superior to most other children in his class and was counting the days to when he could leave this babyish middle school and attend a senior school. Most of what he was taught he thought pointless. The only subjects he valued were those involving science and maths. He could see a use for them. Why didn't they teach computer programming and engineering instead of history, English and religious education? RE was particularly pointless he thought to himself as he sat waiting for the teacher to arrive. Religion was for primitive people who had a need to explain the unexplainable in a pre-scientific universe. Now that we have science, he believed there was no need for such superstitious beliefs. And why inflict those beliefs on him? As if he wanted to know about how Muslims pray. Or, how to label the inside of a church? Nobody went to church now anyway. And Hinduism, what was that about? Their heroes seemed to be skinny men sitting around meditating, just so they could be reborn as something better. Ridiculous!

He leant over to his friend and suggested they play a game on their phones while the lesson was on. The teacher bustled in. She wore tweed suits and a blouse that was too tight. Too much cake! Wouldn't it be funny if her buttons popped off? Jacob shared this thought with his friend who sniggered. Miss Preston was always disorganised and late. She claimed she had been seeing a parent, but Jacob reckoned she had been in the staff room having another cup of tea and a biscuit. Her breath always smelled of tea.

She moved a few books around the desk, dropped a pen on top of them and began hunting around the floor for it. Face flushed from bending low, she stood up, pushed her glasses down her nose, stared at the children in front of her and finally started the lesson, "Today we are going to talk about miracles. Can anyone tell me what a miracle is?"

Felicity's hand shot straight up. Felicity's family went to church. She was annoying.

Jacob decided to interrupt, "If my mum lets me have a lie-in on a Saturday," he shouted rudely. There was laughter, he sat forward pleased with the attention.

Miss Preston looked at him, annoyed, "Jacob don't shout out! Put your hand up. Felicity, you were first."

As expected, the tedious girl had the right answer, "It's when something happens against the laws of nature, Miss Preston. Like when Jesus healed the man with the withered arm."

"Yes, that's right. Well done! We are going to read about a miracle, and I want you to create a newspaper article of the event, writing about it as if you were there."

Jacob groaned inwardly. This was just the sort of task he hated. He had to do something quickly to distract her and get some fun out of the lesson. "Miss Preston, as there is no proof that miracles do happen, can I write the article in such a way as to describe Jesus as a con man who tricks people?"

The woman clicked her tongue, exasperated, "No, you cannot Jacob. The point of the exercise is to describe accurately what you have seen and to use your imagination. Think about how the people might have felt. They were poor, they had no doctors, and a man with a withered arm would not be able to work. This was a great act of kindness and would have changed his life and circumstances forever."

Jacob was enjoying himself, "Well, that's the point Miss Preston; I haven't seen it have I? It's not like writing about David over there picking his nose. I can see that with my own eyes." The class tittered and some laughed. Jacob sat back in his seat and picked up his pen. He began tapping it on the desk. He did this when agitated as it helped calm him down.

The teacher was becoming flustered, "Look David, I mean Jacob…this is not a philosophy lesson. If I wanted to discuss whether miracles happen, then I would set you a different task. You need to be able to describe a miracle."

"But Miss, I can't describe something that I haven't seen or don't agree happened. Do you have any proof that miracles still happen today?" he sat back in his chair tapping his pen on the table.

Miss Preston was becoming increasingly flustered and two little pink marks appeared on her cheeks just underneath her eyes. "Well, there's the miracle of creation and the wonderful miracle of birth."

"But Miss, didn't you just say that a miracle is against the laws of nature...there's a perfectly natural explanation for birth." He paused for effect, looking around the class with a knowing grin. "And the earth was caused by the Big Bang not God."

The class were listening attentively, enjoying the entertainment. Then, the annoying Felicity came to her beleaguered teacher's defence. "There's a man in our church who was healed of cancer after we prayed for him. The doctors said it was a miracle because he only had a few days to live, and they had given up on him."

Miss Preston mopped her brow and nodded with relief, "Yes! Good! That's a wonderful example Felicity, thank you. Now class, let's get on with the task, we only have a few minutes left. That includes you, Jacob. In fact, I shall be reading yours first."

Jacob opened his mouth and then shut it.

He would get Felicity later.

3 REBEKKAH AT SCHOOL

Rebekkah loved school. She had a little crush on her teacher who was calm, kind and enthusiastic. Whatever Rebekkah did she seemed delighted with. This was in stark contrast to her mother who was always critical and was hard to please. Rebekkah ran into school and found her peg. There was the usual chatter and excitement interspersed by squeals of delight when someone showed something especially cute on their phone.

"Look Rebekkah, Grace has a Labrador puppy, isn't she adorable?" Rebekkah hung up her coat and dropped her bag on the floor. She adjusted her ponytail and then peered at the tiny image on the screen as it was thrust into her face.

"Mmm…oh she's so beautiful. What's her name?"

"Honey."

"Awww that's so cute. I'd love a dog." The bell went for morning school, Rebekkah slipped her arm into her friend's, and they ran towards the classroom door expecting to see Miss Bates who usually stood in the entrance to greet them. Instead, there was a different teacher whom they had never seen before.

"Hello girls I'm your teacher today. Miss Bates is unwell." Rebekkah's heart sank. Her feelings about the day ahead immediately took a nosedive. The teacher turned to Rebekkah and Grace.

"That's not really an appropriate way to come into the classroom, is it? We are 11 years old, not babies. Go back into the cloakroom and come in properly as befits girls of your age."

Grace and Rebekkah unlinked arms and slowly went back into the cloakroom. They looked at each other and Rebekkah pulled a face. "She's a bit of a witch, isn't she? Miss Bates never minds us linking arms. Who does she think she is? Old bat, she looks about 90 and did you see that wart on the end of her nose? Wouldn't want to get too close to her on a dark night..." Rebekkah tailed off as she noticed the look of horror on her friend's face. Slowly she turned round to find the battle-axe standing right behind her. She had a weird look on her face.

"Get in the classroom both of you; we haven't got all day. Your parents are not paying for you to stand here gossiping. I thought you would have better manners than this. I shall be keeping my eye on you two and don't think you are sitting together; collect your things and sit away from each other."

Rebekkah felt tears prickling at the back of her eyes. "But Miss..." she realised she had no idea what the teacher was called. "Miss Bates always lets us sit together."

"Miss Bates is not here, and she is clearly far too soft with you. Hurry up or you will be sitting in the corridor. And my name is Miss Cannon."

The lesson did not improve. It was clear Miss Cannon had no intention of forgetting and forgiving. She took every opportunity to pick holes in Rebekkah's work. In English she stood at Rebekkah's shoulder reading every word. Every so often she would point out an error in punctuation or tut loudly when she spelt something wrong. At one stage she threw a dictionary at her. In maths she asked Rebekkah to answer the most difficult questions and when she stammered that she did not understand, rolled her eyes upwards questioning whether she had been awake in any of her lessons. By lunchtime Rebekkah was a nervous wreck. She and Grace went off to the nurse together but to their horror found Miss Cannon sitting with Mrs Band chatting and drinking a cup of tea together. The nurse looked up expectantly at the two girls as they came in.

Grace looked at Rebekkah and rather lamely said, "Rebekkah has a tummy ache."

Miss Cannon fixed her small piggy eyes on Rebekkah. "These two are hypochondriacs, Stephanie. I have been teaching them all morning and neither of them complained of anything wrong. I think they are just trying to get out of their afternoon lessons. Don't worry; I shall make sure they have plenty to do to keep their minds off themselves. Don't be so pathetic girls."

The nurse looked at Miss Cannon and then back to Rebekkah. Impatiently she waved them both away. To her horror Rebekkah realised Mrs Band was also scared of Miss Cannon and there would be no refuge in her office.

The afternoon was no better. In science she was forced to work with Freda. How did Miss Cannon know that no one wanted to work with Freda? Freda was a loner and preferred to work on her own. She tried to control everything and would not share. She also went into long complicated explanations about things that were completely irrelevant and used long words that Rebekkah did not understand. Once, Miss Bates had gathered the class together and had tried to explain that Freda was a bit different to other children. She found it difficult to make friends and they should all make a special effort with her. Rebekkah made a special effort to avoid her.

In this lesson they were studying the body's circulation system. They had to find each other's pulses and explain why, after exercise, the pulse rate got quicker. As evidence, they had to take each other's pulses and write down the resting rate and then the new rate after exercising. With Grace this would have been fun, but Freda hated anyone touching her and insisted on taking her own pulse rate. Initially, she could not find it and pulled back sharply from Rebekkah when she tried to help. When she did find the little beat in her wrist, she went white as a sheet and had to sit down.

"What's the matter now?" Rebekkah was getting really

frustrated and worried that Miss Cannon would tell them off if they did not complete the task.

Freda looked at Rebekkah with a pained expression on her face, "I don't like the feeling of it."

Frustrated, Rebekkah grabbed her wrist, "Come on; don't be so silly. You can't see the blood. It's underneath your skin."

Freda snatched her hand away from Rebekkah and started screaming. "Don't touch me. I told you not to touch me."

Then the dreaded thing happened. Miss Cannon strode over to them both. Legs astride, hands on hips, piggy eyes glaring, she descended on Rebekkah. "What have you done to Freda, you wicked girl?"

Freda was now building up to a crescendo. Miss Cannon moved towards her. Scared that she might be touched again, Freda ran out of the classroom and down the corridor wailing.

"This is all your fault," hissed Miss Cannon. Pointing at Grace, she ordered her to go and get the nurse while telling Rebekkah to sit down, "I'll deal with you later."

Rebekkah really did feel sick now. The class was completely silent and stared at her. It seemed an eternity before the nurse arrived, red in the face and out of breath. Rebekkah wondered what her pulse rate would be at this moment in time.

Miss Cannon stepped outside the classroom so no one could hear the conversation. Meanwhile from the classroom window Freda could be seen running down the road towards the bus stop. A few moments later the nurse could be seen running down the road after her. It would have been funny had Rebekkah not been so scared. Miss Cannon came back in and closed the door. "That's it, girls, the show is over."

"But Miss, will Freda be alright?" asked Claire.

Miss Cannon brushed her off, "Of course, she will be. The nurse is with her." She turned threateningly towards Rebekkah, "That's no thanks to you though, Rebekkah. The bell is about to go. Pack up everyone but not you Rebekkah. I am not done with you yet."

Everyone rushed out. Rebekkah slowly packed her things into her bag. Her hands were shaking; she wished she were on the bus and a zillion miles from school.

Miss Cannon wandered around the room tapping her stubby fingers on the tabletops. She was humming to herself. It suddenly dawned on Rebekkah that she was stretching the moment to create maximum tension. Torn between fear and anxiety about missing her bus she eventually plucked up the courage to speak. "Miss Cannon, I have a bus to catch, and my brother will be waiting for me." She looked up at the woman standing just two desks away from her. She had a strange smile on her face, almost menacing. "Rebekkah, today has not been a good day. You have got off to a very bad start with me. Miss Bates will be away for some time, and I shall be your teacher. I don't like what I see of you, but you must have some redeeming features. So far, you appear to me to be dim, rude, and impossible to work with. I don't think you should be here. You need to show me that you deserve your place at this highly academic and well thought of school. We don't want numbskulls like you bringing down its reputation. Over the weekend you will do some research on the circulation of blood in the human body. I expect a three hundred word essay on it.

No cut and paste from the Internet. It will be your own words. Do you understand?"

Rebekkah nodded glumly, picked up her school bag and ran out of the door. Hurtling down the road, bag in hand she fleetingly noticed a large magpie perched on the branch of a tree. As she jumped on the bus, the bird cackled with laughter. Startled, she settled into her seat breathing heavily. As the bus pulled away, the bird bounced off its branch and pursued the vehicle until finally it fell away and disappeared into the woods. Uneasily Rebekkah followed it with her eyes, it was bizarre but, it reminded her of her dream.

4 THE JOURNEY HOME

On leaving school, Jacob stopped by the school garden to collect a few unmentionables. He still had revenge in mind for Felicity and her friends. The bus arrived and he noted with glee that the driver was Old Spike. He was only interested in getting them home as fast as possible. He would stop for nothing.

The bus journey proved to be hugely entertaining. Jacob had somehow got hold of some worms and spent the journey dropping them onto various unsuspecting girls. Soon, the bus was in uproar with children squealing and shrieking. The bus driver had tried yelling for everyone to sit down and be quiet, but this only added to the pandemonium. In the end, much against his instinct to just drive on regardless, he was forced to pull over and find out what all the fuss was about. He was a tall, thin man with heavily greased spiky hair that stood on end. His face was already red and sweaty from the exertion of shouting. He marched down the aisle of the bus halting only to pick up a few of the wriggling creatures that he ejected through an open window. It did not take long for him to find out that Jacob was the culprit. He had ill advisedly (as Jacob knew his rights) grabbed the boy by his arm and dragged him down to the front of the bus where he shoved him onto an empty seat. Muttering about rude, middle-class twerps with too much money, the driver had demanded to know his full name.

When Jacob got home his mother was standing at the door waiting for him. She did not look at all happy. Apparently, the bus driver had phoned school and they in turn had phoned home. Jacob was sent to bed without any tea. When Jacob protested that the bus driver had manhandled him and called him a middle-class twerp his father cuffed him across the ear and said that he was a spoilt brat. He then got a lecture about how lucky he was because when his father was a lad, they used to cane boys like him. Anyway, time out in his room wasn't so bad as he had stashed away a box of sweets and biscuits for just such an occasion as this and it was better than lamb stew any day! It also got him out of the agony of dinnertime conversation and nags about manners.

Rebekkah, left on her own with her parents, found dinnertime interminable. They were arguing and bickering about plans for

21

the weekend. Apparently, they had all been invited to a christening. Her father did not want to go because he said it would be boring and he had loads of work to do. Her mother had snapped back at him that she had had to sit through his mother's 70th birthday with all his dreadful relatives and at least this was a celebration of the beginning of life, not the end when his mother was going senile.

Rebekkah was quite interested in the event itself. "What's a christening?" she had asked. She was quite horrified by the answer - a child, against her will, was splashed with cold water and oil but apparently (according to dad) this was preferable to circumcision which Jews and Muslims did to induct their children into the faith. Part of her wished it was a circumcision as it would have been fun to see Jacob's reaction. She carried her plate to the sink and excused herself as she had a lot of homework to do. That always worked.

Saturday passed uneventfully. Jacob was grounded and spent the day in his room. Rebekkah did her homework and then sat watching TV. She liked Saturdays as she could catch up on all the programmes missed during the week. Wistfully, she wished her mum would come and watch something with her. But she was always too busy.

That night she slept fitfully and dreamt extensively. She was constantly being chased, by whom she had no idea, but there was an ominous presence, a darkness from which she could not escape. She would run but seemed to make no progress. The darkness just got closer. Afraid, she called out for help. Then, as if from nowhere, a huge bird descended from the sky and caught her in its talons. Moving soundlessly through the air she was aware of being tightly held and very safe. After a while a tree came into view and the bird dropped her into it. The branches shook and snapped as she bounced from one to another.

Then a voice broke into her dream. "Rebekkah, Rebekkah, wake up! We need to get going." She opened her eyes to see her mother's face looming over her. The shaking was caused by her mother who had her by the shoulder and was roughly pushing at her. Rebekkah groaned and turned over. At least it was not Monday.

Over breakfast she tried to talk to Jacob. He was grumpy and uncommunicative,"Jacob, have you ever had a dream that you can remember?"

He reached in front of her and grabbed some toast. He slapped some butter on it and then stuck the buttery knife in the honey leaving yellow streaks in its golden syrup. Normally she would have told on him, mother would be cross that he had not used the honey spoon. However today she swallowed her indignation and tried again,"Jacob? Have you ever had a dream that you can remember?"

"No." he said shortly, munching his way through the toast.

She watched as the over laden bread released a trickle of honey down the side of his hand,"Jacob, lick your hand before it goes on the cloth." For once he did as he was told. She pressed on, hoping his compliance might mean a conversation,"Last night I dreamt that a large bird saved me."

"Saved you? From what?" Jacob mumbled as he licked the honey off his hand.

"Well, that's just it. I don't really know. I was being chased by something. Something dark and horrible and the bird scooped me up in her claws and saved me. It was so real."

Jacob stared at her. He lowered his voice to a whisper and leaned in close. "Something dark and horrible," he whispered. And then he paused for effect, "LIKE THIS!" He roared; twisting his face into a grotesque shape, tongue out, teeth bared. Rebekkah screamed.

Their mother peered at them from behind the Travel section of the Sunday papers and yelled at them both to go and get ready for church.

5 THE CHRISTENING

It was a beautiful warm and sunny day. Everyone looked smart if a little grumpy as they drove to the church. Jacob was ominously quiet; *Probably planning something*, thought Rebekkah. She was upset that he had not taken her dream seriously; she had also been told about the worm incident and was not at all surprised as Jacob frequently played tricks on her. It served him right and she hoped he would get punished at school as well.

The church was old with beautiful stone arches. The inside smelt musty and was cool after the warmth outside. Rebekkah waited for her eyes to adjust to the light. It was very beautiful with sweeping arches made of a rich, dark wood. Her eyes were drawn upwards to the ceiling that was extremely high and shaped like an upturned boat. The family were welcomed by a smiley lady who gave them a sheet of paper and a book. Her mother was busy scanning the congregation, looking for a familiar face while her father stood and scowled. His mood was as dark as the wooden pews they were ushered towards. Jacob picked up the cushion that was at everyone's feet and sat on it. Mother jabbed him in the ribs and bringing her face very close to his so others could not hear, hissed at him to put it back. Apparently, it was for kneeling on not sitting. Rebekkah thought that on this occasion Jacob was right. She would have had a better view if she had been elevated on the cushion. She sighed audibly when a very tall man and his family sat in front of her.

"Great," moaned Jacob, "can't see anything, can't speak, can't play games; welcome to the house of fun!"

The man must have heard because he shifted sideways so that he was sitting in front of their father.

The service was a sandwich of hymns, prayers and readings. The vicar, a jolly man dressed in a white dress with a collar was doing his utmost to be entertaining. But he was not. Instead, Rebekkah found herself fascinated by the lectern from which the Bible was read. It was made out of brass and perched on top of it was a magnificent eagle standing with its wings spread out and its neck raised. It looked up into the ceiling as if it longed to be free of the burden on its back. As she stared at it, she realised that it was very similar to the bird in her dream. She found herself zoning out from the vicar's voice. Closing her eyes she imagined what it would be like to fly with the Eagle. The church slipped away with its musty smell and hushed voices. Instead, she could feel the air rushing into her face, the rhythm of its wings, while beneath her the earth rushed by. "Oh Eagle," she murmured. "Take me away from school so I don't have to see Miss Cannon again."

Jacob poked her in the ribs, making her jump, "Look! This is more like it!"

Snatched rudely from her reverie, she glowered at Jacob, but her attention was immediately grabbed by the spectacle of the child who was soon to be christened running gleefully along the front of the church. His mother, uncertain what to do and not wanting to draw attention to herself, bent down low as if avoiding divine fire and ran after him. He, thinking it a game ran even faster and began to chuckle. Rebekkah looked at the vicar who carried on talking while his eyes followed the little child. All eyes were now on the chase. The toddler, finding his way barred by adults, dropped to his knees, scampered up the stairs, past the wrought iron rail where worshippers had knelt before their God for centuries and up to the altar. Spotting a place to hide, he scampered under the white tablecloth, which swallowed him up. His mother, now a deep shade of pink dropped to her knees and peeped under the table. He shuffled backwards on his bottom in order to avoid her grasp. Loud giggles emanated from the tablecloth. No one was listening to the vicar.

"The only way she is going to get that kid is if she goes under the table herself," whispered Jacob. He was sitting forward in his seat, eyes glittering with enjoyment.

Sure enough, the woman, after several wild sweeps of the hand under the cloth, ducked her head and crawled under the table. There was a scream of rage; the cloth bulged to the left and then, out they both came, like Jonah from the mouth of the whale. She was red in the face, and he was absolutely furious at losing the game. The vicar, undeterred, cleared his throat and bellowed above the noise, "Now, as we move into the next bit of our service there's something I would like to show you all." Seemingly oblivious to the uproar around him, he scooped his hand under his cassock and triumphantly, as if he were God himself and had just created it from nothing, held up a small bottle.

"This," he said, "is holy water, brought from the River Jordan itself." He paused dramatically for effect. One or two adults looked up but most continued to watch the pantomime of mother with struggling child who had now reached the pew from which the escape had been made. Pressing on, the vicar asked, "Now children, who can tell me what is special about the River Jordan?" Silence followed, only broken by the hiccoughing of the star of the show, who had been given some chocolate to eat as a distraction.

His father leaned towards Jacob. "It's where Jesus was baptised."

Jacob glowered at his father, "I'm not saying that I'll look like I'm a member of the God Squad. You say it."

Rebekkah had her hand up. "It's where Jesus was baptised and it's in Israel."

The vicar beamed at her. Her father looked at her and winked. Jacob raised his eyes upwards in disgust. Mother smiled indulgently at her daughter. The private education was paying off. She looked around to ensure that everyone had noticed that it was her daughter who had answered the question.

The vicar raised his arms and swept to the back of the church. "Follow me," he called, "we are now going to baptise young David using drops of water that have come from the very same river in which our Lord Jesus was baptised. Children, come to the front so you can see what's happening. Adults, please make room for the children."

Rebekkah shyly joined the children while Jacob hung back. The vicar stood behind the font, which looked to Jacob like a large birdbath. The parents of little David joined him. David's dad was holding him tightly lest he run off again. The child had a chocolate dribble emerging from his mouth. Jacob watched, fascinated by the gooey mess that dripped into the waters of the font. An older lady in a white smock reached forward with a tissue and tapped the mother on the arm. Confused, the mother looked at the lady who nodded encouragingly towards the child's mouth while touching her own lips.

Little David, however, was distracted by a large, swinging chain at the bottom of which was a bauble containing incense. It was

31

perilously close to his fingers and Jacob willed him to grab it and swing from it. The boy, distracted by the large ornate silvery bowl was taken unawares when the vicar began daubing his forehead with oil and then splashed some water over his head. The little boy's lips puckered, and he reached over to his mother calling for her. The vicar quickly lit a candle and gave it to the dad to hold while mum turned sideways to allow David a better view of the light. The toddler, once again made bold by distraction, reached over to grab the candle that dropped from its holder and with a loud plop fell into the font. There was an audible gasp from the watching congregation. Jacob grinned. The vicar, ever the true professional, pressed on regardless. A steamroller came to mind.

Finally, it was over, and they could eat.

Jacob and Rebekkah sat in a corner as near to the food as they could get without being conspicuous. They did not talk; they had nothing to say to each other. Rebekkah got up to help herself to more food and as she re-joined her brother at the table, he groaned, "Look out, that vicar's coming this way!"

Sure enough, he stopped at their table. "Enjoying the chocolate cake?" He enquired.

Jacob took a huge bite and nodded hoping this would deter the man from asking him any more questions.

Instead, he pulled up a chair and turned to Rebekkah. "You're the girl who answered my question about the River Jordan aren't you?"

Rebekkah nodded.

"Have you ever been to the Holy Land?" He enquired?

Jacob could not resist having a pop at this man who held such ridiculous beliefs. His mouth, now empty, blurted out: "The Holy Land. Why is it called that? No land is holy. All land is the same."

The vicar looked at him. "Well, it's where our Lord was born and so that makes it unique and special to God."

"I don't believe there is a God and if there's no God then it's not holy, is it?" Jacob was belligerent, his chin jutted out and two red spots appeared under his green eyes.

Rebekkah squirmed with embarrassment, "Jacob, that's not very polite."

The vicar smiled kindly at her, "No, that's all right. I can understand why you might think that. What's your name?"

Jacob reluctantly told him his name.

The vicar pressed on, it occurred to Rebekkah that Jacob would be no match for a man who could talk over the top of a screaming toddler. She relaxed a little.

"Jacob, why don't you believe there is a God?"

"Because I can't believe in something I can't see." Jacob's fists were clenched as he answered. This subject mattered to him, thought Rebbekah.

The vicar looked thoughtful, and then waved his arms around as he spoke, "When we look at a beautiful painting, we don't have to know or see the artist to know someone painted it. Isn't it the same with earth? It is a beautiful and well-designed place. Surely a being with creativity and imagination must have created it?"

Jacob looked disdainfully at him, "Why? Science tells us that it evolved. Anyway, the earth isn't well designed. There are earthquakes and volcanoes. Would you excuse me for a minute, I need to go to the bathroom?"

Jacob stood up and went to the toilet. On his return he found the vicar in earnest conversation with his sister. He tripped as he approached the table and put his hand out to save himself from falling to the floor. In so doing his hand pressed against the vicar's back.

The vicar jumped, but recovered his composure and asked, "Are you okay Jacob? Good job I was here, or you could have had a nasty fall. Anyway, nice talking to you both, enjoy the rest of your day." The man stood up and as he turned away Rebekkah could see that a piece of paper appeared to be stuck to his jumper.

On it were written the words: *I think stupid things therefore I am stupid.*

"Oh, Jacob that's so rude," gasped Rebekkah.

"He's an idiot," sneered Jacob. "Don't tell me you believe in all those fairy stories too?"

"No! Of course not," she stammered, "But my teacher Miss Bates says that she has seen an angel and she talks to God."

Jacob mimicked her: "My teacher says...Miss Bates says...but you haven't, have you? She's just as barmy as that vicar and so are you. It's because you are a girl, girls are soft in the head."

"Jacob!" His father's voice interrupted him; "I want a word with you."

6 THE FLIGHT

Jacob was sent to bed as soon as they got home. Apparently, he was a disgrace and an embarrassment. His sister on the other hand was the best daughter any parent could wish to have. "Little do they know," thought Jacob, "She makes things up and lies."

He reached under the pillow for the small electronic gadget he had hidden and switched it on.

He could hear his parents talking loudly downstairs. If Jacob had been more sensitive, he would have listened in and heard them arguing. However, the adult world was of no interest to him. He was briefly aware of a plate being dropped on the floor and a shout, which he assumed was of annoyance at the breakage. There were some clanking noises as mum emptied the dishwasher and then, silence. He guessed they were both working; at least they would not be back upstairs and bothering him.

Absorbed in his game he was unaware of the strange glow that appeared outside his window and was startled by a gentle tapping against the frame. Curious, he swung his legs out of the bed and peeked underneath the curtain. Two unblinking hazel eyes looked back at him. Startled, he dropped the curtain and drew back into bed. His first inclination was to shout but something held him back and he did not. Dad was in no mood for jokes and if he called out and it turned out that nothing was there, he would be grounded for a million years. No, he would have to look again. Slowly he pulled back the curtain and then he saw it, a beautiful golden eagle was peering through the glass at him.

"God! You scared me," he said and then to his surprise the bird answered him. "Don't be afraid, Jacob."

"You spoke! You can speak! I must be dreaming. I can't believe this is happening to me." Jacob rubbed his eyes. And stared.

"Jacob? Jacob? Who are you talking to?" It was Rebekkah. Excited, Jacob jumped out of bed and ran to the door. "Look out of the window, there's an eagle outside." It was odd, when he later replayed it in his mind, that he never thought she might scream or scoff at him. They so rarely shared any moments of childhood intimacy or affection that he suddenly felt shy and a bit embarrassed.

Rebekkah, unaware of her brother's sudden discomfort, ran to the window and looked out.

"Oh," she gasped and took a step back in shock. "There's a huge bird outside; it's trying to say something."

"You can hear it too?" Jacob looked at her in shock. His little sister, usually so babyish and infantile suddenly seemed older and surprisingly unafraid. He was not sure what he expected when he invited her into his room; screams perhaps but not this.

Rebekkah turned to her brother, a shy smile on her face, "This is the same eagle that I saw in my dream. You know the one I told you about this morning, over breakfast. Oh, Jacob this is amazing!"

Jacob opened his mouth to say something sarcastic and then promptly shut it. He turned back to the window and looked at the Eagle waiting patiently for a response. Gingerly he flicked the catch on the casement and pushed it open. The Eagle stepped to one side, her claws balancing on the window ledge.

"Hello Rebekkah, we meet again. Are you ready to fly?"

"Oh yes, please," said Rebekkah instinctively, "Can I climb on your back? Come on, Jacob!"

"Wait a minute," stammered Jacob. *What is all this about?* He thought quickly. *I must be dreaming. That's it. I fell asleep and now Rebekkah is in my dream. A bit weird especially after we had been talking about dreams.* He pinched himself.

Meanwhile Rebekkah had climbed onto the Eagle's back and settled herself deep within the soft feathers. "Oh come on, Jacob, it's like being in a gigantic feather bed."

Carefully he edged out of the window and placed a cautious foot on the Eagle's back. The huge bird as if waiting for him to make the first move, reached behind her picked him up with her beak and placed him behind Rebekkah on her back. He then felt the tension in her muscles as she sprang off the windowsill and soared into the night sky. Terrified, he grabbed as many feathers as he could and crouched down into the downy forest of bony fluff. It was hard to keep still as the motion of the wings meant he could feel his seat moving up and down.

"Relax!" called the great bird. "The more you fight the movement the more tired you will become. You won't fall. Let go and lie back. Copy your sister!"

Sure enough, Rebekkah seemed to have done this before, she was lying back and gazing up at the stars. "Isn't it beautiful, Jacob?" she whispered.

"Where are we going? Where are you taking us?" Jacob shouted, unable to relax and still holding on for dear life.

The Eagle turned its head slightly so Jacob could hear her above the rushing wind. "To the nest."

And that was it. Air rushed past Jacob's head. He was glad it was dark so he couldn't see the ground. He didn't have a great head for heights and his stomach was surging between feelings of excitement and terror. At one point he thought he was going to be sick but fortunately this subsided. He was bemused as to how his baby sister could be so calm. He would have liked to talk to her, but he was scared of moving in case he fell off and tumbled to the ground. He examined the Eagle as she flew; her wings were enormous and well out of proportion to the rest of

her. She had a short neck, which she kept steady while flying.
He suddenly realised why the flight was so smooth; after the
initial flapping to get them aloft she was gliding. His mind, ever
questioning and curious became detached and observant; she
appeared to be using the minimum of effort to soar. He
remembered reading somewhere that eagles used updrafts and
thermals to move. Her centre of gravity was between the wings,
his dad had told him that sitting over the wing on a plane was
statistically the safest part of an aircraft. As his mind began to
work once more, logic took over and he began to relax. They
were lying between the wings; they were safe.

In what seemed like an age, they just lay and watched the stars.
He had a sense of being very small in a wondrous universe. He
had never felt like that before. A shooting star careered across
the sky and headed into the enormous vastness of space. He
wanted to cry with the sheer joy of it all. And then, as abruptly
as it had started, the journey ended. The Eagle suddenly
adjusted her position and began to flap her wings; she appeared
to be descending. After several moments of complete and utter
terror she lowered her feet and swooped at speed into a tree.

Crashing through the branches the children held on for dear life as the Eagle seemed to accelerate. Jacob heard himself shouting but the words were snatched from him drifting upwards into a different world. Rebekkah, white as a sheet, was crouched deep into the backbone of the bird's body holding on for dear life. And then, mercifully, it stopped. The canopy of the tree opened and welcomed them into what appeared to be a large nest. Landing gently She shook her feathers vigorously and deposited them both on the floor. They appeared to have arrived.

"Now sleep," She said. "You must both be exhausted. There will be plenty of time for talking in the morning." With that She gently picked up each child by their pyjama tops and placed them carefully onto a feather bed. Both children slept.

7 JACOB AND THE NEST

Jacob was woken by a nudging movement. Slowly, he opened his eyes and then shot bolt upright on his bed. A few feathers floated lazily up in the air and just as slowly descended back to earth. The Eagle stared at him with her big hazel eyes, only this time it was daylight, and he could see her hooked beak and talons. He edged himself into a corner, arms hugging his folded knees.

Please don't hurt me, he thought.

The Eagle laughed a rich sonorous sound that reverberated around the nest. "Jacob, if I had wanted to hurt you, I would have already done so. You are my friend and my guest. Your sister is already awake. Come let us take a walk together."

The Eagle bounced from one foot to another, her claws spread like starfish on the uneven ground. Jacob stole a sideways look at her. He had never been so close to such a majestic bird of prey. Her head and neck pushed forward as She strutted along.

Her legs were strong, the feathers hung like baggy trousers. Her wings were pressed against Her sides. Jacob thought She looked far less intimidating than She had done last night. Her head was large for a bird, Her beak and eyes moved from side to side as She walked. He could see that She was taking everything in, constantly assessing all about her. Jacob had to run to keep up.

The Eagle told Jacob that as Her guest he could go wherever he wanted and eat whatever he wanted. However there was one rule. In the centre of the garden grew a tree. This tree had the appearance of holding good fruit but eating from it would bring dire consequences. Jacob wanted to know why, his instinct was always to challenge any instruction that came without a clear and reasoned explanation. The Eagle stopped and turned to face him. Breathing deeply, he looked deep into Her eyes. Her gaze was steady, unblinking and uncompromising. What he saw filled him with fear and he looked away.

After a long uncomfortable pause the Eagle finally spoke, "You will know the tree by its golden trunk and silver leaves. There are no others quite like it. Jacob, listen to me! Do not eat

45

anything that you find growing on that tree however attractive or tasty it may appear. Do you understand? If you do, then I can no longer protect you here."

Then with a flap of Her wings she was gone.

Jacob was troubled by the way the Eagle had spoken to him. He was accustomed to being told off, but this was different. It was as if the Eagle had looked deep within him and found a dark shadow in his soul.

He shook himself. It was time to stop this ridiculous introspection. He did not believe in a soul anyway. He wasn't sure where he was nor whether he was dreaming but decided to make the most of it anyway. He looked around him. There were trees to climb. His parents had always told him not to climb trees in case he fell or tore his trousers. But here he could do what he liked. Joyously he ran to a tree and grasped the gnarled trunk. His fingers found a crevice, he lifted his right foot onto a knobbly bit and up he went. Exhilarated he climbed and he climbed until he found himself swinging in the very tops of the trees. The view was fantastic, he could see for miles. To his right he caught sight of a river with a boat. Another thing his parents had told him he could not do was to swim in a fresh-water river in case he got a stomach upset or a chill. Excitedly he dropped from branch to branch and landed with a thump on the ground. He ran towards the river, untied the boat, grabbed the fishing net and pushed off. Under the seat was a hamper. Opening it he found all his favourite food inside; hot chip butties and ketchup, crisps, little sausages and jelly all to be washed down with real lemonade. He had a great feeling of liberation as he ate the food and tucked the hamper back under the seat. He peered over the side of the boat into the glistening water. Fish darted under the boat and out the other side as if to say, 'join us.' Ignoring his mother's voice which was telling him he had to wait a full hour after eating before he could swim, he pulled off his clothes and jumped into the water gasping at the delicious coolness. This was fun!

He took a deep breath and dived to the bottom of the river touching the smooth stones with his hands. He was a good swimmer. He picked up a large flat one and burst up into the open water. Grabbing the boat, he hauled himself in and flopped down inside. He examined the stone; it was beautiful and would make a good skimmer. He popped it into his pocket and dried off in the warm sunshine. *This place is like heaven* he thought to himself. Lazily, he picked up the net and poked it over the side of the boat. A fish swam into it and he lifted it out of the water. As he reached into the net, he thought the fish spoke to him.

"Now put me back. Everything here must live."

He hesitated for a moment and then tipped the net upside down and watched the fish wriggle away. It seemed to pause and turn back to him before disappearing under a stone. He squeezed his eyes shut and tipped his head on one side to empty the water from his ear. *This place is weird,* he thought to himself. *Talking birds and fish. Weird.*

8 REBEKKAH AND THE NEST

Rebekkah had woken before her brother. Deciding not to wake him, she wandered outside. A beautiful scene greeted her. There was a meadow to her left with a carpet of pretty wildflowers and, to her right, was a wood. She could hear the trickling of a stream in the distance. To her delight, there were animals everywhere and none of them seemed afraid of her. There were lambs in the meadow darting in and out of the carpet of flowers shaded yellow and blue. She watched as they gambolled around their mothers nudging at their nipples and trying to access milk. She gasped as she noticed a lion in the distance. He looked at her and then opened his mouth and yawned. Lazily turning onto his back so his tummy faced the sun he stretched and rolled in the dust and then flicked himself over onto his haunches. *Just like a huge pussy cat*, she thought to herself.

"Good morning Rebekkah, are you enjoying the nest?" She jumped at the unexpected interruption and turned to see the Eagle standing nearby.

"Oh Eagle," she said, "you made me jump. This place is amazing! Why doesn't the lion eat the lambs?"

The Eagle laughed her rich, throaty laugh and with a jerk of her head indicated that Rebekkah should follow her. She ran to catch up and then the Eagle paused to allow her to walk beside her. "So, Rebekkah, you and I have met before."

"We have?" she responded, puzzled. And then light dawned, "Oh yes! You mean in church and in my dreams? But you weren't real then as you are now."

"What's real Rebekkah?" The Eagle stopped and looked at her with those unblinking hazel eyes.

"Well, Jacob would say something is only real if you can touch it or see it with your own eyes."

"Ah! Jacob," mused the Eagle, "and you, what do you say?"

"Well, unless I am dreaming, this seems to be real. I can touch you and see you. So, you are real. But..."

"Yes?" The Eagle waited patiently.

"It's not normal. All this is not normal. The lion should be eating the lamb. The lamb should be afraid. You shouldn't be able to talk. We shouldn't be here. We should be at home in bed…"

"Ah," interrupted the Eagle, "and here's the thing. It's normal for you because you only see things from your world's point of view. Here in this world these things are normal. Come, let me show you around. Are you hungry?" The Eagle hopped over to a table and tapped three times with Her beak. In an instant the table was filled with all her favourite food. She gasped in astonishment as chocolate croissants, fresh and soft, burst out of nowhere. A jug of strawberry milk tipped itself into a glass. Toast and marmalade piled itself up onto a plate.

"Tuck in Rebekkah and enjoy this place. You may go anywhere you like and eat anything you like, except, in the centre of the nest there is a tree. You will know the tree by its golden trunk and silver branches. You must stay away from its fruit. It is the tree of knowledge of good and evil. If you eat of its fruit, however appetising it may seem to be, you will be unable to remain in the nest. Is that understood?"

Rebekkah nodded vigorously. Her one thought was that she could avoid going back to school and seeing that dreadful Miss Cannon again. "I won't Eagle. I promise I will be good."

The Eagle looked at her long and hard and then with a bounce and a flex of Her long muscular legs shot up into the air and flew off. Rebekkah breathed deeply and smiled. She ate her fill of breakfast and then wandered into the woods.

She was in heaven.

9 THE TREE OF KNOWLEDGE

Meanwhile, Jacob was growing tired of the water. Picking up the oars he rowed to shore and jumped out. His thoughts turned to his sister who he had not seen that day. Not usually given to much affection for her he found himself wondering whether she was all right and headed off into the woods. "Rebekkah!" he called. "Rebekkah!"

"Over here," came the reply.

He followed the sound and as he came into a clearing he saw her seated on a large trunk playing with squirrels and rabbits.

"Oh, look Jacob! Aren't they cute? Come and play with us."

He approached her warily biting back the cutting remark that would normally flow from his lips about rabbit stew and cotton buds. He sat down next to her and watched her feed a carrot to one rather substantial rabbit. "Rebekkah, what do you think of this place? Don't you think it's weird? It's like…" his words trailed off.

"Heaven," she finished the sentence for him, patting a squirrel on its head.

"Well, yes, except I don't believe in heaven," he said, rather lamely.

"No?" She looked at him out of the corner of her eye. "So how do these creatures talk? How did we get here? What is this place?"

The logical and rational side of his brain hunted for an answer. "Maybe it's a dream that we are both sharing. You know, you exist in my dream."

Rebekkah looked at him and sighed. "Oh Jacob you are annoying, why can't you just believe?"

He changed the subject. "Hey! Why don't we play hide and seek?"

Rebekkah smiled, even Jacob was prepared to be kind and friendly in this beautiful place, "Ok, you go and hide and I'll count."

Jacob ran off into the woods. He couldn't be sure but he thought he saw a flash of yellow in the undergrowth and then it was gone. *Probably a snake*, he thought to himself and for some reason a shiver moved down his spine. *What if there were snakes in this place? What if the Eagle was lying and there were dangerous things in the woods. What if there were poisonous snakes and dangerous creatures? Why should he trust the Eagle?*

"Eight, nine, ten... coming, ready or not," his sister's voice broke into his thoughts. A thought came to him. *Would not it be fun to hide and then scare her?* Looking around him he saw a golden tree in an open glade in front of him. He ran towards it. He looked up at its delicate, lung like branches. They sparkled and shimmered in the sun like silver. And then it came to him. This must be the tree that the Eagle had told him about. He hesitated but then curiosity got the better of him. He approached it and laid his hands on the golden trunk. It was smooth and shiny. Surprisingly he felt no fear or anxiety. Surely, if this was such a dangerous tree then he would feel something? He looked up into its silvery branches and there high above his head he could see an enormous pear. It appeared to be made of chocolate.

55

Certainly, it was not a normal pear but then nothing was normal here. He looked furtively over his shoulder and could hear Rebekkah crashing about in the woods behind him. The thought occurred to him that the Eagle had said nothing about climbing the tree only about the fruit itself. No sooner had the thought entered his brain than his eyes fell upon some golden whorls on the tree that were rough enough for him to climb onto. Without further thought he reached up and grasped a whorl just above his head. As if by magic a ladder appeared attached to the trunk. Gleefully, he grasped a rung and stealthily climbed up into its branches where he sat and waited. As he looked around, he could see the chocolate pear was easily within his grasp. Sitting next to the pear was a bird. It appeared to be guarding the fruit.

Rebekkah meanwhile had started to run along the path where she had seen her brother disappear. This was such a lovely place and there was so much to see that she frequently became distracted; stopping to stroke an otter or a badger. It was a while before she got to the tree. Oblivious to her brother sitting above her she called out for him. No answer. But then something dropped on her shoulder making her jump. It was a dead bird. She screamed and looked around her. "Jacob!" She shouted. "Please come out, I don't want to play anymore."

Silence.

She looked at the bird closely and gingerly touched it with her finger. It was still warm. It seemed odd and out of place. It marred the sense of paradise. She wasn't expecting to see death in this wonderful place. Then she saw him, perched above her. She cupped her hands over her eyes to get a better look. Shards of bright light stabbed their way through the leaves of the tree and hurt her eyes. Jacob was holding something in his hand. Something dark. And next to him, wound tightly around the branch was a yellow snake with red eyes. A shiver ran down her spine.

"Jacob," she screamed, "There's a snake next to you!"

Jacob slowly made his way down to her. Dropping the last metre, he turned and looked at her, an odd gleam in his eye. Colouring slightly, he wiped his mouth with the back of his hand. There were dark stains above his lips. He reached into his pocket and pulled out what looked like a chocolate fruit. Hesitantly he offered her the dark thing. She looked past him and up into the tree. She was looking for the snake, but it had gone. In its place were branches laden with chocolate covered apples. It reminded her of the Christmas tree at home laden with chocolate gifts. A memory flashed across her mind of the two of them, peeling the silver paper from the hanging chocolate bells one Christmas and eating all the chocolate baubles. Mum had taken their Christmas presents away for two whole days as a punishment.

"Jacob, what is this tree? Did the Eagle tell you about the Tree of Knowledge of Good and Evil? We aren't to eat from it. How do you know what this tree is? You might have broken the Eagle's rules."

He grinned. "Well, yes and you know what, that Eagle lied, nothing has happened to me and this chocolate is lovely. I'd go so far as to say, 'heavenly'" and he laughed an odd, lopsided laugh. "Try some."

Rebekkah backed away as if he was offering her a snake. "You idiot," she shouted. "You idiot; now you've ruined everything!"

"Aw come on Rebekkah how can eating a little bit of scrumptious chocolate ruin everything? Hey! Did you have a hamper of food too? I had chip butties in mine. It was all my favourite food but there was no chocolate. I think the Eagle likes a joke and we were meant to find this tree. She wants us to enjoy this place and do as we like. It's an adventure. This is a test to see if we are brave enough to take a risk. You like chocolate and she didn't say exactly what would happen to us, did she?"

Rebekkah looked at the chocolate. It was true she loved chocolate and she was very hungry. It seemed hours since she had eaten. What was it the Eagle had said about this tree? She couldn't really remember. Jacob was so logical and what he said made sense, she so wanted some chocolate. She reached out and took the piece he offered her and ate it. It tasted good. And then she waited. Nothing bad happened.

"Oh I feel sick now," said Rebekkah.

She looked at Jacob who also looked a bit green. And then it happened. A shadow flew across the sun and the silhouette of a giant bird descended on them. They were grabbed in two mighty claws promptly lifted out of the nest and into the sky. They flew like this for some way before the Eagle descended and dropped them onto the ground. They both rolled some way before they came to a halt. She landed next to them and fixed her unblinking stare on them both.

"What did you do?" She demanded.

Jacob took one look at Her, dropped to his knees and vomited up the contents of his stomach.

"Eeuuw," Rebekkah screwed up her face, "That stinks." And promptly followed suit.

The Eagle spoke to them both, "Listen carefully to what I am about to say. You could have had anything you wanted in that perfect world of the nest but you were disobedient. You did the one thing you were told not to do. Jacob, you were tempted by greed and as a result allowed the snake to kill the bird guarding the fruit. Rebekkah, you too gave in to greed. You were unwise to listen to your brother. Now you are free once more, but you can't go back to the nest until you have learnt to be less selfish."

"Oh Eagle," sobbed Rebekkah, "I am so sorry; it was Jacob, he made me do it. I wasn't even sure if it was the Tree of Knowledge. Please give us another chance. I don't want to go home."

Jacob, still crouching on all fours, said nothing.

The Eagle looked from one child to another and then, picking them up more gently this time, flew up into the sky. As they flew it became darker and darker until at last they reached the outskirts of their town. Finally, the Eagle hovered above their home. Bending Her elegant neck, She picked Jacob up by his collar and pushed him through the bedroom window. He collapsed onto the floor in a heap. Rebekkah was gently deposited on the window ledge and then nudged through the window with a push of the beak.

"Goodbye both of you. I shall be with you always. Don't worry, we shall meet again." And with that She was gone.

Rebekkah looked at her brother who was slowly

getting to his feet.

"I'm going to bed," he said gruffly, "I'm tired."

"Aren't we going to talk about what happened?" She demanded.

"Talk about what? There's nothing to talk about. Now get out of my room, you silly little twerp." Jacob opened the door and shoved her onto the landing. His door closed with a click, and she found herself looking at the smooth white painted surface. She raised her fists to bang on the door but then realised that this would wake her parents. Thinking better of it she headed into her own room, quickly undressed, took to her bed and slipped into an uneasy sleep full of dreams of snakes, dead birds and chocolate.

10 MONDAY MORNING REBEKKAH

Rebekkah opened her eyes and was overwhelmed by a sense of sadness. She squeezed her eyes shut and tried to re-enter her dream. As hard as she tried, she could not get back to the joy of the nest. All she could see in her mind's eye was the rigid body of the dead bird. Tears ran down her face. *What had they done? Jacob, it was Jacob's fault, he had ruined everything.* Then almost simultaneously another thought ran through her head like an engine pulling a carriage of anxiety. It was Monday morning. School! Would Miss Bates be back, or would they have the old battle axe again? Groaning she pulled the covers over her head and tried to retreat into her own little world.

"Rebekkah! Get up!" her mother had grabbed the covers and pulled them off, dumping them on the floor. No time seemed to have passed in her world although Rebekkah figured they must have been at the nest for at least a day.

Breakfast was a silent affair. Neither child spoke. Jacob avoided looking at his sister and thankfully Mum seemed preoccupied and was working on her iPad. Dad had gone to work early. It was a dull grey day; the sort that meant wet play. It mirrored their feelings. There would be no sun to brighten up their Monday morning.

On arriving at school her heart sank when she walked into the supply teacher, Miss Cannon. Menacingly she greeted her by name and said she was 'delighted' she would see her later in her lesson. She also demanded the homework that had been set and made Rebekkah stand in the classroom while she read it. On completion she screwed it up and threw it in the bin.

"That took me two hours to write." Rebekkah was horrified.

"Really? Well, it looked like it had taken you ten minutes. Do try in your lessons today. And remember, I shall be keeping my eye on you. Right, it's time for registration, come on!"

Smarting with anger and humiliation, Rebekkah followed the woman, her dyed black hair sat like a helmet on her head. She felt hatred welling up in her. She could taste it in her mouth. She wanted to slap her.

Freda was back. She sat on her own by the window reading her book. She looked up at Rebekkah, but could not hold her gaze, her eyes shifted sideways and then back to her book. Cannon walked up to her and grabbed the book. Peering at the title she scoffed loudly, "Beatrix Potter! That's a book for babies, can't you read, girl? Do you still require a book with pictures?"

The class held its collective breath, waiting for the meltdown that was sure to follow. Without looking at the woman, Freda sprang to her feet and grabbed her book. Miss Cannon was quicker and held the book aloft, just out of Freda's reach. Freda began to yell. A strong sense of injustice flooded into Rebekkah's heart. She could not bear this. Miss Bates had always been kind to Freda; this woman was horrible to everyone. It wasn't fair. She watched with horror as the teacher took the book to her desk, placed it very precisely in the drawer and sat down. Freda was now beside herself with rage. Cannon simply watched her, finally she stood up and ushered the class out into the corridor and into an empty classroom, leaving Freda alone.

The class filed obediently after the horrible woman, but Rebekkah could not, instead she returned to her form room and stood in the doorway. Instinctively she moved across the room to the desk, opened the drawer picked up the book and gently handed it to the sobbing girl. Groping in her pocket she produced a tissue and handed that to her as well. Gradually the sobbing subsided, and Freda was able to wipe her eyes and look at her book, "Thank you," she murmured and then blew her nose very loudly.

"We probably should get back to class," Rebekkah said unenthusiastically.

Freda emitted a peculiar sound that was halfway between a sob and a hiccough, "I can't go back in there not with that bully."

Rebekkah was surprised, the woman was a bully, but it had not occurred to name her behaviour in such a way. Children were bullies not teachers, but Freda was right, the woman's behaviour had been bullying. She made her mind up, "Come on Freda, let's go and tell the headteacher what has happened."

The two girls made their way down the corridor, avoiding the classroom where their classmates had been taken. The receptionist looked at them both with a smile, "Can I help you girls?"

"Yes," said Rebekkah politely, "we would like to see the

headteacher please."

The woman looked at the computer on her desk, "she is very busy and has meetings all morning, she might have a small window at break, would you mind giving me some idea what you wish to talk with her about?"

"Ah there you are!" The girls jumped at the terrible sound of Miss Cannon's voice behind them. "You should be in class girls, I was worried about you." Miss Cannon smiled sweetly at the receptionist who smiled back and tried to usher them out of reception.

Undeterred, the receptionist raised her eyebrows and persisted, "What is it you wanted to see the headteacher about?"

Rebekkah panicked, but then an idea popped into her head, "Freda and I have an idea for a charity event, and we would like to ask her what she thinks of it."

The receptionist nodded, "I think she will be able to see you at 11.00, perhaps your teacher could release you from your lesson a few minutes early so you can be prompt."

As they walked back to the classroom Miss Cannon glowered at them, "A charity event? I can't believe that you two would be capable of doing anything so altruistic. I think you are up to something. If I find out that you lied to get to see the head, you will be in big trouble!" With that they entered the classroom which fell silent as they took their seats.

11 MONDAY MORNING, JACOB

Jacob had also woken up feeling depressed. The memory of the events in the nest troubled him. He did not want to admit it to Rebekkah, but he felt guilty for the first time in his life. Pushing the unwanted thoughts away he rationalised the experience as a dream. No time had passed so it must have been a dream. He chose not to talk to Rebekkah because he wanted the thoughts to fade. It was with relief therefore when he climbed out of the car and walked away from her to the bus stop.

When Jacob got to school, he was summoned to the Head's office where he was questioned about the bus incident. No, he did not know why he had done it. Yes, it had been a silly and immature thing to do. Yes, he was sorry for bringing the school into disrepute. No, it would not happen again. Yes, he would write a letter of apology. Yes, he would do it now. As he sat in the outer office he went to that place in his head where his lips and his thoughts were separate. He laughed out loud at the memory of the girl's squealing and the bus driver posting the little worms through the window. When finished, he went to the toilets on the way back to the classroom taking an extra-long time. It was only French.

On returning to his classroom, Jacob settled into his chair and stared out of the window. His thoughts turned to the nest. Not usually given to fanciful thoughts, he struggled with the vivid nature of his memories. He could still feel the rhythm of the Eagle's wings beneath him. He blinked and then in his mind's eye, he saw the little bird crushed by the evil yellow snake, and his own hand reaching up through the shards of sunlight to take the chocolate pear. He squeezed his fingers into his lids trying to get rid of the snapshot in time. He opened his eyes and looked around the classroom. The boys around him were working steadily, heads bent, industriously focused on the essays they were writing. His gaze turned to the board where the teacher had written the task.

Racontez une histoire sur un aigle. (Tell a story about an eagle)

Was this a joke? Had the class agreed to play a trick on him while he was out of the room? He looked furtively around the room. Were they pretending to work? Was anyone trying to stifle a grin? Any moment now would they all simultaneously put down their pens and laugh at him? He looked around the room trying to catch the eye of his friend. It was not logical. He had not told anyone about the nest. And then, it came to him. Rebekkah must have been blabbing about the dream and somehow the boys had heard about it. The little twit! What was he to do now?

Then the teacher's voice cut through his musings. "Taylor, get on with your work, stop gazing around the room. Boys, you have ten minutes left."

No one was laughing. Slowly he sucked the pen and started leafing through his French dictionary. Painfully he began to write.

L'aigle est un grand oiseaux. Il habite dans un nid. He had to look up the words: big, bird, live, and nest. By the time he had worked out the verb endings the lesson was over. Subdued, he sat quietly at his desk.

A boy punched him playfully on the arm, "Hey Jay, what did the Hedgehog do to you?" Hedgehog was the nickname of the

Headteacher, so named because of his spiky black hair. "Rumour has it you've been expelled."

"What? Nah, he's soft as putty. I had to write a grovelling letter to the bus company and that was it."

They walked down the corridor together and headed out into the playground. A group of lads were playing football, Jacob watched them for a few minutes before he slipped away to the bike sheds. Leaning with his back to the brick wall, he pondered the night's events. He was inclined to convince himself it had all been a dream, somehow it was easier to manage his conscience if he did this. As he idly surveyed the tree canopy above him, he noticed a flock of magpies darting from one branch to another. Fascinated, he watched them; they clearly enjoyed being together and rarely sat still. Then, without warning, one broke away from the group and headed straight for him. Thinking it would just fly past, Jacob continued to stare until the bird began to dive at him beating its wings ferociously at his head. Letting out a yell and raising his hands to protect himself, he began to run. Only when he reached the safety of the school doors did the thing fly off. Once inside, he stopped to catch his breath. He wasn't fit and the run had taken a lot out of him, he was also scared. *Was this normal? Did magpies often attack human beings?* As oxygen flowed into his lungs his heart rate slowed and he regained his composure, but he still jumped as the bell rang directly above his head for afternoon school. He made his way slowly to the lesson, for once he was glad to be in the comparative security of a classroom.

12 REBEKKAH AND THE BANG ON HER HEAD

Reluctantly Miss Cannon released the students at one minute to eleven so they had to run down the corridor to make it in time. As they approached reception the lady looked at them apologetically,

"I am so sorry, girls, the Head had to attend to an emergency, can you come back tomorrow?"

The girls looked at each other in despair, how much longer would they have to put up with this bully?

"Well, I'm not going back," Freda was determined. She sat down on one of the chairs in reception, opened her book and began to read. Rebekkah felt anxiety begin to rise in her chest, panic filled her throat, and she couldn't swallow. She looked around desperately for somewhere safe to sit as she felt she might faint. Then she noticed it, in a dark corner of the room, a small glass cabinet containing a stuffed bird. Curious, she headed over to it and peered inside. In the centre was an eagle, it stood to attention, on a smooth branch, talons open and beak slightly ajar. Leaning in, she peered into the lifeless eye; fascinated by the black pupil, she edged still closer until the eye filled her vision, sucking her in. Feeling dizzy, a rushing sound filled her head and then sharp zig zags of light entered her vision. Losing her balance her body tipped up and she headed for the empty black pupil like a bullet. Terrified, she cried out. What was going to happen, would she hit the eagle's brain? As suddenly as it started, the noise stopped and she found herself lying flat on the floor, staring into the anxious face of the receptionist who was leaning over her and calling her name. She answered but her voice was small and thin as if she was a long way away and in a tunnel.

Then she was aware of a conversation on the phone, it was the nurse, and she was talking to someone, about her. As she struggled to her feet, she was urged to sit down; Freda was nowhere to be seen. Mumbling incoherently, she asked what had happened and was told she had fainted, hitting her head on the glass case. Gingerly she felt her forehead; there was indeed a large bump for which she was offered an ice pack and a glass of water. She was informed she was not to go back to lessons as her mother would be collecting her and they had to watch out for a concussion. Rebekkah's heart lifted at the thought of avoiding lessons but then sank again as she considered how her mother would react at being dragged away from work. Then, Freda appeared at the door, awkwardly holding her school bag, shyly, she made her way over to Rebekkah and handed it to her. She didn't look at her but mumbled, asking if she was alright. Rebekkah thanked her and nodded, wincing as she did so, her head did hurt.

"Right, Freda," said the receptionist kindly, "I think Rebekkah will be fine, she is going home to rest and recover. You need to go back to your lesson now."

Rebekkah looked at Freda, she could see the anxiety in the girl's face, and the receptionist noticed it too. She paused, thought for a moment, and then continued, speaking to the nurse, "Freda has had a bit of a shock, seeing Rebekkah faint, I wonder whether she might spend the rest of the day with me, I have some filing jobs she could do. Would you like that, Freda?"

Freda looked at the kind woman gratefully. The nurse's phone buzzed urgently, "Yes, that's fine, I must go, we seem to have an outbreak of norovirus, I haven't got time to deal with hysterical girls." She bustled off and both Freda and Rebekkah breathed a sigh of relief.

Saved from the battle-axe for at least 24 hours it felt like they had been freed from prison.

Just at that moment, the main door- bell buzzed, it was Mrs Taylor, Rebekkah felt a sharp pang of anxiety, but thankfully the egg on her head was growing and her mum gasped as she saw it. At least she could see she wasn't pretending.

As they sat in the car on the way home, her mother quizzed her about what had happened. Rebekkah nearly told her the whole story, but something made her hold back, she thought her mother would be less sympathetic if she told her the full truth, so she stuck to the story she had told Miss Cannon, that she and Freda had gone to see the head about a charity event, she had felt faint and while looking at the stuffed eagle had passed out, banging her head on the case.

"There's a bad attack of Norovirus in the school, mum, perhaps

I have that and should stay home for a few days." Rebekkah looked at her mother hopefully. Her mother cast her a sideways look and then focused on the road. "You may not be going back to that school at all, Rebekkah."

"What? What do you mean?" Rebekkah was puzzled.

"We have been meaning to tell you, but this is as good a time as any; your father and I are splitting up."

Rebekkah felt as cold as the block of ice pressed to her forehead. She wasn't accustomed to talking about feelings with her mother and she didn't know what to say.

"How does that affect school?" she queried.

"Your father lost his job a few months ago; we can't afford to pay the school fees."

"He was at work this morning," Rebekkah's voice tailed off.

"Yes, he has been lying." Her mother's voice was bitter. "He lost his job three months ago. He hasn't been paying your school fees. The first I knew of it was when the Bursar phoned me to talk about non-payment of fees. I confronted him last night and he told me. He didn't want to tell us and so has been pretending to go to work. He has been unbearable to live with, I knew something wasn't right."

"But what about me? Can't you pay the fees? Dad will get another job." Even as she said the words, there was a small part of her that didn't actually mean it. Her heart leapt at the thought she might never have to see Miss Cannon again.

Her mother was quiet for a while and then she continued, "We may be getting a divorce, we are going to have a trial separation; and so we shall need to rent another place, as we can't afford to have both of you at fee paying schools."

Something about the way her mother had phrased the sentence raised a doubt in Rebekkah's mind, "Can't afford to have both of us at fee paying schools," she repeated, "What about Jacob?"

Her mother paused once more, choosing her words carefully, "Your brother is less adaptable than you, he doesn't make friends as easily as you do, also he only has one term left in the middle school, and you have three years. We shall find the money for Jacob's fees for a term and then you will both go to state schools."

Had not Miss Cannon blasted her way into Rebekkah's world she would have protested vociferously but she had to acknowledge a feeling of relief that she didn't have to go back. The state school might be fun, she enjoyed new challenges her mum was right, she did make friends easily. A question bounced into her mind, her brain felt muzzy and she wasn't as sharp as usual, maybe the bang to her head was affecting her?

"If you and dad split up, where will we go?"

Her mother kept her eyes fixed on the road ahead, she was driving slowly; the car behind revved its engine, roared past, tooting its horn as it did so. Her mother made a rude sign at the driver and mouthed a word that Rebekkah had often heard her parents utter in a row. She waited for her parent to calm down; fearful she might crash the car if she pushed her too far.

"Well, you will spend half a week with me and half a week with dad. That's why he needs to get a flat with three bedrooms. And it has to be close enough for you to get to school."

"Oh, so we become suitcase kids!" Rebekkah had tried to keep her feelings under control, but this was too much. "I lose my bedroom, my school, and have to cope with packing everything up twice a week. Why can't you just live separately in the same house? This is going to be so awful."

Her mother's face set in the hard lines that she knew meant no further discussion, "Oh don't be so dramatic, Rebekkah, loads of families live like this, you will be fine."

 And that was it! Her mother had just dropped a bombshell, made an almighty mess, refused to help clear it up and just walked away. Rebekkah was glad of the ice bag she was clutching as it hid the tears that rolled silently down her face. She could not under any circumstances let her mother see she was upset. On arriving home, she walked slowly upstairs and flopped heavily onto her bed. She felt a bit sick and her head hurt, but after a while she dropped off to sleep.

13 REBEKKAH'S NEW SCHOOL

Rebekkah did not return to her old school. She took the rest of the week off while her mother bought her new uniform. She tried to talk to Jacob about the break-up, but he had closed down completely since the flight to the nest. He retreated more and more into his on-line games, refusing to engage with any of his family.

The following Monday came too quickly for Rebekkah and not quickly enough for Jacob. He and Dad had moved into a small flat while Rebekkah had stayed in the family home with Mum. This seemed unfair to Jacob even though he marginally preferred his father to his mother. He liked his bedroom in the old house, it had been his haven on many occasions. Still, living with Dad meant he got to eat the food that he liked. Dad ate takeaways and loved his fat and sugar whereas Mum always insisted on fruit and healthy food. Rebecca was secretly quite glad at the way things had turned out. Seeing less of her big brother was a bonus and although sorry to say goodbye to her friends, she was glad to see the back of Miss Cannon.

By the end of the week both children would wish they had never been born.

For Rebekkah it started on Thursday. The first three days had gone well. The other girls in her class seemed friendly enough and wanted to be her friend. Her new class teacher was delighted with her. She found most subjects easy and discovered that she was way ahead in maths and reading. Eager to please and to make a good impression, her hand was constantly in the air. Gradually the atmosphere in the class began to change. Other students exchanged looks when she answered a question and made faces behind her back.

Rebekkah found herself increasingly isolated. The other girls shunned her, and she began to feel terribly alone. She considered telling someone but whom? Her mother was preoccupied, dealing with work and the divorce. Her dad was distant and depressed. Jacob behaved as if he was on another planet and hardly spoke to her. The teachers were all nice but very busy. So, she went to the library most lunch times and joined the swimming club hoping to make friends there.

One Monday it was raining heavily, and she had made a dash for it as she emerged from one building and entered the sports block. Ahead of her she could see a small group of girls sheltering from the rain. They were sitting on the radiators chatting and sucking lollipops. She recognised one of them as being Kirsty; a particularly unpleasant piece of work who often made her life a misery. Her heart sank, normally she would have turned around and gone a different way, but they were sitting right outside the changing room doors. Taking a deep breath, she straightened her shoulders, quickened her pace and walked through the doors. They followed her. Looking around she had hoped there would be others getting changed but she was alone. Avoiding the communal changing area, she pushed open a cubicle door and locked herself in. She could hear the girls talking outside, changing quickly she planned to place her clothes in a locker and get into the pool as fast as possible. They couldn't get at her there.

Emerging after a few minutes, clothes clutched under her arm she avoided looking at them and made her way to a locker. Kirsty stepped in front of the locker door, obstructing it.

Rebekkah moved to another locker, Kirsty stepped in front of that one too. Rebekkah stood up straight and looked the girl in the eye. "Excuse me, Kirsty," she spoke politely.

"Excuse me, Kirsty," sneered the girl as she mimicked Rebekkah's posh accent. "Why, what did you do? Did you fart? I can smell a bad smell can't you girls?" The others gathered round. Some smiled menacingly, others pushed to see what was going on.

"Please, could you just let me get to the locker?" Although terrified she stiffened her chin and looked defiantly at the other girl.

"Why?" Kirsty was a large girl, and it would not have been easy to shove her to one side. Besides which she had her cronies with her. Rebekkah didn't answer. It was obvious why she needed a locker she wasn't going to give her the satisfaction of an answer.

"Use that one over there." Kirsty pointed to a large locker at floor level. It was much bigger than Rebekkah needed but it would do. Obediently she moved to the unit and bent down to put her things inside. As she did so someone tripped her up and gave her a hefty shove. Rebekkah fell. Two more girls got down next to her and manhandled her into the locker and shut the door.

Kirtsy's voice thrust itself through the metal door. "So, geeky girl, if you think you are so smart, get yourself out of there." There was a squeal of laughter and then lots of giggling. After a while it became quiet as the girls moved away.

It was dark inside the locker. It smelt of stinky socks and shoes. She tasted panic in the back of her throat. She began to hammer on the door. "Please let me out! Oh! please let me out!"

But no one came. She hammered wildly against the door. Panic flooded over her, tears poured down her face and her nose ran. *What if she used up all the oxygen and died of suffocation? What if she was left here over night?* She could not breathe. Her thoughts turned to Jacob - logical, rational Jacob. He would not panic he would say something scientific like, sit still, calm down and take deep breaths. Then she felt it. She became aware of a presence with her in the locker which seemed to expand and fill the entire space, it grew and grew until the back of the locker disappeared altogether and she could see a beautiful field. Unsteadily, she stood up and walked out into the fresh air where a beautiful golden eagle was waiting for her.

"Rebekkah, climb on my back. I am getting you out of here." Joyfully she ran to the Eagle and buried her head in its rich soft downy feathers. "Oh Eagle. Is it really You? Can You help me?"

The Eagle reached over to her and gently stroked her hair with its long, hooked beak. "I can't stay long but I want to show you something."

Rebekkah climbed onto her back and together they soared up into the deep blue sky. Up, up they went until the top of a mountain came into view. The Eagle circled it several times and then dropped down onto the flat stones. She arched Her back and stretched Her wings before folding them carefully so as not to hurt Rebekkah.

Rebekkah drank in the gorgeous bucolic scenery. "It's so beautiful," she breathed.

"Yes," replied the Eagle. "Be at peace. Help is on its way; you are not alone. You must be strong Rebekkah. It won't be much longer before you are out of here."

"Oh Eagle, it's hard. Everything is changing. Dad, Mum, Jacob, school and those girls were so mean."

The Eagle looked at her with her unblinking eyes. "And it will continue but there are a few on your side. Jealousy is a powerful emotion, Rebekkah. Things will get worse before they get better. You must be brave. Now take one last look at the view and then we must go."

The world faded from view as Rebekkah found herself back in the dark, smelly locker. Breathing more slowly, she waited. Before long, there was a grinding sound and then the locker door flew open. A girl that Rebekkah knew from her class was standing there. She looked furtively around. "Come on. Get out and be quick about it before the others come." She thrust a bag at Rebekkah as she crawled out of the space.

"Thank you," stammered Rebekkah. "I will never forget this."

The girl looked at her. "Don't say anything to the others and keep your mouth shut." She then turned and walked away leaving Rebekkah to get dressed.

Panicking, Rebekkah dressed quickly. She was late for her lesson, and she hated being late. Grabbing her bag she shoved her feet into her shoes, jammed her heel down on the back of the shoe and half-walked, half-ran, down the corridor. She burst into the classroom and gasped out a, "Sorry miss for being late."

The class tittered and Rebekkah caught Kirsty looking at her. She mouthed, "Don't say a thing, or else."

The teacher was staring at her. "Rebekkah what have you done to your shirt? Did they not teach you how to button a blouse at that independent school of yours?"

"She probably had a servant to dress her," sneered a girl with a big nose and dyed orange hair. The class roared with laughter. With a pang of embarrassment Rebekkah realised that they had been waiting for her humiliation and were glad. Tears stung her eyes; she looked helplessly at the teacher. She did not want to go down in her estimation, she had been taught that teachers were kind and fair and if you told the truth against bullies, they would help you. But then a vision of Miss Cannon floated before her eyes. She found herself looking for the girl who had released her, but she was nowhere to be seen.

"Well, Rebekkah, I had thought more of you than this but in the light of an inadequate explanation I am going to have to place you in detention. Come back tomorrow lunchtime, the hamster needs a clean out and you can pick the chewing gum off the bottom of the desks. Be grateful I am not going to make you eat it!"

The class laughed again. Rebekkah dropped her head and slipped into her seat, cheeks aflame with embarrassment. She began to re-button her shirt as the lesson continued and attention turned away from her to the board. For the rest of the day, she kept her head down and answered no further questions.

Later that afternoon, as she walked to the bus Kirsty pushed up behind her. "Well done, geek! At least you aren't a snitch as well as a show off. But don't think I'm finished with you yet. I don't like you. You need to get in tomorrow early and do my homework for me. Got that? Be in the dining hall at 8 o'clock."

Rebekkah looked at her in horror, "But my mum doesn't drop me off until 8.30."

Kirsty put her face up to Rebekkah's so close that she could smell stale breath on the bigger girl. "I don't care. Tell her you have a club or something; make it up. Use that brain of yours. Just do it or else something worse will happen to you." With that she popped a bubble gum into her mouth, grinned and walked off.

Feeling miserable, Rebekkah climbed onto the bus, settled into a window seat, pulled her school bag onto her knee and stared out of the window. What was happening to her? Her nice safe world had turned upside down. It all seemed to stem from the nest. Was the Eagle friend or foe? Was the bird real? Sometimes she seemed as real as Jacob and at other times just a fantasy. She could not make sense of it all. She leaned against the bus window, which was misted with breath and steamy coats. It was raining heavily outside. She drew a bird into the haze in front of her and then with a swipe of her hand rubbed it away. The Eagle was like that.

14 JACOB MAKES A RUN FOR IT

A week had passed since the worm incident. Jacob was enjoying living with his dad. If he had thought about it more deeply, he would have had to admit that he didn't really want to see his sister; she reminded him of the nest and what had occurred there. It was much easier to lose himself in computer games and his dad seemed preoccupied, so didn't bother him.

He had kept his head down at school and since the magpie attack, avoided the bike sheds. Old Spike, the bus driver had refused to have him back on the bus, so he was cycling to and from school... until Friday morning. He had gone to get his bike and noticed the rear tyre had a puncture. Swearing, he kicked the bike and returned to the house. His dad appeared at the bedroom door. He was dressed in a smart suit for a change and was tying his tie as Jacob called out to him.

"What's up?" dad asked.

"My bike's got a puncture," Jacob moaned, "Can you take me to school?"

"I have an interview this morning," his dad checked his watch, straightened his tie and grabbed his coat. "You'll have to walk."

"What?" Jacob complained, "It's three miles, it'll take me ages and I'll be late."

"Can't help that," his dad was already moving out of the door, "if you hadn't been such a brat, you could have gone by bus. Come on, I'm locking up." Jacob was shunted out of the door and stood watching as his dad drove off in the opposite direction to school.

"Idiot!" shouted Jacob after the car, "No wonder mum left you!"

Grumbling to himself, he began the journey to school. He was only missing registration and then PE so he wasn't too bothered although he did wonder what Hedgehog would say about him being so late. He had been put on a warning for good behaviour which expired at the end of the week. He had to report to Hedgehog daily which was a pain.

The sky was dark and heavy with rain clouds. Jacob noticed how dreary everything was in the rain. It matched his mood. The wind howled around him and a single blast nearly knocked him off his feet. A half empty can of lager dribbled a dark liquid onto the path as it rolled back and forth in the wind. He kicked it covering his shoe in stickiness. As he finally approached the school gate, he noticed a commotion on the street in front of him. Getting closer he could see two lads surrounded by a group of boys. One was dangling a mobile phone high above a small boy's head and, as he jumped up to take it from him, the older boy threw it to someone in the crowd. The owner darted uselessly over to the recipient just in time to see the phone fly through the air again and land in the hands of another boy. He was getting desperate. Jacob felt sorry for him and waded in. He intercepted the phone as it flew through the air and handed it to the small child who muttered a 'thanks' and quickly tucked the precious item into his pocket and ran off.

Angry, the lads turned on him, "Who do you think you are, posh boy?"

"Suppose you think you are better than the rest of us."

"Who told you to interfere, mister high and mighty?"

Jacob was shoved and pushed. He looked around him for the

lad whose phone he had saved but he was nowhere to be seen. He held his hands up and reasoned, "Look he was only a small kid. He was on his own, there are loads of you."

"Yeah, but you're not though are you?" sneered a big lad, "There's quite a bit of you," and he took a swing at Jacob punching him in the stomach. Jacob doubled up in pain. There was a laugh and then another boy grabbed his bag and dumped the contents on the ground. His iPad was grabbed and that was the last Jacob saw of it. He had no idea who had taken it. Furious he swung blindly at the nearest boy. His hand caught the lad on the chin, and he fell to the ground. Gasping, he turned and crouched like a tiger, eyes narrowed in pain, breath coming in short gasps.

"Give me back my iPad!" he yelled, much to the amusement of the boys surrounding him.

Then a cry went up, "Quick! Run, someone's coming," the crowd melted away leaving Jacob next to the boy whom he had knocked out.

Jacob looked at the teacher who was running towards him, he

had a radio grasped in his hand and was speaking urgently into it. As he reached Jacob, he yelled at him to stand still and then dropped to his knees to check out the unconscious boy.

"You'll be in big trouble for this, that temper of yours has got the better of you this time, Jacob. It looks like you have really hurt this lad."

Jacob began to pick up his things. "It wasn't my fault; I was attacked first. And they've got my iPad."

"Go inside and wait for me there. The Head will want to see you."

"Why? It's not my fault. Didn't you hear me, they have got my iPad? You should be calling the police, they are thieves, those idiots!" Jacob was now shaking uncontrollably with the injustice of the situation. His iPad was his most precious possession.

The teacher shouted at him, "Go inside. Now! You don't want to get into any more trouble than you are already."

Jacob looked at him. Rage overwhelmed him. He did what Jacob always did when he was filled with uncontrollable anger.

He yelled, "This is a horrible school; I hate you and everyone in it. You are all idiots!" Picking up his bag he ran out of the school gate and out onto the road. He didn't look back.

15 REBEKKAH AND KIRSTY

Rebekkah's Friday was also going badly. When she had told her mother that she needed to be at school for eight o'clock, Mrs Taylor had gone into meltdown. No, she could not get Rebekkah into school at that time. She had a phone call arranged at eight. Did Rebekkah not understand that she was organising her time around her for this week? She could not just shift everything around at the last minute.

Rebekkah had then burst into tears and yelled at her mother. Did she not understand how hard it was starting a new school? She missed her friends and was trying to make new ones. This was a club she wanted to attend. At that point her mother had softened and agreed to take her earlier, she changed the call only to receive a message from Dad just as they were leaving. This left her grumpy and irritable and made them late. Now she was rushing through the gates at ten past eight.

She arrived in the dining hall; her face red with the exertion of running through the school with a heavy bag and stood anxiously at the door looking for Kirsty.

"So, there you are," muttered a voice in her ear. She jumped. Kirsty must have been hiding in a nearby classroom, as she had not been there seconds before.

"You are late, geek. No one makes me wait. I've got a punishment lined up for you but for now let's get this homework done." She dragged Rebekkah by the arm into a classroom and got out her books.

"Maths first, let me see your work," she demanded. Rebekkah reached into her bag and produced her exercise book and opened it at the right page. Kirsty quickly scribbled down the answers. "Now English, blimey, you've written a lot," she moaned, "this will take me ages to copy."

She thought for a minute and then made a decision. "We don't have English until this afternoon. I'm not copying all that out. You will type it up for me on the computer, you should have thought about this yourself, you selfish girl. And then you can print it out and give it to me."

"But," stammered Rebekkah, "our work will be the same."

"No, it won't," grinned Kirsty, "Cos you are going to do a new one for yourself."

"But I won't have time. I have detention at lunchtime. Remember? You made me late by locking me in that locker. Now I have to pick chewing gum off desks. Probably you put it there in the first place." Her words tumbled out in a rush. She had not meant to speak so forcefully. Something instinctively told her that the bigger girl would punish her for her insolence.

Sure enough, Kirsty thrust her face into Rebekkah's and hissed, "No? Well, that's your problem. You should have thought about this last night. In future you write two pieces of work. One for you and one for me or else worse will happen to you. The locker was just the beginning. Get it?" With that she stuffed her books back in her bag and strode off.

Now wretchedly downcast, Rebekkah checked her watch, noting it was already time for registration. She repacked her bag and headed off to her form room. The girls inside were laughing and joking. They ignored her completely. She felt tears welling up in the back of her eyes. Turning her head away she dropped into her seat and opened a book. She had never felt so lonely.

Registration was a rushed affair. Their form teacher was apparently away, and the very flustered Head of Year bustled in loudly exclaiming that they were late for assembly and needed to get a move on. Rebekkah suddenly felt a shaft of hope. If the teacher was not here, then maybe the detention would be cancelled and she could do the homework. She waited behind after everyone had gone. The teacher was just finishing adding absence marks to the computer.

"Yes?" he looked at Rebekkah expectantly.

"Please Sir, I have a detention at lunch time with our Form Tutor, will it be rearranged when she comes back or do I still need to come here at lunch time?"

"Mmm, you are the new girl aren't you? In detention already? What did you do?"

Rebekkah had not expected an inquisition. "Er, I lost my shoes in PE and so was late for her lesson." she said rather lamely. She could not look the teacher in the eye and shuffled awkwardly from one foot to another.

"Ah," said the man kindly, looking at her. "Rebekkah it can be hard starting a new school. There's a lot to take in, new routines and so on. I will speak to your tutor when she gets back and say you were keen to do the detention. We'll sort it out. Don't worry for today. Now better get yourself to assembly." With that he logged out of the computer and dashed off.

His kindness comforted Rebekkah and sustained her until lunchtime. She decided to miss lunch and get the extra homework done. She did not want to get into any more trouble. Afternoon registration was less rushed. The register was called, and the students were quiet. It was therefore really noticeable when the Head of Year appeared and asked for Rebekkah. Turning pink she got up from her desk and began to make her way towards him.

"Bring your bag Rebekkah," he said. "You won't be attending lessons this afternoon." Turning back to collect her bag she caught Kirsty's eye.

"Say nothing, or else," mouthed the girl.

Mystified and a bit scared, she followed the man out of the room and down the corridor. He paused and shortened his step so he could walk beside her.

"Rebekkah," he said very solemnly, "I have some bad news, your brother Jacob has gone missing. Your mum is waiting for you in my office, she wants you to be together with your father and the police would like to interview you."

"What about?" she asked anxiously.

"To see if you have any idea about where he might have gone."

Her first feeling was one of relief that she would escape from school for the afternoon. Then she felt guilty. What if something terrible had happened to her brother? Although she did not like him very much he was still her brother. As these thoughts tumbled through her mind they arrived at the Head of Year's office where her mother was waiting. She looked worried.

"Oh Rebekkah, darling!" She jumped up and threw her arms around her daughter. Rebekkah, unaccustomed to such a display of affection felt hugely embarrassed but nonetheless allowed herself to be entwined by her mother's skinny arms. Her body, bony and thin wasn't very comforting. Rebekkah shifted in her grasp and pushed her mother away. "Where's Jacob, Mum?"

Her mother burst into tears, the Head of Year swiftly moved to the table and deftly passed her a box of tissues.

"We don't know. He has run away."

16 JACOB AT THE FACTORY

Jacob gazed at the derelict factory in front of him, it would be a good place to hide. Besides he was soaking wet, it had not stopped raining since he had run away from school. He pulled up the hood on his jacket and squinted right and left before sprinting across to the grey building. He ran round it; occasionally jumping up to get a better look at a boarded - up window. At last, he found what he was looking for: a window that had been forced open by a previous visitor. Hunting around for something to stand on, his eyes settled on a crate. Giving little thought to the possibility that someone else had already used this method of entry, he dragged it across to the window. He climbed onto the crate and then hauled himself up onto the wide window ledge. Puffing and panting he lay sprawled like a beached whale. The frame of the window pushed into his gut, he needed to move quickly. Catching his breath, he hauled himself to a crouching position and peered through the open window. It was gloomy inside, but the way seemed clear and the drop wasn't too far. Taking a deep breath, he jumped, but landed awkwardly. His ankle bent underneath him, and a sickening sharp pain shot up his leg. He gingerly felt his ankle which was already tender and swollen. It really hurt and he was afraid to walk on it.

The window was way above him and there was no friendly crate on this side of the window. The only way out was through the warehouse. His ankle was throbbing, and water was dripping from his hair into his eyes. Unable to walk, he shunted across the floor on his bottom, wincing at the pain. Swearing softly to himself, he was aware of dust and dirt sticking to his wet trousers. He felt very exposed and knew if there was anyone else in the building, he would have no chance of escaping them. Panic rose in his chest like bile, he didn't like the dark and wished he hadn't jumped through that window.

Just as he felt he might be losing control a shaft of sunlight burst through the broken window illuminating the room. There was a door just in front of him. Jacob shuffled as fast as he could towards it. He levered himself up onto his left knee, his right foot extended to one side. Panting with the exertion he grabbed the handle and pulled. The door creaked as it opened into another dark room. It stank of beer and death. When riding his bike, he had caught a similar whiff of decay as he passed a roadside ditch where an unsuspecting animal lay rotting. Curious he had got off his bike to get a closer look and had been fascinated by the way nature acted to decompose a body. The stench was off- putting though. He wondered what had died in that room and hoped it wasn't a human being.

He sat very still and waited for his eyes to adjust. To his right he could just make out a mound of something.

The mound moved. *This is it*, thought Jacob, *there's a zombie in here, it's going to attack me and suck out my brains.* Then a voice came from the mound. Jacob looked around for something with which to defend himself. He saw a plank of wood and started shuffling towards it. The mound suddenly grew feet and arms and a head. A man stood before him.

Jacob could not make out his features, he stammered, "Don't hurt me please. I meant no harm."

"Who are you and how did you get in?" asked the man. He had a deep voice, and he sounded kind.

Jacob squinted at him through the gloom, "My name is Jacob

and I fell through the window."

"Are you ok, Jacob? You seem to be struggling with that leg of yours?" The man remained in his part of the room.

Jacob was aware of how vulnerable he felt. He was standing like an ostrich on one leg. He knew he could not possibly make a run for it. "Erm it's just a little strain, I landed awkwardly when I jumped through the window." He gulped, wondering if he had given away too much information for his own good.

"I might have something that could help with that," the man knelt on the floor and began rummaging through a bag. Jacob began to sweat despite the cold, what if the guy had a weapon?

"It's alright, Jacob, I won't harm you, but I do have something which might help with the pain. If you'd like to sit down and take off your shoe and sock, I have some healing ointment. You can put it on yourself if you would rather."

The man seemed to be genuine. Jacob was in a lot of pain with his foot and the thought of anything that might help ease it was attractive. He dropped to the floor with a grunt and tried to remove his shoe. His foot was too swollen.

The man edged towards him, "May I help?"

Jacob nodded. The man knelt before him, removed the laces and holding the heel gradually eased the shoe off. It hurt like hell and Jacob winced as the shoe finally came away.

"Good! Well done! Just one more bit, we need to get your sock off so I can apply the cream directly to the skin."

Jacob was afraid of more pain. He felt faint and very sick. Closing his eyes, he gritted his teeth and allowed the man to remove his sock. Finally, it was done.

"Last bit," he said cheerfully. He applied some foul-smelling ointment to Jacob's foot. A deep heat squeezed its way between Jacob's skin and into his ankle. The ligaments, swollen and torn were engulfed by throbbing waves of energy. Jacob yelled in agony, swore at the man and pulled his foot away from the agonising touch. "You idiot!" he shouted.

The man laughed. "Is that the way you say, thank you?"

Jacob scooted into the corner cradling his ankle in his hands. "What have you done to my ankle? That really hurt and it's stinging."

The man stood up, "It will feel better soon. Sometimes things that hurt bring healing. Think about a vaccination, or stitches when you cut yourself. How about trying to walk on it?"

Jacob stared at him and then at his ankle. It was still throbbing, but the pain was lessening. Gingerly he wriggled his toes and then moved the foot from side to side. It felt strong. He stretched out his leg and then carefully put some weight on it. Again, it felt strong despite the heat which lingered deep within the bone. "How did you do that?" he whispered.

The man was packing the ointment back into his bag, he smiled, "Ah, it's a miracle, Jacob."

Just at that moment the door at the end of the warehouse was flung open. Jacob jumped. Standing silhouetted against the light was another man.

"What's going on here? Who's this? I go out for an hour, and you have a boy in tow." The man ambled up to Jacob and leered at him. Jacob shrank back in disgust, his breath smelt of cigarettes and beer.

The Healer, as he now became known in Jacob's head, pushed the newcomer away and marched him down to the end of the room. The two men huddled close together and seemed to be arguing. Jacob looked at the open door considering whether his ankle was now strong enough to make a run for it.

The first man came back. "What's your parents' phone number Jacob? We want to phone home and let them know you are safe."

Jacob looked from one to another. There was something odd about them. The second man was grinning and licking his lips. The first man looked really serious as he held out his hand for the phone. Jacob felt very uncomfortable. He thought quickly, "I will phone my dad to let him know where I am. Ok?" He began to dial the number, while the two men watched him. His dad answered but before he could say anything the mean man grabbed the phone from him.

"Hello, is that Jacob's dad? Yeah? Just to let you know we have your son and if you want to see him alive you need to pay us ten thousand pounds by tonight."

Jacob's mouth dropped open. The person on the other end replied and the man offered the phone to Jacob. "Tell him that it's true and that you are okay."

Jacob took the phone, "Hello! Dad? Yes, it's me. Yes, it's true. I am in an old factory..."

The phone was snatched away from him, and the man spoke into it. "So, that was your son, now let's make arrangements for the transfer of money. Ten thousand pounds, no police and your son will be returned to you safe and sound. You tell the police, and you will only see your son in a box. Get it? You get the money and when you are ready phone me again on the number, I am going to text you. It's a sim only phone and you can't trace it. We will arrange an exchange." He terminated the call with a flourish. "I am so good at this kidnapping lark; I think I might make a habit of it." He laughed and strode to the back of the warehouse where he produced some ropes. Kneeling in front of Jacob he tied his hands and feet together. "Don't want you running off now do we?" He surveyed his handiwork and then turned to the man who had treated Jacob who was standing watching them both. Taking a mobile from his pocket he changed the sim card and text a number from Jacob's phone. He then grabbed a beer and sat on a box, watching Jacob carefully. The Healer said nothing but also took a beer and sat down a little distance from Jacob. They waited.

****

In the meantime, the school had already alerted Mr Taylor to his son's disappearance. He was not best pleased as he had just completed an interview for a job that morning and was enjoying a mocha with full cream milk and three sugars. *Flipping selfish kid*, he thought to himself.

Certain that Jacob was just attention seeking, he finished his coffee and then tried to phone his son. Unsurprisingly Jacob failed to answer. Mr Taylor could well imagine his irritating son laughing to himself as he saw his father's number come up on the screen. He decided not to waste any more time and instead sent him a text message to phone home. Muttering to himself, he pulled on a jacket and tried to phone his wife as he drove home. She too was irritated by Jacob's disappearance but blamed her husband. Apparently, he was not providing his son with the emotional support he needed. This had evolved into a full-scale argument, about who was going to look for Jacob. It felt like she always won any argument to do with the kids, and this occasion was no exception. She had humiliated him by reminding him that she was working while he was not and had cut him off before he could argue. Angry, he determined to ground Jacob for a month once he came home.

Driving a little too fast for the wet conditions, he phoned the school and asked to speak to the Head. He felt uncomfortable, last time he had spoken with Hedgehog as Jacob called him it had been to beg him not to expel his wayward son from the school. Now he was having to apologise once again. Humility did not come easily to Gerald Taylor.

When he finally got through to the man, he was nearly home; the Head was concerned to hear that Jacob was still missing and suggested he call the police. Mr Taylor was shocked. He was unaccustomed to taking much notice of his son's antics; his policy had always been to ignore any bad behaviour in the hope that it and Jacob would go away. Sending him to his room seemed to work well and it got him out of his hair. So, the suggestion that he should call the police seemed a bit extreme. As he pulled into the drive, he turned off the engine and sat for a while deep in thought. And then his phone rang. It was Jacob. Thank goodness. Relief quickly turned to anxiety as the rough voice on the other end told him that he had kidnapped his son. Every parent's nightmare suddenly became a reality. Guilt overwhelmed him. Why had he not taken this more seriously? He was in an agony of indecision. Should he phone the police?

****

Back in the warehouse, Jacob felt sick and shaky. He was shivering with fear and the smell was really getting to him, he was not sure how much longer he could last without throwing up. He did not want to show weakness, but he also wanted to cry and above all he wanted his dad.

He looked directly at the man who had healed his foot.

"Why did you help me when you also planned to hurt me?" he asked.

"Shut up," shouted the man from the back of the warehouse. "You speak again, and I'll stamp on your mouth."

115

The Healer walked over to him and bent down to check the ropes, as he did so he slipped Jacob a broken piece of glass. The other man stood up and half ran over to Jacob. He looked suspiciously at the two of them and also checked the ropes. As he bent his dark head over Jacob's feet and checked his wrists Jacob thought again of a magpie. His eyes were small and widely set, almost on the side of his head. His nose was long and thin, tapering to a beak like end. Thin lips barely covered his tobacco stained, misshapen teeth. Jacob physically recoiled from the smell of his breath.

"What's up boy?" he cawed, pushing his face up against Jacob, "part of me hopes your daddy don't come up with the money 'cos I'd enjoy cutting off your finger and sending it to him."

In his mind's eye Jacob suddenly thought of the Eagle. He imagined the bird swooping down upon this magpie like man and grabbing him with her strong talons. In his head, the strong, honourable bird took the dark headed vermin to a dustbin, having dropped it into a box and shut the lid. Despite himself he found himself praying, "Oh Eagle, if you exist, please help me."

The Healer spoke in his deep soothing voice, "that's enough, leave the lad alone, can't you see he's terrified?" He placed his hand on the Magpie's shoulders, pulling him backwards. The man yelled in fury and swung out at the Healer hitting him square on the chin, causing him to stagger backwards. Seizing his opportunity, Jacob began furiously working at the ropes using the shard of glass. Hands occupied, he watched terrified as Magpie man picked up an iron bar and stood over the Healer, he tapped the bar slowly into his palm, working up the fear that he could see building in his victim's eyes.

"First, I am going to kill you and then I am going to take all the money I get for this little geek myself."

****

Mr Taylor turned the phone over in his hand. What should he do? He had seen these things happen in films and had always felt irritated with the victims. It seemed so obvious you should call the police. But now he was in the situation himself, he was not so sure. He clambered out of the car and stood uncertainly at the gate his eyes raking the road hoping to see his unruly son striding towards him.

As he stared a police car drove quickly down the road and came to a halt outside his house. A female officer opened the car door and looked up at him, "Mr Taylor?" she asked.

Shocked, he simply nodded. His thoughts were racing, what should he do? How much should he tell them? She explained that the school had contacted the police and asked if she and her colleague might come inside to get a photo of Jacob and get a few details. Once inside, he found himself explaining about the phone call. They immediately became very grave and serious. One got straight onto the phone while the other asked a barrage of questions about Jacob's friends, habits, hangouts. He realised how little he knew about his son. His wife was called. She was to go to the school to see if Rebekkah might have any idea as to where Jacob might be.

He was sitting with his head in his hands when she and Rebekkah both arrived. She had whirled in demanding to be given an update and then had burst into tears. He reached out a tentative hand expecting rejection but instead she buried her head in his shoulder and sobbed. For the first time in months, he held her, and a bridge was built.

****

Jacob sawed at the ropes as if his life depended on it. He watched with deepening horror as the Magpie swung the iron bar at the Healer. It came crashing down onto the floor with a loud bang as the man rolled out of the way and rugby tackled his attacker to the floor. The vile man swore and struck out at his prey with the bar hitting him on the side of his shoulder. The victim cried out in pain and then quickly rolled sideways avoiding further blows. Jacob sawed more urgently at his wrist. His thumb and finger were bleeding as the sharp glass cut into his flesh, but he was making progress. He could feel no pain as one by one the entwined bits of braid frayed and popped. Finally, they dropped away from his wrists, and he frantically set to work on his feet. He glanced fearfully at the writhing bodies and began to shuffle away from them towards the door working hard at the same time. He was aware of loud yells, shouts and screams. The abuser was now standing over his quarry and raining blows down on his head and body, kicking him in the

119

groin and head. The poor man was curled in a foetal position trying to protect himself from the bombardment. As Jacob reached the door, he clambered to his feet and clawed desperately at the handle, trying to open it. Behind him he heard a cry of fury and a claw like hand gripped his arm, pulling him away from the door. Instinctively Jacob stabbed at the man's face and neck with the shard. Howling in pain the man let go of Jacob to protect his eyes, this gave the youngster a moment to yank the door open and hop through. Finding himself in a cool, dark room he slammed the door behind him and wedged a substantial lump of wood under the handle. Grateful for fresh air, he gulped it into his lungs and hopped, feet together as fast as he could away from the door.

Adrenaline fueled, he seemed possessed of super-human energy. He could feel that the airflow was becoming stronger, and he figured that there must be an exit at the end of it. Groping his way along the wall, his fingers found an old sign with the letters 'E it' on it and an arrow pointing left. There were now loud banging noises coming from the locked door. Sobbing with exertion and fear Jacob hopped in the direction of the arrow and then with relief found the door. He pushed against it and it flew open releasing him into a large yard. He dropped to his knees and rolled onto his back hugging his legs to his chest and panting with exhaustion. As he moved his head from side to side, his eye was drawn to a heap of rubbish in the corner of the yard. He was sure he could see a rusty old saw. He rolled back up and hopped over to the pile. The saw made quick work of the remaining ropes and as the last thread was broken, he staggered to his feet and ran towards the stairs at the end of the yard. Emerging at the top he found himself in a busy street, he grabbed the nearest person, begged them for help, and passed out.

17 JACOB, THE MAGPIE AND THE VICAR

When Jacob opened his eyes, he was surrounded by people. He had a rushing sound in his head and voices clamoured for his attention. A voice was asking him if he was hurt or had pain anywhere.

He shook his head and murmured, "The Healer, please help the Healer." Then more voices penetrated his head asking the crowd to move back, a man's face swam into view and Jacob muttered again, "the Healer, please help the Healer."

Jacob's voice seemed to be coming from far away. The man moved his ear nearer to Jacob's mouth to hear him, "What's that son?"

Jacob repeated the words and added, "He is in the factory."

The paramedic was looking at him, "Have you been hurt son? You have blood all over you."

Jacob shook his head, "Please help him, he might die."

The ambulance man looked at him and then spoke to his companion. "Phone the police and get another crew here. It's all right son, we'll look after your friend. Now let's sort you out." The man was examining his hands, which were covered in lacerations.

Another siren approached and a police car screamed to a halt. A burly police officer got out and asked him his name. He then spoke into his radio. "Missing boy, Jacob Taylor has been found in Windsor St."

The ambulance man said something to the officer who beckoned to his companion and they both ran off towards the warehouse. Relieved, Jacob allowed himself to be bundled into the back of the ambulance and they sped off towards the hospital. Then what occurred was a bewildering set of events. He was questioned by several police officers who were concerned about what the men had done to him in the warehouse. They seemed disinterested in the well-being of the man who had saved him and disbelieving when Jacob told them about the ankle.

"Stockholm syndrome," said one young woman to her

companion. "The boy has obviously got fond of his captor."

"A bit quick for that, don't you think?" said the other officer.

Jacob was irritated by the exchange and told them so. He was even more irritated when his parents arrived, and his mother burst into tears and sobbed all over him. Such a display of emotion had never happened before as far as Jacob could remember and he was intensely embarrassed. His dad stood to one side his arms hanging limply by his side and a goofy smile on his face. In a brief moment of respite, when his mother lifted her face to plant a kiss on his cheek, his dad stepped forward and patted him on his shoulder.

"Glad that you are safe, son," he said. "You gave us a bit of a scare. Good news though, you know that job I went for this morning, well, I got it."

Jacob smiled wanly, he felt exhausted, but he was hungry. "That's good," he said simply. "Can we get something to eat, I am starving."

Much to Jacob's delight he was given a few days off from school to recover emotionally and physically. He couldn't hold a pen as his thumb and forefinger were badly cut but he was told he could use a computer to help him write.

On return to school, he had been subjected to a long meeting with the Head and his parents. He had had to give an undertaking to be polite and to stay in school. His parents had also had to sign a contract to say they would support the school in their attempts to support him. He was given an amber time out card that he could show to any teacher that allowed him to leave the room if he needed to. It all seemed a bit over the top, but he liked the fact that he had an excuse to get out of his least favourite lessons.

At last, he was allowed back in form where he suddenly found he was a bit of celebrity. The other boys crowded around him wanting to know what had happened. He resisted the temptation to exaggerate his own role and enjoyed showing off his wounds. As he stood in the playground and told his story for the hundredth time, he looked up and saw a magpie perched on the tree above him. There was something almost human about the way it looked at him, and he was filled with a sense of foreboding.

Sure enough, that evening as Jacob walked home, he heard footsteps running behind him. Someone pushed into him and pressed him against the wall. He could not see the face as it was hidden behind a scarf and a hood. But the smell was unmistakable, Jacob shouted at the top of his lungs for help. People turned to look, and some began to run towards him.

His attacker leaned in close and croaked into his ear, "I will get you Jacob, no one escapes from me, have no doubt, I'm coming back for you." Giving the lad a mighty shove, he ran off, leaving Jacob doubled up with fear.

Not again, he thought. *Why me?*

Then a kind voice spoke to him asking him if he was all right. Jacob looked up at him. His face was vaguely familiar.

"It's Jacob, isn't it? We met at the christening of David a few weeks ago. Let's go inside and take a few moments to get your breath back," said the vicar. Jacob looked at him, tears streaming down his face; the shock of a second attack in a week was making him shake. The man took him by the elbow and led him to the church building opposite. Inside it was cool and dark. Jacob sat down on a chair near the door.

"So, do you want to tell me what happened?" asked the vicar. And despite himself, out it all came: the bullying, the fight, running away, the factory and now the attack. The vicar was a good listener; he didn't interrupt and revealed little through his expression. When Jacob finished, the man looked at him. "You have had a tough time, Jacob. And you need to report this second attack to the police. I will ring them now." He paused as he waited for the phone to engage and continued, "do you know what happened to the man you call the Healer?"

Jacob waited while the vicar spoke to the police officer on the end of the phone.

"I am to keep you here, Jacob. They will come and collect you. What about the man who helped you?"

Jacob looked at his feet, "No, I don't know what became of him, but I did try and get him some help." He looked again at the vicar and then lowered his eyes to the floor.

The vicar looked at him and then stood up. "Come on, let's get you home, I'll come with you in the police car."

Rebekkah was at home when they got back. She was delighted to see the vicar again and made him a cup of tea. They sat and chatted about birds and books while Jacob spoke to the policeman.

"You think it was the same man who kidnapped you?" The police officer had a book open and was scribbling furiously.

"Yes, I'd know that smell anywhere. And he threatened me, said he'd come and find me."

The police officer paused in his scribbling and spoke for a while into his walkie talkie.

Jacob wandered over to his sister and the vicar who put his cup down very carefully on his saucer and looked at Jacob with concern. "You have had a terrible experience and need to take care over the next few weeks. This man sounds very dangerous. I am sure the police will know what to do." He paused and then persisted, "I can't help thinking about the man who helped you in the warehouse. He must be very unwell. Do you know how he is?"

Jacob looked at him and realised he hadn't given the guy a

128

second thought. Guilt flooded through him, he resolved to talk to his dad about it.

Steve, the vicar, checked his watch, picked up his coat, said goodbye to them both and left.

18 JACOB AND HIS CONSCIENCE

That night Jacob slept badly. His stomach was sore, and his thoughts were troubled. He dreamt of eagles and magpies; they were battling together, and it was bloody. The Eagle had a nest, and She was defending Her young. The nest was under attack by hundreds of magpies. They wanted to kill and eat the little ones. The Eagle was unable to defend Herself because She needed to protect Her young. Outnumbered She perched on the edge of Her nest and spread out Her enormous wings to cover Her babies. She lifted Her proud head and cried, a loud yelping call that sounded more like a sea gull than a noble bird. He woke with a shout; his hands were bunched together, and he was crying. He knew immediately what he must do.

The next morning, over breakfast he broached the subject that had been troubling him with his father. "Dad, what happened to the man who helped me escape from the warehouse?"

His father looked up from his paper, "The police arrested him. Well, they will do once he recovers."

Jacob immediately felt guilty, why hadn't it occurred to him to ask about the man before now.

"But that's not fair, he tried to help me."

"Why do you care? They are both losers." His father looked at him. "By the way, the police called, they want us to go back into the station this morning. They want a more detailed statement about last night's attack and coincidentally, they want to ask you a few more questions about that bloke."

"Why? I told them what happened." Jacob was impatient.

"They seem to think you were emotionally connected to the guy and now you have had a few days to think about it, they want you to give a clearer account of his involvement with your kidnapping."

"He didn't kidnap me, I jumped into the warehouse, and he tried to help me. It was that other guy, the Magpie one that tried to harm both of us. That's why the Healer is so ill; the guy beat him to a pulp. I won't testify against him. Dad, you have got to help me. This is just not fair." Jacob's face was pink, his chin jutted out in defiance and his green eyes glistened.

His father looked at him and slowly put down the paper. "That guy really got to you, didn't he? Listen Jacob, there is something called Stockholm syndrome, which is where the people who have been kidnapped become emotionally attached to their kidnappers. We will need to get you some trauma therapy if you aren't able to tell the truth."

Jacob shouted and banged his fist on the table making the salt and pepper pots jump. "I do not need therapy. I am not an emotional wreck; I just want to tell the truth and I want you to stick up for me and him!"

His dad looked at his watch. "Let's go Jacob."

Jacob looked at him and folded his arms. "I am not going with you unless you promise to support my account."

His father sighed, checked his watch, and folded his paper. "How about you do as the police ask and then we can go and get you a new iPad? I don't want to spend all morning doing this."

Jacob stood up, his fists were balls in his hands, and anger like bile rose in his throat. "You think you can bribe me to lie? Just for an iPad, to say things that would put a man in jail. He is already down on his luck and now this. It's all because I tried to run away. I won't do it Dad and you will just have to sit with me until the police see sense!"

His dad looked again at his watch and sighed. "Okay. Now get in the car."

Once they arrived at the station Mr Taylor asked to speak to the police officers in private. On returning to the interview room the officer was accompanied by a smart woman with a briefcase. They were then moved to a room that was more like a lounge and sat down together. The smart woman introduced herself as Dr Seymour and said she wanted to ask him a few more questions about the incident in the warehouse. Jacob looked at her and then at his father who shrugged.

"Are you a shrink?" He demanded.

"Jacob! Manners!" Exclaimed his father.

'It's all right Mr Taylor. Yes, I am a psychiatrist, and I would like you to give me your account of what happened. It's quite normal in these cases in order to help the victim come to terms with what has happened."

Jacob looked at her with disdain. "You won't change my story. I have already told the officers. I ran away from a fight at school. It was raining. I jumped into the warehouse to shelter and then I hurt my foot. The Healer was there. He healed my foot with some ointment and then this other bloke arrived..."

"Ah yes," interrupted the woman, "healed your foot. Can we talk a bit more about that? What makes you so sure that your foot was badly hurt? Did he tell you it was?"

"No! It hurt. In fact, I was in agony, and I couldn't walk. I had to drag myself along the floor and hop around on one leg."

The lady turned to his father. "Mr Taylor, has Jacob ever hurt his ankle before?"

Jacob's father looked at her. "Not that I am aware of. Why?"

She was looking at the papers in front of her. "Well, the report from the doctor who attended Jacob in accident and emergency said that he x-rayed the foot and there definitely was a break, quite a nasty one, but it had healed. He said it was recent, within the last couple of months."

Mr Taylor looked at his son. "No, Jacob has never broken his ankle to my knowledge." He shuffled awkwardly in his chair. "Look is this necessary? Jacob may actually be telling the truth. Weird things do happen."

The psychologist looked at him. "It's understandable that you want to protect your son Mr. Taylor but we do need him to testify to keep this dangerous child abductor off the streets. Otherwise he might do it again."

"But Jacob was not abducted. He jumped into the warehouse. The guy happened to be there."

"Ah but can we be sure? The behaviour of the man he calls Healer leads me to believe they were in this together. He abducted Jacob and pretended to be his friend. This is quite common in abductions, one kidnapper pretends to be the good cop and the other the bad cop." She laughed, "present company might recognise this technique in policing." The officers smiled.

Jacob jumped up. "This is ridiculous. You are twisting my words. He did not abduct me. I ran away from school because I was accused of starting a fight. The Healer tried to help me.

Why won't you listen?"

The lady rustled through her papers. "It says on page four of your statement that the man you called the Healer did not protect you from his companion and colluded with him when he phoned your father. Is that true?"

"Yes," said Jacob through gritted teeth. "But he obviously was planning how to help me because later he gave me some glass to cut my bonds. I don't know why he didn't help me earlier but have you considered that he might have had a plan and was waiting for a time when he could safely help me to leave?"

Dr Seymour was scribbling rapidly into a little red book. She looked up just once and smiled at Jacob and then went back to her writing. Then she stopped and fished out a photograph. "Who is this, Jacob?"

Jacob looked at the photo. It was the man he called the Healer, but his face was broken and bruised.

"The Healer," he whispered in a small voice.

She fished out another picture and gave to him. "And who is

this?"

Jacob expected to see the Magpie in front of him. Instead, he saw a different man, clean shaven and smiling. His arm was raised and perched on a leather sheath was a large golden eagle. His eyes however were unmistakably the same as those of the Healer. "I, I, I am not sure," he stammered. "I think it might be the same man."

"You are right," she continued, "This is Robert Cameron. Formerly, he worked as a bird-keeper at Beaulieu in Hampshire. He cared for the birds of prey there."

"What happened to him?"

"Well, he was accused of killing a falcon and then poisoning a golden eagle. Both birds were in his care at the time. He was sacked." She paused.

Jacob opened his mouth to argue but she held up a hand to silence him. "The eagle was later found. It had been poisoned, not as it happens by Robert, but by another bird-keeper who had been neglectful and left out meat with poison in it intended for rats. The eagle smelt the meat and ate it. The perpetrator,

137

knowing he had been careless, allowed Robert to take the rap. So you see this is not the first time your friend has had a brush with the law."

"So why are you telling me this? What has this got to do with my story?"

Dr Seymour paused and tapped her pen against her teeth. "Let's just say that your friend Robert, before he was sacked, had been experimenting with healing ointments that he used to mend fractured wings on birds. So, it may not be entirely inaccurate to say he helped your ankle."

The police officer seated to her right shifted slightly and stared at the doctor.

"Jacob, I find nothing in your story to lead me to believe that you are lying. In my expert opinion you have not got Stockholm syndrome and my recommendation is that your statement should be allowed to go forward as it is."

The police officer stood up with Dr Seymour and the two of them walked out together. Shortly afterwards the officer returned alone. "Just to let you know, based on your testimony

Jacob, we are dropping charges against Robert Cameron but not against the man you call the Magpie. However, it may be of interest to you that when we entered the building Mr Cameron was on his own, the other man was nowhere to be seen and is still at large. So, without wishing to worry you, our advice is to be careful."

Jacob smiled, he felt good for the first time in ages.

His father shifted in his seat, "It's a pity you lot haven't found this evil kidnapper because he attacked my son again last night. What are you going to do about him?"

"We have put out a description to all units, sir, based on what Jacob has told us, it's only a matter of time."

Jacob looked at the man, all the joy he had felt ebbed away, he knew he would meet the Magpie again before the police managed to catch up with him.

19 JACOB AND ROBERT

"Can I have some money, Dad? I want to go into town, I am meeting John and some of my friends from school." Absent-mindedly his dad placed some coins onto the table from his money purse and went back to watching the snooker.

It was Monday, two days after the interview in the police station. He took the number sixteen bus down to the hospital and walked into reception. He asked if they knew of the whereabouts of Robert Cameron. A distracted receptionist waved him towards a door at the bottom of the corridor. Nervously, he entered the ward and was asked by the nurse at the desk to apply some disinfectant to his hands. Rubbing his hands together he marvelled at the way the slimy stuff just disappeared into his skin. As he passed through the ward, he examined the occupants of the beds. Would he recognise the guy? Finally at the very end he saw him. His face was still swollen, his right eye puffy and black and one leg suspended in a cage above the bed. Jacob paused before walking purposefully on. He arrived at the bed and stood hesitantly to one side and waited. The man slowly turned his head and looked at him. He smiled revealing three cracked teeth. "Hi Jacob," he greeted him. "It's good to see you again. Sit down, sorry I can't get up."

Jacob looked for a chair and spied one at another bed. As he collected it, he noticed the bedside cabinets of other people's beds were laden with fruit, sweets and soft drinks, Robert's was empty.

"I am sorry, I should have brought something for you," he stammered.

Robert smiled, "That's okay, you brought yourself; I wanted to thank you, for your testimony. The police have dropped all charges, I am free to go," and he laughed, the deep laugh that Jacob remembered from the warehouse and waved vaguely at his leg. And then Jacob saw it. Robert was wearing a sleeveless vest exposing a muscular shoulder on which had been tattooed a beautiful golden eagle.

Robert followed Jacob's eyes and smiled. "You are wondering about the Eagle? She protects me."

"Protects you!" Jacob blurted out. "How can you believe that she protects you? You have lost everything; your job, your home, your... teeth!" He looked at Robert who burst out laughing and stuck his tongue out through the gaps in his teeth."

"Yes. She protects me. Life often isn't fair and there are some tough things along the way, but we are both alive and free. Also, I am lucky to have met you Jacob, because through your story Steve your vicar friend came to see me. He has offered me food and accommodation if I look after the gardens at his church. So, all is well that ends well."

Jacob looked at Robert, "Thank you for helping me to escape. I am sorry you got hurt. But who is the Magpie? He seemed to be your friend. Why didn't you warn me of him before he came back to the warehouse?"

Robert looked away and appeared to be thinking. A long time passed before he answered. "Jacob, I was deceived too. I had met him before, never much liked the fellow, but I was down on my luck, without a home or a job and I bumped into him. He said he might be able to help me. When things are hard you jump at chances. It was only after I saw the way he treated you

142

that his true nature was revealed, and I knew I had to get you away from him."

Jacob wasn't convinced, "Why didn't you attack him straight away? Why did you go along with the phone call and frightening my dad? And why…" Jacob was growing more indignant as the memories flooded back, "why did you allow him to tie me up? I had no chance of escaping."

Robert looked at him sadly, "Jacob, I am not proud of myself, but I was scared too. There's something vile about him. I had no idea what he would do and no real plan until I found the glass on the floor. I slipped it to you so you could saw through the rope. He was strong but not quite strong enough. And you acted quickly. You did well, Jacob."

Jacob flushed at the praise, he knew what Robert meant about the man being vile, he felt repulsed every time he thought about him. He paused then continued, "He's still around Robert, he attacked me again last night, said no one escapes from him and he would come and find me."

Robert looked concerned and then touched the tattoo on his

arm. "You are going to need protection, Jacob. Do you believe in the Eagle?"

"Of course not," Jacob scoffed. But a memory came back to him; whilst in the warehouse he had reached out and asked the Eagle for help. Robert stared at him for a long time until finally Jacob stood up and said he needed to go.

Chapter 20 Rebekkah and Jacob

Just as Jacob put his key into the door it flew open and his sister was standing, hands on hips, waiting for him. It was as if she knew that he wanted to talk to her.

"Where have you been?" she demanded. "You can't just go off like that. The Magpie is still around you know."

He looked at her in astonishment. "How did you know?" he asked her.

"Dad told me that we need to be careful because one of your abductors had run off, the one you called Magpie."

"Oh, that makes sense then. Rebekkah, can we talk?"

He pushed past her and into the kitchen. She trotted after him expectantly. He was starving and began raiding the fridge and cupboards. He opened a packet of biscuits and shoved two into his mouth.

"Jacob that's really greedy," Rebekkah reprimanded him. He hesitated planning to eat another two and then offered her the packet.

Shocked at this unusual act of brotherly kindness she took one and sat down with him at the table. He told her about the conversation with Robert at the hospital. She listened gravely. When he had finished, she took another biscuit and then asked the question that had been on her lips since the journey to the nest.

"Jacob, what do you think happened at the nest?"

He looked at her turning a shade of pink at the memory. "What do you remember?" he asked cautiously.

She told him her account of what happened. Stunned at the accuracy of her memory he finally had to accept that they had both experienced something together in another world that transcended their own.

After she had finished, they were both quiet, lost in their own thoughts. Then Rebekkah spoke, "Jacob, since that experience everything has changed. Do you think it's linked?"

"Just a coincidence," he said gruffly. "What else could it be?

How can a fantastical world in another time zone have an impact on our lives here? It doesn't make sense."

"No, I suppose not, but it's weird how Robert believes in the Eagle too. And he rescued you."

"So?" Jacob was closing down, she could see it. "I helped myself, Robert agrees. Nothing supernatural or magical about it." With that he stood up and walked to the fridge. "Fancy a strawberry milkshake? Let's go and watch a film together." Rebekkah looked at him in exasperation, she wanted to pursue the conversation further, but something deep down inside held her back. For now, she was content that one day they would talk further. She bit back the words about chocolate pears and dead birds that were on her tongue and followed him into the lounge instead.

The Eagle and The Magpie

PART 2

SIX MONTHS LATER

1 THE DREAM

The cat crouched motionless on the patio. Its unblinking eyes were transfixed upon the bird resting in the centre of the lawn. Suddenly, it arched its back, raised its tail and wiggled its haunches before unleashing its attack. In a flash, it had the hapless bird clenched between its teeth and was darting to a hedge where it sat crouched stealthily, mouth full, alert to any who might come to steal its prize. Then, as if from nowhere, the air was filled with the raucous sound of angry and urgent chattering. Rooflines and trees were filled with birds all identical in their black and white plumage. They had flocked together to protect a fellow magpie and to intimidate the feline aggressor into dropping its catch. Furiously and plaintively, they protested, moving up and down branches, beaks flapping.

Suddenly, three birds, as if bound by a chord, jumped in unison from their perches and dive-bombed the cat. Completely taken aback by this daring move, the cat dropped its catch and scampered off deep into the undergrowth out of harm's way; the hunter now feeling hunted. The prisoner, realising it was free, half hopped half dragged its way across the garden, its wing damaged and leg broken. The watching birds in the trees raised their cries to a deafening crescendo, furious at the damage done to one of their own. The three rescuers bobbed anxiously around their wounded friend urging it to fly up into the trees and to safety. It did its best but after several failed attempts flopped helplessly back onto the lawn.

From another corner of the garden darted a different cat that grabbed the wretched bird and dragged it out of sight. The great cacophony of protest was raised even higher as the birds witnessed the end of one of their own. Protest quickly turned to realisation and resignation. One by one the doleful birds departed leaving a blanket of silence.

In his dream, Jacob moved towards the hedge and pulled up the branches to get a closer look at the bird. The predatory cat had gone, bored now that its prey was dead. The bird lay on its side, mangled and motionless, its existence at an end.

Jacob recognised the purplish–blue iridescent sheen of wing feathers and the unmistakable green tail of a magpie. He moved in closer, picked up a twig and poked the bird's body. As he did so the chest moved and the bird turned its head, its small orange beady eye fixed on his own. To his total shock and horror, the face began to swell, change and distort. Within seconds it had morphed into the face of a man, his face twisted into a terrible sneer, "I am coming for you Jacob," he snarled.

Jacob woke with a start. He was sweating and terrified. He could feel his heart palpitating in his chest.

The face was not unknown to him. The man in the dream had trapped him in a warehouse and threatened to cut off his finger unless his parents paid a ransom.

He had no desire to meet the man again.

2 HOLIDAYS

Swinging his legs out of bed Jacob sat up. His red hair, washed the night before, was now dishevelled and twisted into all sorts of weird shapes. Passing his hand over his sleepy green eyes he squeezed them tightly, trying to shut out the terrifying memory.

What did the dream mean?

Being a rationalist and materialist, Jacob did not really believe in fanciful things but meeting the Eagle had challenged this worldview. His thoughts turned to a memory of a night six months ago. Dropping off to sleep, a soft tapping on his bedroom window had roused him and drawn his attention. This was his first encounter with the talking bird that they called

the Eagle. On that occasion she had flown his sister and himself to her nest. What a beautiful paradise it had been!

Reliving the experience afresh, his mouth watered at the thought of chip butties for breakfast. He smiled at the memory of swimming in the clear river waters with the silvery fish. For a moment, he was transported back to the nest and a sense of peace settled his anxious thoughts. He found himself thinking about the Eagle. Then, his rational consciousness cut in. *Was she real? Or was it all inside his head, another realistic dream?*

"Jacob!"

He jumped at the sound of his sister's voice. She was banging on his door and then pushed it open without waiting for a reply. "Jacob! Mum and dad have invited Robert Cameron for tea tonight."

"What? Oh! Great!" He looked at his younger sister as she hopped excitedly from one foot to another. She was a neat, petite, eleven-year-old with a button nose. Her hair was tied back into a ponytail. As usual, his smarmy sister was first to be ready and was chasing him. But something wasn't right.

"Rebekkah, why have you got your jeans on?"

"Because, silly boy, it's school holidays. No more school for six weeks. Yippee!"

Of course! He had been so wrapped up in his dream that he had forgotten that today was the first day of the summer holidays. A sensation of pure joy flooded his heart. Freedom!

He jumped out of bed and grabbed his iPad and then lay on his back, legs doubled up, playing *Fortnite*.

"Jacob. Get up! You can't play that all day. Come on let's plan what we are going to do." Rebekkah made a grab for his iPad but he deftly moved it to the left and carried on.

"Oh, please yourself. I am going downstairs, Mum and Dad are going to tell us where we are going on our holidays, remember?"

Yes, he did remember, and he was dreading it. Holidays with his parents were always so tense. They spent most of their time bickering over who was going to supervise them while the other one read the latest book recommended by the Times. They also produced a list of books recommended for him to read too. Naturally, they were never the books he would choose. He swung his legs off the bed, pulled on some shorts and a tee shirt and headed downstairs.

Rebekkah was seated eagerly at the table. He joined her and began surveying the options on the table. Decision made, he reached for the *Chocolate Weetos*, his favourite. At the same

6

moment Rebekkah made the same move. With a swift flick of his hand, he slapped her away and grabbed the packet for himself. Rebekkah yelled at him.

"I got here first; you should let me have the cereal. It's not fair! You are so greedy and rude!" protested Rebekkah.

Their father peered at them both over his paper.

Jacob had already started shovelling *Chocolate Weetos* into his mouth. His dad reached across the table and moved the bowl away from his son, slopping chocolate covered milk over the cloth as he did so. Rebekkah smirked triumphantly as she reached passed her brother and took hold of the packet.

Jacob quickly moved the milk away from her reach and smirked back.

Their mother joined them at the table, frowning at the mess, "Gerald, did you have to make quite such a mess?"

Gerald looked at her, "Your son, needs a few more manners."

"My, son!" she exclaimed. "You're the one who has ruined him by buying him all those gadgets. When he was living with you,

7

he learnt all sorts of bad ways."

As soon as the words were out of her mouth, all three of them looked at her. She stood, hands on her hips glaring at them all. Both children knew not to quarrel with her when she was in this mood. She was dangerous. Rebekkah longed, not for the first time, for the peaceful days when it had just been her and her mother. Shortly after Jacob's warehouse experience her parents had got back together again. The atmosphere had not improved.

Breakfast continued in silence apart from the slurping noises that came from Jacob's mouth. Gerald went back to his paper and Susan Taylor busied herself with the coffee machine. When she finally sat down, she looked like she was chewing a wasp.

Rebekkah spoke first, "Mum, where are we going on holiday this year?"

There was a momentary silence. Their father lowered his paper, "Er, we're not."

Jacob looked up from his slurping. Milk flecked his chin. A shred of hope dawned in his brain.

"Rather, we are not going away together as a family. You are going to your cousins and your mother and I are going away… on our own."

Jacob couldn't believe his luck. What a relief, a holiday without his parents nagging at him all the time. Fantastic! His cousins lived in a large country house in the middle of nowhere, in Lincolnshire. Their parents took no interest in them at all. It was all very Darwinian. He who was strongest and most deceitful survived. He could do what he liked. He grinned and looked at Rebekkah. She was looking upset.

"Where are you going?" demanded Rebekkah.

"Spain," replied Susan Taylor.

"Why can't we come too?"

"Because…" said their father, "Your mother and I are going on our own. We both work very hard and need some time together."

Rebekkah moved her spoon around her bowl. She didn't want to go to her cousins and felt angry that her parents were being selfish again. "I would like to go to Spain too. I hate going to Uncle David's house."

Jacob threw her a disgusted look. "Well, I like it there. I don't mind if you go away without us."

Rebekkah pulled a face, "Well I don't. There's no order in that house, they just do what they like. I never know when I am going to eat, and they have those horrible rats as pets. Ugh!" She shivered.

Jacob grinned. He liked rats. "I heard they now have snakes and lizards too." He said airily. He got the desired reaction from his sister.

"Mum! That is so gross! How can you send us to a place where they live in a zoo?"

"Don't be selfish Rebekkah. We need this time, your father and I, anyway, guess who we have invited for tea tonight?"

Rebekkah already knew and she was not happy about the obvious attempt to distract her.

"Robert?" interrupted Jacob. "Rebekkah told me. That's good.

I haven't seen him for ages. What time is he coming?"

"Six p.m.," responded his father and went back to his paper.

The day passed slowly. Jacob was looking forward to talking with the man he really thought of as the Healer. He had met Robert six months ago in a disused warehouse. It was the day he had run away from school after a fight with a fellow student. Seeking shelter from the driving rain he had jumped through the window of the warehouse and injured his ankle. Hurt and disorientated in a dark void, he was initially terrified to find that he was not alone. But Robert had emerged out of the gloom and had helped him by rubbing some mystical ointment onto his ankle that to his amazement had healed the broken bone. At this point another man, an associate of Robert called the Magpie, seeing an opportunity to make some money for himself, decided to kidnap Jacob, tied him up and forced him to phone his parents. A ransom was demanded for Jacob's return.

Robert had pretended to go along with this plan but then slipped a piece of broken glass into Jacob's hand, which he had used to saw through the rope. Robert had hurled himself at the Magpie

11

allowing Jacob to escape. He was later found unconscious and seriously injured. The Magpie however had disappeared. It was Jacob's greatest fear that the man would seek him out and kill him or worse.

While Jacob was lost in his thoughts Rebekkah was battling with her own demons. She had been upset by the news that the family were not going on holiday together. She suspected that the real reason her parents did not want them to go on holiday together was because they were still having problems in their marriage. They had actually been living apart until the incident in the warehouse when Jacob had been kidnapped. She wondered about the reason for their poor relationship. Was it her fault or Jacob's? Did they think that they would get on better if they were not around? She could not shake off the feeling that she was somehow to blame. It made her feel sad.

Six o'clock arrived and there was a loud knock at the door. The children rushed to open it and greeted the rather odd-looking man who stood waiting for them. Rebekkah hung back shyly while Jacob tried to hide his delight. She noticed the twinkle in the older man's eye as he presented his right hand to Jacob and then turned to her. He stooped, removed his beanie hat and bowed ever so slightly to her. Rebekkah thought him a bit awkward and old fashioned. Who today bowed to girls and shook hands with boys?

Their mother emerged from the study looking slightly harassed. There had been an argument the previous night about who was going to cook. It was clear that Susan Taylor was less keen on Jacob's new friend than her husband. Gerald Taylor declared that he found Robert Cameron an interesting man, a bit of a scientist. Susan had said she did not like the look of him and was suspicious of why he had been in the warehouse with the Magpie in the first place. The upshot of it was that Gerald had been persuaded to cook.

"Good move, mum," thought Rebekkah who preferred her dad's cooking.

"Good evening, Cameron," said Susan Taylor formally, "I hope your journey here was an easy one. Would you like to come through? Gerald is just serving up."

3 DINNER

They all went through to the kitchen where a rather red-faced and harassed looking Gerald was dolloping spaghetti onto the plates. Rebekkah giggled as all the spaghetti slid onto one plate in a large pile.

Irritated, Gerald picked up a knife and large spoon and viciously chopped at the worms of pasta moving it in chunks to the various place settings.

"Oh Gerald, you are an embarrassment. Why didn't you use the spaghetti spoon?" Susan laughed awkwardly.

Robert came to the rescue. He reached into his coat pocket and pulled out a bottle of wine from one pocket and two books from the other. He presented the wine to Susan and the books to Jacob and Rebekkah. Jacob turned it over in his hands, muttered a quick thank you and then sat down at his place at the table. Rebekkah read out her book title, "*The Time and Space of Uncle Albert*" by Russell Stannard. What's your book Jacob?"

Rebekkah nudged her brother indicating the book that he had

placed on the table next to him. He passed it to her, upside down. Turning the book, she read out the words, "'*Black Holes and Uncle Albert*'. Who is this Uncle Albert?"

Robert started to say, "The books are about Albert Einstein, a famous scientist who…"

"Wrote about time, black holes and quantum theory," interrupted Jacob. "Don't you know that?" He sneered as he said the word 'that.' His lips lifted a little showing his teeth, his nose moved, and his nostrils flared.

Rebekkah felt incredibly irritated. "Ugh Jacob, you are such a show-off."

Robert had hoped to rescue the situation caused by the obvious tension between the Taylor adults. He could see that all the Taylors were out of sorts with each other. He shifted awkwardly in his seat, took a bite of garlic bread and continued. "I remember your interest in science Jacob from our conversation in the warehouse. Did you know that Einstein was also a believer in God?"

Gerald Taylor ladled the last bit of Bolognese onto his plate and sat down. He reached for the bottle of wine that Robert had brought.

"Thanks," he nodded to Robert as he levered off the top and poured three glasses. "You believe in God do you Robert?"

"Yes, I do. Many people think belief in God does not fit with science, but I don't agree. I know that Jacob has a very thoughtful and questioning approach to these things, so I thought I'd get him a book about Einstein."

"Thanks," mumbled Jacob unenthusiastically as he shovelled as much food as he possibly could into his mouth.

"Jacob!" said his mother, disapprovingly.

"And…" Robert smiled at Rebekkah; "The hero of the stories who travels in a thought bubble to investigate Einstein's theories is a girl."

Jacob made a strangled sound as he shovelled more food into his mouth. Red sauce dribbled down his chin as he sucked in several strands of spaghetti.

Gerald raised his glass to his lips and looked at Robert

thoughtfully, twirling the glass around in his fingers. He took a sip.

"Odd the way you were able to mend Jacob's ankle with that ointment you use on bird's wings. Do you think God did it? Would you call that a miracle?"

"Dad!" Rebekkah cast a warning look in her father's direction. She knew her father had strong atheist views and could see this leading to an argument.

Robert took another bite of garlic bread and chewed for a few moments before answering.

"What I think is … God can use our brains to find scientific ways of helping others. We just have to be open to the possibility of God existing."

"Ah," said Gerald, swooping in, "I am afraid I shall never believe in God because of the existence of evil. For me, the fact that suffering exists is good evidence for the non-existence of God. If a loving God existed, then surely he would do something about it?" He paused, glass mid-air, looking pleased with himself for having made such a clever point.

17

Rebekkah knew her father well and realised that his desire to argue had been fed by his irritation with having to make the meal and the spaghetti sliding everywhere. Jacob, on the other hand was enjoying the possibility of a heated debate between the two men.

"Good point dad, and what about wars and murder and torture and terrorism? I saw on the news the other day how …"

"Jacob," warned his mother, "Not while we are eating!"

"Your mum is right, this is not a good topic for the dinner table," said Robert wiping his mouth on his serviette and looking apologetically at the children's mother.

Gerald however was not to be put off; he had the bit between his teeth, "It seems to me, that you religious people are all the same. When it comes to the tough questions you avoid answering them."

"Gerald! Robert is our guest." Susan Taylor scolded her husband, while waving her fork at him.

Rebekkah looked at Robert and he winked at her, "What do you think Rebekkah?"

"I think that all the things Jacob mentions are caused by humans being mean. I don't think it's anything to do with God." She said defiantly, looking at her father and brother, willing them to challenge her. "Even when things are perfect some human being will want to spoil it, that's just the way we are." As she said this, she looked directly at Jacob.

He blushed as a memory of himself in the beautiful paradise world of the nest flashed across his mind. He had killed a bird in that wonderful paradise. Why had he done that? It seemed a totally mindless thing to do now he thought about it. Lost in his thoughts he failed to hear his mother talking to him. "More food Jacob?"

Rebekkah nudged him in the ribs and repeated the question. She knew that Jacob was remembering and was glad at his discomfiture. She had been very angry with him and the way his selfishness had got them both thrown out of the most beautiful place she had ever known.

His thoughts then inexplicably swam to the dream he had had

19

the previous night about the cat and the magpie. An idea occurred to him. "What about the evil in nature? Cats, for example, they just kill birds for the fun of it. They aren't hungry – they just play with the prey until it's dead and walk away."

"Yes, that's an interesting one," agreed Robert. "Most of my work is with birds of prey but I have heard a theory that cats toss their victim around in order to disorientate it so that when they do kill it, by severing the spinal cord at the neck, then the creature can't bite or scratch the cat. Cats have small, flat faces and their eyes are very easily scratched."

As if aware that she was being discussed Rebekkah's cat strolled over to the table and began weaving in and out of Rebekkah's legs. The girl tilted her shoulder slightly and tickled the cat's back allowing her hand to be nudged gently by the cat's nose.

"Rebekkah, don't play with Tipsy at the table, you don't know what she has been doing with her mouth!" Susan was neurotic about hygiene.

Jacob grinned. "Licking her bum, I expect. That cat has got the smelliest breath ever." Imperiously Tipsy walked off with her tail in the air; a few seconds later they heard the cat flap bang as she disappeared into the night.

Susan glared at Jacob, cleared her throat and turned to Robert. "How is your job going down at the church?"

Robert opened his mouth to answer but before he could there was an ear-piercing screech and hissing outside the back door. Susan shouted at her husband. "Gerald! Go and break up those cats. Last time it cost £300 in vet's fees!"

Gerald threw his chair back and marched to the door. He yanked it open, strode out into the garden yelling as he did so, hoping to break up the catfight.

Then everything went silent. A voice could be heard saying, "Oh my God!"

4 THE MURDER

All three Taylors jumped up on hearing the alarm and fear in Gerald's voice, but it was Robert who got to the back door first. "Stay here and don't move. Wait until I return." His voice was authoritative as he ran through the open door and into the darkness beyond.

Mrs. Taylor hesitated, torn between her desire to know what was going on and the authority in Robert's voice.

"Mum, I'm scared." Rebekkah caught her mother's hand and held onto it tightly. "What's happened to Tipsy?"

Jacob ran to the door and balanced on the threshold. He peered into the darkness unable to see anything because of the lights shining from the house. "Turn the lights off so I can see what's going on."

Then, shouting out into the darkness of the garden, he called for his father and Robert. The lights went out and his mother and Rebekkah joined him. All three of them gazed into the shadows, straining to catch sight of the two men and the cat.

"There," said Rebekkah pointing, "can you see them?" Two men walked back towards them; one held his hand to his head while the other had something cradled in his arms. Rebekkah was first to realise that something awful had happened to Tipsy and leaving her post at the door ran to meet them.

The silhouetted men stopped and conferred. One continued his way towards them; the other with the bundle turned away and disappeared behind the back of the garage.

Mr. Taylor came in view and as he approached the back door it was possible to see the blood streaming down his head from what looked like a deep laceration near his right eye. He stumbled as he entered the room and dropped into a kitchen chair. His wife grimaced, grabbed a piece of kitchen roll and gave it to him. "What on earth happened out there?"

Mr. Taylor held the paper towel to his head and muttered, "Damn bird nearly took my eye out, I could hardly see it in the dark and then it swooped on me out of nowhere and started pecking at my face."

"You had better get that wound seen to at A&E and get a

tetanus injection."

Everyone jumped at the sound of Robert's voice. He stood in the doorway, pale and thin. Somehow, he looked older and more tired. Moving towards the little family he sat down heavily at the table and looked at Rebekkah as he spoke, "I am so sorry Rebekkah but Tipsy is dead. A magpie killed her with its beak. It was, it seemed, er… quick," he said rather lamely.

Rebekkah's hand shot to her mouth and tears welled up in her eyes, "Oh, poor Tipsy! This is awful."

Jacob was standing next to Robert. He too had been disturbed by the events but his instinct for the macabre made him curious. "How can a magpie kill a cat?" Remembering his dream, he continued, "Surely cats are the predator, and the bird is the prey?"

Rebekkah looked at him in disgust, "Jacob! How can you be so uncaring? Who cares how it was done? Tipsy is dead. Killed by a vile bird. Poor, poor Tipsy, she must have been terrified. I hope she didn't suffer." She began to cry.

Robert hesitated, he wanted to comfort her but felt her parents should be doing that. He looked at Mrs. Taylor expecting her to move towards her daughter and cuddle her but instead she was staring at the wound on her husband's face. "I do hope this won't affect our holiday." Her voice was brittle.

It was impossible to tell if she was about to cry over the cat, her husband or the holiday. Robert suspected it was the latter. From what he had seen of the Taylors they were pretty self-absorbed. He cleared his throat and asked, "Have you got a first aid kit? That wound should be washed and then I think you should go to A&E and get it stitched."

Mrs. Taylor moved towards a cupboard and extracted a small first aid box, which she handed silently to Robert. As Robert opened the box he looked directly at Jacob, "I have known magpies attack people. They are vicious birds. But the attacks usually take place in the nesting season when they feel that their young chicks are threatened in some way. They always go for the eyes."

He pulled out a piece of gauze, filled a bowl with water and added some salt. He carefully cleaned the wound above Mr.

Taylor's eye. He was gentle and reassuring. Rebekkah watched him methodically clean the blood away from the wound and thought of all the birds he must have helped using his healing hands. Watching him at work was soothing. Finally, he took a step back and looked at Mr. Taylor, "I have done as much as I can for now. In my opinion, you need stitches and a tetanus injection and maybe some antibiotics. The beak of a magpie is full of mucky bacteria. You were lucky not to lose your eye."

Turning to Mrs. Taylor he asked, "Would you like me to stay here with Jacob and Rebekkah while you take him to casualty?"

Mrs. Taylor sighed heavily, stood up, grabbed her handbag and muttered grudgingly, "Yes, thank you that would be very helpful. I don't know how long we shall be though. Casualty is always a complete nightmare. This is not exactly how I wanted to spend my Friday night after a week at work. Come on Gerald."

Mr. Taylor got shakily to his feet Robert stepped forward and caught him as he staggered forward. "Steady up there my friend, I know it's been a bit of a shock, but they'll soon patch you up. And you'll be as right as rain by tomorrow." He helped Mr.

Taylor into his coat while his wife marched off to the car rattling her keys. She held the door open as Robert walked her husband to the car. She gave him a dark look as she slammed the door shut. "Drama seems to follow you around, doesn't it?" she said sarcastically looking him in the eye. He smiled demurely and took a step back as she brushed past him and opened her own door.

"Now don't worry about Jacob and Rebekkah, they will be fine with me."

"Thanks," she said a bit too curtly, got in and drove off.

5 THE DARK SIDE

Robert walked slowly back into the house and quietly shut the door. He methodically went through every room locking doors and windows and pulling curtains. Only when he was satisfied that nothing could see in and the house was secure did he sit down in the lounge with the two children.

Rebekkah looked at him, her face was blotchy, and she looked scared. "There's something going on isn't there Robert? You don't think Tipsy's death was an accident, do you?"

Robert looked at her without answering. He was clearly weighing up what to say.

Rebekkah felt cross. Why couldn't grown-ups just treat her as an equal? She knew a lot more than they gave her credit for.

Before Robert could answer her Jacob blurted out, "Robert, I need to tell you about a dream I had last night."

Robert looked at him and then at Rebekkah. "Go ahead. I'm listening."

Jacob told them about the dream. When he got to the bit about the magpie in the dream morphing into the face of the man who had tormented him and nearly killed Robert in the warehouse six months ago, the man known as the Magpie, Robert's face became grimmer and grimmer. "And then he said, 'I'm coming to get you Jacob'. It was at that point I woke up terrified."

Rebekkah was watching her brother as he shared his dream. She could see that he was very disturbed by the night's events and was trying to be brave. She also felt very upset by what had happened and wanted reassurance from an adult that all would be well. Clearly traumatised by the night's events Robert could see that she needed comfort, but he was torn between his desire to protect her from any further distress and a growing sense of foreboding that this attack was a just a warning and there would be more to come.

"Are these things connected, Robert?" she asked.

He studied them both for some time, debating how honest to be. "That's pretty smart of you Rebekkah. Yes, I think they are. After the incident in the warehouse, I conducted a few enquiries of my own. The man you know as the Magpie is still active. He is a bad man and is angry that Jacob got away from him. He despises me too and I have experienced a couple of attacks from his birds whilst working in the church garden. He has this special connection with magpies, in fact, he has his own group of magpies that he is able to control. I think that one of his birds attacked your dad and killed Tipsy."

Jacob was unhappy at Robert's compliment of his sister and also cross that he had not received more sympathy for the effect the dream had had on him. "Huh. That's unbelievable. It was an accident," said Jacob grumpily.

Robert studied Jacob and waited a while before speaking, he chose his words carefully, 'There's no place for disbelief here Jacob. You have met the Magpie you know how dangerous he is. I think you have been warned. He is on the look-out for you. You must be careful. Both of you. Very, very careful." His face was deadly serious, and he spoke earnestly.

Jacob felt a shiver of fear pass down his spine. He had no desire to meet the Magpie again and tonight's events were sinister.

Robert continued, "I think it might be a good idea to go away for a while. It's summer holidays, isn't it? Have your parents any plans for a holiday for you?"

Rebekkah looked down at her fingernails and replied unenthusiastically, "We are going to our cousins in Lincolnshire. Our parents are going somewhere else."

Robert looked at her and grinned, "I gather you aren't too pleased about the idea?"

Jacob interrupted, keen to recover the limelight, "I am looking forward to going. They are fun. Their parents don't bother much so we can do what we like."

Rebekkah wrinkled her nose and said nothing.

Robert looked at her and asked, "Do you feel safe there?"

Not wanting to look weak in front of her brother she chose to lie, "It's ok. I would just have liked to have gone away with Mum and Dad, that's all."

Robert looked at them both; his fingers were forged into a steeple with the two indexes just touching his lips. He began tapping his fingers on his top teeth making little clicking sounds as he did so. Finally, he spoke.

"If the Magpie is out to get you then he will send his birds to find you. The magpies act like scouts. They will follow your car. Fortunately, they can't fly as fast as a car, their top speed is about 30 mph, and they average between 10 and 15mph so, traveling a long distance for you is a good thing."

Rebekkah stopped him, "I don't understand why the Magpie wants to get us. What have we done to him?"

"You have visited the nest and are followers of the Eagle. He hates the Eagle and will do whatever he can to attack Her followers. Jacob, he has a particular hatred for you as you

got away from him. He thought you were his and then you escaped. He won't ever forgive you for that."

Jacob was looking at Robert with a look of incredulity on his face. "This is complete rubbish. I chose to go to that disused factory/warehouse place. It was coincidence that I met you and the Magpie. Had I made a different choice then things would have been so different. Also, I am not a follower of the Eagle.

She may be," he looked at Rebekkah and then defiantly back at Robert, "but I am not."

Robert rounded on him angrily, "Jacob, your disbelief and constant rejection of evident truth is going to get you into further trouble. Do you think you are in charge of your life? Do you think the choices you make are completely random? You need to read that book on Einstein I have just given you. He talks of how all things have a cause and an effect. You ended up in that old factory because of your nature. Once those boys took your precious iPad you were always going to hit out at them. Admittedly running away was a choice but a likely choice for you, given how unfairly you were treated by that teacher and also given your character which has little regard for authority or rules. It was raining, so, hiding in a disused warehouse was also highly likely given how wet you were. Shall I go on?"

"Actually, you have something to answer too," retorted Jacob. "It doesn't explain what you and the Magpie were doing there and how come he thought you were his friend? You have never really explained that." Jacob also spoke with anger. He was ruffled by the suggestion that he was part of some cosmic game where he had been moved into position like a pawn on a board.

"Ah yes, I wondered when you would come back to that again." Robert looked at Jacob and then turned to Rebekkah. "What happened in the nest Rebekkah? Why were you asked to leave?"

Rebekkah was completely taken aback by Robert's question. She had no time to think of a fake answer, so she told the truth. "Well, Jacob and I ate a chocolate fruit from the Tree of Knowledge of Good and Evil." Rebekkah went red as she said the words, shame flooded her heart and face. "How do you know about the nest Robert, have you been there?"

Jacob interrupted, "You two have been talking together. Stop pretending you didn't know, Robert. There is no such thing as a nest. This is just a story you two have hatched up between you to make me feel bad."

"Is that really what you think Jacob? Why would we want to make you feel bad?"

Jacob was getting redder and redder, the blood was pumping into his scalp and his face against his red hair seemed to be on fire, "Because she hates me, and you are just a weirdo!"

"Jacob!" Rebekkah yelled at him. "That's so rude!"

"No, Rebekkah, it's all right. Jacob has a right to know what I was doing in that old factory. I was down on my luck. I had been working with birds of prey in Beaulieu, Hampshire but was accused of poisoning a golden eagle and was sacked. I had no job and had also lost my home because I was living in a tithed cottage on the Beaulieu Estate; it went with the job you see. I couldn't get a reference, had no address and so couldn't get work. I was living in the disused warehouse and that was where I met the Magpie. He seemed a reasonable guy at first. He was in a similar position to me. He claimed he had been working in stables but had been falsely accused of neglecting the horses. He had left the office doors open on more than one occasion and jewellery had gone missing. The other staff left their valuables, watches and things in the office for safekeeping while they mucked out the stables. He claimed that magpies had got in and taken it. The thing is, he was blamed and lost his job. I know how magpies work; the story was plausible. They are famous for stealing so, I felt sorry for him."

"So, that's it? You two just happened to bump into each other in that warehouse? I've always felt that bit of your story was unlikely." Jacob's tone was thick with disbelief.

Robert looked at Jacob. It was disappointing how quickly a relationship of trust could evaporate. "I suppose it does seem a bit of a coincidence, but he challenged me to work with him. He said he had a dream to open a bird sanctuary. He said that he wanted to save all the birds that no one else liked or wanted - seagulls, magpies, and crows. I believed his heart was in the right place and reckoned he needed someone to listen to him and take an interest in him. As time went on, I also became a bit scared of him, there was something sinister about his behaviour and he was very strong."

Jacob looked at Robert as if he could not believe what he was hearing. "You were so naïve! Either you are a liar and are in this with him in which case Rebekkah and I are in real danger here with you. Or you are more stupid than you look." He looked around frantically as if expecting the Magpie to leap through the door at any moment.

Rebekkah stood up at this point and yelled at Jacob to shut up.

Robert held up his hand. "I will leave now if that's what you want but you need to phone your parents to let them know that you are on your own."

Rebekkah stood between her brother and Robert, her pony- tail swung from side to side as she stood, hands on hips glaring at them both.

She would be a formidable woman when she grew up, thought Robert. She was very agitated. Her mouth was working hard as if she wasn't sure what to say but then the words tumbled out. "You know about the nest. I haven't spoken to you about that. I have told no one except Jacob. How do you know?"

"Because everyone who has met the Eagle has been to the nest in some form or another."

Rebekkah looked at him quizzically, "Have you been there too, Robert?"

Robert smiled but did not answer straightaway.

"Yes, I have but I suspect I had a different experience to you. We meet our perfect world in the nest but are always confronted with a choice. That choice is always in the form of a temptation to disobey the Eagle. Everyone who goes there thinks they will never want to leave and that the temptation will be easy to resist. But it's almost impossible and then you have to leave." He paused for a moment and looked directly at Jacob who had gone pink.

Rebekkah looked at him too. Jacob looked at them both defiantly, "Well that's just stupid!" he yelled, "fancy creating a perfect world, which you know is going to get spoilt because no one can pass the test. What sort of a creature would do that? It's nuts! You are bonkers Robert if you believe that!"

Robert shrugged, "I know it seems that way, but you learn stuff about yourself."

"Like what?" Rebekkah was interested; she had just felt a terrible sense of shame and an overwhelming sense of sadness that she had let the Eagle down. It made her feel better when she realised that Robert had also failed the test.

Robert passed his hand wearily over his eyes and down his nose as if trying to exorcise a painful memory. "You learn that you are frail and weak and even if you think you are strong you actually are not. The Eagle uses the nest to expose the dark part of our character. I believe it's part of our growth as humans. Afterwards you feel bad but then you realise the Eagle does not leave you. She forgives you and goes with you wherever you are."

Rebekkah nodded slowly. What Robert was saying touched her deeply and made her feel much better about herself and her own weakness. She smiled and squeezed Robert's arm affectionately. "Thank you, Robert, that helps doesn't it, Jacob?"

Jacob looked at them both disdainfully. "No! For a start the nest isn't real. You are just sharing fairy stories and making up things. I think we just have to get on with things on our own without the help of some dumb bird who sets tests that it knows we are going to fail."

"Fair enough," Robert changed the subject. "Anyway, I am sure you can agree that the Magpie is a real threat as can be seen by what happened to your cat tonight. There are forces out there, forces of good and evil. Whether you like it or not, you both have the mark of the Eagle on you. She has chosen you. I don't know what Her plans are, but She will make them known. He, on the other hand, will stop at nothing to distract you from following your true path. He knows where you are weak and will use that weakness. So, beware."

"This is such rubbish," yelled Jacob. "You two are completely deluded. I'm not staying here listening to this nonsense. Why don't you both have a cosy little chat about your precious Eagle? I'm going to watch telly." With that he hurled himself out of the room, slamming the door behind him.

Rebekkah and Robert sat in awkward silence for a while. Eventually Rebekkah spoke, "Robert, I do believe that the Eagle is real but ever since she has come into our lives some really bad things have happened. Why is that?"

Robert looked at her thoughtfully and rubbed his chin. "What sort of bad things?"

"Well, Dad lost his job, Mum and Dad split up. I had to go to a different school and I…" she paused; she had never spoken of her experience at her new school to anyone.

Robert leaned forward, his eyes sympathetic, "Go on."

Rebekkah looked down at her feet, two pink spots emerged on her cheeks; "I was bullied by this girl called Kirsty. She and her gang pushed me into a stinky games locker and then she made me do her homework for her. I am really scared of her."

Robert nodded slowly, "I am so sorry Rebekkah, that must be tough, you must be glad it's holiday time. By way of an answer, let me ask you a question. How much of that would have happened anyway even if you hadn't met the Eagle?"

Rebekkah thought for a moment. "Well, probably all of it. I can't see how the Eagle could have caused all that upset."

Robert persisted, "So, in all that upset did you find your faith in the Eagle to be of help or a hindrance?"

Rebekkah still didn't look at him when she finally answered. She said, rather shyly, "I suppose She has been a help. I sort of speak to Her when I am upset, and I have these experiences where I am flying on her back." She stopped. Her face was now very pink. She wasn't used to talking in this way with another adult. Her parents never took an interest in her

41

thoughts and feelings and it felt really awkward to share them with this man whom she hardly knew. She looked at him to see if he was going to dismiss her like most other people did. But no, he was looking at her with a wry smile on his face and as her eyes met his he nodded in encouragement. "I understand completely, I have had a similar experience. The Eagle rarely takes us out of difficult situations, but She will give us strength to cope when we are in them. She can give you the power to do the right thing."

A tear of relief ran slowly down Rebekkah's cheek. "I don't always feel I do the right thing. Mostly I feel all wrong."

Robert chuckled. "Join the club. But you are brave, and you have a good heart. The Eagle can see that, and She has chosen you for a special task, Jacob too, but he will take a bit more persuading. Anyway, enough of all this heavy stuff! Have you a game we can play? How about Monopoly, I love that game."

Rebekkah jumped up in delight, "Oh yes me too. I'll go and get it."

Several hours later, following much dice throwing and house

purchasing, they heard the key turn in the lock and their mother's voice called out. Robert stood up as the parents entered the room. "I must be going, thank you for having me, lovely dinner."

6 HOLIDAYS BEGIN

"Sorry it ended the way it did," Mr. Taylor was sporting a set of stitches over his right eye. He looked tired. "I'll show you out." Jacob and Rebekkah went to bed without speaking further. Their family holiday was due to start the next day and bags needed to be packed. In Jacob's case the only thing he wanted was his iPad. Rebekkah packed her books.

Breakfast was also a silent affair. Dad had buried the cat in the garden thinking this was best. When Rebekkah heard of this she scolded him for not waiting for her. Predictably, Jacob had sneered at her for being soft even though he too would have liked to be present at his pet's burial. He was still smarting from the revelations of the night before. Instead of showing gratitude to his sister for not spilling the beans and telling Robert about the bird he had killed, he felt angry and vindictive. He was unwilling to examine his mood and recognise that the conversation with Robert had uncovered feelings with which he was uncomfortable. These were linked to an image of himself that he did not want to confront. He had been avoiding doing so for months and had no intention of doing so now.

He did however feel a little thrill of victory when Rebekkah threw the cereal at him over breakfast and was told to leave the table. Jacob only smirked. At last, Miss Goody Two Shoes was in the doghouse rather than him. Or was it, all things considered, the cat basket?

They were to stop off at their grandparents on the way to their cousins. They lived in a sweet little cottage in what seemed like the middle of nowhere. It was actually near a village called Toft in Cambridgeshire. Grandfather loved his garden and Granny seemed to spend all her time making cakes and cutting flowers from the garden to distribute to the sick and lonely. Both children were very fond of their grandparents, although both were a bit eccentric.

The journey passed quickly - mercifully for Jacob he had headphones and an iPad. Rebekkah settled down to read a book but she struggled to concentrate. She had been more deeply affected by the events of the night before than she realised. Snapshots of her cat, and then her dad walking through the door with blood running down his face, filled her mind. She squeezed her eyes shut and tried to think of something else.

The conversation with Robert replayed itself. She was afraid of this man called the Magpie. She had never spoken about her own feelings when Jacob was kidnapped and then released. Her family did not talk about feelings and so she kept most of what she felt to herself. She did not feel that she had a right to talk things through and much of her silence the night before had been not so much a sense of loyalty for her brother as a reluctance to give voice to her own feelings about the nest and what had happened there.

She had loved the nest; it was the most beautiful place imaginable. The Eagle had given them both permission to go anywhere they liked and sample any of the land's gifts except to eat from the Tree of Knowledge of Good and Evil. She had been very happy to obey this instruction as she trusted the Eagle and wanted to please her. However, Jacob had found the tree and had eaten the chocolate fruit.

There had also been an odd and disturbing incident that she had never spoken about. In fact, she had buried it in her memory until the night before when Robert had asked Jacob what he had done before being asked to leave the nest. Jacob had been hiding from her in the branches of the tree. As she approached the tree a dead bird had fallen from the exact place where Jacob was sitting. She was uneasy with the thought that he might have killed the bird. She disliked her brother but had not thought him capable of killing such an innocent thing.

She had then found out that Jacob had eaten the chocolate from the tree, and she was persuaded to do the same. Also, the more she thought about it the more she was sure that Jacob had killed the little bird. That part of the garden had felt different to the rest, and she was sure she had seen a snake in the tree. Afterwards the Eagle had carried them both away and dropped them back into their own world. They had never spoken of the incident, until last night.

She felt a deep sense of shame as she remembered the Eagle's anger and sadness with them both. She suddenly had an urge to say sorry, to start again, to talk it through with someone. But who was there? Who would listen? Her parents would think her mad and just tell her to stop imagining things. Jacob would shout at her or use some clever argument about it all being a dream. Robert was the only human being who understood but it would be some time before she saw him again. And bad things seemed to happen when he was around. She suddenly felt terribly alone and afraid. She was not looking forward to spending a week with her feral cousins and a grumpy brother. A tear oozed out of her eye and ran down her cheek. Furtively she wiped it away hoping no one had seen her cry.

7 THE GRANDPARENTS

Rebekkah woke with a start – she gazed blearily through the car window at the little cottage, uncertain as to where she was. Then, it dawned on her. They had arrived at Granny's house. She tugged at the door, frustrated by the child lock. Jacob opened his door, slammed it shut and walked around to her side of the car, made as if to open the door for her and then stuck his thumb on his nose, grinned and walked indoors.

"I hate him," muttered Rebekkah to herself as her mother opened the door for her. She picked up her book and ran inside. The place, as always, smelt of lavender. Granny was already on her way to welcome the little family. As soon as she saw Rebekkah she held out her arms in welcome and Rebekkah threw herself into her embrace. She breathed in deeply and felt the tension easing out of her as she relaxed in this wonderful place where she always felt safe. Her grandmother gently pushed her away and held her face between her hands. "It is so lovely to see you, but you look a little tired my dear." The old lady gave her arm a gentle squeeze and then gestured for them all to come to the table to eat.

Just then her grandfather appeared from the garden. A wisp of pure white hair poked out from under his peaked cap. "Rebekkah!" He laid down his trowel and held out his arms. She ran to him and kissed his soft bristly cheek. His skin was like brown crinkled paper. He headed for the bathroom to wash his hands while they settled into their seats. Lunch was always the same at Granny's – ham sliced from the bone, salad and potatoes mashed with mayonnaise followed by chocolate cup-cakes.

Once lunch was over Grandfa, as his grandchildren called him, suggested that the children might like to join him in the garden. Jacob declined, but Rebekkah skipped off happily with the elderly man. The garden was huge and lovingly tended. Grandfa spent most of his time with his beloved plants. He knew every type by name and always loved sharing his knowledge. As they wandered along the windy path down to the apple orchard Rebekkah stopped by a beautiful, red-leafed tree. "What's that Grandfa?" She asked.

"It's an *Acer Rubrum* better known as a red maple."

"Why do plants have Latin names, it is so confusing."

'Well, naming plants is a science called botany. All plants have a genus and a species. It helps us to identify where the plant is from and what family it belongs to. If everyone uses Latin then it is the same system wherever you are in the world regardless of language. Did you know that we humans use the same system? So, you are of the genus Taylor but your species or your specific type of Taylor is Rebekkah. It's the same with this plant here it is of the genus maple but it is specifically a red maple."

"I wish I wasn't the same genus as Jacob sometimes."

Grandfa looked at her sympathetically, "You and Jacob fallen out have you?"

Rebekkah looked at her feet and shifted awkwardly from one to the other. The old man waited. Then, out it all came, in a rush; the events of the previous night, Robert's warning about the Magpie and Jacob's anger about … she stopped. Grandfa waited. Jacob's anger? How could she explain that? It would mean talking about the nest. Grandfa would never believe her.

She sighed and bit her lip.

Grandfa looked at her and then tapped her gently on the arm. "Come along young lady, follow me," he said simply and together they headed towards the orchard. Threading through the apple trees Grandfa reached up and picked her a little apple. He rubbed it on his jacket and gave it to her. He then pointed to a shed and they walked in silence towards it. He opened the door, reached inside and pulled out a soft brush with which he brushed down the seat. He gestured for Rebekkah to sit while he walked a little way down the path to a large shrub. He had also collected a stick from the shed and he hooked it around a sturdy branch and pulled the bush towards him. It was like a leafy curtain. Rebekkah sat forward, suddenly alert. She could see something in the bush. It looked like a giant statue of an eagle.

"Grandfa," she blurted out. "Why have you a statue of an eagle hidden in the bush?"

"To remind me, that even though I can't always see the Eagle, She is always there. I just have to look carefully for Her."

"You know the Eagle, Grandfa? You have met Her too?" Rebekkah said with astonishment but yet delight.

"Oh yes. And I know that there is something that you are holding back from me. What is it?"

The rest of the story tumbled out, the nest, Jacob's deceit and her anger at him. He listened carefully, until she had finished. "Rebekkah I have been a follower of the Eagle most of my life, the things you have described to me suggest that you and Jacob have been chosen for a special task. There is something She wants you both to do. Yes…" He held up his hand to stop her protesting, "Especially Jacob. He is rebelling at the moment but his place in the plan is just as important as yours. You must help him to believe again. You need to work together."

"You believe me, oh Grandfa! You have no idea what that means to me. You don't think I am going mad?"

"Absolutely not, my dear, you see reality more clearly than most."

Rebekkah looked at him, puzzled, "You think the Eagle will forgive us both for messing up?"

"Oh yes! She already has. The Eagle wants you to learn from your mistakes. She won't abandon you."

"But she was so cross and actually I was a bit scared of Her. She seemed so disappointed in us both."

"Ah yes, disappointed, but you could not stay in the perfect world of the nest. I too have eaten the fruit from the Tree of Knowledge of Good and Evil. This has been the case every time I have lost the faith, been mean or self-centred or have hurt others in order to get my own way. Oh yes Rebekkah, I have done many bad things but the truth is the Eagle has never lost faith in me. If you had stayed in that perfect world you would not have learnt about yourself. How would you have grown? How would you have used your knowledge to help others? Perfection when we are still imperfect is impossible, more to be desired than attained. Remember, the light can only be seen through the cracks in a wall not the wall itself."

Rebekkah could not believe her ears. It was as if a great weight was lifted from her. She suddenly felt free. She threw her arms around the old man and hugged him tightly. He laughed and hugged her back. "Come now, we need to get back to the others."

"Can you speak to Jacob too, Grandfa?"

"He isn't ready yet. He is incapable of listening at the moment,

but his time will come. The Eagle will make sure of it. Come on." He held his hand out to her, nails short and blackened with soil, gratefully she grasped it and hand in hand they walked slowly back to the house, he a tall, slightly bent, willowy figure in a hat; she, half his size, pony-tail bobbing.

8 THE IPAD

That night Rebekkah resolved to talk to Jacob about her conversation with Grandfa. She waited for the grown-ups to settle into their night-time routine. The TV was always on loud as Granny was a bit deaf. Mum moaned about it but Rebekkah found it quite comforting having the noise in the background. It also hid any noise of floorboards creaking when she moved about. As the news headlines pumped their way up the stairs Rebekkah slid out of bed and into Jacob's room. He was sitting up in bed playing *Fortnite*. He had headphones on and ignored her.

"Jacob," she began.

"What?" he replied gruffly without looking at her. He continued to tap on the screen.

"Jacob, listen, I've got something really important to say." She spoke earnestly and purposively. She pulled his headphone away from his ear, he growled at her, fingers hovering above the screen.

"Grandfa believes in the Eagle too. He talked to me about Her. He has a statue of Her in the orchard."

Jacob stared at her for an extended period. She could see the conflict that was waging inside him in his face. Finally, he answered. "What do you mean, he believes in the Eagle?"

"He talked to me about Her. He understood about the nest and," she hesitated but then carried on determinedly, "he understood about, you know, the tree and the bird and the chocolate."

Jacob's face twisted into a dark scowl. They had never spoken about him killing the bird in the garden. He had convinced himself that it was all a dream. He didn't like being reminded of it.

"Jacob," she said urgently, "We have a job to do. The Eagle has chosen us. Grandfa says…"

He interrupted her, "A job? What kind of job?"

"I, I don't really know," she stammered, suddenly uncertain. The confidence she had felt after speaking to grandfa was beginning to evaporate in the face of Jacob's questioning and hostility. She thought about going back to her room. She didn't want his cynicism to squash her and tarnish the hope and faith she had felt after speaking to her grandfather.

"He's nuts," said Jacob rather too vehemently, "And so are you. He's got that memory loss thing that old people have – dentures or something."

"Dementia," said Rebekkah indignantly, "And no he hasn't, he is as clear as you and I. He really knows what he is talking about. Oh Jacob, you are so frustrating, why don't you speak to him, if you don't believe me?"

"Because you and he are in this together, you're playing fantasy games like you always have and he is just going along with you because he doesn't want to hurt your feelings."

Even as he spoke Jacob knew he was not facing up to the truth of Rebekkah's words. But he didn't like being confronted by his little sister. He was a stubborn boy. Rebekkah picked up his slipper off the floor and threw it at him in anger. "You stupid, stupid annoying little idiot!" She shouted.

Quick as a flash he picked up the slipper and threw it back at her. Before she knew it, she was on the bed pulling his hair and hitting him. All the pent-up frustration and anger that he aroused in her poured out through her fists. She pummelled him, tears flowing down her face. As he struggled to get out of her way, his iPad slipped out of his hands and fell onto the floor. There was a crunch as it did so.

Pushing her to one side and howling with rage he sprang off the bed and knelt next to the device. The screen was cracked. Just at that moment their father burst through the door, drawn by the sound of World War III breaking out in the bedroom. He surveyed the scene; Rebekkah, seated on the bed, back against the wall, hair awry, snot coming from her nose and Jacob; cradling his cracked iPad on the floor, crestfallen.

"What the devil's going on here?" He shouted. Gerald Taylor was never good in a crisis. He always made things worse. He tried to get a better look at the iPad but Jacob snatched it away from him. "Rebekkah's broken my iPad." He yelled. "Look at what she's done, she's cracked the screen!"

"No, I didn't," Rebekkah protested, "You dropped it."

"You attacked me for no reason!" Snapped Jacob, his fury not subsided.

"Right, you are both grounded," blurted Mr. Taylor without seeking to enquire further. "You shouldn't be up at this time of night anyway! You are both as bad as each other."

"What's going on here?" Mrs. Taylor said on arriving at the door.

Jacob yelled at all of them. He was getting hysterical. "It's not my fault. She came into my room. She broke my iPad. That's so unfair."

"I was against him having another iPad. I said he wouldn't look after it properly, you never listen to me, now look at what he's done." Mrs. Taylor joined in, speaking without understanding. She was making things worse.

Rebekkah watched both her parents turn on each other. It was an all too familiar scene. Her father squared up to her mother. "That's it, make it all about me. It's all my fault, as usual. What about you? You're always on your iPad you are a bad example; he gets that from you. You set up the *Fortnite* account for him."

Jacob screamed at his parents, "You are not listening to me! She has broken my iPad."

His mother marched over to her son and grabbed at him, "Don't speak to us like that. You probably deserved it. The way you have been behaving recently – you are an ungrateful, spoilt brat!"

"I wish you weren't my parents you don't know how to be good parents; you are both rubbish." Jacob was getting into his stride.

Rebekkah knew that once her brother started on this road, he was likely to dig a big hole for himself and fall headfirst into it. She wanted to scream and run away, instead she surprised herself by what came out of her mouth, "It's my fault, Jacob is right, I hit him and he dropped his iPad. I am sorry Jacob."

Her mother rounded on her. "Well, I am sick of you both and I will be glad to get shot of you at your cousins' tomorrow. You are both as bad as each other. Rebekkah go back to your room and Jacob turn that blooming thing off and go to sleep."

Jacob opened his mouth to argue, but Rebekkah caught his eye,

widened her eyes in warning at him and shook her head slightly.
He sat down heavily on the bed with his back to everyone. Mr.
Taylor brushed past his wife and walked down the stairs leaving
Mrs. Taylor alone with the two children. She folded her arms
aggressively and waited while Rebekkah slunk off to her own
room. She then slammed Jacob's door so the house rattled and
followed her husband downstairs. Rebekkah, now alone in her
room, climbed into her bed and laid her head on the pillow. The
fragrance of lavender drifted into her nostrils and calmed her.
As she drifted off to sleep, she dreamt she was back at the nest.
It was beautiful.

9 THE ARRIVAL

Breakfast was a subdued affair. Jacob hardly spoke, Grandfa had his head in his paper and Granny and Mum talked about which jams they would like to take to their cousin's house. Mr. Taylor was agitating to get going as they had a plane to catch after dropping the children off and so by 8.30 am the children were packed into the back seat of the car with a box of homemade jam between them. As Rebekkah waved goodbye, her grandfather winked at her; Rebekkah cast a look at Jacob who rolled his eyes upward as he mouthed, "silly old fool." The journey passed without incident and it was late morning when they arrived at their cousins in Lincolnshire.

The house was a large, rambling 18th century building with lots of corridors and places to hide. The grounds were huge and largely unkempt. Gerald always muttered about his brother not looking after the place. Their uncle had come into some money through his wife's side of the family and Mr. Taylor had often grumbled that his sibling had all the luck.

Jacob was told to pull the chain on the bell that hung to the right of the large green wooden door. The paint was peeling off the door adding to the general feeling of neglect that the house communicated. As the children stood side-by-side Rebekkah thought she could see a face at the window in one of the bedrooms. Despite the warmth she shivered slightly. She did not trust her cousins. They played tricks on her, sometimes pretending to be friendly and kind and then at other times behaving as if she was the last person on earth that they wanted to see. Jacob cared less about what his cousins thought as he had learnt from bitter experience to tough it out. If they did not like him then, who cared? He would find something else to do. He liked the lack of interest shown by his uncle and aunt in his activities. He craved greater freedom from his parents. He was looking forward to his stay.

There was a sound of footsteps approaching the door and then a grating noise as a key was turned. The person behind the door was making loud grunting noises as he or she tried to pull open the door. It trembled slightly but did not budge. After several minutes a frustrated voice came through the letterbox instructing them to go round the back.

"Typical of this chaotic place," grumbled Gerald as they picked up their bags and moved to the back where their Uncle David was waiting for them. He looked harassed; his glasses perched on the end of his nose slightly lopsidedly. Physically, he was a taller version of his younger brother but with significant differences. His red hair was long, flecked with grey and tied back in a ponytail. He was dressed in shorts and a baggy tea shirt which said, '*Don't tase me bro'* while his feet were bare, displaying some rather long yellowing toenails.

"Greetings bro' and family." He grinned as he slapped his brother on the back and ruffled Jacob's hair. Jacob hated having his hair touched and very obviously smoothed down his fringe.

"So, what happened to you?" He pointed to the stitches above Gerald's right eye.

"Oh, nothing much, walked into something," muttered Gerald vaguely.

Uncle David turned on his heels and sauntered into the house, hands in his pockets, whistling. Their father nodded at Jacob and Rebekkah to follow inside whilst checking his watch for the time. "Hey David! we haven't got long before we need to get to the airport, is it ok if we just leave the kids and go?"

Mrs. Taylor stood on the doorstep she had no intention of going inside. She hated the house it was old and dark and smelt of greens. Rebekkah looked at her mother, anger rising in her throat. Why couldn't she have normal parents who would take their children on holiday with them instead of leaving them in this house with a load of wild and unruly cousins?

"Sure thing brother," Uncle David's voice was getting fainter as he disappeared into the bowels of the house. "Have a good trip."

"Bye then children." Their mother quickly embraced them both, but the hug was lacking in warmth and they knew she was keen to get away.

Mr. Taylor's face still scarred by the encounter with the Magpie twisted itself into what he thought was a suitable expression for saying goodbye to one's children. "Yeah, cheers kids, try not to get kidnapped Jacob because I'm not coming back to rescue you. Look after your brother Rebekkah, you know what a clot he can be. Have fun."

With that they were both gone. Jacob and Rebekkah followed their uncle through the kitchen and into the house and up the stairs. Neither spoke until Rebekkah asked where their cousins were.

"Oh, around somewhere." Their uncle waved his arms in a big circle as if to emphasise the point.

"Here's your room Rebekkah, hope you don't mind but Phillip keeps his rat in here. You are fine with rats, aren't you?"

Jacob grinned, he knew that Rebekkah loathed rats, "Oh yes Uncle," he said smiling sweetly at his sister, "Rebekkah loves rats."

Rebekkah looked at her brother and silently mouthed, "I hate you!"

"And, this is your room Jacob, you are sharing with Phillip. Hope that's ok but we only have one spare room as we have a friend of mine staying in the other one. You will meet him at dinnertime. Right, make yourselves at home and we will see you downstairs at 6pm." He had a habit of rubbing his hands together as he spoke and then clasping his fingers together. He unclasped them and wandered away down the corridor. Once

he was out of earshot, Rebekkah rounded on her brother, "Love

rats do I Jacob? You know I can't stand them. You will have to

take it into your room."

"Mmm let's see, what can you trade in return? How about you

pay for my iPad screen to be fixed?"

Rebekkah looked at him, she knew he had her. She had a real

phobia of the creature that was sitting staring at her from its

cage. Its pink glassy eyes were fixed steadfastly on her as if it

knew her thoughts. "Alright, it's a deal, just take it out now.

Please!" She was so desperate that her voice took on a pleading

tone.

Still grinning, Jacob picked up the cage and slowly moved it past

her face. She shrieked in terror.

"What's going on?" said a voice from underneath the bed. The

children jumped and Jacob nearly dropped the rat. Rebekkah

stooped down to see under the bed. There, lying on his tummy,

was her cousin Phillip surrounded by toy cars. "Hello 'Bekkah,

don't you like Ratbag?" He always called her by the shortened version of her name, it came from a time when he couldn't pronounce all the syllables.

"Not much," said Rebekkah, instantly regretting the fuss she had made. She knew from bitter experience that the rat thing would now be used against her.

"Well, don't worry, let me show you my cars. Come a bit closer so you can see this amazing Mini Cooper I've got here."

As she lay obediently on the floor and turned her head sideways to see him better, he bent his head towards her and then inhaled deeply and puffed out a large breath. It was very dusty under the bed and it seemed to all end up in her face. She began coughing while the two boys laughed at her. She was furious with herself for falling for the trick. "You wait," she spluttered, "I'll get you for that."

Phillip wriggled his way out from under the bed and stood up. He was the same age as Rebekkah and the same height. He had small eyes, with the same monobrow owned by Jacob and her dad. His skin was darker than Jacob's, and tanned from running about outside. He was skinny and looked tiny next to Jacob's swelling stomach and robust frame.

"Oooh now I am scared!" He was balanced on his toes, moving from one foot to another, his hands formed into fists. "Come on then, if you think you can."

She figured it was better to stick up for herself rather than to appear weak. She had managed to tackle her brother last night so Philip would be a piece of cake. She gave him a firm shove in the chest. Surprised, Phillip fell backwards onto the bed and lay there for a while looking at her. She prepared herself for a fight, but none came.

He sat up on the bed and looked at them both. "I can't be

bothered to get you back now. But we have prepared a little welcoming party for you. Be in the garden at midnight and don't get caught by a grown up." With that he jumped off the bed and disappeared under it leaving Jacob and Rebekkah wondering what lay in store for them later that night.

10 THE GUEST

Jacob and Rebekkah whiled away the afternoon exploring the house and garden together. Now that their parents had gone, they were united in an uneasy truce. Jacob stuck to his word and placed Ratbag in his room. Rebekkah, grateful for this, decided to open a conversation about the midnight meeting. "Are we going to go to this meeting, Jacob?"

Jacob stooped and picked up a cane like branch from the ground, "Why not? It sounds fun."

He used the branch to move some nettles and brambles to one side so they could walk through.

"What if they have planned something horrible? What then?" Rebekkah felt the need to plan, she did not trust her cousins.

He didn't look at her, instead he hit out at a particularly sharp bramble that crossed their path at face height. "If they try anything, we'll get our own back," he responded with a grin.

She liked the use of the word 'we' as it somehow drew them together. She looked shyly at him and felt a sudden desire to

71

build a bridge towards this brother of hers who was usually so distant and cynical. "I'm sorry about your iPad Jacob."

He said nothing but thrashed more vigorously at the vicious brambles. "Don't think that being nice gets you out of paying for a new screen," he said gruffly.

"No, of course not, a promise is a promise. But I can't get at my money just yet."

"Come on, let's have a good look round the garden so we know where things are. I don't want to be completely blind when we meet our cousins later. I wish we had a torch. We'll need one."

And so, the afternoon passed. The two children mapped out the garden in a rare period of intimacy and unity. Rebekkah could not help wondering if Jacob would have been so keen had his iPad not been broken. Nonetheless she found herself enjoying her brother's company. She saw a different side to him. He was methodical and thorough taking her through the points of the compass and how to fix on various landmarks and orientate herself by them. It was a large garden and took some time to explore. Just as they felt inclined to stop and go back to the house, they came across a wooden door in the garden wall. It was locked but clearly in use. The path leading up to it was well trodden and the handle to the door was shiny.

"I'd like to know where this leads," said Jacob as he jiggled the handle and tugged at it. Rebekkah took a closer look at the latch. She stiffened as if someone had just grabbed her. "Jacob! Look at this!"

"What?" He looked carefully at the latch plate. There, etched into the black metal was an image of a magpie. He jumped backwards and looked around him as if expecting something or someone to jump out at them both. Clearly disconcerted, he stood chewing his lip, his eyes darting from side to side, his face pale as ash. For the first time Rebekkah realised how deeply the incident in the warehouse had affected him. She laid her hand gently on his arm. He brushed it to one side and began pacing up and down. "There has to be an explanation for this. It's ridiculous. It can't be true."

"What can't be true?" Rebekkah was getting caught up in his anxiety.

"The Magpie, the Eagle, Grandfa, you, Robert, all of it and now this!"

Rebekkah thought for a minute before speaking. Something told her this was an opportunity to get through to Jacob. She chose her words carefully. "Jacob, listen. What if we are affected in some way by our contact with the nest? What if there is a battle going on for our loyalty? What if there are secret followers of both the Eagle and the Magpie and we are somehow caught in the middle of some kind of battle between them?"

Jacob looked at her in disbelief. "Battle? Why? This is not something we have chosen. It's just happening to us. I don't get it."

"Neither do I but Grandfa is a follower of the Eagle and so is Robert. These are adults not children. What happened to Tipsy, our cat was real enough."

Jacob was thinking deeply. Then something dawned on him. "You know what I think? Somehow our cousins heard about the attack on me at the warehouse. Dad must have told his brother and Uncle David told them. This is some kind of sick joke. They carved this on this door and tonight they are going to show it to us in the hope that I will be scared and turn into a gibbering wreck. Well, I'll show them. Two can play at that game."

Turning on his heels, his mouth set in a taut grim line, he marched back to the house. Rebekkah ran after him. "What are you going to do, Jacob?"

"I'm thinking," he said tersely.

As they reached the back door, they were greeted by the middle of their three cousins, Jazz, short for Jasmina. Jazz was 13 years old; tall and graceful with black shoulder length hair. One would describe her as beautiful except for her eyes, which were small, like Philip's and too close together. Her mouth seemed permanently contorted into a disconcerting smirk. She raised her hand in greeting as they moved towards her. "Ah, it's the Taylor kids!" she drawled. "I was just about to send out a search party for you. Dinner is ready."

The children followed her into the house. They were hungry, not having eaten since breakfast. As they emerged from the long dark corridor into the dining room, Rebekkah looked anxiously around for the remaining cousin, Jack. He was the one she most disliked. Tall and thin, he could be mean to the point of cruelty. Her heart was beating fast as she scanned the table. Her eyes settled on him, but he was not looking at her. Instead, his eyes were fixed on his mobile phone. Jazz gestured to the Taylors to sit on the far side of the table. Phillip was next to Rebekkah and he grinned at her. "Hello Ratty Rebbekah!"

Rebekkah forced a smile and retorted, "Hello Pathetic Phillip!" She instantly regretted the insult as she saw the smile freeze on the boy's face. He kicked her under the table. She kicked him back. Fortunately, they were saved from any further contact by the entrance of their uncle with a stranger. He had a beer in one hand and was talking animatedly to their uncle. Rebekkah looked at Jacob who was staring at the man in disbelief. She could see that he recognised him. She leant across the table. "What is it, Jacob?"

He looked at her, his face ashen, "I will tell you later," he whispered. "Let's eat and then get out of here."

Dinner was awkward. Phillip was still smarting over the exchange with Rebekkah and did his best to annoy her by eating with his arms spread out, wing-like so that his elbow jabbed into her arm every time she tried to put her fork in her mouth. He ate noisily, spoke with his mouth full and slurped his drink. Mum would have had something to say about his manners, thought Rebekkah with a pang that she instantly ignored. She needed to be strong to survive.

Jack ate quickly but was constantly texting and appeared to be playing some kind of online game. His parents completely ignored him. Rebekkah and Jacob were introduced to the strange man whose name was Pete Maghi; Rebekkah watched intently as he shook hands with Jacob. It did not seem as if he recognised her brother. His hands were rough with short stubby fingers. The nails were broken and black. Rebekkah looked him in the eye as she was introduced. And that was when she experienced her own sense of unease. The man's eyes were orange.

Rebekkah had tried to engage Jazz in conversation, but the girl had responded with short, disdainful comments that made it clear that she despised her younger cousin and could not be bothered with her. Eventually Rebekkah gave up and focussed on eating. The food was surprisingly good, and she was hungry. Jacob on the other hand picked at his food and appeared to be listening to the conversation between the adults. At one point his aunt turned to him to ask where his parents had gone on holiday.

"Erm, not sure, but they flew." Jacob wouldn't look at his aunt as he replied.

"You don't know!" drawled Jazz. "I've been meaning to ask, why didn't they take you both? Don't they like being with you?" Venom oozed from her. Rebekkah wanted to punch her nasty spoilt mouth. She didn't want to tell her cousin the truth, which was that their marriage was on the rocks, and they were trying to fix it. But what was she to say? "They have gone to Spain," she responded. "We didn't want to go. It's very hot this time of year and, Jacob's skin is easily burnt." She finished lamely.

Jacob glared at her, and Jazz laughed. She turned to her cousin and pinched him on the cheek.

"Yes, you are very ginger and freckly. How unfortunate for you."

Jacob recoiled from her touch and his face had flushed red. "At least I am not a stick insect," he growled.

Jazz smiled sweetly although her close-set eyes were hard and mean. "Ooh sensitive *and* ginger! You need to watch that temper Jacob, or else people will confuse your round head and red cheeks for a tomato."

Aunt Patricia laughed. "Aw come on your two, be friends. You've got a week together, so you need to get along." And with that she returned to her conversation with Pete and Uncle David. The children finished their meal in silence and then one by one left the table. The adults seemed hardly to notice their heads were bent close together in conversation. Jacob beckoned to Rebekkah to follow him outside. The tips of his ears were still red, and he walked fast into the garden. Once well away from the house he stopped and dropped to his haunches indicating to Rebekkah that she should do the same. She waited, watching Jacob as he gathered his thoughts. "That man, Pete, I think I have met him before although I am not sure." He chewed on his lip. "I think he is the Magpie!"

Rebekkah's hand flew to her mouth to hide her horror. Jacob had described his experience in the warehouse when he had been trapped and held to ransom by the homeless man whom he had called the Magpie. He had only escaped because Robert Cameron had helped him, who was badly beaten up in the process. He had never been caught.

"Oh Jacob, we should go to the police."

"The thing is," her brother frowned, "I can't be sure. It was dark in the warehouse and he was dressed differently, his hair was greasy and long and he had a beard. This man is clean-shaven and he doesn't appear to be homeless."

"And, how come he is a friend of Aunt Patricia and Uncle David?" mused Rebekkah. "Also, there's something odd about his eyes. Did you see? They seem orange."

"Yes, orange is the colour of a magpie's eye. He must be wearing some sort of contact lens."

"What about his voice? Did you recognise his voice?"

"Well, here's the thing, his voice in the warehouse was low and husky and he had an accent like a West Country accent; but Pete sounds Scottish."

"Is it possible he is putting on the accent? If he is able to change his appearance, then he might be skilled at changing his accent too. Actors can do that."

A magpie suddenly appeared in a nearby tree and began to chatter. Rebekkah jumped at the noise. Jacob stared at the bird and then, quick as a flash picked up a nearby stone and threw it. The bird took off into the air raising the alarm as it did so.

"Oh Jacob, this all feels really spooky. What shall we do?"

"Well, we need to phone Robert, he'll know what to do."

Neither child thought of contacting their parents.

11 MIDNIGHT, END OF DAY ONE

They were not able to get hold of Robert but did manage to leave a voice mail. Rebekkah had insisted on Jacob giving him their uncle's address. To find it they had wandered out of the front gate and down the lane. They had been deeply troubled when they discovered that the house was placed in Magpie Lane. The knowledge only added to their sense of foreboding.

And so the children began the preparations for the midnight meeting. Jacob was convinced that the cousins were planning some sort of trick or attack. Consequently, he found a couple of sturdy branches in the garden and, using a penknife, whittled them into a weapon. They also retraced their steps around the garden. After this it seemed there was nothing more to do except to wait.

Rebekkah wandered up to her bedroom and shut the door quietly. Nervously she checked under the bed and found it was clear. The cars and Phillip had gone. She tentatively opened the wardrobe doors and peered inside. She wasn't sure what she expected but just felt the need to check. Then a thought occurred to her. She went back to the bed and stripped back the covers. There, sitting in the centre of the bed was a very realistic rat. Stifling a scream, she took several steps back and then stopped. The creature did not move. Picking up the stick Jacob had made for her she gently poked at it. Nothing. With relief she realised it was plastic and deftly flicked it off the bed and onto the floor. *Pathetic Phillip*, she thought to herself. And then the enormity of the last few days flooded over her in waves. Her memory rewound to her Dad's face and the awful sounds of squawking as her cat was killed. Then the news that they were to spend a week with their unpleasant, bullying cousins and now this weird, orange eyed stranger. It all felt too much, and she fell onto the bed pulling the pillow over her head.

As she lay there in the sombre darkness an image came into her mind of an eagle soaring high above her. Gazing upwards she could see the bird effortlessly gliding, wings outstretched. She imagined herself nestling into the thick downy feathers; her head resting as the bird moved soundlessly through the blue sky. Above her she noticed fine feathery cirrus clouds set against a light blue sky and below her a landscape of soft colours. Brown,

83

suede like fields newly ploughed blended into velvety green
pasture dotted with little brown trees and divided by snake like
tracks. She inhaled deeply, enjoying the clean fresh air that filled
her lungs as the huge bird sailed through the thermals. She
stayed like this for what seemed like hours, resting, enjoying the
sensation of being held, safe within the majestic wings. Then
suddenly the motion changed, and the bird began to descend. In
her dream she landed and clambered off the back to face the
Eagle. She looked into its beautiful golden eyes and thought
please help us. In response, the bird lifted its head and then slowly
dropped its beak. *Oh Eagle,* she thought, *is that really you? If only
you were here, you could protect us.* The huge bird tilted her head
upwards towards the direction of the sun as it burst through a
dark cloud and then turned back to face the young girl.

She stepped forward and wrapped her arms around the feathery
neck and buried her head into its chest. The Eagle nibbled her
ear gently with her beak. She stood, enfolded in the Eagle's love
but gradually a noise crept into her dream. A soft tapping which
gradually became more insistent followed by the sound of a door
opening and a voice saying her name. Reluctantly she drew

herself away from the Eagle and pulled the pillow away from her head.

Jacob was standing by her bed. "It's time to go," he whispered urgently.

She swung her legs off the bed somehow refreshed and strengthened by her dream. Jacob thrust the stick into her hands and together they tiptoed down the stairs and out into the garden. Jacob had found a torch from somewhere, but it was a full moon, and it was fairly easy to see. The garden had changed its mood and was now a silvery grey with shadows and noises. Something twitched in the bushes and a shape darted across their path. An owl hooted and a little bird flew out of a tree pursued by a large, winged creature. The children paused, uncertain of where to go when a human shape suddenly stepped out from the shadows and materialised into Phillip. "Come on, follow me," he whispered.

Tightening her grip on her stick she followed behind Jacob and Phillip. They made their way in single file through the shrubbery in the direction of the small door. In the light of the full moon, as their eyes adjusted, the adventurers could see the path ahead quite clearly. The door was open.

Jacob looked at his sister and stopped. Phillip continued and passed through the door. Looking back, he could see that his cousins were no longer following. "Come on," he urged. "What are you waiting for? Are you scared?"

"Of course not," Jacob's response was clear and strong. He was determined not to appear weak. Stepping through the gate, he waited for Rebekkah to catch up. "If we are attacked, stand back-to-back and use your stick," he exhorted. Rebekkah nodded, indicating that she had heard him, and they walked on. Phillip was moving quickly, and they almost lost sight of him as the path twisted and turned. Jacob was aware that the path was well-used, and he wondered where it led. He was about to find out.

The children could see lights flickering in the depths of the woods. Phillip veered off the path and led them towards the light. As they got closer a bizarre scene met their eyes. A table had been laid in the middle of a clearing. It was set for five people. Each place setting had a nest and in the nest were some eggs. It was hard to make out the colour, but Jacob knew they would be blue with brown speckles. Rebekkah cast a sideways look at him and noticed his clenched jaw and pale skin in the eerie light. "What is it Jacob?" she whispered apprehensively.

"Magpie eggs," he muttered between clenched teeth. "I will destroy them all."

Rebekkah's eyes swept over the scene and finally settled on her cousin Jack, who was sitting at the head of the table watching them. To his right lounged Jasmina also watching intently, a sneer twisting her face. Phillip moved to stand between his older siblings. For once he was silent. Then, quick as a flash, Jacob raised his stick above his head and began smashing at the nests. He didn't stop until the last egg was broken.

"You violent thug!" spat out Jack. "You have destroyed loads of potential little birds."

"Like you care," panted Jacob. "Those eggs wouldn't hatch. Where's the mother bird?"

"Jacob, look at this," intervened Rebekkah in a hushed voice.

She was crouching on the ground and had a piece of shell in her hands. "The shell has been painted. These are just chicken eggs." She stood up and looked accusingly at her cousins. "That's really mean. Just because Jacob was kidnapped by…"

"Rebekkah!" warned Jacob, "That's enough."

"Jacob? Kidnapped?" said Jasmina feigning surprise and concern; "Tell us more."

"You know already, or else you would not have planned this. Who told you?"

"Told us what?" Jack was staring at Jacob. He got up from his seat and walked around the table. He was at least a head taller than his cousin. Jacob took a step back and gripped his stick tightly. "You are a filthy, rotten liar, Jack. Don't pretend you didn't plan this. Your parents must have told you."

"As far as I can see, Jacob, you are the one I should be calling names. We, your good and kind cousins, have arranged a little welcoming feast for you." He clicked his fingers. In an instant Phillip reached under the table and brought out a large cake. "*WELCOME COUSINS*" was written on it in icing. "It seems that you are the rude ones, not us! How ungrateful and violent you appear to be. You always had a temper, Jacob."

"Goes with the red hair," sneered Jasmina.

"Come now Rebekkah, surely you can see that your brother has behaved badly. You seem more sensible. Would you like some cake?" said Jack.

Rebekkah didn't know what to do, she had been shocked by the violence shown by her brother, but she understood why he had behaved in the way he had. Lots of things didn't add up. A thought troubled her. "Why the eggs? Why the painted eggs? Why were they painted to look like magpie eggs?"

Jasmina smiled sweetly but insincerely, "Oh are they? I just thought they looked pretty. Phillip was bored this morning, so we decided to do some egg painting. We thought you might like to see them. Our real surprise was the welcome cake. Do you like it?"

"And the nests?" Rebekkah wasn't finished.

"Duh! Eggs are laid in nests, aren't they?" retorted Jack

scornfully. "Jazz, cut the cake, there's a darling. I'm starving."

Jasmina cut the cake into five pieces and handed one to Rebekkah, who waited for her cousins to eat first. Jack grinned at her and deliberately took a huge bite of the cake. He signalled to the others to do the same.

Jacob refused to eat and stood sullenly by, watching as they ate their bits. Rebekkah nibbled at hers. It was surprisingly good. She loved chocolate cake. "Try some Jacob, it's good." She had been disturbed by the presence of the nests and her brother's behaviour, but she figured that one of them needed to be polite especially if they were to spend a week there. Also, she wanted some answers. Everything was not as it seemed. If she pretended to be friendly, then she might get more out of the others.

He shook his head, "I'm going back. You coming? Or are you staying here with your new chums?"

"I'll come with you. Well, thanks very much for the cake and see you tomorrow. Er, sorry about the mess," she said rather lamely and then trotted off after Jacob. As they approached the door in the wall, they could hear their cousins laughing.

"I hate them!" Jacob exclaimed. "And you! How could you eat that cake? You know what they were up to. They wanted to humiliate me."

"I know Jacob, but I figured one of us needs to appear a bit gullible. They are not telling the truth. They know more than they are letting on. They wanted to get under your skin."

"Well, they succeeded. I don't like this Rebekkah. We will need to keep our eyes and ears open."

"Do you think we are in danger, Jacob?"

Jacob paused. He was afraid but something inside him wanted to protect his sister. He thought quickly. "No. I don't think we are in danger. I just think they have heard their parents talk about what happened to me in the warehouse. I do think they are liars and bullies. They like playing jokes on people. That's all."

Rebekkah looked at him. She could hear the fear in his voice, but she appreciated him wanting to protect her. It made a change. They let themselves in through the back door and crept

upstairs to their respective bedrooms. It took a long time for

Rebekkah to go to sleep and when she did manage to, her

dreams were full of magpies and cats. Likewise, Jacob slept

fitfully. He carefully placed the stick in the bed next to him. It

gave him some comfort.

12 DAY TWO, THE CANOE

Rebekkah awoke. The sun was streaming through the un-shuttered windows. She was used to curtains so it hadn't occurred to her to close them before going to bed. The rays picked up a cobweb in the corner of the room. Fascinated, she watched as a fly struggled to escape from the webby prison. A spider sat on the outer circle waiting for its prey to exhaust itself.

Isn't nature cruel? She thought to herself. And then another thought, popped into her head. Does it not depend on your point of view? The spider needed to eat, and the fly was its breakfast. The fly on the other hand, had probably already had breakfast feeding on some dog poo somewhere. She disliked spiders but flies even more. Her sympathy for the fly quickly disappeared and she was left with admiration for the spider and the hard work it had put into creating its flycatcher. The thought of breakfast made her feel hungry. Swinging her legs out of bed she padded across the floor and carefully opened the door. She had no idea what time it was. She softly made her way down the corridor to Jacob's room and pressed her ear against the old black wood and listened. She could hear him snoring. Gently opening the door, she tiptoed inside. His room was dark and cool. The shutters were closed. Phillip's bed was empty the bed had not been slept in. That struck her as odd but perhaps he had gone to sleep with Jack after the events of the previous night. Ratbag sat up in its cage and looked at her.

"Ugh!" She had forgotten about that creature. She shivered and moved over to the bed.

"Jacob," she whispered and shook his shoulder. He jumped and instinctively grabbed the stick. Seeing his sister, he visibly relaxed. "What you do that for?" He grumbled, propping himself up onto an elbow, yawned and then asked, "What time is breakfast?"

"I don't know. You are always thinking of food. What's the matter with you? I've been thinking. What are we going to do today?" He peered at her anxious face and swung his legs out of the bed. He felt tired. "I don't know. I expect P, J and J will have something exciting lined up for us."

Rebekkah giggled.

"What?" Jacob looked at her.

"The PJs, let's call them the Pyjamas."

"More like the three turds," suggested Jacob. His mood was no better for a sleep. He was tired and some of the anxiety he had gone to bed with had returned. However, there were noises coming up the stairs and he concluded that breakfast was nearly ready. He was hungry not having eaten much the night before. "I'd better get dressed. That sounds like breakfast, and I can smell bacon. I wonder if Pete Maghi will be joining us?"

The children headed down the dark rickety stairs. Rebekkah noticed the carpet was threadbare. It ran, like a stripe, down the centre of the stairs, held in place by black iron rods.

Aunt Patricia greeted them as they entered the dining room. She cheerfully asked them how they had slept and encouraged them to help themselves to the food that had been prepared. It was all waiting on hot plates. There was no sign of their cousins, their Uncle or indeed Pete Maghi.

"At least the food is good," mumbled Rebekkah with her mouth full of bacon and egg. "Pass the toast Jacob."

Jacob was enjoying his food, and he relaxed a little as he helped himself to crispy bacon and scrambled egg. He threw a piece of brown toast at his sister and laughed when it fell on the floor.

"Jacob! That's so rude!" She grumbled as she picked the toast up and placed it back on the toast plate. Avoiding that piece, she reached across her brother and selected another one, sticking her tongue out at him as she did so. He grinned and, reaching across her, stuck his knife into the honey. The jar was quite a distance from his plate, so his knife left a sticky trail as he wiggled his way back to his piece of toast.

"I can see your manners haven't improved with sleep," drawled a voice behind them. The children turned to see that Jasmina had entered the room and was helping herself from the tureens on the sideboard. "Mum, this dirty boy has dripped honey all over your tablecloth."

Aunt Patricia disappeared and came back with a wet cloth that she rubbed vigorously over the honey trail.

"Sorry Aunty," said Jacob apologetically, avoiding Jasmina's disgusted look.

"Jasmina! I hope you will look after Jacob and Rebekkah today." Their aunt paused, dishcloth in hand.

"Oh, we don't need looking after, Aunty," said Rebekkah hastily, noting the way her cousin had rolled her eyes at her mother's request.

"Don't worry, Mum, we will make sure they are kept entertained." A shiver ran down Rebekkah's back and she buried herself in her toast. She decided not to tell Jasmina that the piece she had just taken was actually the one that Jacob had thrown on the floor. It was what she deserved and gave her a small feeling of satisfaction as she saw the girl eat it.

"Be in the garden, by the door, at nine a.m." And with that Jasmina opened a book and buried her nose in it. Rebekkah would have liked to ask what she was reading but then thought better of it. Her cousin had turned her back and she did not want to aggravate her further. Finishing breakfast they headed to their rooms and prepared for the day.

Jacob and Rebekkah were on time, but their cousins were already waiting for them. Indicating that they should follow them, they passed through the door and into the woods. The mess from the night before was still there but they turned away from the path and moved deeper into the trees. Jack set a fast pace and the children had difficulty keeping up. Neither was very fit; Jacob was tubby and spent most of his spare time on his iPad and Rebekkah attended dance classes but that was about it for exercise.

At last, they emerged onto a clearing and in front of them was a large lake with a couple of canoes moored on the edge. The cousins made their way down to the boats and climbed in. The only time either of the Taylors had ever been in a boat was in the nest. The PJs watched to see what Jacob and Rebekkah would do. It was clear they thought they would be unable to even leave the shore, but Jacob surprised everyone, even himself, by moving the boat out into the centre of the lake. Rebekkah was clutching the side of the boat terrified of falling in. The water was dark and sludgy. "I didn't know that you could canoe Jacob?" she spoke, admiration in her tone.

Jacob was enjoying himself and almost before he could think about what he was saying he responded, "I learnt to canoe when we visited the nest."

"So, you do remember being there! Jacob, it had to be real if you learnt to canoe."

Jacob said nothing. He was concentrating on moving the canoe in a straight line. There was another paddle in the bottom of the boat which Rebekkah picked up.

"Like this," he said, indicating that the paddle needed to be placed in the water and dragged backwards to get the canoe going forwards. "And now the other side, you steer using the head of the paddle."

Rebekkah copied him and fairly soon they were moving quite quickly through the water. Their cousins were arguing over something and had not left the shore by the time the Taylors got to the centre of the lake. They stopped to listen, taking the opportunity to have a break. The only words they could make out were, "Stay behind."

Then Phillip was left on the shore while his older siblings paddled out to join Jacob and Rebekkah in the centre of the lake. Phillip disappeared into the trees. As Jack drew close he deliberately slapped his paddle into the water wetting Jacob and Rebekkah. Immediately, the Taylor's responded. Jasmina howled and placed her hands over her neatly straightened hair. Jack shouted at his sister to paddle while he tried to get close to the other canoe. It was clear that he intended to hit their boat. Jacob yelled at Rebekkah to push her paddle at the enemy boat while he rowed as fast as he could. Rebekkah jabbed at the other canoe with her paddle trying to push it away. She was not strong enough and Jack grabbed her paddle and yanked her towards him. Losing her balance, she fell forward and into the bottom of the boat dropping her paddle at the same time. There was a loud bang and grinding sound as one boat struck the other. Jacob swore and jabbed at Jack with his paddle pushing him away. What saved them was Jasmina's desire to protect her hair. As the boat rocked dangerously, she let out a loud screech and began beating her brother with her own paddle. Unable to fight a war on two fronts, he turned away from Jacob and grabbed his sister's paddle twisting it out of her hands. Rebekkah clambered back onto her seat, reached over the side and picked up her oar that was still floating on the surface. She was breathing heavily and had a large bruise on her knuckles where Jack had hit her. Jacob was paddling backwards doing his best to put some distance between the two boats. She copied him. Before long they reached the relative safety of the opposite shore. Jacob was pleased with the way things had turned out. "One nil to us!" he said gleefully.

Rebekkah sucked her bruised knuckles and turned her attention to her cousins who appeared to be in a mess; Jack and Jasmina were going round in circles. Jasmina was screaming at Jack and he in turn was bellowing at her. Rebekkah started to laugh. "She's not so cool when her hair is wet. Did you see her wallop Jack with her paddle, I almost felt sorry for him."

Jacob began to chuckle. "Yes, he thought he had us when he grabbed your paddle, but he hadn't banked on his sister whacking him over the head. That was hilarious! Sabotaged by his own crew."

It was the first time in ages that they had worked together successfully without arguing. It was fun to laugh together and it helped to get rid of some of the tension they had felt since arriving at their cousins' house.

"Let's go off and explore on our own without them. I'm sick of their tricks and meanness."

"Yes, let's," agreed Rebekkah. They jumped out of the boat and pulled it up onto the shore. "I think we should hide the paddles," said Rebekkah thoughtfully, "in case they come over and try and pinch the canoe."

Jacob nodded his approval, "Good idea." They walked up into the woods and buried the paddles under some leaves. Jacob hauled a large branch on top of them as a marker so they would not forget. It was dark in the woods. They had been so preoccupied with escaping from their vicious cousins that they had not noticed that the sky had got darker and darker until they emerged into a clearing. As they looked upwards, they could see storm clouds gathering.

"Do you think we had better get back Jacob, before it pours with rain?"

The sky was menacingly dark, the wind dropped and the trees became still. The atmosphere in the woods was heavy as they waited for the rain to fall. A little mouse scurried into the undergrowth. A bird called out a warning and then crashed its way up into the sky. Something had spooked it. The children huddled together, peering through the gloom. Was there someone behind the tree? Thunder rumbled in the distance and the atmosphere became more oppressive.

"We should move away from the trees. Dad says that if you get caught under a tree when lightning strikes you can get hit too."

Jacob nodded. "The electricity in the lightning takes the easiest path to earth. It connects with the trees because they are tall and provide the quickest route to the ground. Although the tree acts as a reasonable conductor of electricity the lightning prefers us because we have salt in our bodies."

Rebekkah looked around fearfully, "Thanks for the science lesson, Jacob, but what do we DO?"

Jacob was looking around; a short distance away was a clearing. "Come on, let's go over there." He started to run to the clearing. As soon as he got there, he dropped to the ground and crouched low, instructing his sister to do the same. It made sense to keep away from the trees and to hide from the lightning. Great drops of rain fell from the sky splashing onto the hard dry ground. Dirt and dust soon began to turn to mud but still they crouched hoping and praying that they would be safe. Lightning flashed and thunder roared, together.

"The storm is overhead," shouted Jacob. Gradually it moved away, the time between flash and thunder became longer and the rain slowed to a patter. Relieved, the children stood up. They were both soaked but pleased to be alive.

"Phew, that was really scary," Jacob blew out through his lips and picked up his stick. "Let's get back." As they made their way back to the boat, Rebekkah had an intuitive sense that they were being watched. She found herself looking over her shoulder and her pace quickened. They found the paddles much as they had left them although the leaves had been disturbed.

"The rain must have moved the leaves." It was if Jacob had read her thoughts.

"Hmm," she responded, "let's get out of here. I can't shake the feeling that we are being watched."

Jacob looked at her. "I know what you mean but I think it's just the rain dripping off the trees and the storm has made us both a bit jumpy. Here! Grab one end of the canoe."

Grunting with the effort the children pulled the canoe bit by bit down into the lake. Rebekkah clambered in and Jacob pushed off, jumping in as the water lapped around the boat. They both set to work and soon were at the opposite shore. The other canoe was already there. "I wonder how the PJs got on in the storm?" Rebekkah stared at the canoe, it had a lot of water in the bottom of it.

"Hopefully got struck by lightning." Jacob jumped out and indicated she was to do the same, they pulled the canoe up onto the bank.

"Jacob! That's a horrid thing to say."

"Well, I'm still angry about that trick they played on us last night with the magpie eggs. If the Eagle exists why doesn't She zap them?"

Rebekkah was just about to reply when she saw a figure ahead of them darting behind a tree. And then she jumped as a bird fell

to the earth and then another and another. They lay motionless
on the wet soil.

13 THE BIRDS

The children dropped to the ground and examined one of the birds. It was a blackbird and just ahead of them on the path was a robin. The blackbird was still warm to touch. Rebekkah looked anxiously around for the mysterious man. Then she heard them before they came into view. At first it was a distant sound; then it was as if a cloud of birds had descended from the sky into the treetops; it was the unmistakable cackle and chatter of magpies. Panic cut across her mind like a knife. Jacob too had gone very pale. They stared up into the trees where they could easily pick out the white breast and bluish plumage of hundreds of magpies. It was as if they were laughing at the children. Jacob began to look for stones and sturdy bits of wood buried beneath the carpet of wet leaves. Motioning to Rebekkah to do the same he stuffed his pockets. She understood; they would use them to throw at any bird that came their way. Once her pockets were full, they moved cautiously forward. The magpies cackled incessantly as the children made their way along the path. Little dead birds dotted the woodland floor, watery eyes staring up at them. Rebekkah choked back her fear, an image of Tipsey's lifeless body swam into her mind as she kept her eyes peeled for danger. Any minute now she expected an attack either from the mystery man or, a magpie. Her fingers were clenched around a large stone, adrenalin coursed through her veins, every muscle in her body was finely tuned to act quickly and to run if needed.

Suddenly they emerged into the clearing where they had eaten the night before. In front of them was the door to the garden. A dreadful sight met their eyes. The table was covered with magpies feeding on eggs. The nests from the night before had been refilled with more eggs. Who would have done that? As the children approached one large bird lifted its head and raised its wings as if to fly at them. Rebekkah let fly her stone hitting the bird on its chest. A cackling alarm went up from the remaining birds that immediately flew up into the sky and into the nearby trees where they sat and cackled ferociously at the two human beings.

Looking to their right and left, the two ran swiftly to the garden gate. Thankfully, it was open. They passed through, entered the garden and slammed the door behind them. Were they safe?

Turning away from the door they continued to watch the sky for further magpie attack and so failed to notice the figure standing a short distance away in the garden. As Jacob turned and saw him, he jumped in shock and caught hold of his sister's arm. They both stopped. It was orange eyes. Jacob could not move; it was as if his feet were concreted into the ground. Rebekkah looked around seeking a place to escape. The man spoke, in his harsh Scottish accent. "They are noisy, aren't they? Something's upset them. Or someone?" He smiled but the smile didn't reach his eyes, which were alert and watchful, like a bird.

"Have you been following us?" The words blurted out of Jacob's mouth.

"Now what makes you say that little man?"

Rebekkah watched him intently. There was definitely something really fake about him. He was also soaking wet. It could have been him hiding in the woods. He was ignoring her, his orange eyes fixed on Jacob.

"Who are you?" Jacob spoke loudly, fear making his voice sound harsh.

"I am a friend of your uncle. What interests me more is what you two have been up to? Out in a thunderstorm, it's a wonder you weren't hit by lightning. Weren't you scared? And where are your cousins? Your aunt has been worried about you all."

"Ah well, we had better go and see her then. Let her know we are ok." Rebekkah began to edge her way round the man. He moved as if to block the path and then thought better of it, smiled and stepped to one side. The children made their way past him and ran into the house, closing the door with relief.

"Phew, that was really scary, I've had enough adventures for a whole year!" Rebekkah spoke lightly but Jacob could see that she was shaking. He nodded, and they both climbed the stairs. As they neared the top their aunt emerged from a bedroom, a pile of laundry in her arms. "Oh, Jacob and Rebekkah, I am so pleased to see you. I have been so worried. That storm came on unexpectedly. You are absolutely soaked, poor things. Have you seen Jack, Phillip and Jasmina?"

"No Aunty, we got separated at the lake when we went canoeing." Jacob's face was the picture of innocence. His aunt didn't need to know why they had separated.

"Oh well, I am sure they are fine. They probably sheltered in the old cottage in the woods and are on their way back now that the rain has stopped. Get out of those wet cloths and I will pop them in the washing machine." Their aunt spoke to the wall and without looking at them as she headed down the stairs.

The children walked into Jacob's room and sat on the bed in relief. Jacob was silent. Rebekkah looked at him. "I am going to try and get hold of Robert again. That man is a weirdo and a fake; I think he was following us in the woods. Those dead birds were really sick and then all those evil magpies cackling like witches. This is just a nightmare. Do you think the magpies killed all those little birds?"

"It looks like it. Well, you can try and phone Robert." Her brother responded gloomily. "He hasn't been much good up until now. It feels like we are totally on our own with this. What I don't understand is how he, the Magpie, got here? How can he be friends with Uncle, and how did he know we were coming?"

Rebekkah shrugged as she picked up her telephone and checked

the messages. Her heart leapt; there was one from Robert. It

simply said. "I am on my way."

14 DAY 2, THE ACCUSATION

"Jacob! Rebekkah! Come down here at once," shouted their uncle from the bottom of the stairs. Something about the tone of his voice made them act quickly. As they entered the dining room everyone was gathered around the table including Pete Maghi. Their uncle was standing by the sideboard looking grim. In front of him was a pile of stones and twigs and a dead blackbird. "These stones were found in your pockets when your aunt tried to wash them."

It hadn't occurred to either child to empty their pockets before giving their wet clothes to their aunt. Their uncle continued, "When Jack, Jasmina and Phillip returned they told us how deeply upset they were by the sight of many woodland birds lying dead along the path in the woods. This is one of them. What have you to say for yourselves?"

"It wasn't us Uncle; we saw them too. They fell from the sky. It happened after the storm, after the magpies came. We were really scared!" Rebekkah's words tumbled out in a rush.

"So, you didn't use these stones to throw at any birds?" persisted their uncle.

"No!" said both children together.

"You know that's very interesting, because Pete saw you Rebekkah, throw a stone at a magpie. It hit the bird on the chest. Didn't you Pete?"

"I did indeed." Pete was watching the children intently, "You were outside the garden door and threw a stone at a bird that was feeding."

"Yes, but that was only one and it didn't die, it only flew up into the trees. I thought it was going to attack me like it did my ..." Rebekkah stopped before saying the word cat. She didn't want to go into all that now. "We would never harm all those little woodland birds. Uncle, you have got to believe me!" pleaded Rebekkah.

"Bird murderers!" said Jack accusingly. "You should have seen the way they attacked us with the paddles from the canoe. I can well believe they killed all those birds. These town kids are vicious."

A strangling sound emerged from Jacob's throat. He was pink with rage. Before his sister could stop him, he hurled himself at Jack and began pummelling his chest. He was shouting, "You liar! You know that's not true. You attacked us! We were defending ourselves."

Jasmina screamed hysterically, "Dad, get that ginger brat off Jack! See how violent he is."

Pete Maghi and Uncle David both grabbed at Jacob and pinned his arms behind his back. Jacob continued to struggle, shouting at both men and trying in vain to free himself. Rebekkah had seen this before. Once Jacob was in a rage it was very hard to control him and he became oblivious to consequences. Phillip was dancing from one leg to another, obviously enjoying the drama. "Put him in the fridge, put him in the fridge, that'll cool him down! Bird murderer, bird murderer!"

"Shut up Phillip!" Rebekkah shouted at him. "You don't know what happened, you weren't there!"

"Let me go!" shouted Jacob as both men obligingly dropped him onto the floor. Jacob lay still for a moment and then got to his feet. He ran to the door and out into the corridor. In the silence they could all hear the sound of his feet as he stomped up the stairs. Rebekkah made as if to go after him but her uncle barred the way. "You stay here Rebekkah, he needs time to cool off. Perhaps you can tell us a bit more about what happened out in the woods."

Rebekkah resisted the desire to run after Jacob and away from these hostile people but thought better of it. Perhaps she could calm things down. "It's as Jacob said, Uncle David. We went canoeing but got separated from," she paused, "our cousins and then a storm came along. Once it was over, we noticed all the little birds. It was really scary because there were a lot of magpies in the trees. I don't trust magpies because they attacked our cat Tipsy and killed her. Dad was also attacked at the same time. You saw the stitches above his eye? So, in case we needed to protect ourselves we collected some stones. When we got back to the garden door there was a table with loads of magpies on it. They were feeding on eggs, it was disgusting. One looked like it was going to attack us, so I threw a stone at it. Then, we met him." She pointed at Pete.

"They are lying Dad," interjected Jack. Rebekkah looked at him with distaste. She had deliberately left out the bit about Jack and Jasmina's treachery. She wasn't a tell-tale.

Their uncle began to laugh, "So, that's how Gerald got that nasty cut above his eye? He wouldn't tell me what happened. Attacked by a bird, that's almost as funny as having one poo on your head!"

Rebekkah felt she had somehow betrayed her father and her cheeks flushed pink. The others joined in the laughter.

All except orange eyes who continued to stare at her. "Anyone who throws stones at a bird has a cruel streak in them and your brother has quite a temper. It seems to me he is very capable of committing such a crime. Maybe you copied what you had seen your brother do to those little birds in the woods. Magpies are much maligned. They are beautiful birds."

"Jacob can stay in his room while we investigate this further, let's eat." Their aunt had remained quiet throughout but now she moved towards the tureens on the sideboard and began heaping piles of lasagne onto everyone's plates. Rebekkah's stomach was churning, she felt upset and picked at her food. If a trap had been laid for Jacob, then he had fallen into it. He did have a bad temper and he should not have attacked Jack. On the other hand, Jack was a liar, and she had a sneaking admiration for the way Jacob had launched himself at the bigger boy. Served him right. Jack excused himself after dinner complaining of a headache caused by his cousin's behaviour.

Oh please! Rebekkah thought to herself. *What a wimp!* She was about to leave the table herself when Jasmina sidled up to her. "You will be on your own this evening," she drawled. "How about we play a game of hide and seek? I'll hide and you and Phillip can come and find me."

Phillip hovered nearby grinning like a Cheshire cat. "Ok, I'll count. 1,2,3…"

Jasmina shot out of the door leaving Rebekkah with her cousin. She would rather have gone upstairs to Jacob but thought it might be best to at least try to be friendly, so she stayed with Phillip while he counted. "Coming! Ready or not!" He called out and then trotted off, beckoning Rebekkah to follow him.

He headed along the corridor and then down some stairs to a door.

"What makes you think she is down here?" asked Rebekkah suspiciously.

"Because there's a fridge in the cellar with ice cream in it and she will be sitting in the dark working her way through the choc ices. Look, go and see for yourself." He opened the door and Rebekkah peered into the gloom. She suddenly felt suspicious but as she began to turn away from the door Phillip gave her a shove. Off balance, she stumbled forward giving him sufficient time and space to shut and lock the door behind her. The dark enclosed her. She was alone. It reminded her of the time she had been shoved into the PE locker, and she started to panic.

15 JACOB

Jacob sat on the bed staring at Ratbag. He was fuming. Thoughts tumbled round his head all mixed up with feelings of extreme rage. He was not at all sorry for what he had done to his cousin. Towards Jack he felt only anger and a strong resentment grounded in a sense of unfairness. It reminded him of how he had felt when he was at school. On that occasion he had been trying to protect another student from some bullies. In the process the bullies had turned on him, tipped everything out of his bag and taken his iPad. In a rage, he had lashed out wildly and caught a boy on the chin knocking him unconscious. In a gross act of unfairness, a teacher blamed Jacob for knocking him out rather than recognise that he was only defending himself.

As a consequence, he had run away rather than be put in the cooler. That was when he had met Robert and the Magpie in an old disused factory. He was becoming more and more convinced that the man downstairs with orange eyes was also the man who had kidnapped him called the Magpie. How on earth had he got to know his uncle and aunt? Did they know who he really was? It was all very confusing. He wished Robert would turn up as he wanted to talk to him. After a while he made his way to the top of the stairs and tried to listen to the conversation. The door was closed, and he could not hear so he gave up and went back into his room. He heard Jack run up the stairs and go into his room, this was followed by voices in the hall, then a door opened and closed, followed by silence. Jacob stood up and walked over to the window and stared out into the garden. A thin figure with a rucksack on his back emerged from the side of the house and hurried across the garden and passed out of sight. It was Pete. What was he doing?

Contemplating the mystery of Pete Maghi caused his mind to spin and whirl. Then it suddenly became clear and he understood. Pete Maghi was an anagram of The Magpie!

Without thinking he jumped off his bed, made his way downstairs and out into the garden. He carefully opened the garden door. He could just see the shape of a man moving along the path ahead of him. Jacob followed, hiding behind trees as he had seen them do in the films. After about ten minutes the figure moved up a side path that looked like an unmade road. It was harder to keep hidden from view, but Jacob could see a building in the distance. He decided to make his own way through the woods to the house, avoiding the road altogether. Jumping over branches, tramping through bits of twig and fallen leaves he was aware of the silence around him. It was getting dark, so it was harder in the gloom of the trees to see where he was going. He had no plan and no idea what he was going to do when he got to the house.

Suddenly there was a cracking sound to his right, Jacob dropped to the ground and froze. Immediately the trees were filled with chattering, cackling birds – magpies calling out an alarm. Lights and voices were coming his way, he crept backwards until his hands and feet found a large tree trunk. Feeling his way along the bark he found an opening where its inside had decayed away. Gratefully he squeezed inside and kept still. The voices became louder and he could hear shouts of, "There he is!" and, "Quick over here!"

His mouth was dry with fright and he thought his heart would burst through the wall of his chest it was beating so fast. His breath came in short shallow gasps of fear. Any minute he expected rough hands to grab him and haul him out of his

hiding place. But to his great relief they became less distinct and the crashing noises moved further away until it was clear they had gone. He crawled out of the trunk and brushed himself down. Bending low he moved sideways until he could see in the distance a group of men half dragging a struggling figure towards the house. Once they got to the front door, they pushed him inside and that was it. Then silence. Jacob made his way back down the road to the path and ran all the way back to the garden gate. Only when he was through and climbing the stairs did he feel safe. He needed to talk to Rebekkah.

16 THE CELLAR

It was dark inside the cellar. Rebekkah panicked and hammered on the door calling Phillip's name as she did so. After a few minutes she stopped and put her ear to the door. Immediately his voice drifted through the keyhole, "Watch out for the rats Ratty Rebekkah, there's loads in the cellar."

She let out a scream and pleaded with him. But there was no reply. *Hateful boy!* She hammered on the door again but then dropped, exhausted onto the floor and wept.

It wasn't fair, why couldn't she have normal cousins like everyone else that she could play with and be friends with? Why was her life so difficult? Why were her parents so distant and uncaring? What was the point in anything? Feeling sorry for herself, she sat for a long time waiting for her eyes to adjust. Waves of panic flooded over her as she imagined rats nibbling at her feet. Her skin felt itchy and she slapped at her arms picking at her skin with her fingers.

Just as she thought she might go mad she became aware of a presence. It was neither in her head nor in the room it was more in her heart and soul. It was gentle and warm. It entered her

thoughts and calmed her. It bathed her in its light. She had felt
this presence before, once when locked in a locker at school by
some bullies. The memory of the experience came pouring back
into her thoughts and she relived it. Eyes closed she was
transported to another world, the world of the nest. She was
playing with lambs and lion cubs. She was drinking strawberry
milkshake. She was running through trees alongside a beautiful
clear stream that gurgled and sang to her as she skipped along its
banks. In her dream she stopped and whispered, "Where are
you Eagle?"

"I am with you in the darkness," came the reassuring reply.
Rebekkah opened her eyes and the scene instantly disappeared.
Yet now she felt calm and was able to order her thoughts.

He said there was a fridge down here with ice cream in it. But then, just
as quickly, arose another thought, crushing the hope that was
rising in her chest. *Maybe they were lying just to get me down here.*
And then, immediately, quick as a flash, a reply. *But maybe that bit
was true, maybe there is a fridge and where there is a fridge there is light! If
there's a fridge it will hum.*

As the thought flew across her mind there was a click and then a slight humming vibration perceivable in the oppressive darkness. Listening carefully, she followed the sound, edging her way across the floor, arms outspread. She bumped into what she assumed was a chair and it moved a few inches across the tiled floor making a scraping noise as it did so. Feeling the shape of the chair with her outstretched fingers she steadied herself against the back of it, held on and moved one foot in the direction of the noise. She could feel something hard and shiny and flat. Sliding her other foot forwards, she began moving her hands to right and left until she felt the edge. Slipping both hands to the right she gripped the corner and pulled. Nothing. Moving over to the other side she repeated the movement. This time the door opened, and light poured into the room. She gave a little squeal of relief.

From the interior light of the fridge, she could see that she was in a small room with a table and two chairs. To her left was a door and to the right of the door was a switch. She let go of the fridge door and darted across the room. Just as the door swung shut enveloping her once again in darkness, she reached the switch and flicked it down. Light!

She knew she could not escape through the door into the hall, so she turned her attention to the other door that had been revealed by the light. Trying the handle, it opened easily, and she passed through into the other side. The room was empty apart from four boxes. Curious she opened the first to find some blankets inside. Moving to the next she uncovered piles of what looked like children's clothes. The next box was much smaller. Kneeling on the floor she reached inside and pulled out some small booklets. Turning them over in her hands she noticed the writing on the front. It was in gold leaf. There was something written in squiggles. Underneath the squiggles were the words, 'Syrian Arab Republic' and then under that, 'Republique Arabe Syrienne'. A gold bird sat under the words and then more words. More squiggles but then a word she recognised, 'Passport'.

Opening it, she found a picture of a pretty girl looking out at her. She was about her own age with black hair partially hidden under a scarf. Closing it, she picked up others; there were more photos. There were about twenty in all. Puzzled and with questions racing into her mind, Rebekkah put them back. What were her uncle and aunt doing with all these passports? She had heard of the country Syria. At school they had raised money to send clothes to a refugee camp where thousands of people were living in tents, having had to leave their homes. She had been touched by the stories of children fleeing from war to preserve their lives. But that was in another country, miles away. What were these people doing here and where were they now?

It was time to talk to Jacob about all this. She looked around the room and noticed a small window. It was slightly ajar. There was no other way out apart from the way she had come in and she knew that door would still be locked. She went back into the room with the fridge, grabbed a chair and moved it underneath the window. Climbing onto it she peered through the grubby glass. She could see that it opened onto a small walled area below the garden. She was in cellar, so the window was at ground level. Pushing it open as far as it would go, she heaved herself up pushing her head through the opening and flopped out onto the patio like a great big fish. She lay still for a moment trying to catch her breath and then jumped up, dusted herself down and climbed over the wall dropping into the garden below. She was at the back of the house, and it was getting dark. She moved slowly looking around her as she did so. She did not want to run into her cousins or that man, Pete. Safely inside, she dashed up the stairs and into her room where Jacob was waiting for her, sitting on the edge of her bed.

17 THE WALK IN THE WOODS

Both children shared their stories. Rebekkah was particularly troubled by Jacob's disclosure that Pete Maghi was the Magpie, but it made sense and was obvious now she thought about it. She wanted to leave immediately and head for their grandparent's house. Jacob was torn between anxiety about what the Magpie might do to him and curiosity about what the guy was up to. He reasoned with his sister that they could not be in any immediate danger, as Pete had not done anything to them and had the chance to if he was so minded. As long as they kept up the pretence of believing he was Pete rather than the Magpie then he considered that they were relatively safe. Secretly, he was not sure who he was trying to convince – himself or his sister – but he had to find out what he was up to, who the people were in the woods and what was the connection with the passports?

Reluctantly, not totally convinced by her brother's reasoning, Rebekkah agreed to give him until morning to find some answers to their questions before she contacted her grandparents. Not wanting to waste any time he suggested they might go back into the woods that night and visit the cottage when everyone was asleep.

So, they waited. Midnight came and went, 12.30, 1.00 a.m..... Rebekkah had just nodded off when she felt her brother shaking her shoulder. Blearily she followed him down the stairs and out into the night. A wind had blown up and the clouds were scudding across the moonlit sky. The trees in the woods waved back and forth as if they were masts on a galleon being buffeted by waves. It was both eerie and exciting to be out at night. Rebekkah thought back to how things had changed for them both over the last year. The Rebekkah Taylor of a year ago would never have considered an adventure in the woods at 1 o'clock in the morning, and definitely not with her brother. She stole a look at him, his face looked older, his mouth was set firm and she felt a sense of pride at his courage and joy in the growing closeness in their relationship.

As if aware of her eyes on him, he gave her a diffident and slightly embarrassed look and stuck his tongue out at her. She laughed and gave him a playful punch on the arm.

Picking their way carefully through the woods, their eyes became fully adjusted to the gloom. It was surprising how much it was possible to see by the light of the moon. As they drew near to the cottage Jacob slowed down and dropped deeper into the woods away from the path. She followed him. At night, it was much harder to walk without tripping over tree roots or getting tangled in the shrubs. Rebekkah was concentrating on where to put her feet when Jacob grabbed her arm, making her jump. There in front of them was a fence, and behind the fence, a cottage. The lights were on in an upstairs room and as they gazed, face upwards, a shape passed in front of the window. Rebekkah stuck her hand in her mouth and stared wide eyed at Jacob. "Now what?" she mumbled.

Jacob stood still uncertain as to what to do next. "Let's get a little closer, and see if we can look through the downstairs windows?"

They moved stealthily forward until they found their way blocked by a fence and shrubs.

"We could move around the fence, see if there is a gap we can get through." Rebekkah's whisper sounded loud in the silence.

Jacob nodded his agreement and cautiously they made their way around the perimeter. Soon they arrived at a gate, wide enough to permit entry of a motor vehicle. It was locked. As they stood hesitantly by it unsure what to do next Rebekkah's eyes were drawn further up the track. In the distance she could see the headlights of a vehicle. It was driving slowly towards them! Pulling urgently on Jacob's jacket she alerted him to the danger and the two ran back into the woods. Finding a fallen tree trunk, they clambered over it and slid down onto the soft earth behind it. Panting, they both sat with their backs pressed against the ribbed bark. The noise of the engine could be clearly heard now and there was a crunching sound as it swept up to the gate and stopped.

Turning in the direction of the vehicle they tentatively poked their heads above the tree. A man got out of the vehicle, which they could see was a dark coloured van, and punched some numbers into a keypad on the side of the wall. The gate swung open. As he then got back into the front seat, Jacob without saying anything to Rebekkah, hopped over the tree trunk and ran towards the back of the van crouching low, trying to keep out of sight of the rear-view mirrors. As the van moved forward, he ran behind it and followed it through the gate, which then closed. Rebekkah, who had been astounded by this turn of events, crouched paralysed with shock. There was no way she could follow her brother and he had moved so fast she had no time to think. What was she going to do now? How was Jacob going to get out? What would happen to him? Why had he been so rash? She felt overwhelming anxiety mixed with rage at the predicament he had left her in. She knew he had no plan, had acted on the spur of the moment and had not left her deliberately but she didn't like being left behind and was worried for his safety.

Then, a thought took root in her mind; she knew what she had to do.

18 THE COTTAGE

Once inside the gates Jacob dropped back from the van and headed for a shed he could make out to the left of the house. He was banking on the driver being more focused on moving the van forward rather than looking in his mirrors. From behind the shed he could watch all that was going on. As the van came to a halt, the front door of the house opened and a tallish man came out, his silhouette clearly visible in the light of the open door. It was too dark to make out his face clearly. He greeted the driver and the two of them walked round to the rear doors of the van. Unlocking the doors, the men shouted at whoever was inside to get their things and to come out. To Jacob's complete amazement a group of six people tumbled out of the van. As far as he could see, it looked like there were children amongst the group. They were silent for the most part although he could hear what sounded like a whimpering noise coming from one of the small people.

He watched the two men herd the people into the house and shut the door. Jacob had a strong sense that these were not friends and family arriving as guests, he was beginning to suspect something deeply sinister was going on. The intrepid lad waited a few minutes and then edged his way round the shed and up to a window. Peering through into the dark interior he could not see a thing. And then suddenly the lights were turned on in the room. Startled he took a step back and fell, making a dull thud as he did so. Shuffling on his bottom he scooted back towards the shed. But it was too late. He had been seen. His face had been illuminated against the uncurtained window once the lights went on. Why had he been so stupid and taken such a risk? A large man instantly ran out after him. Like a terrified rabbit caught in headlights, Jacob froze as a torch shone into his face and rough hands grabbed his jacket and pulled him to his feet. "What have we here then? A little chicken running away from the coop?"

Thinking quickly Jacob decided to say nothing. Maybe it was best to let them think he was one of the strange people. Besides, he wanted Rebekkah to have time to get home.

"Come on little fellow let's get you indoors with the rest." The man frogmarched him indoors and pushed him into the room he had been staring into from the window and shut the door.

There was a sound of a key turning.

Jacob was now a captive! He stumbled and then fell onto his knees. Resting on his hands he looked up and took in his surroundings. The room was full of people, some with headscarves others bareheaded. There were children and adults. For the most part they all looked as terrified as he felt.

One of the men, with a swarthy complexion and black hair, spoke to him in a language he couldn't identify. He shook his head and spoke in English, "Sorry, I don't understand."

The man tried again, "You, English?" His accent was strong.

"Yes," replied Jacob. "Who are you?"

The man turned to a woman who was half lying on the floor, she was in a sleeping bag and had propped herself up on an elbow. She was studying Jacob with interest. The man spoke quickly to her, words tumbling out like water over stones. Jacob had no idea what they were saying. There were also several children in sleeping bags. All were awake and staring at him with dark anxious eyes. The adults seem to reach an agreement and the man spoke again to Jacob in his halting English, "Why they put you here?" He waved his hands indicating the room.

Jacob thought and then said, "They think I am one of you; that I tried to escape."

The man studied him carefully and then turned to the woman. He conveyed Jacob's words to her and then tried again. "You, not one of us?"

"No," said Jacob. "I am English. I saw you arrive. I was watching when they saw me. I wanted to find out what was going on. They thought I had hidden in the van and that I was trying to escape. I didn't speak. They put me in here with you."

The man nodded slowly and then said, "We refugees. We come from Syria. These men bad, take all our money, clothes, passports, promise us new life in England, lock us up, many days." He pointed to a pencil tally on the wall. Jacob counted 126 sticks, 126 days?

Then it dawned on him. The man had mentioned passports. Rebekkah had found clothes and passports in the house. Were these the people to whom the passports belonged?

His brain was working overtime. He had seen the Syrian crisis on the news but had not paid much attention. It had all seemed far away and pretty irrelevant to a boy of thirteen.

"Are you an illegal immigrant?" He asked.

"No, we refugee family, we escape war, not illegal. Men say they have papers that say we can stay here. But all we do is sleep, work, sleep, work."

"Work? How can you work?" The question came out clumsily. Jacob was struggling to understand. The man was keen to explain.

"We are like slaves, we cannot escape; we are beaten, made to work long, long time. We pick fruit. You help us, yes?" The man looked so sad and dejected that Jacob felt pity and compassion for him, an unfamiliar feeling that swallowed up his own fear.

"I don't know whether I can help you," he said. "I am a prisoner too, a boy. It won't be long before they learn I am not one of you and then…" Jacob stopped. He had not considered what would happen to him once the men realised that they had made a mistake. "Are there more of you here?" he asked.

The man nodded. "Yes, twenty, I think. Bad men have guns. Beat us. Not possible escape." He then turned to the woman again and spoke with her. Jacob presumed he was filling her in on the conversation. He began to feel uncomfortable. They were all staring at him. He wondered what had happened to Rebekkah. What would she do? Who would she tell? Jacob felt powerless and frightened. What had he got himself into?

19 THE STORIES

"Do you know man called Pete?" Jacob jumped, startled out of his thoughts of Rebekkah. The question came from one of the children he was a boy about his own age. He was staring at Jacob.

"Yes," Jacob responded. "What do you know of him?"

"He very bad man. He boss man here."

Of course, thought Jacob, as another piece of the jigsaw fell into place. This was where Pete had been yesterday when Jacob saw him in the woods. He was running this whole racket. It should not surprise him really, having been captured by Pete himself before; he knew what he was capable of doing and it was not a pleasant thought.

"How did you get here?" asked Jacob quizzically.

The boy drew a deep breath and then began his story, "I born in Aleppo, Syria. My father, he a pharmacist and we have good life. I went to school. I play football." He paused, "I support Manchester United," he said proudly. "Who you support?"

Jacob hated football and shook his head. The boy looked at him and then continued, "Then fighting start, much shooting in streets, much blood," he mimed the gesture of shooting an automatic weapon with his hands. The woman reached over and touched his arm and shook her head nodding at the younger ones who were watching with large brown eyes. "My father, he take one morning by government soldiers; he come back three days, much hurt man. He tell me, must leave and go Berlin or England, start new life where safe. My family pay $5000 to smuggler to get out Syria and to Libya. We fly to Sudan and then lorry to Libya. Thirty people in back lorry. No eat for four days, food they give very dirty, no good. Some our people die and people we pay to help just throw off lorry. It hard. We very sad."

The boy's eyes filled with tears, he stopped to compose himself before continuing, "I miss my family so much, I alone, I scared. I not know what happen. My hope was Libya, hope they look after me there."

"And did they?" asked Jacob; he found his interest growing despite his own gnawing fear about his own safety. He could see this boy had been through troubles much worse than his own.

The boy laughed a bitter laugh. "Oh yes, they look after me, in police station. Me prison ten days, they say me an illegal immigrant."

"That's so unfair!" Interrupted Jacob, a strong sense of injustice flooding through him.

"Unfair? Oh yes, much unfair. I only free because my father pay smuggler more money, much more money."

Jacob blanched remembering his own experience of telephoning his father to ask for money when the Magpie had kidnapped him. Thankfully he had escaped. He had never asked his father if he would have paid up had the story ended differently. "So, your father coughed up?"

"Coughed up?" The boy looked puzzled. "No, he not cough."

"I mean, he paid, otherwise you wouldn't be here, would you?" finished Jacob rather lamely.

"Oh yes, he pay money, to same smuggler man that help me escape. I then release; they me take north to coast where I stay in house for few days. One night they come for us and put us, many, many people, on boat, not good boat, not safe. It bad time. Many of us sick, no life jackets, many people for boat, water come in boat. I afraid."

"Wow!" Jacob was astonished. This boy had been through so much. "How did you make it?"

"As we come near Italy, another boat come by us. Take smuggler man who drive boat away. He give one of us a mobile phone and tell him he must call Italy coastguard when we see land and then he leave us. He say not phone too soon or Libya coastguard come take us back Libya. We no want that. We wait. We very afraid, no food, no water and some people very ill, babies and children. After one night and one day like this we phone coastguard, too scare dying to wait more. Italy coastguard come help us, al-Hamdu lillah!"

"And were they Italians or Libyans," asked Jacob completely absorbed in the boy's story and the matter-of-fact way he was telling it.

"Italians," the boy smiled for the first time in his story. "They very kind to us. We given message Arabic which said, '*this not a prison. Do not escape, there is no reason to. The people of this land are happy that you have arrived safe and well.*' They give us hot food and medicine. When they see I alone without my family they tell me I must ask protect from any man who scare or want hurt me. I so happy to be in Europe with kind people. You no understand how good it feel after leaving my home. Much kindness. It a good thing."

"So why did you leave Italy?" Jacob was genuinely puzzled.

"My name Tarek; I no speak Italian, I speak English and Arabic. My father he say I try get England or Germany. I listen him. After time, I see life in refugee camp no good, no future. Many people come and then move on. You learn how escape by talking others. I speak smuggler men, you call traffickers I think. I speak my father, he pay. I then go."

"But how do you know you can trust them?" asked Jacob.

"I no use men who work alone, they not have contacts, I told go to traffickers that work from offices, have many contacts. I not know safe but must leave. I have no choice. I get out Syria. I now here." Tarek looked around the room and spread his hands. "In Italy, I telephone my father. My family happy I alive. My father pay more money to another trafficker who get me in back of a lorry. We drive then arrive Calais in France. I lucky I think. English family, they give me passport and drive me to England in car on ferry. When arrive England, I pass over to Pete and keep here. Trapped, not allow leave. I no lucky. We work long hours in factory and they keep us here like chickens in cage. Nothing to do except work, sleep, work, sleep."

He stopped his story finished. He looked exhausted. Jacob felt very sorry for him but also angry. The same anger he had felt when he had been wrongly accused of starting a fight when some boys had taken his iPad. It was not fair.

Another man who had been watching and listening now joined in, "I want work, earn money for my daughter school. I promise good job in England, so me and two my friends we pay. We drive in lorry to port; then ferry to England. When we arrive they say we get work for good money, so we work very hard, for long hours, do job well. But when we finish, they no pay us. Instead we lock up here." He scratched his beard and then continued smacking his right fist into his open left hand. "They force us do more work. They beat us and threaten us if we don't finish work. We no leave because they take our passports, papers and money. We in trap."

"Why don't you all gang together and attack these men?" asked Jacob.

The man looked at him sadly, "We think that too but they catch us and they have guns. If we try escape, they bring us back and punish us. We feel hopeless; we weak, they strong."

Jacob remembered the image of a struggling child he had seen the day before when he was hidden in the tree trunk in the woods. He shivered.

"Please, you help us? You the first person from outside we see in weeks?" The man was pleading with him. Jacob shifted uneasily. He wasn't sure how much to tell these people. Should he build their hopes up by telling them about Rebekkah, his grandparents and Robert? Would they be able to keep it all to themselves? He didn't want Rebekkah hurt by Pete.

"I really don't know. I have met this man before and when he

147

recognizes me, I shall be in as much trouble as the rest of you."
This was the truth.

Tarek yawned and the man nodded slowly before turning away
and back to his bed. He was disappointed but did not question.
"We must sleep," he said sadly. "Tomorrow we have work long
day. We pray that Allah uses you to help us."

Yeah, right, thought Jacob cynically. *Another religious nut case who
thinks life can be magically sorted out by an invisible being.* But for once
he kept his thoughts to himself, these people had been through
enough and they didn't need him arguing with them in the
middle of the night. The woman was tugging at something
under her mattress; she said a few words to the man who
nodded in agreement. Together they pulled out a rug that had
been between the mat and floorboards and gave it to Jacob. She
reached for a coat and passed it to him, then, placing her hands
together she pressed them to the left side of her head and smiled
at him. Jacob's eyes filled with tears and his nose stung. Her
kindness had taken him by surprise. Embarrassed, he busied
himself with laying the rug on the floor so that the strangers
could not see his eyes. Turning his back to the room he laid on

his side eyes closed and tried to think. Despite himself he

drifted into an uneasy sleep.

20 THE NEST

Jacob slept fitfully but dreamt vividly. He was back in the nest, that beautiful home of the Eagle where he could eat as much as he wanted of crisps and chocolate and play for hours in the water. It had been a kind of paradise. But in his dream the nest had changed. Jacob remembered the extraordinary light that had pervaded everything but now there was only a dark sense of foreboding. The trees were empty of leaves. There wasn't an animal in sight. No flowers to break up the dull, lifeless ground. Jacob hunted desperately for the river where he had fished and swam but all he could find was a dark lake on which floated a huge rubber dinghy full of people. As he watched they shouted and cried, some fell in the water while others hung onto them. Magpies flew overhead cackling disdainfully.

Then the scene changed, and he was back at the tree – the beautiful golden tree where the chocolate fruit had been. Jacob stretched out his hand searching for the golden whorl that had released the little ladder that allowed him to climb up into its branches. He could not find it. He was searching and searching but it was not there. He dropped to his knees, hands outstretched and bowed his head.

His thoughts turned to the last time he had been in this place, when he had climbed the ladder against the Eagle's orders and grabbed the chocolate pear. *This is my fault entirely,* he thought, as despair and sadness overwhelmed him. *All this darkness, I have spoilt this beautiful place just because I was greedy and selfish, thinking only of myself.*

Like a dog who had lost his owner, he threw back his head and howled into the night sky, "I am so sorry, I didn't know what I was doing. I didn't mean it. Please help me to make it right." As soon as the words were out of his mouth a shaft of light shone down through the trees and lit up a little door in a tree to his left. Jacob got unsteadily to his feet and made his way towards the light. On the door was an old-fashioned knocker shaped as an eagle's head. He studied the door carefully looking for a handle but could find none. It would appear that this door could only be opened from the inside. He knocked gently; the door swung open and Jacob stepped inside. He found himself bathed in startling bright light so bright that he had to shield his eyes. It was like looking at the sun. He knew he had to walk deeper in towards the light but it hurt and so he turned to look back. The door was still open and through the light Jacob could see the wizened trees with their lifeless branches. Uncertainly he took two steps back towards the door.

Irresolute, he hovered in the hall, at the threshold between the harsh but known world outside and the bright but unknown world within. One he could see the other he could not. At least he knew what to expect of the forest outside. However, he had no idea what to expect if he was to walk blindly into the light. What lay there could be far worse. His rational mind was working overtime. He teetered on the point of indecision like a tightrope walker caught by a sudden breeze.

Maybe I should go back into the gloom and take my chances with what I know and what I can actually see. But I hate the darkness so maybe what lay cloaked within the light would be better.

He hesitated and then moved away from the door closing it firmly behind him. A feeling of relief poured over him, but he still could not see into the light. Taking a deep breath, he closed his eyes and felt his way along the wall. Finally, the wall turned right, and he had the impression of a much larger space. He stopped, uncertain what to do next. He still could not see but then a familiar voice came out of the light. "Jacob!" the voice was deep, rich and reassuring.

"Eagle," he stuttered. "Is it really You? What has happened to the nest?"

"Nothing," she said, "the nest is still here; it is your perception that has changed."

"I don't understand; the trees, the darkness, those poor people in the boat and the magpies, it is all so different. It's terribly sad."

"You are seeing things differently," She said, "you are beginning to care about others, and you are seeing the difference between darkness and light. Your reality is changing."

"I don't get it. The nest was beautiful, but now it is damaged, broken, sick," he was searching for words. "The nest has actually changed, not me."

"I thought you did not believe the nest existed," persisted the Eagle, "So, how can it change?"

Jacob thought frantically. "This is a dream, right? You are just in my dream?"

"Jacob, are dreams real? What are dreams?"

"No!" said Jacob firmly. "They are just parts of our subconscious talking to us when we are asleep."

'Then, I am in your subconscious and so is the nest, but it doesn't make what you are beginning to understand any less true or real. Tell me what happened outside the tree before you came through the door."

"I…" Jacob was struggling to find the words, "I thought, that is I felt, that the nest had changed because of something I had done. I felt that it was because I had taken the chocolate from the tree. Is it, is it all my fault?"

"You could say it is also my fault Jacob, for trusting you, for bringing you into the nest, for giving you freedom of choice. You could say that it was a great risk, knowing the sort of boy you are. The temptation to take the chocolate was always going to be too great. You could argue that I should have protected you from that."

"Then why didn't you?" Jacob found himself beginning to shout with frustration. "You know I killed a bird as well? Why didn't you stop me?"

"And if I had, what would you have learnt? If I controlled your choices like some kind of robot what good would that have been to you?"

Jacob nodded slowly, his eyes were still closed against the light, but it was helping him to focus and think. "Yes, I would have been furious, a choice has to be a real choice or else it's no choice at all. But it all seemed so pointless. I didn't see the consequences of my decision until…" His voice trailed off.

The Eagle was silent as if she was waiting for something more.

"But it's not real, is it? You aren't real? You are just in my imagination. I am just talking to myself."

The Eagle said nothing.

"And what about all the bad stuff that's been happening since I visited the nest? The Magpie, Mum and Dad's relationship falling apart, me being kidnapped, moving schools and those horrible magpies?"

The Eagle spoke softly, "Tell me about the bird you killed."

He did not want to talk about it, he felt ashamed. "The bird was trying to peck the chocolate and I didn't want to share it. It looked so good and the bird was spoiling it. I tried to shoo it away by flapping my arms, but it kept coming back, every time I tried to pick the chocolate the bird tried to stop me so in the end, I got mad and just grabbed it and twisted its neck until it was dead. And then I picked the chocolate and ate it."

The Eagle was silent again. After a long time she spoke, her voice heavy with sadness. "Yes, I know; in fact that was worse than taking the chocolate. To be so fixated with what you want to the exclusion of any other living thing is the source of evil."

"Evil?"

"Yes, it is only when you begin to understand the potential for doing bad things that exists in all of us that we are in a position to consciously choose to do good."

Jacob turned his head back towards the light and tried to open his eyes but the light was still too powerful. He felt exposed and vulnerable almost as if he was naked and that the Eagle could see deep into his heart. He wanted to hide. He thought about running back out through the little door. He hung his head, lost for words. Then something of his old belligerence came back to him. "Why did you bring me here? Why did you allow me to spoil your home? What was the point?"

"Jacob, you and Rebekkah are part of a battle between good and evil. In this battle there are those who choose to walk in the light and those who prefer the darkness. The light walkers are many but sometimes they seem too few, whereas the walkers in darkness can seem too numerous and powerful. However, as you grow in understanding you will become stronger, braver and wiser. You will learn to connect with other followers of the light, and you will resist the darkness together. The nest was just the beginning. You are now more aware of your own weakness and the depths to which you will go to get what you want. You know there is darkness within your soul, and this disturbs you.

You want to be different and are choosing to walk in the light because you dislike what you see of the darkness. You are beginning to reject that part of you that demands to have its own way, and in its place you are learning a new way."

Jacob frowned, "I really don't get what you are talking about? What do you mean? Give me an example."

"The man you call the Magpie, he is a walker in darkness. You have already challenged him and he is angry with you. But he senses the struggle between light and darkness that is taking place in your heart and soul. He understands your fear and has no time for faith in higher things. He would seek to crush all that is good from you like an orange in an orange squeezer. But do not be afraid, help will come when you least expect it."

And that was it; the dream ended abruptly.

21 DAY 3 – JACOB AND PETE

Jacob could feel someone shaking him and when he opened his eyes, he suddenly found himself staring into the beaky face of the Magpie. He was hauled roughly to his feet, his eyes still blurred with sleep, and for a moment he could not work out where he was. Then the awful truth dawned on him. He was in the cottage and all the refugees were staring at him. He could see the terror in their eyes and sense the tension in the room.

"So, this is the boy you caught last night," the Magpie was staring at him while he addressed a tall man who was standing in the doorway. The room was crowded, and Jacob was pushed towards the door. He stumbled and fell on top of Tarek who whispered in his ear. "The Eagle be with you."

"What?" Jacob was so shocked that he thought he must have misheard. Before he could say anything, he was grabbed by the tall man and dragged into the hallway. The door was closed behind them, and Jacob found himself alone with the two men. The Magpie spoke, "You know who I am." It was more a statement than a question.

"Of course, I don't," said Jacob sullenly. "One minute you are Pete, friend of my Aunt and Uncle and next I find you are a people smuggler. Do they know what you are up to here?"

"That's for me to know and you to find out." Pete smirked. He was clearly enjoying Jacob's discomfort. Pete stared at him for a long time as if contemplating what to do next. Jacob met his gaze and then looked away. What happened next was a complete surprise. Pete walked away from him and opened a door into a kitchen area, whereupon a wonderful aroma of bacon drifted along the hallway. He could see a man cooking rashers on the grill. Turning round Pete beckoned to Jacob to follow him into the kitchen. Once inside he pulled out a chair and helped himself to two rolls and some bacon. He set one before Jacob and the other for himself. Pouring some coffee, he asked Jacob what he would like to drink. Shifting uneasily in his seat Jacob realised how thirsty he was and asked for some orange juice. Pete sat down opposite him and bit into his roll indicating to Jacob that he should do the same.

Chewing on his bacon, his mouth full of bread, Pete started to speak, "You are a clever boy Jacob. And brave. Not like your cousins. You are not very keen on them, are you? I can see why, they are idiots compared to you."

Jacob was completely taken aback. This was totally unexpected from the Magpie. He took a swig of orange juice and then placed it carefully on the table in front of him. Despite himself he experienced a warm feeling of satisfaction that this man had sized up his ridiculous cousins and could see that he was better than them.

Magpie continued in a friendly tone, "I can see you have many questions Jacob, ask away, I'll do my best to answer them."

"Well," Jacob thought quickly and decided to play along for the time being. He really wanted to know more about the relationship between Pete and his relatives. Maybe if he asked a question about their house, it would cause the man to give away the true status of his friendship with his uncle.

"Um, I was wondering about the magpies. They seem to be following me, like when we went out with our cousins and after the storm there were hundreds in the trees calling out. And then there were those nests with the bird's eggs in them. And I've noticed the magpie symbol on the gate at Uncle David's house. And he lives in Magpie Lane, it's all very coincidental."

"Good questions, just what I'd expect from a smart and observant lad like you. The house has been a refuge for followers of the Magpie Order for centuries. The Magpie is a symbol of freedom and rebellion against the all-controlling Eagle and all that She represents. Followers of the Magpie believe the Eagle puts needless restrictions on human knowledge and progress. I can see that you have met the Eagle, haven't you?" A smile appeared on his face. Jacob was completely wrong-footed; he wasn't expecting this at all. His mouth dropped open and he just stared at the Magpie.

The Magpie laughed; he was clearly enjoying himself. He reached across to the side of the kitchen and grabbed a bag of sugar. He tipped three heaped teaspoonfuls into his coffee and stirred it rapidly banging the spoon against the side of the cup before laying it down on the table. Jacob watched the brown liquid drip onto the wooden surface. He didn't know what to say, all he could think was that his mother would not approve of all that sugar.

"You know Jacob, you and I, we could work together. I've been watching you, you hate your cousins and why would your parents leave you with them while they go off on a nice holiday in Spain? Deep down inside you don't understand why they would do that to you. Rebekkah? Well, you tolerate her, but she destroyed your iPad and the only reason you talk to her is because there is no one else. You don't really like her, and you have nothing in common. Instead, you could come along with me to Europe. You could pretend to be my son and help me win the confidence of these refugees. No more school, just a business arrangement. You would be rich by the time you're 18."

Mistaking Jacob's silence for agreement Pete warmed to his subject. "I know you hate being told what to do, just like me. We have a lot in common, you and I."

Jacob pulled the bacon out of his roll and began pulling the fat from it. He hated fat. It gave him time to think. "These poor people, how can you imprison them and make them work for you like this? They are slaves. I don't want to be a part of this."

Magpie's eyes narrowed very slightly but then he carried on. He reminded Jacob of a boxer darting around jabbing his opponent with his arguments, waiting for the knock-out blow.

"What did they tell you? Some sob story about being in Syria, caught up in a war and then being captured and brought here against their wishes? It's rubbish. These people were without hope, left to die in a detention camp in Europe. They wanted to come to the UK. I have made it possible for them. Without me they'd still be rotting in Italy. And it's expensive moving around human cargo; the risks for me are very great. I could go to prison for a very long time. They all owe me money. Once they have worked and paid back their debt then they will have new lives and go free. Freedom comes at a price. It's not an easy business you know."

Jacob was torn. The Magpie's ideas seemed to have a ring of truth about them. He was appealing to Jacob's own sense of rationality and rebellion. It was true; he did feel angry and trapped by school and home. Maybe the Eagle was controlling? The thought of travelling across Europe was appealing. And it sounded like he could do some good as well.

Pete could see that he was making progress with Jacob. He nodded amiably and pushed the tomato ketchup towards him. 'Think about it Jacob, you don't have to make a decision right now." He wiped his lips with the back of his hand and stood up. "Look I've got to take these people to work and speak to the foreman. I'll be back in an hour. Why don't you take some time, and we'll talk again on my return. Help yourself to the chocolate biscuits. Make yourself at home and I will see you later."

With that the Magpie was gone.

Jacob sat still for what seemed like an hour, but it was probably only a few minutes. He felt numb; having built himself up for a nasty confrontation with the Magpie the meeting had not gone anything like he had anticipated in his imagination. He wondered what had happened to Rebekkah.

22 REBEKKAH

After Jacob had darted towards the house Rebekkah had stayed put, uncertain what to do next. She watched through a parting in the bushes to see what would happen. She saw the torches in the grounds, and she could hear voices. But it was all too dark to really know what was going on. What was clear was that Jacob was locked inside that gate with some strange and possibly dangerous men who very likely would see him as a very unwelcome visitor. Reluctantly she made her way back to the house and decided to phone her grandparents as soon as it got light. She did not want to disturb them in the night.

Back in her bedroom, she sat on the edge of her bed and chewed at her nails; she was deeply worried and unsure what to do next. Morning seemed a long way off. Should she wake her aunt and uncle? What if they were in league with the Magpie? Then, she would only alert them to the fact that Jacob had gone to the cottage in the woods. They would prevent her from phoning her grandparents and Jacob would be caught. Her hope was that he might have found a place to hide and could escape once the gates were open again. Slightly comforted by that thought she stood up and began pacing the room. She had never felt so alone. Where was Robert when you needed him? He had said he was on his way. Why was he not here?

At least Robert existed, she thought bitterly. Jacob was right, the Eagle was a figment of her imagination. What other explanation could there be for all the bad things that kept happening to them? The more she thought about it, the more angry and desolate she felt. Her thoughts were like balloons, the more she focussed on them the more inflated they became until they filled her entire brain.

Life had been fine before the Eagle flew into her life. Mum and Dad were properly together, and she had attended a school where she had many friends. Since the flight to the nest, everything had gone wrong. Dad had lost his job, her parents had separated and she had been sent to a new school where she had no friends and had been bullied by a horrible girl called Kirsty. Then, Jacob had been kidnapped and her cat had been pecked to death by some magpies. Now she was stuck, alone in her cousin's house with people she disliked and distrusted. She hated her life. Tears rolled down her cheeks. She sat like this for a long time.

Then, the sound of a stone pinging her bedroom window made her jump. *Jacob*, she thought, and darted across the room. Peering out into the moonlit sky she could see a shadowy figure. She pushed open the casement window and leaned out.

A familiar voice drifted up to her, "Rebekkah, it's me, Robert."

Immediately her mood lifted. "Finally!" she said out loud as she ran down the stairs and out into the garden to meet him.

Robert was waiting for her. He placed his finger on his lips and beckoned to her to follow him. Once away from the house he stopped and turned to her. "What's been going on?" his eyes were concerned, but his voice calm.

Rebekkah told him everything. When she got to the bit in the story where Jacob had realised that Pete was actually the Magpie his eyes narrowed, and he muttered something that Rebekkah could not catch. Her story finished, she stopped and waited. It was such a relief to tell someone.

"Your aunt and uncle, do you think they are in league with this Pete?" asked Robert.

"I don't know, that is something I keep asking myself. They don't seem interested in anything that we do. Except…"

"What?" Robert looked at her, "except, what?"

"Well, when the birds were killed, and Jacob was blamed they did seem to care then. Oh, and there's a magpie image on the garden gate."

"What? Show me!" Robert spoke sharply. Rebekkah responded by leading him to the wall where the gate was locked shut. Robert stared at the metal image. It was clearly a magpie someone had painted it in the tell-tale black and white colours.

Robert turned to Rebekkah, "I think we are best not to tell your uncle at this stage, this symbol means that the house has been used by followers of the Magpie Order for years. Your family may not be aware of this ancient connection and Pete may have simply wheedled his way into their company because of it. Let's hope it is just coincidence that he was here when you came to stay. Or …"

"Uncle David is in on the whole thing, whatever that is."
Rebekkah finished his sentence for him. "Has it something to do
with the cottage in the woods do you think?"

"Possibly," said Robert thoughtfully. "The passports and
clothes; what do you make of that find?"

"I really don't know except it said 'Syrian Arab Republic' on the
front and had a few squiggles next to it. Oh, and a bird that
looked like an eagle."

"Yes, it does, but it's actually a hawk." Robert chewed his
thumb thoughtfully his eyes were focussed on the magpie
knocker. Then he reached into his pocket and pulled out a
mobile phone. "We should phone the police. Jacob isn't safe
and we can't trust your relatives." He began to dial but then said
in exasperation, "Damn, I've got no signal. Rebekkah, can you
go back into the house and phone from there? You seemed to
have signal when you text me. Once you have spoken to a
police officer try and come back here to let me know how you
have got on."

Rebekkah made her way back into the house. It was dark so she waited in the hallway while her eyes adjusted to the gloom. Then she made her way slowly up the stairs trying to avoid the creaky steps. She was concentrating so hard on not making a noise that she failed to notice a shadowy figure standing on the landing until it was too late.

Stifling a scream, she jumped backwards nearly falling down the stairs in the process. Her cousin Jack stepped forward and grasped her arm. Pushing her into her room he closed the door and turned to face her. "What are you up to, little cousin?" he stood in front of her, arms folded waiting for an answer. "You, and that idiot brother of yours, been out killing more sweet little animals have we? And where is he? That brother of yours, his bed is empty and cold."

Rebekkah thought quickly. She could not trust Jack with the truth, and she wanted rid of him as quickly as possible so she could make the phone call. Anxiety spread through her chest and rose up into her throat making it difficult to speak. That was it she thought to herself, I will fake a panic attack. She began to hyperventilate, her breath came in short gasps and she spoke a word in between every sharp intake. "I ... can't ...

breathe… help… me!" She fell onto her bed, hands grasping her throat. Disbelief changed to alarm as the boy watched her become increasingly distressed. "I will go and get Mum," he said eventually.

"Yes… yes… good!" gasped Rebekkah.

As he left the room she shot across to the other side of the room and grabbed her phone. Dialling 999 she felt as if her heart would burst through the walls of her chest. "Hurry up! Hurry up!" she exclaimed.

A voice answered. "Emergency Operator, which service do you require?"

"Police. Please help me; I haven't got much time. Can you send a police car to The Old Lodge, Magpie Lane. Now!" She could hear voices coming down the corridor and quickly ended the call. She had no idea whether the call would bring the help she wanted but could not afford to warn her aunt in case she was in league with the Magpie. She fell back onto the bed and continued with the panic attack as her aunt entered the room and knelt next to her.

"It's ok Rebekkah, breathe and hold your breath, now count to three and breath out." She was very calm and Rebekkah found her presence soothing as she paced her breathing to her aunt's rhythmic voice.

Jack stood hesitantly behind her. It was the first time she had sensed any kind of compassion or concern in him. As her breathing returned to normal, she sat up on the bed and stared at the floor.

"What happened Rebekkah?" asked her aunt gently.

"Jack frightened me, Aunty," she said truthfully.

Jack interrupted, "She was wandering round the house Mum. I saw her coming up the stairs."

"I sleep-walk." Rebekkah was surprised how easily she told lies. "It happens at home too. If you wake me up, then I get a panic attack."

Jack snorted, "I don't think so, look at you, you have your day clothes on."

"Yes, that's all part of it. I get dressed and then go outside. I don't know what I am doing. My Mum should have told you, but I guess she wanted to get away."

Her aunt squeezed her hand and stood up. "It would have been a good thing if she had told us as we would have locked the doors, it's lucky you did not come to any harm."

Rebekkah breathed a sigh of relief as her story appeared to have been accepted although Jack was still looking at her suspiciously. She yawned widely.

Her aunt moved towards the door and wished her good night. Jack followed her and closed the door behind him. She then heard what sounded like a key turning in the lock. Two doors closed in the distance. She crept over to the door and turned the handle. It was locked. How was she going to tell Robert what had happened?

She picked up her phone, but it too had no signal. All she could do was wait and hope for morning. Surely they would let her out for breakfast!

23 ROBERT

After Rebekkah had gone to the house Robert began pacing up and down the path. He knew how dangerous the Magpie could be and he was keen to get to Jacob before harm befell him. But he would be no match for several men whom he suspected were people traffickers. As he waited for Rebekkah his thoughts turned to the past week and what he had discovered.

After visiting the Taylor home for dinner, he had started his own investigations into the whereabouts of the Magpie. He was deeply suspicious of the attack on the family cat. He knew enough of the man to realise that Jacob was in real danger and now the family was a target. So, he had visited a few men whom he had met while living rough on the streets to see if they knew what had happened to him. They knew who he was talking about and also knew that he, Robert had been wrongly arrested for child abduction. It always amazed Robert how news travelled on the streets. They were reluctant to talk to him at first, but when he explained what had happened, they opened up.

The Magpie had hidden amongst the homeless for a few days before disappearing. In that time he had gained a bit of a reputation because some of the company he kept. When Robert had asked more about this they had told him that he would meet with men who spoke with a foreign accent. These guys were well dressed and spoke about human cargo. The Magpie always had food and drink and he bought the silence of the homeless community by organising plentiful supplies for everyone. He was known as the birdman because in the early morning he would head out from under the bridge where they were living and feed the local magpies. One homeless woman had remarked that she thought it spooky, it was almost as if he was talking to the birds and they were giving him information. Then one day he had just disappeared. No one knew where he had gone. The food had dried up and so now they were willing to talk.

It was at this point that Robert had received the voicemail from Rebekkah asking for his help. The message was broken, it sounded like she was drifting in and out of a poor signal area, but what he had picked up was the address. He kicked himself for not coming immediately. If he had known what he now knew he would have phoned the police himself.

Unfortunately, he had been delayed by a work commitment. He was working as a gardener at the local church where he had been asked to help dig a grave ready for a funeral the following day. When he had finished the job, he had then bought a train ticket for the evening train. It had not been a straightforward journey; after changing in London, he had been delayed by a tube strike. He had walked to Kings Cross where he got a late-night train to Grantham.

On arrival it was very late and he wasn't sure whether to go straight to the house or to wait until morning. The map he had downloaded before departing suggested that the house was a good five miles away and there were no taxis to be seen so, he had decided to walk. He was accustomed to sleeping rough so that did not bother him; it would be easier to sleep in the woods rather than in the town, so he headed off towards the house where Rebekkah and Jacob were staying.

As he drew closer to the house a feeling of foreboding pushed him to make his way to the building itself. He had taken a risk,

177

throwing stones at the windows and unfortunately the first window he had tried had woken a boy who at first he thought was Jacob. Silhouetted against the light in the room he could see he was much taller and thinner than Jacob so he had said nothing and silently slipped back into the shadows of the tree. The next window had thankfully been Rebekkah's. Her news had come as a complete shock to him; he certainly wasn't expecting to find the Magpie had been living here. People trafficking! So, the homeless guys were spot on with their information.

Robert stopped in his pacing and looked up towards the house. There was a light on in one of the bedrooms. Then another light went on. Oh dear, he hoped Rebekkah had not been found out. That boy he had woken may have seen her. Had she had time to make the call to the police? He decided to wait another ten minutes and then, if she did not come back to the garden, he would need another option.

Robert checked his phone for the fourth time, still no signal and the battery was running low. It was now 5 am; no Rebekkah and it was just beginning to get light. He figured that he could either walk back into town, which would take a couple of hours and then contact the police, or he could check out the cottage for himself. If Jacob was hiding in the grounds, he might be able to help him to safety. He needed to get there while it was still relatively dark, as it would give him some protection. He made a decision; if he could not find Jacob then he would walk back to Grantham.

Rebekkah had told him that the cottage was through the garden gate and in the woods. He passed through and picked up the path. It was not long before he came out onto the rough dirt track that led up to the cottage. He could see a light in the window in the distance. His heart was beating fast and he stopped momentarily to calm his breathing. He did what he often did in times of extreme stress; he placed his hand on the eagle tattoo on his arm and closed his eyes. It gave him comfort and strength to believe she was with him. He reminded himself of the way things had worked out after he had met Jacob in the warehouse. Fear was his enemy, it was paralysing; instead he needed to have faith. As if in affirmation the first light of dawn crept onto the scene. The sun was a beautiful red and the clouds surrounding it were tinged with gold. A large bird was silhouetted against the orb, its wings spread in flight. Robert smiled and cupped his hands to his lips whilst emitting a muted sound of marvel and astonishment.

Minutes later a majestic golden eagle descended from the sky and settled on his outstretched arm. He winced as Her claws dug into his flesh. When working with birds of prey at Beaulieu he had had the protection of a leather strap around his arm, but he was not so prepared here. Aware of his pain She jumped a little and shifted Her claws to encircle his wrist. She was heavy but it was good to see Her.

24 THE EAGLE

The Eagle was alert and after greeting Robert, turned Her head towards the gate. Sure enough Her keen hearing had heard something. Moments later the gate swung open and a van emerged. Quick as a flash, the Eagle sprung off his arm and soared up to the sky above. When She had gained enough height to attack at speed she turned and dived at the vehicle.

She swept like a bolt of lightning towards the van. Robert watched in fascination. He knew she could achieve speeds of over 100mph. He also knew that if She were to crash into the van she would break Her neck. She was still gaining speed, Her head vertical, wings tucked neatly behind her body to minimise the drag. She was beautiful. For one moment it looked as if She would collide with the windscreen but just before impact She pulled up and headed back up to the sky.

Startled, the driver, seeing his windscreen filled with the giant bird of prey, lost control of the vehicle and crashed into a tree. He had been in the process of fastening his seat belt as he drove. Unprotected, his head had smashed into the screen; he now lay spread-eagled across the steering wheel. A second man in the passenger seat swore loudly, climbed out and headed back to the house. There were screams and shouts and banging noises coming from inside the van. Running swiftly to the rear door Robert yanked it open. Inside, clinging desperately to one another were people. Robert realised immediately that these were the refugees that had been imprisoned in the cottage.

Thinking quickly, he gestured to them all to sit still. Saying the words, "Friend, friend, I am here to help you," he shut the door and ran to the front of the van. Opening the driver's door he pulled out the injured driver and leapt into the driver's seat. The engine was still running. He threw the gears into reverse and with a loud crunching sound the van kangarooed backwards. Once on the dirt track, he quickly moved into first gear and headed off down the lane. He stole a quick look in the mirror just in time to see a man shouting and gesturing. He was fighting off a large, winged creature. Robert grinned.

He was soon on the road heading down to Grantham. He expected to be pursued but no one followed him. Good old

Eagle, She had done her job well. Next stop, the police station. They would have to believe him with his precious cargo on board. The only problem was that Jacob had not been in the van. He hoped he was safe.

25 JACOB AND THE MAGPIE

Jacob was still sitting at the table thinking when the Magpie burst through the door, blood streaming down his face from a large cut above his eye.

"What happened to you?" exclaimed Jacob.

"Got attacked by an eagle," muttered the Magpie. He turned the tap on and began dabbing at his wound with a dishcloth.

"An eagle? Did you say an eagle? Was it the Eagle?" Jacob could hardly believe his ears.

"Yes! What's the matter with you? Are you deaf? Bloody bird attacked the van. Someone has driven off with it, I couldn't see who it was. I need to get it back. Come on, we need to get to the house so I can grab my car."

Jacob's brain was in a whirl. *What did he say? 'The Eagle,' did that mean She was really here?* The attack was real enough, blood continued to pour down the man's face. It reminded him of Dad. He felt glad. He stood up, he was happy to go back to the house, he had no plan for what he would do when he got there but at least he was not locked in the cottage any longer.

The Magpie grabbed his arm in a vice like grip and held him in this way as he marched him out of the door and back along the track to the house where his cousins lived. They walked quickly; the man continuing to dab at the wound with his free hand. As they approached the gate in the garden wall, he gestured to Jacob to open it. Once inside the garden he headed for the drive where his car was parked.

If I am going to make a run for it, I need to do it now, thought Jacob. And then his heart leapt, for there on the drive was a police car. The Magpie saw it too and cursed. He had to let go of Jacob to reach in his pocket for a key and Jacob took his opportunity, he ran as fast as he could to the back door, pushed it open and shot inside turning the key as he did so. He could hear a car engine start and then a crunching sound as it moved down the drive. He turned pressing his back against the door and let out a whoop of celebration. The door to the dining room opened and out came his uncle.

"Jacob! You are safe! Thank goodness." Following closely

behind him was a police officer, notebook in hand, and then his sister Rebekkah, who threw herself at him. Despite himself he gave her a big hug.

26 THE STORY TOLD AND A MYSTERY UNSOLVED

"I guess this is the young man who disappeared?" The policeman looked quizzically at Uncle David.

"Yes, this is Jacob. Come on in and tell us what happened."

Jacob followed the adults into the front room and stood uncertain what to do next or how to start. He felt like he knew so much and had so much to say but his main concern was for the migrants in the stolen van. He desperately wanted them to be rescued.

The policeman gestured for him to sit, opened his notebook at a new page and addressed him directly. "Rebekkah has already told us about the cottage in the woods, can you tell us what happened when you got inside the gate?"

And so he began, the whole story came tumbling out. When he got to the bit about the Magpie and his true identity, he could not help but watch his Uncle David for any sign of awareness but there was only a deepening horror on his face as he became aware of what harbouring this man might mean for him and his family. Or, thought Jacob cynically, he is terrified of being found out for his part in this.

Just as he got to the bit about the Magpie being attacked by the Eagle, the policeman's radio crackled into life. The officer asked Jacob to pause for a moment. They could all hear the call - a man called Robert had just turned up at Grantham Police Station with a van full of refugees. Jacob and Rebekkah cheered and clapped their hands. The policeman smiled, enjoying their excitement and observing their relief.

"Now, what has happened to this man you call the Magpie?" asked the policeman. "He sounds a dangerous piece of work."

"You need to get after him officer, he has just escaped in his car. That was how I got away. As he reached into his pocket for a key, I managed to twist free and run in through the back door. He is injured because the Eagle attacked him, and his head is bleeding."

The officer nodded and turned to Uncle David, "Let's have a description of this man and the car please sir."

Uncle David gave a reasonable description, but Jacob felt he needed to contribute to the discussion. "He is a master of disguise, that was how I didn't recognise him at first. He will change again. But he can't hide the wound to his head."

The policeman spoke into his radio giving a description of the car. No one could remember the number plate, which was annoying. He looked at his watch and then turned to the children, "He has only been gone about 15 minutes, we should catch him. Don't worry we'll get him," he added kindly.

He spoke to Uncle David, "Sir I would be grateful for a look at the passports and clothes you have in your cellar, and I am afraid I must ask you and your wife to come with me to the station."

"What? Why? We have done nothing wrong," stuttered Uncle David.

"I am not saying you have sir; but you have been harbouring a dangerous criminal in your home and we need to get a statement from you. I am sure you understand. Now let's go and have a look at your basement."

Left alone Jacob and Rebekkah looked at one another. "Tell me what happened after you left the cottage, Rebekkah. How did Robert get hold of those people in the van?"

"I honestly don't know Jacob, but he was here shortly after I got back from the cottage. I told him what we knew and that we suspected Pete was actually the Magpie. He had no signal on his phone and wanted me to go indoors to phone the police, which I did. But Jack found me on the stairs, and I had to make up a story about sleepwalking. I only managed a quick call to 999 and had no idea whether they would follow it up or not. But they did. Thank goodness. I couldn't do much else as Jack and Aunty locked me into my room until the police arrived. The policeman seems kind, but I don't know what's going to happen with Uncle and Aunty. Do you think they knew all about Pete and the refugees?"

Jacob picked at his ear, "I am not sure, I asked the Magpie, and he wouldn't tell me. I do hope they catch him this time, he is a horrible man."

"What do you make of the Eagle attacking the Magpie?" persisted Rebekkah, "doesn't that suggest she is real?"

Jacob did not want to answer. Truth is he had been very disturbed by what had happened in the cottage. He was aware how close he had got to believing the Magpie and following him to Europe. Now, in the cold light of day, he could see clearly how he had been duped but he didn't want to tell Rebekkah. He knew she would not have given the offer of working with the Magpie a moment's thought, but he had. He felt deeply ashamed. He was not as strong or as tough as he had thought.

"Jacob?" His sister was looking at him.

"It suggests that the attack was real in the same way the attack on our cat was real. Robert worked with birds maybe he called on one to help him. Maybe there are some really vicious birds around." He finished lamely.

"Oh Jacob! You are so exasperating, why won't you believe? I am going to phone Grandfa and get him to come and pick us up I have had enough of being here with these horrible cousins and every time I look at that garden I think of the magpies and that man." She shuddered.

Secretly Jacob was pleased; he did not want to stay with his relatives either, but he was too proud to say it. "Do what you like," he said gruffly, stifling a yawn. He had had only a couple of hours sleep and he felt tired.

Rebekkah huffed at him and stalked off upstairs to get her phone.

At the top she met a very bleary-eyed Jasmina, "What's all the noise about? You woke me up you inconsiderate little girl."

Rebekkah sidestepped her and darted into her room, "Not a morning person then Jazz are we?" And then unable to resist it she continued, "you might want to put some make up on as there's a very good-looking policeman downstairs." With that she slammed her door shut and grinned. Little victories were so sweet now she knew this whole nightmare was nearly over. She phoned her grandparents and told them enough of the story to persuade them to come and collect them at once.

After the phone call she sat on the edge of her bed and yawned, she too had had very little sleep but there was one more person she needed to talk to. Picking up her phone she dialled Robert's number. It went to voicemail. She left a message letting him know Jacob was safe and asking him to ring her when he had a moment. And then she lay on her bed and slept.

27 THE MAGPIE AND UNCLE DAVID

"Rebekkah, wake up!" Someone was shaking her. As she opened her eyes her aunt's face came into view. She looked tired and a little scared.

"Your grandparents are here, also there is a man called Robert who wants to speak to you."

Rebekkah jumped up and ran downstairs. She hurled herself at her grandparents who were sitting having a cup of tea in the drawing room.

Standing by the window was Robert. As she turned to him, he smiled, "Well done, Rebekkah!" he said, grasping her small hands in his large rough hands, "you and Jacob have helped to end a human slavery and trafficking ring and have freed at least 20 people who can now start a new life here in England."

"We are so proud of you darling! Robert here has filled us in on just how brave you have been and Jacob too. By the way, where is Jacob?" asked Granny turning to Aunt Patricia.

"He is asleep, David has gone to wake him and let him know

you are here."

At that moment Jacob walked in through the door, he had blood on his shirt and his hair was tousled.

"Jacob, there you are!" exclaimed Grandfa, "well done, lad! You have been very courageous, we are so proud of you."

Jacob coloured, it wasn't often that he received such praise, and he still did not feel that he deserved it. He turned to Robert. "What happened last night Robert? And what took you so long to get here?"

Robert rubbed his chin ruefully, "Sorry about that Jacob, if I had known how bad things were I'd have got here more quickly but I only picked up half a voicemail from Rebekkah. I was making a few enquiries of my own."

He then told his part of the story. When he got to the bit about the Eagle, Grandfa laughed and clapped his hands. "Bravo. She really was watching over you all."

Jacob was shocked. It did seem as if the Eagle had helped save the lives of the refugees and probably his own life as well. This was a bit different to statues in gardens and tattoos on arms. This was real.

"What about the Magpie, any news of him?" he asked, trying to divert his thoughts.

Robert looked grave. "The police caught up with him at a roadblock they had put in place near Peterborough. Apparently, he reversed and shot off in the opposite direction. The police followed him for a couple of miles, by all accounts it was pretty hair raising."

"Like on the films, a car chase. That's so cool, I wish I had been in that police car! Did they get him?" interrupted Jacob, his eyes sparkling with the thought of it.

"No," Robert shook his head, "The police officer told me that the Magpie drove off road up a dirt track and into the woods. The police car hit a tree root and it punctured a tyre. They continued on foot but by the time they got to the car he was long gone. They have set up a search to comb the woods but so far, nothing. He seems to have disappeared into thin air."

Rebekkah and Jacob exchanged looks.

Robert nodded. "You still need to be careful even at your grandparent's house. He has his magpie spies everywhere."

Grandfa put his arm around Jacob's shoulders and Granny reached across and squeezed Rebekkah's hand.

"There was one other thing," Robert paused, "the young police officer was a bit rattled when he told me his account."

"Why?" asked Grandfa.

Robert rubbed his chin as was his habit when perturbed, "I wasn't sure whether to tell you this but I figured you are tough enough to understand the significance of what I am about to say."

"Yes?" said Jacob impatiently.

Robert continued, "When the police found Magpie's abandoned car, they were suddenly surrounded by a whole host of magpies cackling in the trees above. They said it felt like they were being laughed at."

Jacob snorted, "So, he's done it again, got away with it. This is rubbish."

Rebekkah turned to Robert, "What about the other men at the cottage, the ones that were guarding the refugees?"

Robert smiled, "Ah, I have better news there, Rebekkah. The police went to the cottage and found the guy who was driving the van, he had a bit of a sore head and a concussion but will be fit to give a statement. The other guy was found trying to hide the evidence of sleeping bags and so on. He has also been taken to the station for questioning. The police will use their evidence to build a case up against the Magpie."

Uncle David had been listening to Robert's story and cleared his throat, "Your aunt and I are very sorry that we invited this Pete into our home. Obviously if we had known who he was we wouldn't have."

Aunt Patricia had obviously been crying and she dabbed at her nose and sniffed loudly. "Yes, we are so sorry, Jacob and Rebekkah. Your father told us about the warehouse incident, but we had no idea that it was Pete who had abducted you. Oh! How could we have been so naïve, David?" and she started crying again.

Uncle David put his arm around her and then continued, "We hope that this won't put you off coming to stay again; your cousins have really enjoyed having you."

Jacob nearly laughed out loud but stopped himself when he caught a glare from Rebekkah. He could not resist an observation and the question that had been on his mind ever since he discovered Pete's identity. "No doubt you told Jack, Jasmina and Philip about my experience in the disused factory which is why they were so cruel to us when we arrived?"

His uncle opened his mouth as if to speak and then closed it. Jacob continued, "But how did you get to know Pete? And what about those passports and clothes hidden in your cellar that Rebekkah found when she was locked in there by Philip?"

His aunt began to cry again, "We really didn't know about that box of things, Pete must have hidden them there without our knowledge. We don't often go into the cellar."

Uncle David looked at his wife and patted her on the arm, he turned to the children, anger and disappointment in his voice, "Why didn't you ask us for help when you realised that you were in danger? We would have helped you. You took an incredible risk. I don't know what your parents are going to think of us after they find out what has been going on."

Rebekkah looked at Jacob and then at her grandparents. Anger bubbled up within her and the words just came tumbling out, "To tell you the truth, we don't feel safe here. Your children, our cousins, have been horrible to us while we have been here. You were nowhere to be seen. Do you even know what they get up to? Do you even care? The only reason I found the passports was because Philip pushed me into the cellar and locked me in! I only escaped because I used the light from the fridge to find a way out. Otherwise, I'd probably still be there. Would you have noticed? You ask us to trust you! You were the last people we would have turned to. You were friends with the Magpie who had kidnapped Jacob and killed my cat. No way were we going to trust you!" Rebekkah stopped to draw breath, her hands were balled together into fists, two pink spots appeared on her cheeks and she was shaking with rage. Granny placed a comforting hand on her shoulder whilst nodding in agreement.

Her aunt gasped in outrage and David opened his mouth to speak but Grandfa interrupted, "You haven't told us how you came to invite Pete into your home, David."

Uncle David looked at his wife and then at Grandfa. "I met him in the local village pub. He bought me a drink. As we were chatting, he said his family had once lived in this house. I invited him to come over for a meal so he could see how it had changed. We got talking about a business proposition. He owns a fruit and vegetable farm and was looking for someone to do the accounts. He was also looking for further investment. When I had a look at his accounts, I could see he was very wealthy, it looked like a good business to get involved with. So, I persuaded Patricia to let him stay a few days while we drew up the contracts and signed the deal. I had no idea that he was using refugees to work in the packing warehouses linked to the farm. It was just a coincidence that he was here at the same time as you two."

Robert nodded slowly, "I wonder whether you asked the right questions about how he was making so much money out of a fruit farming business or whether it was more convenient to turn a blind eye?"

Uncle David glowered at him, "Get out of my house!" he shouted, "how dare you suggest that I would have turned a blind eye to people trafficking!"

"Well," said Granny grimly, "you were certainly taken in by this man. You were at best greedy and negligent and at worst criminal. No doubt the police will get to the bottom of your links with him. I think it's time to take these children away to a place where they can relax and recover from their ordeal. Grandfa doesn't like driving in the dark and Robert says that one of the refugees, a boy, has asked to meet Jacob before we leave Lincolnshire. Come on children get your bags and let's get on our way."

And so they left. Robert hitched a lift with them. Grandfa said they would take him to the railway station after they had called in at the police station.

28 JACOB AND TAREK

Jacob was surprisingly nervous about meeting Tarek again. As they drove along the country roads, he filled Rebekkah and his grandparents in on Tarek's story. In no time at all they arrived at Grantham Police Station. Tall glass windows stretched above them as the little group climbed the steps. They were greeted in reception by a policewoman, who recognising Robert, immediately led them through into the rear of the station. As she opened the door into a smaller room, she stepped back to allow them to enter. There, sitting on chairs at a table drinking hot chocolate, sat a group of people. As they stood uncertainly in the doorway a young lad pushed back his chair and ran to Jacob and embraced him.

Rebekkah watched her brother intently. How would he react? To her surprise he embraced the boy in return and she could see tears on his cheeks. The boy turned to the others and said something in Arabic. An older man and woman also got to their feet and moved towards Jacob. Hesitantly the man shook Jacob's hand while the woman hung back slightly. Turning to her, the man caught her elbow and moved her forward so she could look at Jacob. She quickly moved forward and kissed him on the cheek smiling as she did so. In hesitant English she whispered, "Thank you, thank you."

Rebekkah found tears welling up in her own eyes.

Jacob stepped back from the boy and asked, "Tarek, what is going to happen to you now?" Tarek shrugged and pulled a face, "We don't know. We ask for asylum and we hope that we shall be able to stay."

"What if you can't? What if they send you back?" Jacob could not keep the anxiety out of his voice.

Tarek looked at him and smiled, "We will be alright, Jacob. Allah is with us. He will look after us."

"How can you say that?" The words tumbled from Jacob's mouth. "Look at all you have put up with - the cruelty and the suffering. How can you still believe?"

Tarek looked at him for a while. He seemed old beyond his years, "Jacob I know you meet Eagle, I see in your eyes, but you not yet reach that place where you let go and trust her to take care of you. Then you understand."

Rebekkah had been listening to the exchange intently but when the boy mentioned the Eagle, she was no longer able to contain herself. "How do you know about the Eagle?" she asked.

Tarek turned to her and smiled. "Allah, God, Eagle, these names for same thing. We spend much time looking things that divide us but not see what unites us. We follow in different ways and use different names, but God known to us all and is in here." He thumped his heart emphatically.

Rebekkah could not restrain herself; she turned excitedly to her brother, "See Jacob, we are not the only ones who believe in the Eagle."

He looked at her, then at his grandparents, then at Robert and then back to Tarek, they were all watching him. All these people, people he had come to respect, they all wanted him to have faith, to believe but he just could not. "What?" he spread his hands, "So, you all believe in the Eagle. Good for you. But I can't, I really can't. This is not for me. Anyway ..." He turned back to Tarek, "I am happy that you are free, and I wish you luck with getting asylum."

Nodding to the remaining refugees he turned and walked out of the door into the corridor and waited. He watched while Robert and his family spent some time saying goodbye. He knew he was being stubborn, but he just could not accept that his life could be entrusted to a winged creature however impressive She was. The only person he could trust in this world was himself. Turning on his heel he walked out of the station and towards the waiting car. His grandfather opened the door for him, and he slid gratefully onto the leather seat. Rebekkah and Robert followed him.

No one said a word but as they drove away, he took one final look at the building and there, perched on the rooftop was a beautiful golden eagle. As he stared, She spread Her wings and soared into the sky. He followed Her path with his eyes until She disappeared into the sun.

Rebekkah had been watching too and she smiled at him.

PART 3

TWELVE MONTHS LATER

1 ROBERT AND THE DEAD FALCON

Robert was woken by a noise. He had a dreadful sense that there was someone in his room. He carefully reached for the knife he kept under his pillow and waited; his heart was pounding so fast he felt sick.

He had been trapped like this once before and it had not ended well. All the old feelings came surging back, like waves pounding onto the shore. He thought he was over it, but fear has a familiar taste. The memories surged into his brain like unwelcome guests.

On that occasion, he had been working at the bird sanctuary and had been asleep in his bunk in the little log cabin where he worked. He was tired after a particularly gruelling day training a difficult and sensitive falcon who had refused to come back when he let her fly free. He had been the last home of all the falconers. Exhausted, he had collapsed onto his bed and drifted almost immediately into a deep sleep.

He had been woken by a bang at the window. He assumed a bird had flown into it, maybe an owl as he lived in the woods.

He had jumped out of his bunk and peered nervously out of the window. Even to this day he struggled to sequence what followed. A dark shadow had passed in front of him and then the knob on the cabin door had turned. It was locked but Robert knew that it wouldn't take long for someone to break in. Did they realise he was inside? Perhaps it was someone wanting a place to shelter? He had decided to call out when the knob had stopped moving. Robert had watched, hardly daring to breath. Then a brick came hurtling through the window hitting him squarely on the head. Reeling from the shock and pain, Robert had staggered backwards and had fallen to the floor, clutching his head. What happened next was a blur, he was only semi-conscious, and the cabin had been dark. There was a breeze from the open door and he had realised with a growing sense of foreboding that his attacker was now in the cabin with him. Through blurred eyes, he could only just make out a shape in the corner of the room. The figure seemed to be moving through his things, but he had not been able to make out what exactly it was doing. The moon had disappeared, and the cabin was dark. Robert had cried out, his voice no more than a croak, "What do you want? If it's money you are after, then take it.

But please leave me alone. I haven't got much, really, I haven't."

The form had then twitched and jerked. He hadn't given it much thought at the time, but it was almost bird like. Then as fast as the thing had come into his cabin, it had left, the door swinging on its broken hinges.

Staggering to his feet, Robert had grabbed the bed post and then sat heavily on his bed. He had reached across to his lamp and had turned it on. His head was bleeding, and he had felt sick. Then he had seen it. Lying on the floor was the falcon he had been training that day, but it was dead. He had crawled his way over to the bird and gently picked it up in his large, comforting hands. She was still warm. He had raised her to his ear and listened for the heartbeat. Nothing. He had gazed at her for a long time, stroking her beautiful spotted chest with his forefinger. He had wept.

Once more in the present, Robert asked himself, was this the same intruder as last time? Different place, different time but it felt the same.

He was determined to face the person. He wanted to know who

3

had killed his beautiful bird. He tightened his grip on the knife whilst fumbling with the torch on his phone. Success! The beam caught a figure standing in the corner of the room.

It was the man he knew as the Magpie!

"You?" Robert steadied the beam on the man's face.

"Yes Robert!" the Magpie held a hand up to his eyes, sheltering from the steady beam, "I want to talk to you."

Robert was filled with disgust for this half creature half man who had caused so much pain for so many vulnerable people. "How dare you break into my home? You've got a nerve after all the terrible things you have done. I don't want to talk to you, but I will ring the police!" Robert began to dial.

The creature shifted slightly to avoid the direct beam of the torch, "I wouldn't do that if I were you. There are things we need to talk about, including your dear falcon. She didn't suffer you know."

Robert paused; the caller on the end of the phone asked him which emergency service he wanted; he ended the call. "You killed her! You evil man, what had she done to you! It was a completely pointless attack."

The Magpie nodded slowly as if agreeing and then continued, "It was a warning Robert so, not pointless."

"A warning?" Robert was puzzled.

"Yes," said the Magpie, "You and I have met before, a long time ago. I was a guard at the Young Offenders Institution. Do you remember?"

Robert felt as if he had been hit by a second brick, he took a step back and sat down heavily on the bed.

Magpie's voice continued, his shadow twitched on the ceiling as Robert's torch moved sideways, "I know all about your shameful little secret. You haven't always been a goody, goody, have you?" The Magpie leered at him. "How do you think your precious little child friends would feel if they knew what you did, all those years ago?"

Robert hung his head, deflated and overcome with shame. The memory still had power over him. "I don't remember you." He mumbled. "How did you find out?"

The Magpie cackled, "I am a shapeshifter. As you know, I can assume different disguises. You were a quiet, withdrawn young man, barely out of nappies as I recall but you did a dreadful thing didn't you Robert and you can't forget it can you?"

Robert's hand began to tremble, and the torch wavered, "That was many years ago, I served my sentence and I have been forgiven. Nothing you can say can change that."

"Forgiven!" The Magpie's tone dripped with scorn, "You know that we can never forget. Our actions will always follow us. They have consequences. When I go to the press with yours, you will never work again, and you will never see those little brats again."

"What do you want?" mumbled Robert.

The Magpie ignored his question, "I am very disappointed in you, I thought we had a deal. We were both working together in that warehouse when we kidnapped that kid, Jacob. What happened to change your mind? I nearly had him. If you hadn't interfered, I would have had a ransom by now. And I'd have

6

shared it with you."

"We never had a deal! I know I've done wrong but I'm not a kidnapper. We were two men who met by chance and Jacob happened to fall in through the window; there was no plan!"

Magpie hopped over to him and grabbed his hand. He twisted it viciously as he removed the mobile phone and shone it directly into Robert's eyes. Robert cowered before his touch, he was surprisingly powerful.

"It wasn't chance Robert, it was fate that brought us back together. You see once a criminal, always a criminal and you did a terrible thing didn't you?"

Robert looked away from the light, he felt exposed, the old feelings of shame surged back into his heart. How come these things still had such a hold on him? Hatred for the man hovering over him rose up in his throat, strangling the good will that he had tried to build into his life over the years. It took all his mental strength not to hurl himself at him and punch him.

Magpie withdrew a little as if he could sense the violence pouring out of Robert. His orange eyes glowed maliciously as he stoked Robert's humiliation, "You see, that Eagle says you can make a new start, but you can't, can you? It's always there; the shame, the weakness, the anger. The only way to deal with it is to give in. Come and work with me. You will no longer have to fight against those urges, there's no need to feel shame. We can put these things to good use and make money out of it."

"Never," Robert was resolute, "Never will I work with you."

"You see Robert, you think you are free to make these decisions yourself, but we all have our weaknesses. You believe in that bird, but what has she done for you? You are still poor, you've made little of your life, you think you can redeem yourself by helping those horrible Taylor children and working in a church graveyard, yet really the past still haunts you. If you work with me, do things my way, then you will have money, influence and power. I don't care what you did years ago."

Robert looked at the man, a foul smell emanated from his breath, his words emerged as if from a tomb. Did he even have a soul? Robert shuddered, repelled by everything about him.

"I have changed, the Eagle has forgiven me, and you are a devil!

Get out of my house or…"

"Or what?" The Magpie interrupted him. "You will never be free of me, I have always been around at the darkest moments of your life, you never know when I'll find you again. And I know your secrets; your weaknesses are those things you love the most, your precious falcons. Last time I killed only one, next time it will be the lot."

"You can't do that," Robert took several steps towards the creature, knife in hand. "You kill my falcons and I'll kill you!"

"Ha, ha, ha! You see, you are just like me really, when something really matters to you, you will kill for it. I don't want to kill our bird friends, but I will, if you don't do as I ask."

"What do you want of me?" asked Robert through gritted teeth.

"I want you to get me Jacob and Rebekkah. And after them,

bring me that Eagle!"

2 THE PARENTAL BETRAYAL

Mr Taylor kerbed the car as he turned into Madison Gardens.

"Watch out!" shouted Mrs Taylor, "You are so careless when you drive."

Rebekkah rolled her eyes at Jacob, who turned his head and stared gloomily out of the window. The adventures of last summer seemed preferable to school holidays alone with his parents. As the car came to a halt outside their front door, they were startled to see a police car drive up their road and stop outside their house.

"Now what?" muttered Mr Taylor under his breath.

He and his wife had just about managed a year together after the kidnapping of Jacob and separation, but if anything, their relationship was worse now than ever before. The atmosphere was thick with irritation. Rebekkah wondered for the millionth time whether her parents might be getting a divorce. She used to dread the thought and often planned conversations in her head. There was an old conversation in which she would say to her parents that she was unwilling to choose which parent she would live with, in the hope that it would cause them to stick together. However, the last few months had changed her, she could see more clearly than ever that they were unhappy and unsuited to each other.

She had settled down at school, Kirsty the bully had miraculously left at the end of term, and she had started to make friends. Some of the girls who had bullied her, either avoided her or became friends. They were impressed when they saw her and her brother on the TV after the Lincolnshire adventure. Some had listened to her account of the terrible suffering endured by the refugees at the hands of Pete Maghie and were keen to join her efforts to raise money for people in a similar situation. Others kept out of her way, muttering about foreigners taking English jobs, but never directly confronting her with hostile views. She had tried to run awareness sessions with the help of a teacher, but the most prejudiced failed to turn up, it was as if their minds were made up and nothing would break through.

She shared her frustration with Jacob who had matured over the last year, since his near miss with the Magpie. He had stayed at his middle school, completing his final year. He too had received a lot of interest from fellow students about his adventures, but he was surprisingly cagey, refusing to say much at all and after a while he was left alone. He had no desire to draw attention to himself in a world of Instagram and TikTok. He wanted to keep a low profile while Pete was still on the loose. As a result, he counselled his sister to do the same and keep her head down. She wasn't sure about this as she felt the need to try and change a world that seemed unjust; having been bullied herself she wanted to stand up for people who lacked an advocate. Jacob's approach was not hers. And she had told him so. He had just shrugged and told her to leave him out of it.

As she swung her legs out of the car, two police officers made their way towards them.

"Mr and Mrs Taylor?" they enquired politely.

"Yes," said her mother. She stood still, looking from one officer to the other. Her father walked towards the door and opened it.

"May we come in?" continued the officer.

"It's not convenient, we have just got back from a weekend away and need to get unpacked and shopping done. Can't this wait?"

Rebekkah felt her face flush with embarrassment, her mother could be so blunt.

"Not really, ma'am," the female police officer smiled politely, "it concerns the safety of your children."

For one awful minute Rebekkah thought her mother might continue to resist, but even she could see it would not look good if she showed no concern whatsoever.

Mr Taylor was standing holding the door open, the two officers looked from one to the other then removing their hats walked through the door and into the hallway. Silently Mr Taylor showed them into the lounge. Everyone else followed. They all stood uneasily in the large room. Rebekkah noticed a cobweb in the corner where her beloved cat had once slept. The empty cat basket sat forlornly underneath. She felt a pang of sorrow as she remembered her beloved Tipsy who had been mauled to death by magpies a year ago. It was probably time to dispose of the basket now, she mused.

13

"Should the children be here?" asked Mr Taylor nodding towards Jacob and Rebekkah.

"Yes, I think it might be best. From what we have heard they are a couple of plucky youngsters, and the conversation concerns them. You are familiar with a man called Pete Maghie?"

"Oh him! Haven't you caught him yet?" scowled Mrs Taylor.

"No, ma'am, I am afraid not. He is still at large, and we have reason to believe your children might be at risk from him. Is there somewhere safe they can go where they are unlikely to be found by this man?"

Rebekkah felt a frisson of fear run down her back, nervously she twisted her fair hair through her hands and retied the ponytail. She glanced at Jacob who had gone white, making his red hair look even redder against the pallor. It had been almost a year since they had last seen the man that they called the Magpie. They had hoped that he had forgotten about them and was up to no good somewhere else in the world. The TV coverage would have made it difficult for him to reappear anywhere near where they lived.

Mr Taylor looked the police officer directly in the eye. "What do you mean, somewhere safe? We aren't made of money. We don't have a little bolthole in the middle of a deserted island surrounded by an electric fence and CCTV. If you lot did your job properly then our children wouldn't need any protection and we could get on with our lives. How about you provide a safe house for them?"

Rebekkah felt as if she had been hit with a sledgehammer. Her father had said, 'them', not 'us'. What was he planning now? She looked at Jacob who was staring intently at the police officer.

"You won't find him easily," he said. "Pete is a shape shifter. He can change into a magpie and back again. That's how he escaped from you last time."

His mother looked at him with disdain. "Don't make up stories Jacob. This is all your fault. If you hadn't run away from school and climbed into that old factory, you would never have met this awful man and we would be able to get back to normal."

Turning to the police officer, she continued, "As you can see officer, my son is still traumatised by what he has been through, so I agree with my husband, until you find this man, I suggest you put the children into some sort of safe house."

"I'm afraid we can't do that. You need to look after them. We can try and arrange some victim therapy to help them deal with the trauma." The police officer looked at Jacob sympathetically.

Jacob clicked his tongue and pursed his lips. "Then you will never catch him, and I don't need therapy. Anyway, why are you worried about him again? It's been a year since I had any contact with him."

The officer looked at his notebook and then at his fellow police officer who spoke kindly to Jacob, "A man answering the description of the man you met in the disused warehouse has been observed in France, we followed his trail to Calais where he disappeared. We think he may be up to his old tricks again, and on his way back to England."

Rebekkah spoke, her voice quiet and tense, "You mean trafficking people again?"

The police officers nodded, "The route from France to England is always busy in the summer months, it's easier for traffickers to exploit."

Mr Taylor emitted a strangled sound from his throat, in sheer exasperation, "This government is so useless at doing anything! These people just run rings around everyone. How come they don't just send in the navy and arrest them all?"

Mrs Taylor clicked her tongue at her husband, "More's the point, we now have to act to sort out this situation because this lot can't get their act together with the French police to sort this all out."

"Here's my number," the young officer reached into his pocket, "If you see anything strange, just ring this number straightaway and we will send a car around immediately. In the meantime, I strongly recommend you give some thought to getting away somewhere safe as a family."

The young man picked up his hat from the table where he had placed it. The two of them walked towards the open door. Mr Taylor hadn't bothered to shut it. The lady officer stopped in the doorway and smiled at Jacob and Rebekkah. Then the two of them headed back to their car. Mr Taylor slammed the door shut and swung on his heels towards them both.

"Your mother and I are so sick of this drama. We took you to your cousins and you managed to turn that into a nightmare. Why couldn't you just stay out of trouble? My brother tells me you were running off into the woods, against his express instructions."

Jacob went red with rage.

Here it comes, thought Rebekkah.

Jacob exploded as expected, "Your brother and his feral children had about as much interest in looking after us as you do. In fact, he had that scumbag Pete, eating at his table. He's lucky he isn't in prison himself for harbouring a criminal. Do you know what happened to us? Do you even care?"

"That's quite enough, Jacob! Don't you dare speak about my brother like that nor to me in that tone of voice. Go to your room!" Dad was as red as Jacob. They looked like a couple of beef tomatoes. Despite her anxiety, Rebekkah had to suppress a giggle.

"With pleasure," spat Jacob, "I'd rather be taken by that devil than stay in this house with you! I hope he comes soon, then I can escape."

Rebekkah followed him. She despised her parents, she felt too angry to stay in the same room with them. She wanted to be with Jacob.

3 DREADFUL NEWS

Jacob had slept badly. He settled down at the breakfast table and surveyed what was on offer, UHT milk and Weetabix. "I hate UHT milk," he grumbled as his father joined him at the table.

"Yes, well, I agree with you, but we didn't have time to go to the supermarket as your mother and I had some planning to do."

His mother joined them, "Yes," she said brightly.

Jacob looked at her suspiciously.

"We have found a nice activity camp for you both to go to. It's got 24 - hour supervision and lots of fun things to do."

Jacob put his spoon down, a look of absolute horror on his face. "I don't want to go," he shouted, "You can't make me!"

"Make us do what?" Rebekkah arrived and stood in the doorway.

"We have found this very nice activity holiday for you both to go to where you will be supervised and safe until you go back to school." Her mother looked at her, challenging her to disagree.

Rebekkah looked at Jacob, "And if we don't want to go?"

"You have to," mumbled her father, his mouth full of Weetabix. "We have no choice. Your mother and I must work, which means you will be in the house on your own. Those police officers made it obvious that we would be regarded as terrible parents if we don't protect you. Given your capacity for notoriety, we don't want the press blaming us as negligent parents if anything goes wrong. So, we've done the sums, we can afford it. Just about. You're going."

"Can't Robert come and look after us?" Rebekkah looked hopefully at her father.

"That scruffy, irresponsible man!" scoffed her mother, "Definitely not! Trouble seems to follow him! It's all done, I booked it this morning. You should be grateful as it's costing us an arm and a leg to pay for."

"When do we go?" Rebekkah asked.

Jacob was wading his way through the Weetabix looking as if the milk was sour.

"Tomorrow, I'll drive you there."

****

The journey was conducted in silence. Finally, the car turned up a large drive, coming to a stop at a small booth. A woman dressed in uniform greeted them cheerily, checked Mrs Taylor's ID, and opened up the barrier to let them through.

"I don't believe it! This is a school!" groaned Jacob as they drove past a sign.

"Yes, that's why we picked it. It's a boarding school with excellent security."

Mother came to a stop in front of reception, "Come on!" she said briskly. The children reluctantly pulled their cases out of the boot and followed her into the school reception area. It smelt of disinfectant.

"Ah, you must be the Taylor family?" The receptionist greeted them with a bright smile. Whilst their mother was signing them in, a troop of yellow tee shirted children ran past the window, shouting, "Hocus Pocus! Everybody Focus!"

Jacob rolled his eyes at his sister who smothered a giggle.

"Well, goodbye you two. Have fun, stay safe and don't get into trouble." Mother looked at them both, for a moment Rebekkah thought she might give them a hug, but she obviously thought better of it and marched away. A few moments later the engine started, and she was gone.

"Right!" said the receptionist, "Let's take you to your rooms. And then you can join the gym session."

4 THE CAMP

Rebekkah was quite enjoying herself, she enjoyed gym and it was good to take some exercise. She had already worked up quite a sweat when, out of the corner of her eye, she noticed Jacob slide into the room and hover at the door. He was flanked either side by two strapping young men, one of whom had his hand on Jacob's shoulder. He propelled Jacob into the mass of burpee jumping young people and indicated that Jacob should join in. She found herself giggling at his uncoordinated and reluctant efforts. Jacob jumped up when everyone else was down. He looked like a Jack in the box with his fiery red hair and new yellow top.

"Ten mountain climbers, five jumping jacks, six butt kickers and a plank to finish!" yelled the instructor.

"Look at that new one," muttered a girl in front of Rebekkah. "He's a slob!"

She realised with a rush of embarrassment, that they were talking about Jacob who was lying prostrate on the floor. One of the young men who had accompanied him, pushed him with his toe, and when Jacob did not move, blew his whistle in his ear. Jacob sprang up, a look of fury on his face.

The guys joked, "Time for lunch Carrot Top, although you haven't done much to earn it."

Rebekkah walked over to Jacob who greeted her with venom. "I am not staying in this place, it's like a prison camp. The rooms have got six beds in them, I had to put on someone else's foul gym shorts and if anyone else shouts at me to burp or kick my butt I shall throw up!"

Rebekkah laughed, "Oh come on it's not so bad, we have canoeing this afternoon, you are good at that. Let's go and get some lunch."

The dining hall was large and noisy. Lunch was a couple of fish fingers, boiled peas, undercooked oven chips, and sponge with lumpy custard. Jacob's mood did not improve. As they finished eating, an older woman approached them. Her dark hair was cropped short, while her blue eyes sparkled with merriment. "Jacob and Rebekkah?" she enquired, "I shall be your coach for this afternoon."

"I think we'll be fine, thank you." Jacob tried his most polite smile, "I know how to canoe."

"Firstly, we are going to do some kayaking, not canoeing, secondly, our safety regulations mean that we have to ensure all new campers are safe. Can you swim? Because we shall start with an Eskimo Roll. Now follow me and pick up a kayak each."

Jacob groaned but followed her down the hill to a stack of kayaks. She pointed out a small red kayak for Jacob and a yellow one for Rebekkah. Marching down to the water's edge she indicated that they should follow her. Lined up in the water, their bows pointing 90 degrees to the jetty were six other young people. All were seated. As they watched, an instructor flipped the boat over, so the occupant was head down in the water and then flipped it upright again. The unfortunate child re-emerged coughing.

"That's stage 1," explained their coach, "Stage 2 is when you do it on your own. You can't take a kayak out until you can roll 360 degrees. Here, put these on."

She pointed to a rack of wet suits and life jackets.

Rebekkah looked at Jacob, she knew he hated putting his head under the water. His mouth was set in a grim, determined line, he was battling with his anxiety.

"Ask the Eagle to help you," she whispered in his ear.

"How can a stupid flying bird help me in the water? That's such a stupid thing to say. You are so stupid." Jacob could be vicious when he was scared.

Even though she knew it was his fear talking she felt like slapping him. Instead, she struggled into the suit and pulled on the life jacket. She was also quite anxious and decided to take her own advice. She offered a quick prayer as she tugged her kayak into the water. She climbed in and the instructor waded out alongside her.

"Now, when I say breathe, you need to take a big breath in. I will spin you, count to three then I will spin you back up. The aim is to get you used to the feeling of having your head under water. Ready? Breathe."

Rebekkah just had time to suck in some air before she was turned upside down. After what seemed like an eternity she spun back up. Coughing, she took in several deep breaths and looked around her. Jacob was pulling on his suit, he seemed to be ignoring her.

"Now, I am going to spin you, but you will need to bring yourself back up. You use the paddle like this." She placed her hands over Rebekkah's and laid the paddle horizontally across the side of the boat. "When you spin over you need to use the paddle to right yourself by pulling the paddle towards you and then sweep out to your right, using the paddle to pull you up through the water. I will do it once with you so you can feel it. Ready? Place your paddle, breathe, and here we go." The kayak span over as before, only this time Rebekkah could feel the instructor moving the paddle for her; twist, sweep, push and up.

"Well done!" The woman smiled at her. Rebekkah felt a rush of pleasure, so rare was it for anyone to praise her that she immediately warmed to the woman. She wanted nothing more than to show her that she could do the roll herself.

"Ready to do this on your own now, Rebekkah? I think you will be fine. If you need me, I am right here to pull you up if you get into trouble. Now, place your paddle, breathe and over we go."

The little boat tipped, she was upside down, clinging to the paddle on the side of the boat. Momentarily confused she began to panic but then remembered the calm, measured voice of her instructor. Twist the paddle round, sweep, and use it to push yourself up. And up she popped! The teacher clapped and touched her lightly on the shoulder. "Hey! What a pro! That was really well done."

Rebekkah beamed at her, "You made it easy for me."

The teacher looked at Jacob, "Your sister did well, it's your turn now."

But then, just as Jacob was wading out to them both, they were startled by a harsh ascending call and out of the nearby woods flew a magpie. It headed straight for Jacob screeching; its claws distended. Jacob quickly ducked, putting his head under the water. The bird flew off.

"Wow, I've never seen a bird do that before, are you alright,

Jacob?" The instructor was concerned and waded over to him. He ran his hands backwards over his hair, squeezing the water down his neck and shoulders. The freckles on his nose and cheeks stood out, his cheeks had turned a sickly green colour.

Bravely, he looked at the instructor, "I'm fine, I want to do this. That Magpie was trying to scare me. I won't let him."

"Him?" the instructor was puzzled. "We don't have to do this, Jacob. That was quite a scary thing to happen, we can try again tomorrow."

Jacob looked at Rebekkah who was biting her lip nervously. "I've done the worst bit, getting my head under the water, I want to do it. Especially as he doesn't want me to."

The instructor looked from brother to sister and back again. "There's something about the two of you, I can't quite put my finger on it, you are different from the other kids, scared but determined. Some kids just do stuff without a care in the world, others freeze and can't move forward but you, you see the danger, are scared of it but are resolved to overcome. That's courage and it's rare. Come on Jacob! Let's get this done!"

And Jacob did it.

He beamed at Rebekkah, and in a rare moment of sibling pride,

she hugged him.

5 ESCAPE

The girls and boys slept in different parts of the building, so it was breakfast before they got to talk properly.

Jacob was already seated, working his way through a bacon roll and a cup of milk. Rebekkah helped herself to some fruit and a yoghurt and sat down next to him. "That magpie attack Jacob, do you think it was him?"

"Yes," mumbled Jacob, his mouth full of bread. "He has found us."

"What shall we do?" Rebekkah tore the top of her yoghurt and licked it.

"We need to get out of here, before he appears as an instructor, or worse."

Rebekkah took a scoop of yoghurt. "I am enjoying it here," she said ruefully.

"You have fallen for that instructor," teased Jacob.

"No, I haven't," said Rebekkah defensively, but she did feel sad at the possibility of not seeing her again. "How will we escape? Security is all over this place like a rash."

"That's what I am trying to figure out, also we haven't got any money. Mum didn't leave us any."

"Where shall we go?"

"I don't know, I was thinking Robert's house, but I don't know how to get there. Also, he's not been answering his phone."

"Why don't we just tell? Mother must have told them about our situation."

"What can they do? They will think we are mad. You saw that police officer's face when I told him the Magpie is a shape shifter and can change between man and bird. He thought I was delusional."

"Well, that lady who was with us, she saw it too, she can support our story."

"Hmmm," said Jacob doubtfully, "Well, I don't have a better plan at this stage so I agree, we will go to her and talk to her."

They dropped their breakfast trays off and strolled down to the lake. They hovered uncertainly for a while, looking for their friend but she didn't come.

"Shouldn't you two be in gym class, now?" A man, half dressed in a wet suit stood in front of them.

"Er, we are looking for one of the instructors, an older lady, she taught us to do an Eskimo roll yesterday." Jacob's powers of observation had always been lacking.

"She's got short black hair, twinkly eyes, is slim and she's nice," said Rebekkah lamely.

The man looked at her curiously, "We don't have any older female instructors, except Jan, she sometimes fills in when we are busy."

"Um maybe, not sure what she is called." Rebekkah wished now that she had asked the lady her name.

"Jan was called away yesterday evening, something about a friend of hers. Robert, I think she called him, had had an accident."

The children exchanged looks, could it be a coincidence?

"Does she live on site?" enquired Rebekkah.

"No, she lives in the town. Right, that's enough now, you had better get back inside and on with your classes."

Just then a tannoy boomed out, "Jacob and Rebekkah Taylor please report for gym in the Dance Studio."

"Dammit! It's like a prison camp." Jacob kicked a stone with his shoe.

"I will walk you back up the hill," said the instructor, "to make sure you get there."

They followed him in silence. It was going to be difficult to leave.

The gym class was exhausting, within 10 minutes both were gasping for air and Jacob looked as if he was going to pass out. He stopped frequently, finally, he went white as a sheet and appeared to faint. Rebekkah ran over to him and knelt beside him. Something was odd about the way he was breathing. The class instructor joined her, turned Jacob over into the recovery position and took his pulse. She smiled at Rebekkah reassuringly.

Jacob began to stir, opened his eyes and groaned.

The instructor continued to hold his wrist, "It's ok, Jacob, you just passed out for a few minutes, but you will be fine."

Jacob rolled onto his back, "I've had this before, I have a heart murmur, I need to go to hospital and get it checked out."

Rebekkah widened her eyes in surprise and was about to interject when she caught a look from her brother. She nodded in agreement, "Yes, he does need to get it checked out, can I go with him?" she asked innocently.

Five minutes later, they were travelling in the school minibus into town. Rebekkah could hardly contain herself, she wanted to giggle hysterically and had to avoid looking at her brother. Instead she stared out of the window, taking in the terrain, looking for signposts.

Once at the hospital they were ushered into A and E and were greeted by a doctor who listened to Jacob's chest. This was the tricky bit. Once they found there was no heart murmur they were going to be sent back. The young doctor asked Jacob a series of questions then, pursing his lips left them alone in the small cubicle.

"Time to leave," Jacob popped his head out of the curtain, the young instructor who had accompanied them was sitting outside, playing on his phone.

"Erm, I need to go to the toilet."

"Me too," smirked Rebekkah.

"Oh, ok be quick then." The young man hardly looked up; he was engrossed.

As the two hurried down the corridor, they hastily followed the exit signs and were soon back in the main waiting area. Fortunately, it was very busy, and it was easy to slip out through the doors. Once in the car park they ran as fast as they could, out of the gates and into a housing estate.

"We must get out of the open and away from here," panted Jacob.

37

"Over here," Rebekkah had seen a large bush, they squeezed their way into its centre, protected by the web of branches. Once enveloped, they sat for a while, to catch their breath.

"Jacob, that fainting trick was amazing! I never knew you were such a good actor."

He grinned, "I used to practise it at school to get out of PE lessons, it worked a couple of times, then they got wise to it. You have to hold your breath until you pass out. You did well not to give the game away though, you caught on pretty quickly."

"What are we going to do now? It won't be long before they contact the police and they will start looking for us." Rebekkah peered anxiously through the tangle of leaves as if expecting a blue light to come screeching down the road at any moment.

Jacob got out his phone, "We can try Robert again." He dialled the number. This time, it was answered.

6 ROBERT IS EVASIVE

Robert had had some business to attend to, he was concerned about Tarek, the young refugee who had been captured by Pete Maghie, otherwise known as The Magpie. The lad was alone without supporters, and he wanted to put himself forward to help him. He had assumed he would be placed in a foster home, but when he enquired of the police, they told him the lad had been placed in a Detention Centre while the Home Office processed his application. Disturbed by this news, Robert had made some enquiries, found out where Tarek had been placed and had fixed up to visit the young asylum seeker the next day.

Jacob and Rebekkah had already texted him with the news that they had to leave and spend the summer in camp, he privately thought it was a good idea and had contacted his friend Jan to keep an eye on them. He was alarmed therefore when Jacob told him about the magpie attack. He had phoned Jan and arranged to meet her to talk through what had happened and to see what could be done to increase the protection for the children. He wasn't expecting the miscreants to run away. As soon as Jacob phoned, he listened carefully. It was clear they would not go back to the camp; Jacob's mind was made up and he was scared. He thought quickly; he was in the area and able to help, he would take the children to their grandparents and then visit Tarek. He made a couple of calls and then drove to the hospital.

As he came to a halt, he texted the children to come out and was amused to see them run out from under a nearby weeping willow. They had been well hidden.

"Phew, it's good to see you Robert," panted Rebekkah as she slid into the back seat.

"Why didn't you answer your phone?" demanded Jacob as he yanked free the seat belt and jabbed it into place.

Robert pushed the car into gear, and started driving, "I did."

Jacob was indignant, "No, you didn't, I phoned you loads of times from that prison camp, left messages and you ignored me."

Robert was concentrating on the road ahead while Jacob

watched him intently, waiting for an answer. Robert looked into the driving mirror and then gave Jacob a sideways glance, "Well, to be fair, I can't interfere in decisions made by your parents, and it wasn't a bad idea to place you in that activity camp, you were relatively safe there."

Jacob was furious, "That's such a poor excuse. We weren't safe at all because the Magpie discovered us."

Robert shifted in his seat, Jacob could see that he was being evasive, and it irritated him. He persisted, "What were you doing that was so important you couldn't even text a reply?"

"Jacob!" warned Rebekkah from the back, "Robert is here now."

Robert ignored the question about his whereabouts and continued, "That's why I came, Jan told me about what happened. She was designated to watch over you."

"Jan?" queried Rebekkah, "you mean she is a friend of yours? But she wasn't there today. How is that looking after us?"

"She left at my request to collect some protection. But you took matters into your own hands," Robert scratched his chin and smiled ruefully. "You weren't to know."

"Can we see her again?" Rebekkah realised she was wearing her heart on her sleeve, and she went a bit pink. Jacob laughed, momentarily distracted from his inquisition of Robert, "Your Jan made quite an impression on Rebekkah, she fancies her!"

"Jacob, I don't. You are so mean." Rebekkah slapped him over the head. He slapped her back, grinning and enjoying her discomfort.

Robert welcomed the distraction away from Jacob's questions and moved the conversation onto Jan, "Yes she too is a follower of Eagle and she said she liked you as well."

"Did she tell you how good I was at the Eskimo Roll?" Rebekkah was basking in the memory of the previous day.

Jacob opened his mouth to continue with his questions, but Robert pressed on, "Yes! Yes, she did, and she told me how brave Jacob was too. Now, I have already spoken to your grandparents. They in turn have spoken to your parents to reassure them you are safe. I think your parents have a view on what should happen next, but I shall leave your grandparents to explain this to you." Robert accelerated as he hit the dual carriageway and turned the radio on.

The journey was spent catching up on news. Robert explained what he had discovered about Tarek and gave the impression that he had been too preoccupied with the asylum system to text. This mollified Jacob a little. Robert knew he was avoiding Jacob's questions, but he had his own demons to deal with, stoked by his meeting with the Magpie. He couldn't tell the children what was going through his mind. It was true he had been busy with Tarek but also his birds. As extra protection he had moved his falcons to a place that he hoped would be safe, but he still wasn't sure what to do. The Magpie was capable of finding them, he had spies everywhere. It was unfortunate that Jacob and Rebekkah had taken matters into their own hands by running away. They were exposed once again and he felt an overwhelming sense of despair about what might happen over the next few days. It felt as if events were moving beyond his control.

The time passed quickly until they pulled up in the driveway of their grandparent's home, where they were greeted with the smell of freshly cooked bread and cake.

7 TAREK

Tarek wiped his plate clean with a piece of white bread. The chicken, rice and gravy had little taste to it. He missed the stuffed vegetables flavoured with garlic, minced lamb and spices that he had eaten almost daily when in Syria. His mouth watered at the memory of Baklava laced with honey. He rested his head on his hands. He felt desperately sad, and homesickness overwhelmed him. He couldn't cry, not here in front of everyone but often did so at night. He would tuck his head underneath the blankets and hot tears would run silently down his cheeks. His heart ached for his mother, and his stomach twisted in fear at what his father might be experiencing. He had been despatched from Syria because the family were being tortured and abused by the Syrian government. His father feared that once Tarek reached 14, he would be given a gun and forced to kill. Tarek knew what that looked like and did not want to be a part of it. He had agreed to travel to England full of hope that he would be made welcome and could start a new life. Little did he know how difficult and traumatic that journey would be. Even now he struggled to recall all the details. He had told Jacob when he had met him last year, but that was the first time anyone had really listened to him. Even now in the Immigration Removal Centre people looked at him with suspicion and questioned his age.

He was full of anxiety about what might happen to him next. He had been in the centre for months. He didn't know what was to become of him, he was afraid of being sent back to Syria, but didn't want to stay in this prison either.

When Robert and the Eagle had set them free, he had been full of hope that he would be well looked after, maybe taken to live with Rebekkah and Jacob. They seemed such nice people. But then the police had taken him to the local Detention Centre. On entry he had been given a full medical examination by a doctor, had his fingerprints taken and then issued with a blue suit and flip flops. He had a cell to himself, but it was tiny and airless. He would have preferred the company of others, but as a child he needed to be safeguarded, or so they said.

He didn't feel very safe. He did feel guarded. Every night, without knocking, a guard would burst into his room, sometimes disturbing his evening prayers, check that he was still there and then leave, locking the door behind him. Some of them were kind and would take a few moments to ask him how he was. Others were miserable and grumpy. He was almost out of hope now. His faith in Allah was a constant support to him and tied him invisibly with his life back in Syria. He kept up the daily prayers or Salat as far as he was able and took comfort from the familiar words and routine. Months ago, he had plucked up the courage to ask for a prayer mat and a compass in order to work out where east was but had been told he might not be there long enough to need these things and to be patient. This had given him some comfort but also some anxiety as he did not know what that meant. The lack of any certainty or predictability in his life was upsetting. No mat had appeared and he was still in detention.

"Tarek!" He jumped at the sound of his name being called.

He signalled with a small nod of his head and a little wave of his hand. He had learnt long ago to be quietly responsive and not to bring any attention to himself if at all possible. A man stood in the doorway, "The Guvnor wants to see you!"

47

Foreboding filled his heart. It had been so long since he had had any good news, he always assumed the worst. He followed the man meekly out into the corridor and outside. He enjoyed the evening air and lifted his face up to feel the sensation of the wind. He entered the reception block. The man knocked at a door, and then stood back to let him in. Seated at a desk was a dark-skinned man he had not seen before. He smiled at Tarek and indicated he should sit down.

"Hello Tarek, it would appear you have some friends who would like to visit you. They are coming tomorrow. I have looked at your file, they are the people involved in your rescue from the traffickers. Are you happy to see them?"

Hope and joy flooded into Tarek's head and heart, "You mean Jacob, Rebekkah and Robert?"

The man nodded.

"Yes! Oh yes! I see them, I see them." Tarek could hardly contain himself.

"Good, I shall phone them and tell them to be here at 10 a.m. You will see them in the lounge. Someone will come and collect you."

He gestured to Tarek that he should go. Uncertainly the lad got to his feet and bowed, "Thank you, sir! Thank you!"

The man nodded kindly, a slight smile on his lips, and waved him out of the room.

Tarek could hardly wait for the next day and, for the first time in days, did not mind being locked into his cell.

8 THE PARENTS

Dinner was a rather gloomy affair and despite the lovely homecooked food, the children were apprehensive when they were told that their parents were on their way to see them. Robert too had seemed withdrawn, picking at his food, whilst staring at his phone. They had talked a little about Tarek and were excited about the fact that he had agreed to see them the next day. Rebekkah was worried that her parents would whisk them back to the camp before they had a chance to see him. Robert reassured her that he would still visit even if they were not able to.

Mr and Mrs Taylor arrived in a foul mood. They seemed to feed off each other in that respect. Mr Taylor was partially mollified after he had been fed. He enjoyed his mother's cooking. Mrs Taylor, on the other hand was furious. She was not impressed by Jacob's story of the magpie attack. "I am getting fed up of the stories you are telling, I can't work out whether you are a fantasist, a liar or both."

Grandfa cleared his throat, he rarely spoke so when he did

people listened.

"I can understand your irritation, Susan," he began. "But what if there is something in what Jacob is saying? You yourselves witnessed a terrible attack on Gerald by a magpie and I believe your cat was pecked to death. These are not just fantastic stories, they do appear to have some veracity. Jacob was captured by this man twice, and he does seem to have some control over these birds. The police have also taken it seriously."

Rebekkah looked at her mother who slapped her fork onto the table in anger. Why was she always so angry?

"That's the point, isn't it? We responded to the advice of the police and found this excellent activity camp, paid a small fortune for them to attend. What do these headstrong fools do? They manage one night, play a silly trick and abscond from a hospital. I had six missed calls from the camp manager and five from the police! It's humiliating!"

'Well, you don't know what it's like to be pursued by this man!" shouted Jacob, his cheeks pink with anger. His eyebrows seemed to be sucking all the blood from his face upwards. "He is a shapeshifter! We weren't safe there. You don't know what he's like. He is a master of disguise. Having found us, he would have wangled his way into the camp and…"

"And what!" exclaimed his mother. "You tell someone, you alert them to the danger! You don't just take the law into your own hands and run off!"

"Your mother has a point," interjected Robert, "You did have a friend on camp. She would have believed you and protected you."

Rebekkah looked at him in dismay, if Robert turned against them, they would have no chance of seeing Tarek.

Mr Taylor turned on him, "Well, a fat lot of good you did, you brought them here. Why didn't you just take them back to the camp? Then we could have stayed at home and got on with our very busy lives!" He glared at Robert who, not for the first time, wondered how these people had managed to bring two such brave and courageous children into the world. But maybe that was it, being so neglected emotionally had made the children more resilient.

This time Granny spoke up. She was gentle but firm, "Susan and Gerald, your children are in danger. It is easy to see that they are afraid, they wanted to be comforted and in a safe place. They feel safe here. They weren't safe at their cousin's house, despite being told they would be, in fact that awful creature duped our other son into thinking he was a friend! How do you expect Jacob and Rebekkah to trust anyone again? I think it's time for you to recognise what is going on here."

Mr Taylor bristled, "And what is that?"

"We are all in a battle between the forces of good and evil. The only way in which we are going to resist this Magpie is by recognising the strength of the threat and placing a protective circle around this house."

"A protective circle?" despite her irritation at her mother-in-law's intervention, Mrs Taylor was curious.

"Yes, it is an ancient protection and can only be used for a short while but Jacob and Rebekkah will be safe here for a few days while we sort out what can be done to thwart this Magpie. We have some ancient books we can consult and some teachers to see."

"Oh! Not this religious nonsense again!" scoffed Mr Taylor. "You haven't still got that eagle in the garden, have you? I gave up on all that years ago. There's no such thing as 'evil forces' and 'ancient protection.' You are just feeding this nonsense."

Despite his own scepticism about ethereal creatures and a spirit world, Jacob warmed towards his granny, feeling a sense of comfort and hope as he looked at her face and listened to her words. She spoke with quiet wisdom, and she inspired trust. He wondered why he had not seen this precious gift in her before, and then with a wince, he remembered the words of Eagle, "You are seeing things differently, your reality is changing, you are beginning to care about others and seeing the difference between darkness and light."

"Are you offering to look after Jacob and Rebekkah?" Mrs Taylor saw a light at the end of a tunnel.

Granny and Grandfa looked at each other then turned to the children. "Yes, if they promise to stay and not go flying off around the country."

"Oh Granny, that would be so wonderful! Thank you!" Rebekkah flung her arms around her granny, who wrapped her arms around the girl and patted her back.

"Yes, thanks, that would be good," said Jacob gruffly. They looked expectantly at their parents.

Mrs Taylor looked at her watch and sighed. "I have an early morning meeting tomorrow. If you are happy to have them and keep them here then that would be acceptable wouldn't it, Gerald?"

Mr Taylor was irritated. "I am not happy that you are filling the children's heads with nonsense, you need to promise not to do that. It's brainwashing and just plain wrong."

A thought occurred to Rebekkah, she desperately wanted to stay so she tried a different tack. "Of course, we won't be brainwashed father dear, we can't possibly believe in anything that can't be proved by science. You have taught us the importance of proof. Until we have scientific proof, we shall continue to be agnostic, even atheistic on this matter." She smiled sweetly, Jacob looked at her suspiciously and then joined in, "You know me dad, I have no truck with non-scientific ideas."

Mr Taylor smiled victoriously and stood up. "Good lad, that's my boy," he looked defiantly at his parents, "Good luck with these two then!"

As the car swept off up the road, Rebekkah breathed a sigh of relief. Jacob went back to the table and helped himself to a large slice of chocolate cake. "Yummy, I can enjoy this now those two have gone! And no burpees or canoes in sight!"

9 THE IMMIGRATION REMOVAL CENTRE

Breakfast was a cheerful affair. The children were given their favourite food - pains au chocolate. As Jacob was about to put his fourth into his mouth, grandfa moved the subject to visiting Tarek.

"Tarek is expecting you both, plus Robert. We believe you will be safe at the Centre and it will give us time to put in place the protective ring around the house."

"Yes, about that," mumbled Jacob, his mouth full, "What did you mean by a protective ring?"

Granny laughed, "It's quite simple, we shall take some of our old CDs and hang them around the boundary of the garden and house. It's not very sophisticated, they glint in the sun, magpies don't like the light."

"Oh!" Jacob was disappointed, "I thought that from what you said, it was going to be a bit more magical than that. You mentioned ancient books and consulting teachers. It all sounded rather mysterious."

Granny responded, "Miracles are possible but rare, we prefer to work within the laws of nature until we have no other choice. This situation with the shapeshifter is beyond our expertise so we need to consult a teacher, someone wiser than us. The CDs are a temporary solution. Now, you need to get going. I suggest you check your mouth before leaving, Jacob." Granny winked at Rebekkah who laughed. Jacob was covered in chocolate.

Once in the car, Robert seemed to relax a bit. He drove quickly and it wasn't long before the Immigration Removal Centre came into view. It was a sterile, utilitarian building with small windows and high walls. The children were shocked to see rolls of barbed wire on top of the walls.

They were stopped by an armed guard who checked his book to see if they were in it and then waved them through.

"Phew that was easy," breathed Jacob.

"You wait," Robert sounded a note of caution, "once we get to the building, security increases."

Sure enough, the receptionist asked for ID, took their photos and they were finger-printed.

"Hey!" Protested Jacob, "This is an infringement of my human rights! I haven't done anything wrong you can't take my fingerprints."

"Do you want to see your friend, or not?" The receptionist spoke in a flat, bored voice, "These are the rules, it's not a hotel, you know."

Rebekkah nudged Jacob who reluctantly complied. They were then ushered through to another door where their belongings were X - Rayed and another machine identified them through their fingerprints. They were also frisked. Rebekkah threw Jacob a warning look, but he was now interested in the machines and seemed to have accepted the layers of security. They were then moved through more doors, told to use yet another fingerprint recognition machine and finally into a large room that resembled an airport departure lounge. There were about forty round tables with four, coloured, plastic chairs around each.

Uncertain, they hovered around a table, a guard stood with his hands folded in front of him by the doors. It made them feel imprisoned. At last, the doors opened at the other end of the hall and Tarek emerged.

Rebekkah ran to him and embraced him, Jacob gave him a high five as did Robert. All were smiling, it was good to see him. The guard who had accompanied Tarek gestured towards a table, looked at his watch and grunted, "Thirty minutes, max."

He then took his place at the other end of the room in effect both exits were guarded.

"It good to see you all," beamed Tarek.

"Are you alright, Tarek, how have they been treating you?" asked Robert.

"Not bad," Tarek's eyes shifted to the guards who were clearly listening. "I miss the air, and I miss my family, I not know what happen next. I afraid, they send me back, but I want to go. Want to see my mother and father." His eyes filled with tears which he wiped away with the back of his hand. "Can you help me? Please!" He pleaded with them. Rebekkah felt her heart would break. She turned to Robert, "Isn't there anything we can do?"

He looked at her, "Yes, this is what I have been investigating, the Refugee Council can help, also the Children's Society. I have been in touch with both and one of them will provide a lawyer and will visit you soon. How old are you, Tarek?"

"Fifteen," he replied. "But some say I older, this why I not get help, they argue over my age."

Jacob looked at the slender young man, he had a bit of growth on his chin, his eyes were hollow, and his limbs were long and gangly. He didn't look over 15. He looked slightly older than himself. Self - consciously he touched his own chin, could he feel a bit of stubble?

Rebekkah shuddered, "I can't imagine being locked up in a place like this. It's so wrong, especially after what you have already been through."

Tarek looked at them all, "Can you get me out of here? Please! I would also like to phone my parents, but I do not have a phone." His eyes filled with tears, his expression was pathetic, pleading. *How could anyone think he was old*, thought Rebekkah.

Robert looked at him and then drew a deep breath, "You need to understand something Tarek. Jacob and Rebekkah are in the middle of something, they aren't the safest of people to be with. Do you remember Pete?"

Tarek nodded.

"Well, he escaped after you were released and he is hunting down Jacob and Rebekkah, he wants them for some reason. Although I hate to say it, you are probably safer in here than with them."

Rebekkah and Jacob exchanged looks, Jacob raised an eyebrow. What was Robert playing at?

"Granny and Grandfa are working out a way to keep us safe," said Jacob with a confidence he didn't really feel, but he wanted to make Tarek feel better. This was an unusual feeling for him, but he felt a sense of responsibility, which was uncomfortable. In the past, Jacob had looked after Jacob.

"Yes, but that might not be enough." Robert seemed very keen to keep Tarek in the centre.

Rebekkah looked at him, "I thought you were contacting the Refugee Association to get Tarek some help. Where did you think he would stay?"

Robert looked shifty, "There are foster homes that are provided. I had thought that he might stay with me, but my DBS check hasn't cleared yet." He felt unable to say more at this stage, but his past was catching up with him.

Jacob looked at Robert and blurted out what he felt, which was that adults were frustratingly cautious and slow to act. He wanted to see his friend freed from this place immediately. "Robert, we can't let Tarek go to a random home with people who don't know him, he belongs with us. Granny and Grandfa will look after him."

Even as the words escaped from his mouth, he realised he had no authority to speak in this way. He hadn't even spoken to his grandparents, and he knew for sure that his own parents would not welcome Tarek. Why was it all so difficult? Why couldn't people just be welcoming? Why did his friend need to be in this prison? It all seemed so wrong and unjust!

"Time's up!" interjected the guard.

"Really?" Jacob rounded on the man, "we have hardly had any time, you said thirty minutes."

"Time's up!" repeated the man.

Jacob looked at him more closely, there was something familiar about him, but he couldn't work out where he had seen him before.

Robert stood up, "Come on," he said, "we have to do as we are instructed."

Tarek looked devastated, "When will I see you again?" he asked.

Robert responded, "I will return soon with a lawyer. Don't worry, we will sort something out."

Rebekkah squeezed his hand and with an assurance she didn't feel, said, "Robert will work something out. Don't worry. We will come and see you again."

The guard moved forward and stood by Tarek.

Jacob looked at him and then at Tarek. "Don't trust anyone in here," he warned.

Tarek looked at him, "Trust!" he exclaimed, "the only thing I trust is Allah, and my parent's love!"

Rebekkah looked at him kindly, "Then, there is hope, Tarek."

10 SHOCKING NEWS

The three drove back in silence. Rebekkah tried to make conversation, but Robert was uncommunicative, and Jacob just stared out of the window. On reaching their grandparent's house Robert said he had some people to visit who might be able to help Tarek and drove off. Once inside, Rebekkah poured out her heart to her grandparents who listened sympathetically. Grandfa turned to Jacob and asked him what he thought.

Instead of answering, Jacob changed the subject and asked about the protection which they had hoped to put in place. In reply, Grandfa stood up and pointed towards the CDs hanging from trees like Christmas decorations. They glistened and glinted in the sun. "Our morning's work," he said proudly.

Jacob was impatient, "Not that!" he scoffed. "The other thing, the supernatural protection."

"Ah!" said Granny, "we are still working on that."

"Oh no!" Jacob placed his head in his hands. Granny rested her hand on his shoulders. "You have been through a great deal Jacob, I can understand your anxiety, but…"

Before she could finish, Jacob shook her off and angrily stood up, "You don't get it do you? This man is after me. Your stupid little CDs rattling in the wind are not going to stop him. Everywhere I go, I see him. Like today, at the Centre, he was there."

Granny took a step back, surprised at his anger.

Rebekkah's hand flew to her mouth, "Oh no! Tarek, will he be safe? You said, 'don't trust anyone.' What did you see, Jacob?"

"The guard," muttered Jacob between clenched teeth. "I wasn't sure at first but the more I think about it, I believe it was him."

Grandfa and Granny exchanged looks and then Grandfa went to the phone. Jacob and Rebekkah watched his face as he got through to the Immigration Removal Centre. He asked to be put through to the Centre Manager. It was clear from his face and replies that something had happened. At last, he came off the phone and sat down heavily at the table.

"Tarek has gone," he spoke gently, but there were tears in his eyes as he continued, "one of the guards took him outside for exercise and they never came back. They are trying to trace them, but they seem to have disappeared into thin air."

"Agh!" screamed Jacob. "This is like a curse! Wherever I go, he is there. What have I done to deserve this?"

Grandfa looked at him sadly and then said, "It is time for you to know your destiny, Jacob. We didn't just hang CDs today; we also visited some wise teachers. We belong to the Order of the Eagle which is a type of church, I don't have much time to explain but suffice to say there is a much wider circle of people than just us. We have scholars, learned people who know much more than your granny and I about our faith. They searched the holy books, and there is a prophecy which I wrote down. I hope it means something to you." He passed it to Jacob who opened it. He read it silently and then out loud, his brow furrowed with anxiety.

"The Golden One surrenders to, and rises from, the destruction caused by the ones who entered the garden. She demonstrates her love, not to punish,

but to turn the heart of stone back to love."

"The Nest, Jacob!" exclaimed Rebekkah, "It's what we did to the Nest. That's the garden, Eagle's world."

Granny looked at them both, "What happened in the nest, Jacob?"

By way of answer, Jacob continued angrily, "This isn't fair, I didn't ask to go there, it just happened. You made me go." He waggled a finger accusingly at Rebekkah, "If you hadn't forced me to climb on that eagle's back, I would never have gone and got mixed up in all this. Everything has gone wrong since that journey! And it's all your fault!"

"No, Jacob!" retaliated Rebekkah, "I didn't make you do anything. You wanted to come, and you didn't respect Eagle's rules, you climbed the tree and ate the chocolate. I just followed you!" And so, they argued, back and forth, until Granny held up her hand.

"Enough!" she shouted firmly. "We have heard enough! Look, there are millions of children in the world, yet she chose you two. She knew what you would do, yet she allowed it. She gave you a great gift and a responsibility, the freedom to choose to obey and to love. She did not want to force you to obey her, this is her strength but also her weakness. You don't have to go through with the next bit. You always have a choice."

"What choice do I have?" Jacob spoke bitterly. "The Magpie will find me wherever I go."

"You don't have to find him, Jacob. He has taken Tarek to lure you to him. Tarek is bait. You are safe here for the time being. He knows you are part of a bigger picture, that you have the mark of Eagle. But he doesn't know what your destiny is. You can both stay here while we figure out what to do next."

"This is all gobbledygook." Jacob stomped off upstairs, clearly upset.

Rebekkah hesitated, then followed him. But his door was shut, so she went to her own room.

11 THE TRACKER

Rebekkah sat on her bed, uncertain what to do next. She was bewildered by the fast pace of events and felt overwhelmed. She lay back on the bed, closed her eyes, took several deep breaths, and thought of Eagle. In her mind's eye, she was lying on the winged creature's back, arms outstretched, looking up at the vast expanse of stars. As she soared on the thermals Rebekkah felt as if she was in a cradle, held like a baby, safe and cocooned. The sensation was soothing, and she fell asleep, exhausted after the trauma of the last few days.

"Rebekkah!" Jacob's face was close to hers. He placed a warm hand over her mouth and put a finger over his own, signalling her to be quiet. It was dark, she must have been asleep for some time. Struggling to sit up, she pulled his hand away from her face, "Ugh, don't put your hand over my mouth, it smells!" She blurted out petulantly.

He had his iPad in his hand and there was a dot blinking on the screen on a map. "This is a device tracker, Robert got me to download it. I can track where Robert is. It follows his mobile phone."

Rebekkah looked at him suspiciously, her mind still clouded in sleep. She was disorientated but something didn't feel right. "Wait! Why would Robert do that?"

Jacob was getting impatient which he always did when he was excited and wanted to get going. He gave the impression that explaining things was a nuisance and he made her feel stupid for asking. "Because he wants us to follow him. Look! He has already set the Tracker going and we can see where he is. Here!" Jacob jabbed a finger at the iPad.

Rebekkah looked at him, still unable to comprehend why Robert would do such a thing. In addition, she was a little jealous, she had seen Robert as primarily her friend. In contrast, Jacob had often been scathing of Robert's unswerving faith in the Eagle. "Why didn't he tell me about this?" Awake now, she sat up and peered at Jacob suspiciously.

"Because you don't have an iPad!" Jacob exclaimed.

"And what's he doing? He only left this afternoon." Rebekkah was still sceptical.

"He went to get some help for Tarek, who has now gone missing, perhaps he has some information about him." Jacob was getting increasingly agitated. He clearly had a plan and was impatient to get going, he was annoyed by Rebekkah's questions.

Rebekkah persisted, she wasn't going to be easily persuaded, "Yes, well, why can't he come here and tell us, he knows we are at risk. Why would he draw us away from this home where we are safe? How do you know it's him Jacob, and not the Magpie?"

"Because it's Robert's phone!" But even Jacob looked shaken by her argument.

He paused for a minute, staring at the iPad, the dot pulsated menacingly. It was mesmerising, like a heartbeat. He felt drawn to it in a way he could not describe. Making his mind up, he looked at Rebekkah, "You are right, it could be a trick. You stay here and if I'm not back by morning then tell Granny and Grandfa, you will need to get them to contact the police."

Rebekkah felt a surge of anger, it was so typical of Jacob to play the hero and to react on impulse. Every time he did that, he got

73

himself into trouble. "No way am I going to let you go on your own. We will write a note to Granny letting her know where we have gone and then they will call the police if we are both not back." She looked at him defiantly.

He grinned. "I knew that would do the trick, come on then!" He quietly tiptoed out of the room and down the stairs. She quickly scribbled a note, left it on her bed and followed, knowing she would regret what she was about to do.

It was two a.m. when they left the house, the Tracker blinked inviting them to turn left.

It was stationary.

Whoever held the mobile phone was waiting for them.

It was a cloudless sky and a full moon cast shadows over the road as they walked. Elongated trees waved at them and whispered in the breeze. An owl hooted and something scrabbled in the hedge. Not for the first time Rebekkah wished she was back in her nice warm bed. She stole a glance at her brother whose eyes were captivated by the small pulsating light. He seemed oblivious to any sound, instead he walked as if entranced. Any attempt to draw him into a conversation was ignored so she gave up and walked silently behind him, her eyes watchful and alert. After several miles, the pulsating dot became very close and the children slowed right down, searching for a building or a car. Jacob headed zombie like into a wood, hesitantly Rebekkah followed him until a distant light could be seen. Instinctively they lowered their bodies and crept stealthily through the undergrowth until a barn like building emerged to their right. Nearby, a creature emitted a howl of pain making them jump. Despite herself, Rebekkah caught hold of Jacob's arm nearly knocking the iPad to the floor. He hissed angrily at her, but both were distracted by a dark shape that moved across the window. The dot blinked menacingly, daring them to come inside. They both stared at the building, it seemed a strange place for Robert to be. Aware of Jacob's hesitancy, Rebekkah took the lead and stealthily stepped towards the part of the building that had no windows. Reaching the barn wall, they flattened their backs against its timbered boards, they felt rough and splintery and smelt of creosote. Nodding towards the door, Rebekkah slid sideways along the wood until she reached it, nervously, she reached out and stealthily turned the handle.

It creaked.

She stopped.

She held her breath.

Silence.

She pushed a little harder.

The door swung open.

It was gloomy inside.

A chink of light could be seen under the internal door. There was no way of knowing whether what lay behind that door was malevolent or benevolent.

They would soon find out.

Taking a deep breath and squaring her shoulders Rebekkah stepped inside, Jacob followed.

A dark shape swooped over their heads and each felt a sharp pinch in their arms. Then, nothing.

12 TRAPPED

Jacob had a cracking headache and his mouth felt like sandpaper. He moved his tongue around his teeth trying to find some saliva so he could speak. On a small table in front of him he could just make out a bottle of water although his vision was blurred. Moving slowly, he crept over to the bottle, unscrewed the top and drank greedily. At once he began to feel better. He sat for a moment cradling the bottle in his hand, then his gaze fell upon his sister who was lying on her back snoring. Grabbing the second bottle he shuffled over to her and shook her hard. She grunted but didn't wake. He trickled some of the water over her face, this had the desired effect. She snorted, and her eyes opened, he observed that her pupils were dilated. He could see her going through the same sensation of running her tongue around a dry mouth, so he presented her with the water and tried to help her sit up. She drank thirstily before trying to speak, her voice was slurred.

"What's happened?"

Jacob shrugged, "I am not sure, we have been given some sort of drug."

"Any sign of Robert or Tarek or the Magpie?" Rebekkah rubbed her eyes to try and clear her vision.

Jacob stumbled to his feet and tried the door. It was locked.

A bird, sitting outside the window began to cackle and chatter. Another bird responded until a cacophony of sound reverberated around the barn. A magpie appeared at the window and tapped its beak against the glass. The window had bars preventing escape but there was a small awning that could be opened. The bird tapped more insistently so Jacob prised it open. It bounced on its feet cocked its beady eye at him and then flew off. The sound receded and Jacob sat back on the floor.

"Definitely back in the clutches of the Magpie," he said glumly.

"Yes! But where is he?" Rebekkah was beginning to feel more awake. "And how did he get hold of Roberts' phone?"

Jacob looked at her, "Perhaps he captured Robert too. Hey! Wait a minute, where's my iPad?" Jacob began a frantic search for his beloved piece of technology.

"You don't think he'd leave us with that do you?" Rebekkah spoke sarcastically. "Anyway, what we seem to be missing is how the Magpie would know about your conversation with Robert about the Tracker. Unless…"

"Unless Robert is working with him." finished Jacob who was visibly upset.

"It would make sense," mused Rebekkah, "Robert has been very odd since he picked us up from that activity place. But why would he betray us? He has always acted on our side as our protector and friend. He even asked that woman Jan to look after us."

Jacob looked thoughtful, "Dad has never trusted him, he always said how weird it was that whenever we got into trouble, Robert was always around."

"That's because we called him. When we were at Magpie House in Lincolnshire, we phoned him he came and helped the refugees escape. He wasn't working for the Magpie then." Rebekkah felt she wanted to stick up for her friend. She liked

Robert as he was one of the few adults in her life who listened to her.

Jacob's mind was racing, not one to be naturally trusting he was already seeing Robert in a different light, "But he was with the Magpie in the warehouse when I was kidnapped by him, I never quite got to the bottom of how Robert came to be there as well."

Rebekkah scrambled to her feet and stood over Jacob, daring him to disagree, "Robert got really badly beaten up while helping you to escape. He ended up in hospital. Remember?"

Jacob wasn't listening, he was distracted by the appearance of a magpie at the window. In its beak was a bag held by a red ribbon. Jacob reached through the awning and pulled the bag inside. He opened it, revealing a bacon roll. Immediately another magpie arrived holding a similar bag. This time Rebekkah pulled it in. It too contained a bacon roll.

"Well, he intends to keep us well fed then," she said sardonically, "A bit like the story of Hansel and Gretel when the witch imprisoned the children in an iron cage and fed them up so they

would have more fat on them when she came to eat them.
Although I think it was just Hansel she wanted to eat, Gretel was
kept as a slave." She paused in her story telling to observe Jacob
taking a large bite of his bun.

"It's actually quite good," he mumbled, his upper lip all covered
with flour. He reached across to grab her bag, "If you don't
want it, I'll have it."

Rebekkah snatched the bag away from him, she was hungry too,
she figured the drug had sharpened her appetite. She tucked
into her roll but felt immensely sad. Was it possible that Robert
had betrayed them? Could it be that he had been grooming
them all the time? She was overwhelmed by the thought.

The day passed slowly. The barn was silent. They would have
had no idea of time were it not for the frequent visits of the
magpies who dropped lunch and dinner through the window.

Despite himself, Jacob felt a sneaking admiration for this man
who could change shape, evade the police, and command
control over these magnificent birds. He seemed to be a winner
despite what had happened at his uncles' house in Lincolnshire.

He recalled the conversation he had had with the man when he tried to persuade Jacob to work for him. It had been an attractive proposition and Jacob was beginning to wonder what he would say if he met him again. The thought of being rich, not having to go to school and getting away from his parents seemed attractive. He didn't share his thoughts with Rebekkah, he sensed she would be opposed to any kind of deal with the Magpie, so he kept quiet.

The day passed and evening came, it was a beautiful starry night and they could easily see by the light of the moon. Eventually, they both fell into a light sleep. Rebekkah dreamt she was being chased by a large magpie that kept dropping bacon rolls on her head. Jacob dreamt he was jumping from tree to tree with the magpies. From his vantage point he could see the world beneath him, and he could control it.

13 THE EAGLE

The night passed. The children woke the next morning to the sound of birds screaming. Jumping to their feet they peered out of the window to see what was causing the cacophony. It was barely light and Rebekkah's first thought was that they had been woken by the dawn chorus. Then she saw it, a majestic golden eagle was swooping her way in and out of the trees. Magpies were flying everywhere, calling and screaming. The children watched, fascinated by the mayhem the awesome bird was causing until finally, she settled on the window ledge. As she steadied herself, she folded her wings neatly by her side and leant forward until she could see the children. In her beak she held a key. Deftly she popped it through the awning, and then was gone. Excited Jacob picked up the key and placed it in the door. The key turned easily in the lock and the door swung open.

Cautiously they made their way out of the room. As expected, the place was empty. No sign of Robert, Tarek or Magpie, but lying on the table was a mobile phone. Rebekkah picked it up and examined it closely. It was switched off. She gave it to

Jacob and asked him whether he thought it was Robert's phone.
Jacob turned it over in his hands but could not be certain.
Pocketing it as evidence, should it be needed later, he made his
way outside and gazed upwards at the magnificent bird circling
above them. Impatiently she flew away from the barn.
Uncertain what to do, they stared after her. She returned a few
minutes later and repeated the movement. It dawned on them
that she was leading them somewhere. Happy to be moving
again, they began walking in the direction she had indicated.

They walked at a fast pace, anxious to be away from the building
where they had been imprisoned. The terrain was easy
underfoot and they made good progress. Most of the journey
was through woodland, however after a few miles the air grew
fresher and the soil under their feet became sandier. Before long
the path in the woods took a right through a gate and they found
themselves in open fields. Ahead of them they could see the
vast blue expanse of the sea.

The golden eagle continued to fly ahead of them until they
arrived at a deserted beach. The children gazed around,
expecting to see a house or something solid where people might

be hiding. It didn't occur to them to look out to sea. Only when the bird flew out to a sailing boat which was anchored offshore, did it dawn on them that she was leading them away from the beach and into the sea. Finally, she perched on the stern of the boat, folded her wings and waited. The whole experience was beginning to take its toll on the children. They were already overwrought from the experiences of the last few days and now bewildered by the behaviour of this raptor. How were they to get to the boat? Did she expect them to swim? Neither of them could sail.

Jacob sat down first, his head in his hands. He felt dizzy and needed a drink. Rebekkah crouched next to him, despite her certainty that the golden eagle was on their side and leading them into the next step, she was also exhausted with recent events and would have liked nothing better than to go back to her grandparents, have a nice breakfast and curl up in the safety of their home. The thought occurred to her that they could use the mobile phone to call them. She was about to suggest this to Jacob when the eagle flew off the yacht and landed on a small rowing boat that was perched on the sand on the beach. It could not have been clearer. The bird was suggesting they take the boat and row out to the yacht. Impatiently she banged the oars with her beak and then flew back to the yacht.

Rebekkah looked at Jacob, he didn't respond, he stared at the boat and the bird as if he had had enough. Then he lifted his head and shouted at it, "I am thirsty! The magpies managed to feed us, if you are so clever, why can't you?"

"Jacob!" cautioned Rebekkah, but he continued to look defiantly at the huge bird. It paused momentarily and then sprang into the air. This time, it turned away from the boat and flew inland. Jacob lay back on the sand, muttering. Wearily, Rebekkah sat with him. She was thirsty too but her belief in the Eagle's goodness sustained her in a way that Jacob could not grasp. She believed the bird was her Eagle, and that She would not let them come to any harm. They waited a long time until finally it could be seen flying rapidly towards them. In its beak it held a large bottle of water. Descending from the sky it swooped down and gracefully landed next to them gently placing the water in front of Jacob.

"Thanks," muttered Jacob as he unscrewed the top and greedily gulped down its contents. The Eagle made a peculiar noise in her throat. Alarmed, he stopped drinking, and handed the bottle to Rebekkah who gratefully drank what was left. It bounced its way across the sand to the boat and waited patiently. This time, Jacob struggled to his feet and made his way to the little vessel. Together they dragged it to the water's edge, climbed in and began rowing out to the yacht. It didn't take long because Jacob was a competent rower.

The golden eagle was waiting for them. She took the rope in Her beak and held them steady while they climbed on board. Rebekkah tied the boat to the back of the yacht while Jacob stowed the oars. Distracted and busy the children did not see the bird leave.

"Dammit!" swore Rebekkah. "There was something I wanted to ask Her. Why is She never around to answer any questions?"

"What?" questioned Jacob. "What did you want to ask it?"

"What are we doing here? Why this yacht? We can't sail." Rebekkah was clearly very puzzled.

Jacob laughed. "You wouldn't have got very far unless you are Rebekkah Dolittle and can speak to the animals. That bird can't speak."

"It was HER, Jacob, The Eagle. Didn't you recognise Her?"

"Not really," he mused, "it was no different from those magpies. It didn't speak, it had a key, which must have come from the Magpie as he was the one who imprisoned us. Don't you think it's possible all these birds are connected to the Magpie? Why are you so certain it's *your* eagle?"

"Because, I just know, and I don't understand why you can't see it." Rebekkah was exasperated, but she was beginning to entertain a sneaking thought that what Jacob was saying made sense. If he was right and this eagle was just another clever bird under the control of Magpie, then they were back under his control.

"But she understood your request for water." She said lamely, knowing this was no argument as the magpies had dropped food off to them too.

"Only when I refused to go on without it," Jacob was more and more convinced that the golden bird was under the spell of the Magpie.

"Do you think we should leave? The boat is still here." Rebekkah was coming around to his thinking.

"Not just yet, let's explore the boat first, see if there are any clues as to what we have been brought here for."

Uncertainly they made their way down the stairs into the cabin where they were greeted by a welcoming sight. Set before them was a small table laden with breakfast food: fresh orange juice, croissants, cereal with fresh milk and fruit.

Tentatively, Rebekkah tried the juice, it was good, Jacob tucked into a croissant.

"We might as well eat before leaving," he mumbled, pouring himself some cereal, "we don't know when we shall eat again."

Rebekkah was hungry too but she also had an increasing sense of foreboding. She quickly climbed the ladder and popped her head out of the cabin door. Scanning the horizon, she could see clearly that there were no boats anywhere near their own, so, breathing a sigh of relief she joined Jacob at the table and ate.

"What should we do next? Do we wait and see what or who turns up? Or do we get back into the boat and row to shore?" Jacob was replete, having eaten his fill of cereal and croissant.

"We have no idea what we are getting into here," mused Rebekkah, "I think we should probably go and see if we can find our way back to Granny's." She yawned widely and suddenly felt very tired.

Jacob agreed reluctantly, it felt like the last few days had been for nothing. He too felt extremely tired, "You know, I am not sure I have got the strength to row all the way back to shore." He yawned too. His eyes were drooping.

Alarmed, Rebekkah got up and grabbed him by the arm. "Jacob, don't fall asleep, we need to go."

It was too late, his head dropped to the table. She was unable to move him, besides, she felt herself becoming drowsy too. Giving in, she lay down on the firm cushion that surrounded the table and drifted into a deep sleep where she dreamt of absolutely nothing.

14 IS ROBERT TELLING THE TRUTH?

Rebekkah was woken by the sound of a diesel engine getting closer. As she drifted between the world of sleep and wakefulness, she was aware that the engine had been cut and the yacht shifted slightly as if someone had climbed aboard.

She stretched over to Jacob and pushed him, "Jacob, someone has just climbed aboard," she whispered.

Jacob sat upright and rubbed his eyes. Rebekkah quietly stood up and opened a drawer in the cabin. It contained several sharp knives which she removed; she presented one to Jacob who nodded his approval. They both waited.

A pair of legs appeared at the top of the ladder and a man climbed down backwards into the cabin. He could not see the two children brandishing knives until he turned around. It was Robert!

"You!" shouted Jacob, contempt in his voice. He wagged the knife at the man. Rebekkah took a step back but held firmly onto her knife too. Robert looked from one to the other and smiled. He slowly raised his hands like a cowboy in a film.

"Hey, you two! It's me! What's going on? Put the knives down, I am on my own, no one else is here."

Jacob pushed past him and climbed the ladder. He poked his head out of the cabin entrance and scanned the deck. It was empty. He walked carefully around the boat looking over the side and into the water. Nothing, except the small dinghy Robert had arrived in. There was a smell of diesel on the air. He turned and climbed back into the cabin. Still holding the knife, he gestured to Robert to sit at the table, Robert did so.

"Right," said Jacob, "you have a lot of explaining to do. How come your mobile tracker lead us straight into the clutches of the Magpie?"

Robert looked Jacob in the eye and said, "I honestly don't know."

Jacob snorted derisively. "You expect us just to swallow that, do you? First, you disappear, then you reappear, then you say you are going to get help for Tarek who, shortly afterwards also disappears, we follow your tracker that you told me to place on my iPad, and when we get to where your phone is, you have disappeared. Now you suddenly appear again. You appear and disappear more times than a magician!"

Robert looked at Rebekkah, "Do you agree with Jacob?" he asked.

She shifted uncomfortably but continued to hold the knife steady. "Agree with what, exactly, Robert? You have been different recently."

Robert slowly nodded. "Yes, I can see why you might be suspicious. I can assure you I have been working hard to try and find Tarek and I have found him. But it's complicated."

Jacob remained unconvinced, "The phone tracker, Robert, what about the phone tracker? You told me to put it on my iPad and it led us into a trap."

"Tell me what happened." Robert seemed genuinely puzzled. He reached into his pocket and pulled out a mobile phone. "Here's my phone."

Jacob pulled out the mobile he had taken from the barn, it was identical.

Rebekkah interjected, "The mobile we picked up could have been planted after we had been drugged, Jacob. It doesn't have to be Robert's. We just assumed it was."

Robert looked down at his phone for a moment, "When did all this happen?"

"Two nights ago, in the middle of the night."

"That's interesting, because two nights ago, I woke to find my phone in a different place to where I thought I had left it. Normally I leave it plugged in. However, it was switched off and when I turned it on it had nearly run out of battery. I thought it odd at the time."

Jacob snorted derisively, "So, you are now suggesting someone crept into your room while you were asleep, took your phone, used it to lure us to the barn and then returned it to your place, all without you waking up!"

"Maybe!" exclaimed Robert. "I don't sleep with my phone

beside me. It's in the other room. After I had put it on charge, I looked at the Tracker and could see you had moved. I phoned your grandparents, and they said you had disappeared. So, I called the Eagle and I am guessing She rescued you and brought you here?"

Rebekkah and Jacob exchanged looks.

Robert watched them both carefully, "Look, you can believe me or not, but I do have news of Tarek and he needs us to work together to rescue him. He was captured by a prison guard at the IRC and taken to a boat which is anchored about a mile from here, just around the headland." He paused, "The dinghy engine is powerful, but noisy, so the plan is to use the engine to get us around the headland. We can tow the rowing boat behind us. Once we get close, we can row across to the boat and rescue Tarek."

"Just like that!" Jacob's lips curled sarcastically. "No doubt the Magpie will be waiting for us. Then he will have us all. How jolly."

"Ah," said Robert, "that's where you are wrong. The Magpie

has a meeting planned tonight with some traffickers. They won't be on the boat between the hours of ten and eleven."

"And how do you know this?"

A cunning look passed over Robert's face, "We have a spy in the trafficking ring."

"Really?" Jacob was incredulous. "Who are, 'we'?"

"The followers of the Eagle, we are everywhere." Robert seemed sincere.

Jacob was angry, he didn't believe Robert's story. He turned on Robert, "Why would your precious eagle bring us here and give us drugged food? As soon as we ate it, we fell asleep! That's the second time in two days we have been drugged. It's getting to be a habit."

"Ah, well, that was my fault, I asked the Eagle to bring you here, it's a safe boat and still within the Protection your grandparents have set up. I didn't want you to run off before I made it. I had a few things I needed to see to, so I put the sleeping powder in the orange juice. Sorry, but no harm done. And I'm here now."

"Great!" said Jacob sarcastically, "Superman is here now, we can all fly off to a new world and he can save the day!"

Rebekkah ignored Jacob. A thought had occurred to her. This would be a test of Robert's sincerity. "Can we go back to our grandparents' now?"

"Yes, of course, you can, you aren't prisoners." Robert seemed sincere, but he did have two suspicious teenagers brandishing a knife at him.

"And what will you do? Come with us?" Rebekkah was curious.

"I will phone your grandparents and they can collect you. I intend to rescue Tarek."

Rebekkah looked at him, "You mean you will go on your own?"

"Yes," Robert looked at her, "Rescuing Tarek is possible. It will be harder on my own, but I will manage it."

Rebekkah wasn't finished. "Why don't you phone the police and get them to rescue Tarek?"

Robert scratched his chin and sucked his teeth before answering.

"I am not sure whether we can trust the police or the coastguard. These boats have been coming and going for a while, my informant has suggested that there are a few police officers who are in on it. If I alert them then they will tell Magpie and we shall never get Tarek out."

The siblings looked at each other. Robert had answered all their questions, his answers seemed plausible, if a little scary. Jacob had no problem believing some of the authorities were in on the trafficking as well. Naturally cynical it matched his outlook on life. Rebekkah being by nature more trusting was genuinely shocked.

"Then who can we trust?" she gasped.

Robert shrugged, pulled a face, and said rather ruefully, "Me?"

Jacob still held his knife threateningly at Robert, "Hmm, we'll find out how true that is won't we? If we decide to come with you, what is the plan?"

"I will need to teach you some boat handling skills so you can manage the inflatable boat while I am rescuing Tarek. It would be most helpful if one of you were to come with me, while the other were to stay with the dinghy and keep her steady, so she doesn't float away. It's too deep to anchor her." Robert paused and waited.

"I think we should talk about this, Jacob, in private." Rebekkah gestured to Jacob that they should go up on deck to talk.

They moved as far away from Robert as they could.

"What do you think? Can we trust him?" Jacob's brow was furrowed. He was anxious.

"It's almost impossible to know what is true." Rebekkah was clearly conflicted. "Yet…"

"What?" Jacob looked at her intently.

Rebekkah continued, "We have come this far, and the Eagle seemed to want us to be here. What will we do if we go back to Granny's? Nothing will have changed. Tarek is still a prisoner, and we live in fear of every magpie that comes near us. And there's the prophecy."

Jacob was looking at her, "Not that again! You can believe in your destiny but if I go it's because I want to rescue Tarek."

He was blustering, but the result was the same, reluctantly the pair agreed. Time went quickly and despite a strong sense of foreboding they enjoyed learning to steer and to power the inflatable dinghy.

15 THE OTHER BOAT

At 21.30 they climbed into the dinghy and set off. The engine purred along with Robert at the helm. The sea was calm. Nevertheless, the boat dipped up and down, hitting the occasional wave. The subsequent spray caused them to gasp.

Under normal circumstances, Rebekkah would have really enjoyed this trip. She loved the taste of salt on her lips, and the feel of the breeze on her face, but her stomach was churning with anxiety. She stole a look at Jacob who sat bolt upright holding on to the black plastic handle on the side of the boat. His red hair twisted around his face and then whipped upright as the boat moved through the water. He looked tense and his mouth was set in a grim line. She could see that he was gritting his teeth. They had agreed earlier that Jacob would accompany Robert to get Tarek while Rebekkah looked after the dinghy.

The little rowing boat bounced along in the dinghy's wake, it gradually filled with water. She found herself wondering how they would get it out.

As they skirted the headland, a boat came into view, its lights twinkling in the dark. Robert immediately cut the engine and they drifted, gently bobbing on the surface of the water. Robert handed Rebekkah a paddle and instructed her to keep the boat in line with a point on the coast. He untied the rowing boat and handed the rope to Rebekkah while he and Jacob climbed in. Under the seat was a cupped shaped baler which he gave to Jacob while he untied the painter (rope). Touching his hand to his head in a kind of salute, he began to row in the direction of the boat. Rebekkah's eyes followed the two of them hoping for a final reassuring glance but Jacob did not look back at his sister instead he occupied himself with emptying the little boat.

Her eyes flicked between shore and vessel. Occasionally she dug the paddle into the water to adjust the position; she was glad of the distraction otherwise the wait would have been interminable. She could barely see them as they drew closer to the large vessel, she thought she could see two shadowy figures climbing up the side of the ship's stern and then they disappeared from her view.

Time passed slowly; she gazed up at the sky, observed the shape of the moon and squinted at the stars. It brought back comforting memories of sitting with Grandfer in the garden with a mug of hot chocolate, studying the night sky. Grandfer had been in the navy and said you could steer by the stars. She knew where the North Star was and looked for it now. Always to the left of the bowl of the Big Dipper. There it was! She checked her watch anxiously they had already been gone 30 minutes. She yawned and checked her watch again. Robert had instructed her to leave and get help if an hour passed. She was beginning to consider this as her only option when she saw a shape on the water, it looked like the rowing boat but how many people were in it? She leant forward, straining her eyes. Just at that point, the moon disappeared behind a cloud and the shape became even less distinct. However, she could easily make out the sound of oars splashing, and her heart rose with expectation.

"Jacob! Robert!" she called in a loud whisper. "Do you have Tarek?"

The boat approached and she could make out the shape of two people, but something was wrong, these were men not boys. Frantically she pulled the cord on the diesel engine: once, twice, three times. Damn it, she had flooded the engine. She began to paddle furiously. The rowing boat was close enough for her to see the faces of the men. One stowed his oars and reached out to her boat trying to catch the black handle. She raised her paddle over her head and slammed it down on the man's hand. He emitted a howl of pain and pulled his hand towards his mouth. She then used the paddle to push the rowing boat away. Turning to the engine she yanked the cord once more, and to her great relief it spluttered into life. She opened up the throttle, pushed the tiller away and roared away from the two men, spraying them with water as she did so. She did not look back but headed for shore as fast as the outboard would take her. She was making an immense racket, but she figured it no longer mattered. As she approached the shallows, she cut the engine and lifted the motor up so it would not catch on the seabed. The boat carried on under the momentum of the engine and finally came to rest close enough to the beach for her to get out and wade to the shore. She hauled the boat after her. Pulling it as high up the beach as she could manage, she reached into the boat, turned off the engine, took the key and safety cord and then ran for her life.

******

Robert and Jacob had reached the boat to hear the faint strains of music coming from the cabin below. Stealthily they had made their way along the deck and then hesitated outside the cabin door uncertain what to do next. There was no one on watch in the wheelhouse, so they let themselves in and listened at the top of the stairs for sounds of movement. They could hear voices and laughter and the sounds of cutlery banging on plates. Jacob was bewildered, he thought the ship would be empty. It hadn't occurred to him what they might do once on board. He hadn't thought about dealing with the remaining crew, he had no idea of the layout of the ship nor where Tarek might be being held. He turned to say these things to Robert when a familiar voice startled him.

"Would you like to join us?" Jacob jumped at the question and whirled round to see the Magpie standing in the doorway. They were trapped.

"You! You aren't supposed to be here! Robert said you had a meeting. Unless ..." Jacob rounded on Robert, "You lied. Again."

Robert looked down at his hands, his face was pink with shame. He said nothing.

"Ah young Jacob. I have missed you. It's been quite a challenge getting you here, I can tell you, but Robert has been very helpful."

"I knew we shouldn't have trusted you. You rat!" spluttered Jacob. "So, I suppose this is all a lie, Tarek isn't here, and you don't have a meeting. What now?"

The man cawed, "We shall continue our chat that we started last time we met, before we were rudely interrupted. By the way, Tarek is here. Robert got that bit right."

A thought occurred to Jacob, "Why here? Why did you need to bring me here? Why couldn't we talk in the barn? It was you who drugged us and left us there, wasn't it?"

"Yes, that's an interesting one, your grandparents put some sort of protection on an area 15 miles from their house. I was unable to move you outside of it without Robert's help. It was he who summoned that bird. Stupid raptor! It thought it was helping you to escape, but it was doing my will. Anyone with it was not bound by the protection."

"Is this true, Robert?" demanded Jacob, "Did you summon the Eagle so that She would lead us to the Magpie?" Jacob realised that he had personified the Eagle, and for a fleeting moment saw it as an act of rebellion against the horrible man who stood in their way.

Robert said nothing. The Magpie stepped forward and slapped Robert across the face. "Tell Jacob the truth Robert, tell him what a traitor you are."

Robert wiped a trickle of blood away from his mouth and looked with dislike at the Magpie. He turned to Jacob, "Look, Jacob, I am not proud of this and I'm sorry, I truly am."

"Get on with it!" snarled the Magpie.

Robert continued reluctantly, "When I was 17, I had been messing about with fire in the woods and it had got out of control. Many animals were killed. I was arrested and sent to a Young Offenders Institution. The Judge supported my plea that the fire was accidental, and that I had not intended to cause harm. But because some damage had occurred to crops and a barn had been destroyed, I was sentenced to a year in a prison for young offenders. This was a reasonably light sentence but every day that passed was like a life sentence for me. I can't bear being confined. In addition, I was badly bullied and very unhappy. When an opportunity came up to do some voluntary work at a local bird sanctuary, I jumped at the chance."

"Hurry up and get to the point," snapped the Magpie.

"I met the man you now call the Magpie at the Institution although I don't remember him well and had no strong memory of him."

He glared at the man who was leering at him with a scornful smile. "Some years later I got a job on the Beaulieu estate as a falconer. They gave me a cottage to live in, but one night someone broke in, attacked me, and killed my favourite bird. I was questioned and given a warning. Shortly after that an eagle I cared for was poisoned and I was blamed, they sacked me believing it was all too much of a coincidence; two birds dead in a short space of time. Following this I was in a very bad way and was living on the streets, when I met the Magpie again. He said he knew someone who might be able to help. Shortly after meeting him, you also turned up at the warehouse. That bit of the story, you know. I realised when he tried to kidnap you that I wanted nothing more to do with him."

The Magpie was looking intently at Jacob while Robert told his story. It felt like he was examining him, looking for signs of weakness. Jacob looked away; the memory of the warehouse still traumatised him.

Robert continued, "But the Magpie never forgets and angry at the way I rescued you and humiliated him, he pursued me. Last week someone broke into my house again, it was him. He told me it had been he who had broken into my cabin and killed my precious falcon and then," Robert paused, clearly overcome with emotion, "He threatened to kill all my falcons. I couldn't bear to let him do that. They are my life, I trained them all. They are like family to me." Robert was pleading with Jacob to understand.

"And?" Magpie was relentless.

"And so, I agreed to bring you and Rebekkah to him. Tarek was used as bait to get you here. I am sorry," Robert tailed off and stood, head bowed, dejected.

"There you are!" Magpie was triumphant. "You think your eagle is so strong, but we all have our dark side where it can't reach us. But I can!" He cackled.

Jacob stared at him, horrified. He felt completely trapped, there was nowhere to go. To whom could he turn? His only hope was Rebekkah, but what could she do against this man? Anger and desperation flooded his heart, he turned on Robert, "You, stupid, stupid idiot!" he hissed between clenched teeth, "I knew you couldn't be trusted. You coward! You traitor!"

Before Robert could answer, there was a commotion outside and two men hauled themselves into the boat, one was nursing his hand. The Magpie moved to greet them. They spoke in low tones but by moving to the door, Jacob could catch what they were saying. Their story made him grin. Good old Rebekkah! She had escaped and broken the guy's fingers into the bargain. The Magpie re-entered the room, "It appears your sister has escaped, but we will find her. Now, come with me."

16 THE CABIN

Robert and Jacob were thrown into a small cabin with a double bed and toilet. For a while, Jacob sat with his back to Robert, arms folded, anger spilling out of every part of him. Unable to contain his frustration, he turned on Robert, "What I can't understand is how you could be so weak. Do you really think he will protect your falcons? Whenever you refuse to do something from now on, he will use them against you. If I've learnt anything about the Magpie, he is a cheat and a liar."

Robert shifted uncomfortably on the bed. "He will keep his word. He has to, otherwise…"

"Otherwise, what? Basically, you abandoned Tarek, me and Rebekkah to the Magpie, just to save a bunch of birds."

As he talked, Jacob was becoming even more angry. Robert didn't know what to say. He could see the searing logic behind Jacob's anger. But he loved those birds like his children. He had nurtured each one from a chick, fed it, taught it to hunt, trained it. He was a loner and did not have many friends. It was true, he had grown fond of Rebekkah, but he found the Taylor

111

family as a whole to be selfish and self-obsessed. In comparison, the birds were fierce and loyal and a part of the natural world which he felt was being destroyed by the sort of materialism he saw in Jacob and his parents. The Eagle's world of the nest had been destroyed by these children, they seemed to care nothing for the animals and trees that formed part of the beautiful, natural world that he loved so much. He saw it now, he did not like Jacob, and he could not understand why the Eagle had invested so much time in him. He gingerly touched his mouth which had swollen up. He ran his tongue over the teeth that had been knocked out in a previous fight with the Magpie when he had defended Jacob so that he could order escape. A rage grew in him too. What did this egotistical young boy know of the world he inhabited and loved?

Then his thoughts turned to Tarek whom he genuinely felt sorry for. He wished there was some way he could help him.

The room was airless, the porthole was dripping with condensation presumably from their breath. Robert felt exhausted.

Suddenly, the engine sprang into life, it ticked over for a few minutes and then the boat began to move. To the heavy thrumming beat of the engine was added the slapping sound of water against the hull. Voices could be heard shouting. Robert strained his ears to hear more but they were muffled. As he peered through the porthole, he struggled to see anything, it was dark, and water slapped against the window making him jump. As the boat gathered speed, he began to feel claustrophobic and a bit sick because he wasn't used to being shut in.

After what seemed like an eternity, the door was thrown open and a man grabbed Jacob's arm and pulled him out of the room. Robert was left staring at the smooth walls of the cabin. To ease the panic that he was beginning to feel, he curled up on the bed and tried to sleep.

17 THE PRISONER'S DILEMMA

Jacob was marched through the main cabin and along a tight corridor lined with wood. There were doors at intervals, all closed. The boat lurched, and he put his hand out to steady himself. The man laughed at his discomfort, as he staggered forward. After a few more uncertain steps they turned a corner where they were confronted by a long, painted metal ladder which stretched down to the bowels of the boat. His guard indicated that Jacob should climb down it. Turning around as he had seen them do in the films, Jacob made his way backwards. He could see the feet of his companion above him, so he quickened his pace to prevent the man from standing on his fingers. Once on the next deck, his way lit by electric lights, Jacob headed away from the ladder to a room at the end of the corridor. As he entered, he saw the Magpie seated at a table.

He indicated to him that he was to sit down. Jacob obeyed. And waited.

The odious man looked at him and said nothing for what seemed like an eternity. Jacob shifted uneasily in his seat, he did not like silence. Anxiety swirled around his stomach, edged it's way upwards and into his lungs, his breathing began to quicken, and he felt dizzy.

At last, the man spoke, "What do you want, Jacob?"

"What do you mean?" Jacob was puzzled, he wasn't expecting this.

"Well, last time we met, I made you a very tempting offer, which was to work with me as my adopted son and to share my success. It is considerable. There is a lot of money to be gained working in my line of business."

"Trading people," sneered Jacob. But despite himself, his heart lifted a little with hope. Maybe he wasn't going to be killed.

"Well, that's one way of looking at it or, you could say, I am giving people a fresh start. They all want to come to England, I don't make them come. For many of them it's the only way they can be safe. And they know, in a few years once they have paid me off by working for me, they will get their English passport and go free. You could also say that I am in the liberation business."

He paused and cackled at his own joke.

"This boat is one of three that operates in the Channel. We have a deal with the local coastguard. They don't want to be fishing refugees out of the water or dealing with small, overcrowded rubber boats that are going to tip up in the waves and cause them lots of grief. No, my venture is safe, I only use solid boats, and the people I look after get food, clothes and somewhere to live when they land. I would say that I am on the side of the weak and homeless." He smirked.

Jacob looked at him properly, the resemblance between him and a bird was extraordinary; his eyes were a peculiar orange colour, they were widely set, almost on the side of his head, his nose was pointed like a beak, while his mouth turned down at the corners. He reminded Jacob of a medieval hooded executioner, he shuddered involuntarily.

"What do you want of me?" even as he asked the question, he felt uneasy.

"The same offer is on the table as before. If you work with me, you can pretend to be my son, to strengthen my cover. You know, father and son, travelling together, a good dad showing his son the world. Who would suspect us of doing anything that others might find…" he paused, grappling for the right words, "distasteful?"

He stood up and walked across to a 'fridge, he opened it, looked inside and brought out a chocolate milk, he placed it in front of Jacob and then continued, "You are also very smart, and I could use your help in navigation, electronics and communication."

Jacob stared at him his mind was working overtime. What about his parents, Rebekkah and school? Even as he thought these things, he realised how unattached he was to them all. He actually despised his parents, school was tedious and Rebekkah, well he had to admit to a sneaking feeling of something for his younger sister, but was it enough to tie him to his humdrum life? As he considered his options his thoughts returned to Rebekkah; while she was free there was hope. If he could somehow play for time this might give his sister, the chance to contact their grandparents and call the police.

Suddenly a phone rang, making Jacob jump. The Magpie

answered it, said, 'yes' a couple of times, and ended the conversation with, "Good!"

Placing the phone carefully on the table, he looked at Jacob. "They have found your sister. She is now on one of the other boats. One of my men is talking to her right now. Making her a similar offer to the one I have made you. If she agrees then I won't need you, I will use her instead."

Jacob's heart sank at the news of his sister's capture. If this was true then all hope of rescue had indeed gone, "She won't agree to work with you. Rebekkah is far too …" he hunted around in his brain for the words, "good and honest."

"And aren't you sick of that?" Magpie leaned in closer. Jacob recoiled at the stench of his breath.

"Wouldn't it be great to be free of her, telling you what's right, what's wrong? Going on about…" he paused and then spoke as if the words were strangling him, "that dreadful bird!" He looked at Jacob, "I know you don't believe in that thing, any more than I do. She's just a clever raptor."

He paused to give time for his words to take effect, "Oh, and you should know, I have put the same proposition to Tarek. I think he will be very easy to persuade as he hasn't got as much to lose as you. I have promised to reunite him with his family. He seemed very keen and I have left him to think about it. Just so you know, Jacob, I only require one adopted child. Too many and you would all become a liability."

Jacob bit his lip. He was very tempted. To save his life, it wasn't a bad offer. He was devastated by the news of Rebekkah's capture, he honestly did not think Rebekkah would give in. But Tarek? He was a different matter. He had little to live for and the offer of being reunited with his family might prove decisive. As doubt began to take root in his brain so his thoughts accelerated towards what might happen if Tarek got in first.

The Magpie looked at his watch and stood up. "Take some time Jacob, but not too long. If your sister or Tarek agree to work for me then we don't need you."

He left the room, locking the door behind him.

18 TAREK AND PETE

Tarek woke to the sound of a dull rumble, the bed he was lying on was throbbing gently. It took him a few moments to remember where he was. He stretched and rolled over taking in the white walls of the cabin. He preferred this boat to the centre in which he had been incarcerated. Pete, the man the others called Magpie, had been very nice to him. It was puzzling because when he had worked for Pete with the other refugees, they had not been particularly well treated. But ever since Pete had helped him escape from the Internment Centre, he had been really kind. He had got him his favourite Syrian foods and given him access to a tablet with games and some films downloaded. The Wi fi was disconnected of course although he had been promised a phone call with his family if he cooperated.

He folded his body into the prayer position and performed the Salat al-fajr, the first of five daily prayers. It calmed him. He sat with his back against the cabin wall and thought again about the events of the last few days.

After the visit of Rebekkah, Robert and Jacob, he had been

returned to his room. He had felt much more optimistic knowing his friends were going to speak to some official people about his case. When the time came for his afternoon exercise, he was escorted by the same guard who had been observing their conversation. Glad to be outside in the fresh air, Tarek had turned his face into the wind, enjoying its cool, fragrant breath on his cheeks. He had been irritated when instead of letting him linger, the guard took hold of his arm and lead him none too gently towards Reception saying that his friends had managed to get a lawyer for him to speak to and he had been instructed to escort him to their offices. It had seemed plausible at the time, although a bit quick.

Excited, he had walked happily with the guard, through the various security checks and out to a waiting van. It was only after they had started driving that he had a proper look at the man. There was something very familiar about him. He had seen him somewhere before. The guard looked at him while he was driving. He reached into the glove compartment and handed Tarek a box of dates. "It will make the journey pass more quickly, eat as many as you like."

Tarek loved dates; it reminded him of home. He popped one into his mouth, it tasted exquisite. He took another but began to feel drowsy.

He remembered little else of the journey. When he woke up, he found he was no longer in the van but outside, he could see the sky and there was a slopping noise that was familiar. He looked around him and realised he had been propped up against the seat of a dingy. Two men were with him, one was the guard from the Centre. In his drugged and sleepy state, it took him a few minutes to realise that the guard had removed his uniform and was sitting in a black beanie hat with a black and white jumper. He let out a cry of fear. "You! You, Pete!"

"That's right, Tarek," Pete spoke gently. "Don't worry, you are quite safe. I have rescued you from that dreadful place. I am taking you to my boat where we shall eat and chat."

Tarek struggled to sit up, the drug he had consumed while eating the dates was wearing off and he felt sick. The last time he had been on a dingy he had been absolutely terrified and very sick. He leant over the side and vomited into the water. Pete handed him a tissue.

"All the more room for supper," said Pete cheerily, "come on, we are here now, up you go!"

The boat bumped against the side of a larger boat which had a ladder for him to climb. Gingerly, he stepped out of the dingy and made his way up the ladder. Reaching the top, he grabbed the handrail and dragged himself onto the deck. Pete followed and took him by the arm leading him into the cabin and down the stairs.

Tarek had never seen such a vessel before, and he had wrinkled his nose at the smell of diesel and salt which assailed his senses. Pete indicated that he should sit and so he slid onto a stuffed, blue cushion and sat awkwardly, elbows on the table, chin in his hand to stop his teeth chattering. He didn't want Pete to see how afraid he was.

"Would you like a drink, Tarek?" asked Pete politely, he opened a fridge and pulled out a drink which Tarek sniffed suspiciously.

"No drugs in this one, Tarek, that was just to get you here, I want to talk to you now. Look I will drink it first." Pete drank half a glass and then pushed it over to Tarek, "Go on, taste it. It's *Jallab*, a fruit syrup made from carob, dates, grape molasses and rose water. Do you want some crushed ice in it or raisins?"

Tarek sipped it and then took several gulps.

"Is that good?" smiled Pete.

"Mm," Tarek quickly finished the drink and set his glass down. He felt better already.

"Would you like some humus, flat bread and souvlaki? I expect you are hungry, the food at that centre was pretty awful." Pete rang a bell on his desk and a man wearing a chef's hat appeared with a plate of food. Pete pushed the plate towards Tarek and then took a bit of souvlaki himself. "Don't worry, it's halal." He said, his mouth full.

Tarek tentatively took a bite, it was excellent. He ate hungrily.

Pete waved a piece of flat bread at him. "You know all this could be yours, all the time, if you agree to work for me."

Tarek stopped eating and slowly put the souvlaki down on his plate. He stared at Pete.

Pete carried on, "I know the last year has been really tough for you. I can't imagine how difficult it was to leave your country, your family and your friends and then to make that journey on your own. You must tell me the details some time. You are an extremely brave and resourceful young man. I could do with someone like you working with me. You know how refugees think. You can speak their language you can reassure them that I mean well. I will pay you well, I will help you to get your family here."

That was it. As soon as Pete said these words Tarek looked at him with hope. "You do that for me?"

"Sure," said Pete conversationally, "if you agree, I can arrange a phone call with your parents almost immediately."

Tarek's mind was racing. He could not connect this new Pete with the one who had held him prisoner at the cottage.

"May I speak with them, so I know it possible, what you plan?"

Pete drummed his fingers on the table, Tarek studied his face. He did not like what he saw, a man with orange eyes and a beak like nose. He looked cruel. He was cruel. The way he had

125

treated he and his fellow refugees was wrong. They had been kept cooped up in a small cottage, forced to work long hours on a fruit farm, without pay. Their passports were removed from them and they had no means of contacting the outside. Tarek was torn. He wanted desperately to speak to his family and to get them out of Syria. This was why he had come to the UK. On the other hand, he did not trust this man and Jacob and Rebekkah had also offered to help him. They didn't trust him either. As he thought of his friends, he made up his mind. "I no trust you," he said.

Pete smirked, "You don't have a lot of choice, my young friend. If you think Robert and co. are going to help you, then forget it. I have Jacob on another boat, and he has agreed to work with me. Rebekkah is on a different boat, and Robert is dead. They can't help you, I am your only hope, your saviour. No God will help you now." He was lying, but Magpie didn't care. It wouldn't be long before these things were true.

He slid out from under the table, *like a snake,* thought Tarek.

"Think about what I have said, I am going to talk to the others now."

He paused at the doorway. "Don't take too long thinking. I have another job coming up. Jacob and I are set to be on it. We could use you too, but once we are gone, the offer is closed." The cabin door slammed shut behind him as if to emphasise his final words.

Tarek had been taken back to his cabin where he slept fitfully. He dreamt of his parents; they were sitting amidst the bombed ruins of his home while vultures circled in the sky. It was a picture of desolation.

As he prayed that morning, he prayed for his family and asked for guidance. At the end of Salat, he knew what he had to do.

19 ROBERT AND THE SEA

As the minutes crept by and passed into hours, Robert became
increasingly claustrophobic. He was not used to being confined
in a small, airless space and he began to sweat. He tried to pray,
but he felt so bad about his betrayal of the Eagle and his young
friends that it made him feel worse. He was glad his birds were
safe, but he had a sense of foreboding about his own future. He
knew what sort of a man Magpie was; immoral, a shapeshifter, a
being without mercy, his actions always had an evil motive.
What he was unable to work out was why the Eagle had listened
to him and moved the children out of the Protection zone? Did
She want them all in the hands of the Magpie? Was there some
sort of weird plan which She was working out? Or, was She also
in the hands of the Magpie and doing his bidding without
realising it? The implications of that were profoundly scary.

He had always assumed She knew everything and could read his
mind. But lately he had had his doubts. If She was all knowing,
then She should have known that the Magpie would threaten his
falcons and also that he, Robert, would be unable to resist the

Magpie's threat. If She was all powerful, She should have been able to stop him from hurting them and if She truly loved him and his birds then She should have wanted to help. The conclusion he had arrived at was that she was not powerful enough. So, he had taken matters into his own hands and hidden them. Just in case.

He now felt he had done the right thing because the Eagle had seemed powerless to work out what was going on. Inexplicably She had gone along with the plan hatched by the Magpie; She had, without questioning him, rescued Jacob and Rebekkah from the barn, then She had willingly led them to the boat. Why? Didn't she know what he, Robert was about to do? The more he thought about it the more he felt he was losing his mind. He was in a rabbit hole digging deeper and deeper into a place of hopelessness where darkness reigned supreme and there was only desperation. The Eagle had not intervened to protect any of them from harm.

Tarek and Jacob had been captured again. He had succumbed to the Magpie and in the process betrayed two people he cared about. What was the point in carrying on? He was useless, everything he touched ultimately disappeared into ashes. Just like those poor animals who had been burnt to death because he, Robert had been careless. He could hardly bear to think about their terror, in his imagination he could smell their fear, even now he could hear their cries. He was tethered to his past. Jacob's dad was right, wherever there was trouble, he, Robert was a part of it. He was a bad lot.

In frustration, he hammered on the door of the cabin and yelled. He had nothing to lose.

After 5 minutes of banging, his hands hurt and his knuckles were sore and bleeding, ashamed, he fell onto his knees; exhausted, tearful and furious.

To his surprise, the door was opened and one of the minders walked in, grabbed him by his arm and shoved him out into the corridor. He marched him up the stairs and onto the deck.

Robert inhaled deeply. It was good to be out of that stuffy, cabin. It was a beautiful night, and a warm breeze ruffled his hair. He suddenly felt alive once again. He breathed deeply and turned to the minder who had his upper arm in a vice like grip, it was then that he noticed that the man had a piece of rope in his other hand. Another man, equally burly stood nearby, making escape impossible.

"On your knees, your back to me," said the man gruffly. Robert dropped to his knees, his heart in his mouth. The man seized his arms pulled them downwards and then tied his hands together. Kicking Robert in the side he indicated he should get up and walk to the back of the boat. Robert slowly got up and lurched slightly to one side with the movement of the vessel. The man gripped his arm again and urged him to move towards the stern. The vertical support which upheld the protective barrier to falling off the ship, was open, Robert looked with horror at the dark swirling waters beneath him and then turned to plead with the man. Wordlessly the other guy looped another rope around Robert's feet and pulled it tight. Robert pleaded with them both, but his captors were in no mood for mercy or pity instead the first man gave Robert an almighty shove and he fell off the back of the boat. Unable to protect himself with his hands, he twisted around so he dropped, feet first into the water. Gasping with shock, Robert gulped and took in a large mouthful of saltwater. Choking, he told himself to keep calm and to float. After what seemed like an eternity, he stopped sinking and began to rise to the surface. As his head popped out of the water, he took in a huge gulp of air before he began sinking again. The air in his lungs provided some buoyancy and he rose more quickly this time. Breaching the surface, he rolled onto his back, his hands underneath him and moved his feet up and down like a flipper. He lay like this for a while trying to breathe and to calm himself down. Gradually he stopped coughing and got his breath under control. Instinctively, he rolled onto his belly and brought his knees to his chest, then quickly stretched his legs out, whilst trying to keep his head above water. Bit by bit he began to make progress and the boat became more distant. When he tired, he rolled onto his back, rested, got his breathing back under control and then rolled over once again. It was exhausting. If death was this, he was going to fight it. Only moments before he had been ready to give up, now his survival instinct kicked in, he determined he was going to try and put things right. He found himself praying despite himself. Knees in, kick out, knees in, kick out and roll onto your back. He was in a rhythm. Gradually, his spirits lifted as he realised by some

132

good fortune, the tide had turned and was pushing him towards the beach. Little by little, metre by metre he was being pulled into the shore.

At last, he could feel waves taking hold of him and moving him forward with the surf. Relieved, he relaxed and rolled over onto his back. Water slapped gently at his face, but the friendly waves held him in their watery arms and pushed him towards the shore. Finally, a particularly muscular breaker propelled him forward and dropped him onto the sandy beach. As it withdrew it tried to suck him back into its foaming mouth, but he dug his elbows into the sand. As the water withdrew, he rolled over, lifted his head and shuffled awkwardly up the beach, snail like until, unable to move any further he collapsed into an exhausted heap. He closed his eyes and drifted into unconsciousness. He dreamt vivid dreams of fires billowing through fields of corn, driving out deer, rabbits, badgers and mice who, terrified by the flames hurtled into the sea. Then the scene changed, and he saw his precious falcons being pecked to death by a murder of magpies. In his dream he was running but not moving, unable to get help and to protect his children. He cried and shouted helplessly as the magpies cackled and cawed. Pete, the Magpie was orchestrating the massacre from the side lines, watching the deathly show and laughing at Robert's grief.

Then a voice, a familiar voice, broke into this terrible nightmare. He shouted to the voice to help him to save his babies. Crying out, he dragged himself back into consciousness and opened his eyes.

A figure was leaning over him shaking him vigorously and calling his name.

It was Rebekkah!

20 JACOB'S DECISION

Jacob was worried and terribly afraid. He was worried that if he left his decision too long, Tarek would beat him to it. He was afraid because he did not want to die. He felt agitated and ill at ease because he didn't know what to do. As he reigned in his thoughts, he tried to sort them out in a logical way, like a scientist would do. He paced the room, chewing his lip, muttering to himself. He could see the advantage to Pete of having Tarek as his adopted son. He understood the mind set of refugees, and asylum seekers. He would be able to empathise with them. They would trust him. Would Tarek give in to Pete's offer for the sake of his parents? Maybe, although Jacob struggled with this idea. He personally was not attached to his family. He would not have made a life changing decision to protect his parents.

As he turned things over in his mind, it occurred to him that Pete might be bluffing. Jacob's natural cynicism returned. How could he be sure that Tarek was even on the boat? How would he even know what Tarek was thinking? Maybe Pete was just

using Tarek in order to bulldoze him into making a decision.
After all, he, Jacob was clever and good with technology, and as
far as he was aware, Tarek was not. This filled him with even
greater uncertainty. He felt his whole life was in the balance.
His head was pounding.

And what of Rebekkah? How could he help her? Had she still
been at large he would have had some hope, but with Robert,
Tarek and Rebekkah all imprisoned what could he do? A
thought occurred to him that he might be able to negotiate with
Pete if he agreed to work with him. He might be able to
persuade him to find a role for his sister and friend. This idea
soothed him a little, but he knew Rebekkah would not give in.
And then what? Pete would not let them go as they knew too
much.

Jacob knew he was talking himself into the role Pete had
outlined for him. Deep down he was very uneasy about putting
his life into Pete's hands, but he didn't feel he had much choice.
Pete was ruthless enough to kill him and chuck him overboard if
he didn't agree. In a scenario like that he wanted to save
himself. The thought that he might be able to speak up on

behalf of Rebekkah and Tarek eased his conscience somewhat.
He did not dare think what would become of them if Pete
carried out his threat.

His thoughts turned to the Eagle, he had to admit that he was
bemused by the magical bird. But She seemed powerless in the
face of the Magpie. Why would he choose to follow a being that
had followers like his grandparents, Robert and Rebekkah? As
he thought of Robert his stomach flipped with uncontrollable
rage. Robert's treachery rose like a bile in his throat, choking
him with contempt. How could anyone choose to betray a
friend over a load of birds? Robert was weak, he had been weak
in the warehouse, uncontactable for most of their time in
Lincolnshire and now he had led them both into the dangerous
hands of the Magpie. He wouldn't have been faced with this
decision if it weren't for Robert. All the emotion of the last few
days poured out in anger over the unfortunate Robert. He
punched a cushion grunting with the force as his fist hit the
thing over and over again.

The door opened, making him jump. It was Pete. He stood in
the doorway looking at Jacob for a long time. His beady eyes

surveyed the room, ranged over Jacob's clenched fist, and focussed on his red face. It was as if he could read his mind. "Well?" he questioned.

"I want to know that my sister and Tarek are safe, can I see them?"

Pete glowered at him, "You don't make the demands Jacob. Decide. It's you or them. You are way out of time."

Jacob's shoulders sagged, he felt trapped, but he didn't have Tarek's courage nor Rebekkah's faith. Bereft, he slowly nodded his assent.

Pete moved into the room and roughly took hold of Jacob's arm, "Sensible choice, I knew you'd see sense. Now come with me and I will introduce you to the work you will be doing and the people you will be working with."

Jacob worked hard all that day, mastering the computer system of the boat. It hadn't quite gone as he expected and when he made a mistake, he found that there were consequences. He was deprived of food. By the time it got to 6 p.m., he was very hungry and thirsty.

He turned to the man who had been supervising him and asked if he might have something to eat. The man had looked at his watch and then shook his head. Jacob needed to finish the work and if he completed it to a satisfactory standard, then he could eat. Jacob had scowled at this. When he had asked who would 'be the judge of a satisfactory standard,' the man had cuffed him over the head and told him to stop being cheeky and just get on with it. Jacob had answered back along the lines of, "How dare you hit me, don't you know that I am Pete's adopted son?"

To which the man had laughed, cuffed him again and responded that sons were the better for a bit of discipline, Jacob should know that he regularly beat his own children if they didn't fall into line. The only thing that would please Pete would be a finished task.

By the time 20.00 hours came Jacob was extremely tired and fed up. He demanded to see Pete, refusing to do any more work until he appeared.

Eventually the man had gone, locking the door as he left. A few moments later he reappeared with Pete who had a thunderous look on his face.

"What's the matter?" he growled. "John here says you have been difficult. And I have just been dragged out of a very important meeting to come and deal with you."

"Difficult?" Jacob yelled, "I have worked all day and I am starving. This meathead won't feed me and every time I ask, he hits me. I can't think without food."

Pete glowered at Jacob, "He tells me you have made some mistakes, that's careless Jacob, we can't afford mistakes. Until you get things 100% right you will only have access to bread and water. John, give Jacob some bread and then send him to his cabin to think. Jacob, you had better be ready to work harder tomorrow as today has not been up to my standards."

Having delivered this bomb shell, Pete turned on his heels and walked away.

John grabbed Jacob by his ear and marched him through the ship to his cabin. Opening the door, he threw Jacob inside and slammed it shut. A few minutes later he returned with some bread and water. As he laid it down on the bed, Jacob asked him what had happened to Robert, Tarek and Rebekkah.

The man paused, looked at Jacob and said with a nasty smile, "All dead." With that, he slammed the door and left.

Jacob stared at his food. He was shocked. He had believed that somehow in deciding to work for Pete he might save his friend and sister. He had hoped he might be able to negotiate with the man. The full realisation of what he had done now hit him.

He felt immensely sad and completely alone. Pushing the plate away he began to cry, something he had not done for years. He had made a big mistake. Agreeing to work for Pete now felt like selling his soul to a devil. Although he did not believe in a devil, such a being, like God, was without provenance.

21 HUMAN CARGO

The next day was far worse. Jacob had slept fitfully and was woken early by 'Meathead.' He was told to get ready as he was going to accompany Pete on a boat trip. He was delivered to the upper deck and stood shivering in the cold morning air while the brute collected a life jacket for him.

"Put it on," said the man curtly.

Jacob struggled into the jacket. He looked around, wondering what he was about to do. He was also very hungry. He was pushed towards the side of the boat. Peering over the edge he could see a ladder leading to a waiting vessel. It was a small metal boat with seats for about 12 people. Gingerly, Jacob turned and climbed backwards down the ladder and jumped into the boat steadying himself with his hands as it tipped sideways.

"Move over," said a voice. He immediately slid his bottom along the seat to make room for a hooded figure. Two more people dropped into the boat beside him and finally Pete joined them.

Jacob desperately wanted to ask Pete about Rebekkah and Tarek. He felt depressed and sad, he struggled to believe that they were all gone. He held onto a shred of hope that Meathead was just being nasty. But Pete ignored Jacob, nodded to the man at the bow to cast off and then stared straight ahead as the boat's diesel engine coughed into life. The boat moved smoothly through the water.

"We shall be picking up some human cargo and bringing them back to the boat," he said to Jacob after some time had passed. "Do not speak to these people, just watch."

The boat purred through the water as Jacob strained his eyes trying to see where they were going. There was nothing on the horizon. Suddenly the walkie talkie crackled into life, making the lad jump. One of the other men sniggered at his discomfort.

"Magpie 2 to Magpie 1. Do you read me? Over."

Pete responded, "This is Magpie 1. Go ahead. Over."

"We have the cargo, we are at collection point Z. What's your ETA? Over."

Pete looked at his watch and raised an eyebrow questioningly at the man on the wheel.

"Thirty minutes," he mouthed.

"Come in Magpie 2. We are 30 minutes away. Over and Out."

Jacob did not know whether his stomach was churning because he was hungry or because he was nervous. Or perhaps a bit of both. He hung on to the side of the boat, leaning forward wondering what collection point Z was. The only objects on the horizon were a sailing boat, a ferry and a rocky island with a circular fort on it. As time went by it was clear they were making for the fort. As they approached, he could make out a ladder going up the rock face to a landing stage. Figures huddled together on the stage, while a tall woman stood next to them. She began to descend the ladder, hooked one arm through a step and turned to face them. The engine noise dwindled as the throttle was turned down and the boat slowed. The man at the bow gathered the looped painter rope in his hand and threw it at the woman who deftly caught it with her free hand and reclimbed the ladder. Once at the top she tied the painter off and threw a second rope to the men in the boat. They tied it through a loop on the back securing it fore and aft. Pete leapt bird like, onto the ladder and swiftly climbed to the top. He chatted with the woman for a while, gave her some money and then indicated to the little group that they were to descend the ladder into the boat. When they refused, he called to Jacob.

"Jacob, my son, come up here and meet our new guests." his voice was silky and insincere. Jacob looked at him suspiciously. "My words will be translated into Arabic, but I need you to smile and look reassuring so they know all will be well. You are young and they will be convinced by your presence that they are safe. If you reassure them then there will be a good breakfast for all when we get back to base."

Jacob stood up and shakily climbed the ladder. On reaching the top, he smiled at the people standing there. They looked terrified, with dark rings under their eyes. The thought of breakfast gave him an idea. He mimed eating and rubbed his tummy then pointed at the boat and smiled. Warming to the task, he pretended to sleep, stretched, yawned, and smiled again. The people turned to each other and began speaking in a

145

language he did not understand. Finally, they seemed to come to an agreement, and one by one climbed into the boat. Pete nodded in approval at Jacob as he also dropped into the boat.

"Good! Jacob, that was well done, you have earned your breakfast."

Turning to the woman he shouted to her to untie the ropes. She did so, and as the dinghy moved away, the man at the front pulled the line in and wrapped it around his arm looping it as he went. Finally, he stowed it in a flap of rubber by his feet.

Jacob stared at the people they had taken on board, there were four of them. They didn't have any luggage. They were all young men. It was difficult to tell how old they were. They could have been anything between 14 and 20. They said very little, one gripped the seat of the boat so hard that the knuckles on his hands went white. Another made an anxious noise every time the boat hit a wave. The third who seemed to be the leader, stared fixedly at the disappearing fort. The fourth seemed more alert and scanned the horizon over and over again.

Eventually their boat came into sight, Jacob had a chance to look at it from the outside, it had been dark when he and Robert had climbed on board, so he'd not has the chance to examine it closely. It looked like a large tug; it's hull was painted blue but badly scratched in places. It was old and tired. Perhaps it had seen a nobler working life at one time. The white wheelhouse stood at one end while the deck was edged with a metal fence that had a gate for access. He was glad to be back. He was looking forward to breakfast.

They all ate together although the refugees only ate the bread and drank the tea. They pulled the bacon from the roll and laid it on the side of their plates. Each piled three or four spoons of sugar into their mugs. *Mum would be horrified*, thought Jacob.

The man who Jacob secretly called Meathead cleared his plate and reached across one of the visitors, he rudely stabbed his fork into the bacon and shoved it whole into his mouth. Jacob stared at him wishing he could have more. Besides, it wouldn't be polite. Meathead grinned at him and indicated that he should do the same with the other plate. Jacob could hear his mother's voice in his head already, but he was still hungry, so he reached across the table and helped himself. Meathead gurgled his approval as he stuffed the remaining pieces into his mouth.

Shortly after breakfast the visitors were taken away and Jacob

was told he was to resume his lessons learning about the boat.

He was to be given tuition in navigation.

He found this interesting, it suited his logical brain, and he

enjoyed learning about angles and map work. It took his mind

off the shock of hearing that his sister was dead. Part of him

didn't believe it. He told himself they were all still alive,

Meathead was just trying to frighten him. This is how he coped,

and the day passed quickly.

He did not see the new people again until it got dark. He was

still working on the maps in the wheelhouse when he heard a

commotion. Pete appeared on deck with the two minders and

two of the refugees. Their hands were in cuffs, and they were

shouting in Arabic. He watched fascinated as they were pushed

towards the side of the boat. The minders held the men by their

upper arm. Pete threw the flexible ladder over the side of the

boat and climbed down first. The first of the minders removed

the cuffs and indicated that his prisoner should follow Pete.

When he refused, he was punched and kicked until he fell to the floor, his hands raised over his head in a plea for mercy. Terrified, the other prisoner obediently descended. The one who had been beaten staggered to his feet and followed his companion. Almost immediately Jacob could hear the sound of an engine and then it became fainter. He guessed they were going to shore, but what would become of the two men? He was shaken by what he had seen. He knew Pete was a violent man, he had beaten Robert to a pulp, but this was a reminder that the trade in human beings that he had got himself wrapped up in was a nasty business. He resolved to try and escape as soon as he could.

22 REBEKKAH AND ROBERT

Rebekkah was struggling to untie the rope that bound his ankles and wrists. Saturated with water, they had become swollen and the knots were tight. At last, she prised loose the knot tying his wrist and the bond slipped off. With relief, Robert stretched his fingers and rubbed his wrists. Once the feeling had come back, he set to work on the rope around his ankles. His fingers were strong, and he gradually worked the knot loose. Slowly he stood up, still a bit wobbly from his exertions in the sea. Rebekkah slipped her arm around his waist and they hobbled up the slope to the dinghy. He flopped down onto the beach, resting his back against the firm, smooth rubber.

"Water, Rebekkah, do you have any water?" He could hardly speak his throat was so dry. His mouth and face felt as though they were caked in salt. She rummaged in the bottom of the dinghy and pulled out a litre bottle. She undid the top and helped him sip the water. Gradually he revived. When he felt able to talk, he shared with her what had happened, he spoke haltingly and with shame. She said nothing as he told her the whole sorry tale of his treachery, the arson, his love of his falcons and fear for their lives. When he came to the bit where his hands were tied and he was thrown over the side, she looked grim, but did not interrupt until he was finished. She was a good listener he thought ruefully. Finally, she asked him what he thought might have happened to Jacob and Tarek.

"I really don't know. Jacob was taken away as I explained and I didn't see him again, Tarek, I didn't see at all. I suspect they are both on that boat or at least Jacob is on that boat and Tarek will be on another."

"Another? You mean the Magpie has more than one boat?" queried Rebekkah.

"Yes, he runs a trafficking ring. He uses boats in relay, so the coastguards don't get suspicious, although I suspect he has some sort of a deal with them, I can't see how he'd get away with what he does, otherwise."

Rebekkah sat still, deep in thought for a long time, Robert said nothing. Glad to get his story off his chest, he rested his head wearily against the boat and closed his eyes.

After a while, Rebekkah spoke, "We can't rescue Jacob and Tarek without help, I think it's time to call the Eagle."

Robert opened his eyes; he dreaded seeing the Eagle. After his betrayal he had no idea what she would say to him, but he knew Rebekkah was right. "Yes," he said wearily, "Yes, that would be the best thing. Can you call Her, I don't seem to have any energy left?"

She stood and called softly, "Dear Eagle, we really need your help, can you come?" She then sat next to Robert who had begun to shiver with cold and shock. "In the dinghy," his teeth were chattering, "there's a first aid box with a survival blanket, could you get it please, Rebekkah?"

She climbed inside the dinghy and found the box. Prising it open she removed the blanket and gave it to him.

"I am going to get these wet clothes off before I get hyperthermia." His teeth were chattering and his lips were turning blue.

Rebekkah nodded and moved away into the nearby dunes to give him some privacy. She nestled into the palm of a dune, sheltered from the breeze. Ever practical, she resolved to get Robert to move to this place as it was warmer and less exposed. She mused upon what he had told her. She was dreadfully disappointed in her friend, she had believed him to be strong and reliable, yet he had revealed serious flaws in his character. Her parents, though selfish and ambitious, never displayed weakness or treachery. They always put themselves first and in that respect were more predictable. What she struggled most with in Robert's story was the betrayal of her trust.

"Yes, that bit is hard, isn't it?" The voice made her jump, she turned and above her perched on the top of the dune was a beautiful golden eagle.

"Oh Eagle, is it really You?" She ran, slipping and sliding in the soft, sugary sand to embrace the majestic bird and buried her face in her soft wings.

After some time, the bird spoke once again, "Look at me, Rebekkah."

Rebekkah turned her head to meet her gaze; the colour of the eye was extraordinary. But it was what she saw deep within that truly startled her. A girl stood with a boy in a beautiful garden, the boy picked something from the tree and handed it to the girl who ate it greedily. The scene changed from one of peace and serenity to destruction and despair. Rebekkah hid her head. "Oh, Eagle I am so sorry for what we did, for what I did to your beautiful garden."

The Eagle looked at her, "Is it any different from what Robert has done?' She asked gently. "I have forgiven you, can you, forgive him?"

Rebekkah felt a surge of anger, "It's different, I trusted Robert and he betrayed that trust for a bunch of birds. Also, this is real and that was…" her voice trailed off, "not," she whispered quietly.

Eagle continued to gaze at Rebekkah. "You both made a mistake, with serious consequences. You made a selfish and greedy mistake; the consequence was that you unleashed the power of the Magpie and destroyed the harmony of my world. Robert made a mistake because he wanted to protect his falcons; the consequence has been the capture of Jacob and Tarek. Do you think his mistake was worse than yours?"

Rebekkah hung her head. "It's all a bit of a mess, isn't it? I don't know what to do. How do we help Jacob and Tarek?"

Eagle looked terribly sad and for one awful moment Rebekkah thought She was going to fly away.

"Don't worry Rebekkah, there is a way through this, but you must trust me. Now I need to speak with Robert." She sprang up into the air and flew out of sight.

23 JACOB PLANS THE PASSAGE

Jacob woke to the sound of his cabin door being unlocked. He was uneasy with the way he was locked in at night, and he intended to talk to Pete about it. It was Meathead.

"Up," he commanded. This was another thing Jacob intended to broach with Pete. He didn't like this man who seemed to have been attached to him. He felt like a prisoner rather than a son.

He was sleeping in his clothes, there had been no attempt to give him a new set. As Jacob made his way, he pondered that he was gathering quite a list of things to talk to Pete about. Not that he looked forward to talking with the man, he was terrified of Pete. But if Tarek and Rebekkah were really dead then he had more to bargain with. If they weren't then Pete would have to tell him. They entered the empty dining room, Jacob looked at the clock, it was 5.30 am. Meathead plonked a bowl of porridge in front of him and then sat down to eat opposite Jacob. His manners were poor, he slurped his way through his food. Although Jacob had often done this to annoy his parents, watching this man filled him with disgust. He tasted the porridge, it needed sweetening.

"Please can I have some sugar or maybe syrup?" He was polite hoping his humility would produce a favourable response. The man paused momentarily, a trickle of porridge running down his chin.

"No," and continued eating.

If Jacob hadn't been so hungry and uncertain of when he might eat again, he might have left the food but, wisely as it turned out, scraped his way through the lumpy glue-like cereal.

At the end, he plucked up courage and asked if he might see Pete.

"What for?" the man was grumpy, maybe he didn't like being up at the crack of dawn eating lumpy porridge with a teenager any more than Jacob liked being with him.

"Er, I have a few things I'd like to ask him." He wanted to add, "you thick twerp." But thought better of it. The man was strong and muscular, and he had seen the way he had beaten the refugee the previous day.

"Pete will want to know. He has asked not to be disturbed unless it's an emergency. He doesn't like being disturbed." He paused menacingly, "My advice is to wait for him to come to you. Anyway," he stood up, "we have work to do."

Jacob was tired, he had already worked two very long days. He decided to try with this man. "How about a shower and change of clothes?"

The guy looked at him, "You can shower in your lunch break. I'll get you some clothes. I don't want to work with a smelly kid."

Jacob bit back a retort about smelly meatheads but decided to quit while he was ahead. They walked to the wheelhouse where Jacob settled down to the chart table which had become his classroom for the last two days. The man plonked a course book on the table, "Do the exercises on pages 10 and 12. They are important, we are sailing tonight, and the boss wants you to plan the route. You had better get it right otherwise, no food. And no shower or a change of clothes."

"No pressure then," said Jacob sarcastically.

The man slapped him across the head, "Don't be cheeky."

Jacob felt his cheeks burning with anger, but he was learning to be careful with what he said. The memory of the night before when the refugees were forced violently to leave the boat was imprinted on his mind.

The guard settled down in a chair, at the second chart table. Jacob watched him. He was also planning a route. He figured that he was doing the same thing as Jacob and if they didn't match, Jacob would be punished. This seemed unfair as he had only been learning these things for a short while. Nonetheless, he enjoyed it and found it absorbing. By 11 o'clock he had completed the exercise and looked expectantly at his minder.

The man was still beavering away and ignored Jacob for a further 30 minutes. Finally, he swung his legs from under the table and looked at Jacob's work. He marked the exercises. Jacob had got them right. He nodded approvingly and then indicated that he should follow him. Jacob was returned to his cabin where a set of clothes had been placed on his bed.

"The shower?" enquired Jacob.

"Strip wash," the man pointed to the cramped bathroom, "you stand by the sink and wash. Hurry up, you have 10 minutes."

He then left, slamming the door shut and locking it as before.

Jacob quickly stripped and washed. The water was cold, and he sucked in his breath as he splashed water over himself. He had only just struggled into his new t shirt and trousers when Meathead came back.

"Bit barbaric, don't you think?" Jacob wasn't impressed.

The man mimicked him, "A bit barbaric! Aren't we the little posh kid? You'll get used to it. Come on, Pete wants to see you. At least you are clean." As he turned round and headed off Jacob stuck his tongue out at the retreating back. It was a small gesture of defiance but made him feel a bit better.

They walked down the familiar route; a wind was getting up and the boat was rolling more than it had previously. Jacob felt a bit nauseous; he didn't mind missing lunch.

They emerged into the wheelhouse. Pete was sitting at the chart table looking at his mornings' work. He looked up when they came in. "John tells me you did well this morning and can be trusted with the route for tonight. Don't let me down Jacob otherwise," he paused, "there will be consequences."

Jacob swallowed, "About that, don't you think it's a bit risky trusting it to me?"

Pete's face darkened into a scowl, he banged the table making Jacob jump, "Of course it's risky, you stupid boy, John here will be watching you like a hawk, and if you get anything wrong, you will be punished."

Jacob looked at Pete and wondered how he could have been so fooled by him, he decided to go for it, "Pete, I don't really understand how this works, I thought, I mean you said, I would be treated as your son."

Pete looked at him with disdain, "You have been. You are being given responsibility and put to work, that's what sons do, they are trained to follow their father's footsteps. Or didn't you do any of that in your namby-pamby, spoilt, soft, suburban four bedroomed house?"

Jacob shifted uncomfortably from one foot to another, this was not going well. "There are rules and rights, children are not expected to work 14 hours a day, deprived of food, nor are their bedroom doors locked at night!" As he spoke, he realised he was sinking, he was speaking to a man who cared little for human rights. Why should he have expected anything different. He felt hopeless, he was also afraid. What might this man do to him? He was trapped on this vessel with these people. He guessed that this is how the refugees must feel. A sudden feeling of remorse and empathy swept over him.

Pete looked at him, contempt oozed from every pore. "Just get this passage planned, and get it right, or else, you may join your friend Robert overboard."

"What about Rebekkah?" Jacob shouted after his retreating back. "What have you done with her and Tarek?"

The Magpie didn't even bother to turn around, "John has already told you."

24 THE DUNE

The Eagle spoke for a long time with Robert. When She landed next to him as he sat with his back to the inflatable, he had wanted to hide. He felt naked and exposed. He was deeply ashamed and lowered his head in anticipation of punishment. Would She peck him with that mighty sharp beak of Hers? Would She lambast him with words? Would She leave him for ever? He realised he would prefer anything other than to be abandoned. He deserved to be punished. Punishment would be just and once done, complete. For Her to leave him would mean the end of hope. He could not bear that. And so, he waited.

"Robert, look at me." She spoke gently.

Slowly he raised his eyes and looked, as Rebekkah had done, deep into the hazel eye. It was unblinking. It was the size of a human eye but much more extraordinary. Despite his anxiety he found himself contemplating its incredible characteristics. Eagles could see things magnified up to five times greater than a human being could see. She would be able to see a small rodent in the grass from high up in the sky. Her field of vision was an astounding 340 degrees unlike a human who was limited to 180. If only he had eagle eyes and could fly, how amazing would that be?

"Robert!" She said again. "Look! Deep into my eye," She emphasised the word, "into."

Obediently he did as she asked. He saw himself as a younger man, surrounded by birds of prey; he was feeding them, caressing them and caring for them. The scene then changed to the inside of a warehouse. It was as if he were looking through a set of binoculars that were wrongly set, the image was fuzzy, but gradually came into focus. He could see Jacob and the Magpie, Jacob was fleeing and he Robert, lay bleeding, badly beaten on the floor. The scene changed once again to a house in the Lincolnshire countryside. He was watching an eagle plummet towards a van. Blinded and disorientated the driver lost control of the van and knocked himself out. Robert saw himself run to the vehicle, pull the driver from his seat, and then drive the van away. The scene rolled forward to him pulling up outside a police station and releasing the precious cargo of human beings into safety. The images stopped. It was like watching a film of a series of events in his life. He was puzzled. Why did the Eagle show him these things?

"Well, Robert? What are you thinking?" She asked.

"Um, well, I am confused, I expected You to be angry with me, I was bracing myself for some sort of punishment. What does this mean?"

"It means Robert, that you have already punished yourself enough, you are deeply ashamed, and I don't need to make you feel worse. Instead, I have reminded you of the good and brave things you have already done. This is necessary because I have a job for you, it is risky, but I know that you are not afraid of danger. I understand that you betrayed Rebekkah and Jacob because you love your falcons. Some would say to sacrifice a human for the sake of a bird is wrong. I make no judgement. But I do offer you a chance to put things right."

"Really? You would trust me once again? How do you know I won't let you down?"

The Eagle blinked. "There is something else you need to get off your chest?" She waited.

He reddened recalling the doubts that had consumed him a few hours earlier.

"Why did You take the children to the yacht?" He voiced the question that had been nagging at him. "You knew it was a trap, you knew I what I was going to do. Why didn't You intervene and take them back to their grandparents where they were safe? Safe from me. Safe from Magpie. Unless…" Robert's questions tailed off.

"Unless…" the Eagle finished his sentence for him, "I didn't know, couldn't know and was just another tool of the Magpie. Is that what you wanted to say, Robert?"

"Yes, yes, I don't understand at all. I know I am weak and powerless, but I always thought You knew everything, and are in control of everything and… love me." The words came out as a whisper as if he feared by voicing his doubts the Eagle would be diminished.

She was silent for what seemed like an eternity, and when She spoke, Her voice seemed to come from a long way away. "You are to take Rebekkah to the boat where Jacob and Tarek are being held prisoner. Whatever happens to Me, whatever you see, you must not interfere, the boys will be handed over to you, you are to collect the boys and leave. Do you understand?"

Robert tried to protest. "Eagle it's dangerous to go to the boat, they will capture You as well, and then they will have all of us. How do you know they will hand over Jacob and Tarek? At least, let me go with you."

She growled at him, "You cannot come with me, I must do this one thing alone. Will you trust me or not?" The abruptness shocked him, She had never spoken to him in such an authoritative manner; he was scared and yet reassured, She seemed powerful again.

Slowly he nodded his assent.

"Good! Now, come, follow me, get dressed and we will go and see Rebekkah."

Robert struggled back into his wet trousers and followed the Eagle who led him up the dune. The sand clung to the bottom of his trousers as if they were covered in glue. He could see

167

Rebekkah sheltering in the bowl and made his way towards her. She was sitting holding her knees. She looked up as he approached.

"I am so sorry to have let you down, Rebekkah." Robert's remorse was clear. Had she not been confronted with her own frailty a few moments earlier she could not have found it in herself to forgive but now it was there, and she nodded slowly, and smiled.

The Eagle took charge, "Rebekkah, we need to get Robert back to the yacht where he can change, and you can both eat. It will be a long night."

Her mood was changing, Rebekkah noticed a heaviness descend. She paused and then said in the most terribly sad voice. "At midnight, you are to make your way to the Magpie's boat. Jacob and Tarek will be waiting for you."

"Where will you be, Eagle?" Rebekkah looked into the wise, timeless eyes that had taught her so much about herself and offered so much recent comfort.

"I will be there, don't worry." She flew off into the azure blue sky.

They headed back to the inflatable, whereupon Robert and Rebekkah dragged the small vessel into the sea. Robert held it steady while Rebekkah climbed in, the little inflatable wobbled like a jelly and for an absurd moment she thought of eating jelly and ice cream. Settling herself into the bench seat by the tiller, she fumbled in her pocket for the key and then inserted it into the lock whilst turning on the diesel ignition. Robert pushed off, sloshing through the water before finally jumping in, causing the boat to wobble most alarmingly until it settled down. Waiting while the boat drifted away from the shallows she pushed the motor down into the water, pulled several times on the cord and the engine sparked into life.

It took some time to get back to their boat by which time, Robert was shivering again. The yacht was well equipped, and while Rebekkah raided the cupboards for something to eat Robert was able to take a hot shower and change. As they ate their meal together, they puzzled over the Eagle's instructions, neither of them could make sense of what She had said.

25 THE LONGEST NIGHT

It was getting dark by the time they finished their meal. At 23.00 Robert and Rebekkah climbed once again into the inflatable. Robert had refilled it with diesel after they had finished dinner. There hadn't been much to do so he had passed the time checking and rechecking the engine. He put a few provisions in the boat including extra lifejackets and torches.

It was cloudy, and a mist was falling. As they set off, Rebekkah felt a rush of fear, she really had no idea what to expect. What happened if they were captured and imprisoned? The Eagle had simply said that Jacob and Tarek would be waiting for them. How did She know? More to the point, what was She going to do to ensure they would be freed? It didn't make sense. Why would Magpie go to all the trouble of capturing them only to let them go? She did not share her thoughts with Robert, she could not entirely trust him after the events of the last few days. They travelled in silence; Robert did not force the throttle as it was difficult to see at times and he was being careful. The boat seemed reluctant to move forwards as it churned through the waves, beating against the tide. *It would be much quicker coming back,* thought Rebekkah. *If they came back.*

After 45 minutes lights could be seen flashing to their left. Robert slowed to a crawl, looked at Rebekkah and headed towards the light. Waves slopped against the boat, and Robert had to zig zag through the water to stop them getting soaked. The silhouette of the slave ship loomed out of the mist and then the detail gradually came into view. The hull stood like a wall of red steel blocking their way. Portholes stared at them blankly. The wheelhouse glowed red against the dark starless sky. Rebekkah felt sick with anxiety. She wanted to ask Robert to turn back, she could see his hand was trembling too.

He looked at her and frowned. "Not sure what we do next, the Eagle wasn't very specific."

As soon as the words were out of his mouth a huge bird flew past them and landed on the top of the wheelhouse. There was a shriek of fear from within and a great deal of shouting. The bird just folded Her mighty wings neatly by Her side and silently waited. A familiar voice emitted a high-pitched cackle and shrieked, "The stupid bird has come! She has come! Grab Her and tie Her up!"

Rebekkah's hand flew to her mouth, she could barely stop herself calling out.

The Eagle raised Her head opened Her beak and spread Her wings. The men who had run out to grab Her stepped backwards, hovering, unsure what to do next. They were clearly in awe of Her.

"Release the boys!" She demanded. Her voice rang out clearly so all could hear. "That was the deal, Rebekkah and Robert are waiting. Do it now!"

Rebekkah's thoughts were in turmoil, what deal? What was the Eagle up to? Surely, She wasn't going to trade Herself for the lads. She waited anxiously, her heart in her mouth, she could barely breathe. Finally, the unmistakable figures of Jacob and Tarek appeared and stood silhouetted against the lights of the boat, next to the Magpie.

Robert edged forward and handed the painter to Rebekkah, the great red hull loomed above them.

One of the men stepped forward to the side of the big boat and looked down at them, he leered and spat at them. She froze, feeling small and vulnerable. *This was it*, she thought, *we are all going to end up captured by these people.* The Eagle shifted on the wheelhouse roof, lifted Her wings and made a sort of eery screeching noise, the men immediately covered their heads as if expecting an attack and withdrew.

Robert moved the boat closer, so it nestled against the side of the bigger vessel. He grabbed the rope ladder that was thrown down to them and signalled to Rebekkah to loop the painter through the ladder. He then held the small boat steady whilst Jacob made his way down the ladder. The rope shook and twisted as the lad moved until finally, he dropped heavily into the inflatable. It rocked alarmingly and Jacob clutched the small black handle before sitting down gingerly in the middle. He smiled at his sister and hugged her tight, "It's so good to see you, Rebekkah, I thought you were dead." Surprised, she hugged him back, noticing his cheeks were wet and salty with tears. Letting go, both turned and craned their necks upwards to watch Tarek's careful descent down the ladder. Finally, he let go and fell into a

heap at the bottom of the boat. He was crying with relief.
Rebekkah hugged him too. Robert indicated to Tarek where he
was to sit to keep the boat balanced, untied the rope and then
edged the boat backwards until they were clear. He turned up
the throttle and raced as fast as the little boat would go towards
the yacht which had become their temporary home.

"Stop! Oh stop, Robert!" Rebekkah was looking back at the
boat where Jacob and Tarek had been imprisoned. "Look at the
Eagle, we can't let them do this to Her."

Robert stopped the engine and they all turned and looked. The
boat was lit up like a beacon. The men had climbed on the roof
of the wheelhouse and thrown a net over the majestic raptor.
She just allowed them to do it. It was as if She had given up.
Why didn't She fly away?

"Bind Her!" shrieked the familiar voice of the Magpie.

The men pulled a mighty rope around her three times. She did
nothing to resist although one peck of that mighty beak could
have cut through the net with ease. A smaller rope was used to
tie Her feet together. Once done, they toppled Her over, so She

was lying on Her back. She said nothing at all while this humiliation was going on.

"Pull out her talons," shouted the Magpie with glee, he was bouncing from one foot to another cackling uncontrollably. "Pluck her wings! She will never fly again!"

There was a raucous shouting and jeering. Now that the Eagle was tied and bound the men seemed to find their courage. They opened bottles of beer and danced around her pouring drink all over her, spitting on her, pulling out her feathers and laughing hysterically.

Rebekkah felt as if her heart would break, this was terrible and horrific and totally unexpected. She kept expecting the Eagle to turn on Her captors and peck them. Surely, She had the power. She found herself willing the Eagle to retaliate, to use Her beak to peck those nasty men. But She seemed deliberately weak, as if She was choosing not to fight back. Overwhelmed with the unfairness and obscenity of it all, she began to cry, big silent tears rolled down her face and onto her chin. She turned to Robert and demanded he do something.

Jacob too looked white and drawn, he clenched his fists and shouted at Robert to go back to the boat. Tarek placed his hand on Robert's arm pleading with him to help the beautiful bird. Robert was battling with his own feelings. He knew the children were looking to him as the adult to rescue, and they would be angry with him. However, he had promised the Eagle that he would not interfere, and he knew he must obey Her in this matter. She had entrusted him with this one last task, and he must not let Her down again. His voice breaking, his face twisted with grief, he vomited the words, "I can't, the Eagle expressly forbade it."

Rebekkah screamed at him and tried to grab the tiller, but he held her hand so tightly she could not move. "The Eagle has made her choice we cannot unmake it for Her."

Rebekkah could hear the emotion in his voice, he was crying too. It made no sense. The Eagle was more powerful than the Magpie, why did She have to experience this humiliation?

She grabbed the oar and tried to hit Robert with it. "This is all your fault," she shouted, grief making her violent and careless of her own safety. He fended her off.

Jacob joined in, "Go on Robert, do something really brave for a change. Or are you just thinking of yourself again, you coward!"

Robert's face twisted in shame and grief, but he was resolute, "I know this seems to make no sense, and I have not behaved well, but now I must do the right thing, the last thing the Eagle said was whatever happened to Her, I was to look after you all. She made it very clear that I was not to interfere."

Tarek came to Robert's defence, "Jacob, Rebekkah stop! What are we going do? We are four against many bad men. I have seen them, they are cruel and strong, they not let you get away. Then what Eagle do for us no good, won't work, bad waste."

Rebekkah slowly put down the oar. She was sobbing. Jacob sat still like a stone, he was deeply shocked by what he had witnessed and somehow felt responsible. Even as he shouted at Robert, he knew he was partly responsible for what was happening on board that boat. He was unable to speak, instead he gripped the side of the boat so tightly that his knuckles gleamed white.

A triumphant scream caused them to all look with horror at the terrible scene unfolding on the boat. The Magpie had a knife and plunged it into the Eagle's chest. For a while time stood still, then he pulled it out, blood running down his arm. He lifted his eyes to the sky and cackled insanely. The madness on the boat increased. The men were dancing and shouting, laughing and cheering. It was like a picture of Hell. The Magpie finally turned towards the little boat bobbing on the waves and waved the knife triumphantly. "Where is your Eagle now, you feeble minded little rats? I am coming after you now! She can no longer protect you!" he shrieked manically, the sound was like a hundred magpies, murderous and insane.

"We should go," croaked Robert. "We are not safe here. It is over and there is nothing more we can do." He turned on the engine, the boat moved slowly through the mist and into the dark night. As the mist enfolded them the gruesome scene faded from view but not from their minds. They would never forget. Could never forget. Should never forget.

26 DAWN

On return to the yacht, they had sat in the cabin for a long time, unable to speak, completely traumatised by what they had seen. Finally, they had all gone to their separate cabins, behind each closed door each faced their demons.

Tarek thought of war and Syria, in his short life he had already seen many terrible things, but this was by far the worst. He longed for comfort and his parents' faces drifted in and out of his thoughts like wisps of smoke. How he longed to embrace them and to be held in his mother's arms once again. He thought regretfully about the Magpie's offer, would it have been different if he had accepted it? Instead of sitting on this boat, uncertain of his future, he could have been working for him now. He would have been on the winning side. Had he made a mistake when he told the Magpie he would never work for him? He had figured the price was too high. His parents would not have wanted him to sell his soul to a devil like creature like the Magpie; a slave trader; a cruel man, much like the torturers he had left in Syria. What was the point in leaving one hell and choosing to enter another? For a short time, he had had hope. His cabin door had opened, and he had been driven from his prison ship to another. His captor was silent, and he had thought he was going to die. Panicking, he had prayed, familiar prayers in Arabic, the Shahadah, eventually brought him peace. By the time he arrived at the big red tug he was ready. He had faced death before and he was not afraid. Pushed roughly by the man who had fetched him, he obediently climbed the ladder into the boat where he had been confronted by the Magpie. The man had seemed agitated and excitable, leering at Tarek and spitting at him, calling him a fool, and a weakling. Tarek braced himself for a violent assault, but none came. Then he had seen Jacob, standing silently at the other side of the walkway. He waved a hand in greeting for the first time in days; Jacob looked scared, white faced and tired, but raised a hand in return. They had been roughly pushed together and there they had stood waiting. He had felt nauseous as he surveyed the men gathered on deck. They had knives in their hands, he assumed they were going to die.

Everyone seemed to be waiting. They were silent for the most part and the air was filled with a violent menace. It felt unsafe. Tarek knew enough of traumatic situations to sense danger in the air. He dared not speak to Jacob, for fear of reprisal, so he stood quietly next to his friend and waited too.

Then the moon had emerged from behind a cloud and Tarek saw a bird silhouetted against its brightness. As he stared, he nudged Jacob. The men around him had seen it too and a slow murmur of anticipation went through the crew. He had felt hope rising in his chest as the bird descended onto the wheelhouse and he realised it was the Eagle. He and Jacob had exchanged furtive looks of relief. She was an awesome, majestic creature, and he found himself gazing in wonder at Her as She carefully folded Her wings and stood like a sentinel on top of the wheelhouse. Expectantly he stared up at Her, drinking in Her presence. Jacob was doing the same.

Then events had moved so fast he struggled to remember precisely what had happened. The awful Magpie had issued the instruction to tie Her up. Shocked, he had looked to see what She would do and was reassured when She had screeched at the men, and they had cowered in fear. Even Magpie seemed afraid.

181

Then those wonderful words which lead to them both being released. He had not believed it was possible, it was only when he hugged Rebekkah and fell into the bottom of the dinghy that he began to believe he might be safe.

As Robert opened the throttle on the outboard, he had allowed himself a small shred of optimism. Sitting with his friends watching the Eagles' torture and death had been the most terrible moment of his life. But unlike the others he understood that She had sacrificed Herself for them, which is why he had supported Robert. He was no coward but equally he understood sacrifice and could see that She had traded Her life for theirs.

The implications of Her great love at once overwhelmed him and filled him with grief. He thought his heart would burst. But now, on the boat with the others, those words of the Magpie ringing in his ears, he was crushed, his faith felt smashed, hope had been cruelly snatched away. He was absolutely devastated. Too numb to think, he had curled up into a little ball and rocked himself to sleep.

Robert too was exhausted. His ordeal in the water and the

events of the night left him bone tired. He did not want to think, he craved sleep so he would no longer be conscious and remember. He had done as the Eagle asked and it had been at great cost. He felt dreadful, but he would complete the task assigned to him and take the children to safety the next morning. Until then he could do no more. He was devastated. Overwhelmed by the responsibility She had placed on his shoulders, shocked by the horrible and unjust death he had just witnessed, he tossed and turned all night waiting for the dawn to come. Finally, just before sunrise, he slept.

Jacob too was drained. He had worked for days in a state of high anxiety unsure of what would happen next. He had become increasingly convinced that the Magpie would kill him, and there had been times when death would have been a welcome release. He was ashamed of the way he had given in and allowed himself to become a slave to a man he despised.

The events of the night spooled in front of his eyes like an endless film. Earlier that night he had been thrown into his cabin, where he lay exhausted on his bed. Having cried himself to sleep he had been roughly hauled awake by one of the henchmen and dragged upstairs to find himself standing next to

Tarek who was shivering with fear. Jacob's pleasure at finding

his friend still alive turned to ashes when he looked around to

see a number of men gathered on deck armed with knives.

Tarek's normally olive skin was tinged a sickly green as he stared

at the men who had imprisoned them both. He acknowledged

Jacob with a wave but there was a haunted look in his eyes, and

he could not smile. Both of them knew something terrible was

about to happen. Were they both to die? Was one to die while

the other watched? Neither boy knew what decision the other

had made with regard to the Magpie's offer. As knives glistened

in the glaring lights, Jacob had felt raw fear rise as bile in his

throat. He couldn't bear to look and lowered his gaze to a point

on the deck. He had distracted himself by focussing on a small

spider scurrying across the painted red metal, consequently, he

missed the first sight of the Eagle. Stirred from his reverie by

Tarek's nudge, he stared up at the moon, and watched with

disbelief as the astonishing bird prepared to land. Her claws

were extended while Her wings pointed heaven wards slowing

Her descent. She landed gracefully on the wheelhouse and

stared regally at the cowering men beneath Her. Jacob could

smell their fear and his heart lifted in hope. Tarek too was staring adoringly at the great bird, a new light in his eyes. He muttered something in Arabic. The Magpie hesitated momentarily, but it was enough for Jacob to see that he too was in awe of this creature. Then he shouted something which sent shockwaves through the young man's chest. He roused himself with a cackle and yelled at his men to grab Her and tie Her up. Then a most bizarre thing happened, the gigantic bird raised Her wings, lifted Her head and screeched, an ear-splitting sound which had Jacob covering his ears, so much so that he only partially heard what She said, but it sounded like, "deal and release the boys."

Rough hands had grabbed him and manhandled him to the side of the boat. Terrified, he had peered over the side expecting to be pushed into the swirling water, but to his great relief he could see the dinghy with Robert and Rebekkah bobbing uneasily in the water below him. Numb with fear, he had climbed down the ladder and fallen clumsily into the rescue boat. For the first time in his life, he had hugged Rebekkah with real joy, while tears flowed freely down his cheeks. Shortly afterwards, Tarek had tumbled into the boat and Robert had pulled away as fast as he could.

His relief at being rescued was short lived as it slowly dawned on him what the Eagle had done to save him. As the grisly scene had unfolded on the brightly lit stage in front of them, he had been stunned and unable to move or speak. It was only after Rebekkah had mounted her assault on Robert that his own emotions overwhelmed him, and he found himself shouting at the traitor. He had not understood or believed Robert's assertion that the Eagle had told him not to interfere. Now as he sat on the edge of his bed in the cabin, his brain seemed filled with sludge, he couldn't think clearly, his heart was in turmoil. He felt both agitated and exhausted. He longed for sleep but also for some relief from the pain that he was experiencing. Guilt and shame took it in turns to assault his frayed nerves, he could not shake off the sense that he was somehow responsible for most of what he had just seen. At one point he contemplated going upstairs and jumping into the sea. Death was what he deserved, and death would end the pain forever. Images reeled through his mind, snapshots in time mostly of

moments when he had behaved badly or selfishly. His cheeks
burned with shame as he recalled the moment when he killed the
little bird in the beautiful garden of the nest. He forced himself
to confront uncomfortable memories feeling somehow that to
relive them with a sense of having wronged forces of good
within the universe, was a form of sorrow. He had never asked
for forgiveness in his life, nor had he ever apologised without an
ulterior motive, but now he found himself kneeling and praying
for help. To whom or what he was praying he had no idea but
he just felt it was the right thing to do. As he did so, he felt an
overwhelming sense of peace, and at last, a few moments before
dawn broke, fell into a deep and dreamless sleep.

Rebekkah had not slept, she cried a great deal. She could not get
the dreadful images out of her mind. She reran them in her
head; sometimes she imagined flying through the air with a gun,
landing on the deck and shooting the Magpie and all his
disgusting crew. In one scene she grabbed the knife from the
Magpie in the nick of time and cut the Eagle free. They flew
away together with Rebekkah on her back like old times. In
another scenario she hit Robert over the head, drove the boat

back to where the Eagle was tied up, climbed the ladder and offered herself instead. Her heart seethed with anger; she was furious with Robert for leading them into this mess. Despite her conversation with the Eagle only a few hours ago, she found herself without compassion for the man she had called her friend. The death of her beautiful Eagle was like losing a parent. All her hopes and dreams had been tied up in that wonderful bird; she had depended on Her, prayed to Her, trusted in Her ability to help her wherever she was and at any time, now there was nowhere to turn, nothing to believe in, her heart was broken.

As she churned through her thoughts, the injustice of it all solidified into a single idea. As dawn broke, she knew what she was to do and stealthily made her way out of the cabin, up the stairs and into the little inflatable. She started the engine and headed back to where the Eagle had been murdered. She had one purpose in mind and that was to bring the body back for mourning and burial. She could not bear to think of her precious friend lying on that boat with those murderous thugs. She could at least give Her a decent send off.

The mist had cleared but the sky looked angry. Storm clouds were gathering and as often happened before a violent squall everything was ominously still and quiet. Grief, and ignorance of the dangers of the sea numbed her senses. Had Robert been around he would not have let her go. But he had fallen into a deep sleep just before dawn and had not heard her get up. Thunder rumbled around her like a bowling ball rolling towards unwitting skittles. She sat upright, hand gripping the tiller, determined, her face set, her hair streaming in the wind. She did not care at that moment in time whether she lived or died, she had one aim and one aim only, to bring back the Eagle's bloody and broken body.

She had not considered what she would do if confronted by the Magpie or any of his men. She hoped they would all be asleep, too drunk to notice a small girl lifting a beautiful bird off the deck.

The sky got darker and more furious. The colours were like a deep purple bruise and they shimmered above the red boat where her dear friend lay. The rising sun disappeared, and it became as black as night. Electricity flickered in the sky like a

189

light with a poor connection. It was terrifyingly beautiful. Despite her grief she found herself in awe of the majesty and power of nature.

Then it happened.

The biggest flash of forked lightning she had ever seen zig zagged from the sky and hit the boat. A sound like a gunshot and the boat was engulfed in flames. Rebekkah watched in horror, she could feel the heat from where she was sitting. Her grief, already overwhelming, had been suppressed by the thought that she might be able to rescue the Eagle's body. Now even that had been taken from her. She screamed in frustration at the heavens from whence the lightning came. It was all too cruel. She wanted to dive into the sea and never resurface. As she stood unsteadily in the little boat, hand clutching the tiller, she was startled by another magnificent flash of light which seemed to emerge from within the sea itself. Stunned, she fell back into the boat and gazed at the tug which was ablaze. There were human cries and shouts, and a few figures fell into the water, like demons plunging to hell.

Then she saw it.

Like a phoenix from the ashes, a huge, winged golden eagle flew out from the fire ball and headed off into the sun which had reappeared as the storm moved away. Then there was silence, a silence so profound, Rebekkah was almost afraid to breathe lest she disturbed the very fabric of the universe.

After what seemed like an eternity, Rebekkah blinked rapidly and rubbed her eyes several times in disbelief at the implications of what she had just seen. Could it be true? Was the Eagle still alive? Had she just seen the Eagle, her Eagle, fly away? She stared and stared until her eyes hurt hoping for another glimpse, but none came. Still unsure of what she had seen, she turned the boat around and headed back to the yacht.

She hardly had time to tie the boat off she was so excited. She tumbled down the ladder shouting at the top of her voice, "Jacob, Robert, Tarek, wake up! I have seen the Eagle. She's not dead, She's alive!"

They all came struggling out of their cabins, bewildered by her excitement. Rubbing the sleep from their eyes they listened, transfixed, to her account of the boat being struck by lightning and the Eagle flying from the explosion.

They didn't believe her, of course. She was overwrought. It was wishful thinking. They had all seen the Eagle die. The more they dismissed her story, the more frustrated she became until finally, they agreed to go and look for themselves. Climbing into the inflatable they headed back towards the place where the prison boat had been. As they navigated around the head land, they could smell smoke and they could see a coastguard circling the wreckage of what was left.

Cautiously, Robert headed towards the coastguard who shouted at him to stay where he was as there was a risk to life.

"What happened?" yelled Robert.

"A boat has been struck by lightning," came back the reply.

"Anyone hurt?" Robert could hardly wait.

"There were no survivors."

They looked at each other with undisguised delight.

"No survivors," repeated Jacob. "That means the Magpie and his cronies are gone."

"And the Eagle is alive."

They turned to look at Rebekkah with amazement.

Could that bit of the story also be true?

27 THE PROPHECY

Back at the yacht they sat around the table and Rebekkah narrated her story once more. Jacob was already trying to find rational and scientific explanations for what had happened.

"Look Rebekkah," he said in his most patronising and know-it-all voice, "boats get struck by lightning. It was a remote chance but not impossible. The storm was forecast, you were lucky to be there to see it. I wish you had woken me up to go with you, I would have liked to have seen it."

"Oh Jacob! You are so annoying! You have to find an explanation for everything. What about seeing the Eagle rise from the flames? Explain that to me."

Jacob was supercilious, "You were overwrought, you didn't sleep last night, you were vulnerable and saw what you wanted to see." If truth were told, Jacob wanted to believe his sister's story, the experience of the last few days had sucked out a great deal of his arrogance and self-centredness, but he could not allow himself to hope that something so incredible could have happened. Dead things don't come back to life.

"Jacob, this no good, you believe your sister, she good sister to you," interrupted Tarek, "Rebekkah say it real, I believe her. What you think Robert?"

Robert had a new light in his eyes and had listened intently to Rebekkah's story.

He looked at them all in turn, finally, he spoke. "I think it could be true," he began, "there is an ancient prophecy."

Jacob rolled his eyes and scoffed, "Not this again, not the one about the ones who entered the garden, the spoiled world and the superbeing who rescues everyone?"

Robert grinned, the first time he had shown any sign of joy for weeks. "Kind of, yes. It goes like this: *"The Golden One surrenders to, and rises from, the destruction caused by the ones who entered the garden. She demonstrates her love, not to punish, but to turn the heart of stone back to love."*"

Rebekkah was bouncing on the bench, "The Golden One is the Eagle, she surrendered to the Magpie, it says, *'she rises from the destruction.'* I saw it, with my own eyes. It's true. It's true!"

Jacob had that look, he wasn't convinced. "So, this prophecy suggests that we; Rebekkah and I, caused all the rubbish things that have happened to us and those around us. We caused Tarek to be enslaved, many refugees to be trafficked by the Magpie, the war in Syria, blah blah blah. All these things were caused by us when we ate a piece of chocolate from a tree in a magical surreal garden. That's just not rational. In fact, it's nuts."

Robert looked thoughtful, "Yes when you put it like that, it does sound ridiculous. Let's think about this in another way. What if what you did was symbolic? Representative of choices we all make as human beings which cause suffering for others and the planet itself? We don't always see the consequences of the decisions we make. If we did have that ability, we probably would not make them. My decision to start a fire for example, I bitterly regret that and will do for the rest of my life. Had I seen the consequences I never would have done anything to harm those creatures. What about you, Jacob, knowing what you now know, would you have eaten the chocolate from the tree?"

Jacob looked at him, he coloured slightly, "Maybe not," he said,

"I would not have killed the bird, that was guarding the chocolate, that was wrong. And I am sorry about that."

Rebekkah looked at him curiously, this was new, an admission that the nest was real and that he had done something terrible there. She decided to remain silent.

Robert nodded slowly, "Telling the truth is a good way to move things forward, Jacob. I do not believe that your actions caused what happened to Tarek, that would be totally out of proportion to what you did, but it shows what all of us are capable of when faced with temptation."

"I no do bad thing," protested Tarek who had been listening intently, "Pete, he said I work for him, I see parents again. I refuse."

"You are a good lad, Tarek, but did you never question whether you had made the right decision?" Robert persisted, "Not once?"

Tarek nodded slowly, "Last night after Eagle die, I think I make wrong choice."

"What do you mean, wrong choice?" Jacob looked at Tarek. "What did he offer you?"

"He say hurry, make decision, he choose you or me. I useful to him as I know how speak to refugees. He say he let me speak to parents, help them come here."

"What about you, Jacob?" asked Robert. "What did he offer you?"

Jacob looked shifty, "He said I could be his son and he would make me his business partner."

"So, you agreed." The disgust was evident in Rebekkah's voice.

"He said it was a choice between me and Tarek. He said that Robert was dead. I needed to buy time, I knew you were still free, and I assumed you would get help. It was only after I had agreed that I heard that you too had been captured and the same offer was being made to all three of us. He said he only wanted one of us, the rest would die."

Rebekkah looked at him with disdain, "You know I would never have agreed to work with that evil man. And neither would

Tarek. How could you Jacob? He was playing you off against Tarek to get you to give in."

Jacob looked at her, lack of sleep and deep remorse had created dark circles under his eyes which were already red rimmed with weeping. Under her gaze, his face crumpled, and he lowered his head onto his arms, his shoulders began to shake. Comfort came from a surprising source, Tarek laid a hand on his shoulder and pulled his friend to him, "Jacob, you brave friend, you were afraid, I know what it is to be afraid. That man is scary, you were alone. It very hard to be alone."

Jacob continued to sob. Tarek's kindness made it worse, he found himself unable to control the tears. "I didn't want to die." he sobbed, "I'm sorry, truly I am."

Rebekkah also placed her hand tentatively on her brother. She had never seen him like this before and it was a bit unnerving. She didn't know what to do. They never showed emotions in their house and here was Jacob in pieces.

After a while he lifted his head, and wiped his nose on his sleeve, "It was horrible, I wanted to set you all free, that was my plan, but, after a while, they told me you were all dead; they starved me, hit me, forced me to work long hours, I was always scared that they would kill me. When you came to rescue us, Tarek and I thought we were the ones to be killed, not the Eagle. The men were there, sharpening their knives…" Jacob's voice cracked with emotion. He was shaking uncontrollably.

Rebekkah held him close and patted him on the back. They were silent, lost in their own emotions.

A tapping began on the cabin roof, making them jump. It stopped, started, stopped and restarted. Cautiously Robert popped his head out of the galley hatch. He grinned and beckoned to the others to follow him upstairs. As they emerged onto the roof they were dazzled by a brilliant light, so bright they had to shield their eyes. It was like gazing into the sun. Instinctively all four dropped to their knees, but it was Rebekkah who spoke first. "Eagle is that you? Is it really you?"

The light buzzed and shimmered then dropped away revealing a beautiful Golden Eagle. She was larger than before, her colour radiant. As she moved, light dripped from her as if she were made of molten gold. She lifted her head and spread her wings showering them with droplets of water that flew over them anointing them with rainbows. And then, Rebekkah noticed that her talons were missing. "Oh Eagle, your poor feet, they are still torn. Those wicked men, I am so sorry, we couldn't help, I wanted to, but it was so dreadful I am so sorry." She could not finish her sentence she was sobbing with grief and pain.

"Come Rebekkah," the bird's voice was different somehow, deeper and softer.

She slowly stood up and walked into the light. The bird tenderly wiped her tears away with her feathery wing and then wrapped Rebekkah tightly and pulled her close.

Like a mother with her chick, thought Robert wistfully.

"You too Tarek, come."

Each was called by name and enfolded by the Eagle. Robert and Tarek went willingly, it was like being absorbed into the very universe itself, surrounded by stars and light. Everything else disappeared as they relaxed into the transformed Eagle's embrace. *This is what love feels like,* thought Tarek. All the tension

201

and fear of the last few months melted away until he felt completely whole again.

Finally, Jacob stood alone on the deck. His head bowed. Releasing her hold on the others the gorgeous creature stepped towards the lad, "Touch my feet, Jacob, feel where the nails once were, see and believe!"

Slowly, Jacob stretched out his hand and touched the foot she extended towards him, he caressed the scaley skin and stroked the holes where the talons had once been. There were four toes in all, three faced forward and one, the hallux backwards. He began to cry. Once he started, he could not stop. As his tears fell onto her wounds, they began to heal until all four were restored.

"Thank you, Jacob," she whispered, "Thank you."

"For what?" he sobbed, "I made a mess, I gave my soul to that devil, I got You caught, I didn't care for anyone other than myself, I was prepared to ditch my family, my friends, You; just to save my skin, it's me who should be thanking You."

The Eagle continued, "Not everything is as it seems Jacob, in the end love wins. And you too can enjoy its power. You have been brave, and you are not the boy you once were. You have made some poor choices it is true, but you did not shirk your destiny and unbeknown to you, other, deeper forces were at work which have allowed Me to release the power of love in a richer more extravagant way. Life is so much harder when you do not believe in the reality and power of Love. You are a part of my family now, Jacob, you need to live like it! Remember, I am with you wherever you go, just call me and I shall be closer than your breath."

With that, she sprang off the deck and shot into the sky like an arrow. A bright cloud enveloped Her, and She was gone.

28 TAREK

They sat gazing into the sky for a while, lost in their own thoughts. Eventually Robert broke the precious silence. "Wow!" he exclaimed.

"Truly amazing!" Rebekkah was lost for more words, to describe how she truly felt.

"That was incredible, I would never have believed it unless I had seen and experienced it for myself," mused Jacob.

"Oh Jacob, you are still so annoying," Rebekkah pushed him gently.

He pushed her back, and grinned.

Only Tarek was quiet, the others looked at him, waiting for a response. He looked at them all and asked, "What happens to me now?"

Robert responded, "We need to get in touch with your family so they know you are safe, I will speak to the immigration people about you coming to live with me while we sort out the paperwork. I found you a lawyer who will represent you and make an appeal on your behalf for asylum."

Tarek beamed with relief, "That would be wonderful, Robert, thank you!"

The others high fived him and they performed a little dance in the confined space of the deck.

"Good, that's settled then. We ought to tidy this boat up, stow everything away and head back to shore. Jacob and Rebekkah your grandparents will be worrying about you as well; they will be dying to know what happened."

"I hope Granny has made us chocolate cake because I am starving."

"Jacob, you are always thinking of your stomach! But I agree, some chocolate cake would be nice."

As they jumped into the inflatable for the last time, the youngsters looked up at the sky, hoping for another glimpse of the wonderful creature She had become, but She had disappeared. They would need to live in the memory of what had happened and remind one another of Her words. And maybe, one day, they might see Her again.

Robert picked up his phone and dialled the number of Jacob and Rebekkah's grandparents.

29 GRANNY AND GRANDFA

The grandparents had faced their own demons; fear and worry about what had happened to Jacob and Rebekkah had consumed them for the last few days. On waking up on that fateful morning when the children had disappeared, they had read Rebekkah's hastily written note and then phoned the police. The next call was to their son and daughter in law who were incandescent with rage. The things that their daughter in law had accused them of were unrepeatable. Sitting in their homely lounge after the phone call granny had wept. She was unable to convince herself that they had done the right thing to persuade their son to let them look after the children. She was inconsolable and could not shake off the feeling that somehow through their desire to protect their grandchildren they had contributed to their capture and possible death. She had raged in her prayers against the Eagle, telling Her that She should have taken better care of Her loved ones. But all that she had got back in return was silence. In the darkness and despair, she blamed herself for being so naïve. Her son was right, how could a bunch of CDs waving in the wind protect two precious children from an evil force such as the Magpie? Grandfa was also devastated, his way of dealing with doubt and grief was to dig in his garden. He also visited his friends from whom he had heard about the prophecy. He tried to encourage his wife with a hope that he did not really feel that this was all part of the prophecy and things would work out. The police had interviewed them, and tried to be reassuring, but even that was empty. The septuagenarians made cups of tea, sat glued to the phone and TV, hoping against hope for some good news.

When Robert phoned, they did not recognise the number. Fumbling for her glasses, Granny nearly missed the call, Grandfa reached across and pressed the green button. Robert's voice crackled through the airways, the reception was poor, and they could only hear a few words, but it was enough. The children were safe. As the phone went dead, they embraced one another with relief, but still didn't know enough to be totally reassured. Searching in her handbag Granny retrieved the number of the police officer who was dealing with their case. She passed on the news that Robert had phoned them, the police officer seemed concerned about that and asked lots of questions that she could not answer. Once she put the phone down, the penny dropped that Robert was a suspect. She shared this thought with her husband, who nodded slowly in agreement.

"I can see why they might think that he is a suspect, he has been involved with Jacob right from the beginning of this thing. I know Gerald doesn't trust him. But the police don't know him like we do, they are looking at the facts."

Granny nodded, "Yes, and the facts don't look good for our friend Robert. Let's see what he has to say for himself when we see him."

"What did he say he was going to do? Where is he?" Quizzed Grandfa.

"That's what the police asked me, I couldn't say, the line was so bad, I only heard the word boat and safe. I am sure he will phone again." She looked out of the window as a patrol car pulled up outside their house, "Here we go again!"

The two police officers removed their hats and sat themselves down at the kitchen table. Granny made them both a coffee and listened while the young man told them that they would stay with them in case Robert made contact again. They were able to trace the call using the cell phone provider and had discovered it came from a point near to a local headland. This fitted with what Robert had said about being on a boat.

The policeman continued, "We have reports of a large boat being hit by lightning in the early hours of this morning. The coastguard who attended the scene said that a small dinghy had appeared with three children on board and a man. They had asked them to move away, but they fit the description of your children and Robert. We are searching for them now."

"Oh, what a relief! It sounds like they are all alive, including Tarek." Granny and Grandfa held hands, both had tears in their eyes.

The police officer smiled, but he was tense, "I can understand your relief, but until we have them all I think we need to be careful about getting our hopes raised, this Robert character sounds at best irresponsible and at worse dangerous."

The old folk gripped hands still tighter, the officers exchanged looks and sipped their coffee. The officer's phone rang making them all jump, he listened, said a few non- committal things, then turned to them both and smiled. "We have them all, they are safe."

"Oh! Thank God!" they both cried, Grandfa did a little dance around his chair, while Granny clapped her hands.

"Can we see them?" she asked.

"Yes, their parents are on their way, but in their absence, it would be good if you would both help us as we listen to what they have to say. I am afraid you cannot question them, but we are happy for you to be present when they are interviewed."

And so that was how Granny and Grandfa heard the story. And what a story it was. The police were incredulous. A psychologist was brought in to assess the impact of the trauma on the youngsters, but all three stories were corroborated. The grandparents were astonished and full of wonder. It appeared as if the prophecy had been fulfilled by their grandchildren. From their point of view, Robert had only done as he had been asked by the Eagle and they felt for him in his struggles over his falcons. But it was to no avail, the law did not take account of the supernatural and Robert had been arrested because of his admission that he had led the children to the Magpie.

While awaiting trial he was not allowed to look after Tarek, so he passed on his notes to Jacob and Rebekkah's grandparents who insisted Tarek came to live with them while they helped him to pursue his claim for asylum. The authorities agreed on the basis that Tarek had already suffered enough trauma.

The Magpie and his henchman appeared to have been destroyed when the ship was struck by lightning, the bodies were not identifiable, and no one knew exactly how many had been on board. One mysterious aspect of the case however, was that the boat did not appear to have a life raft when the wreckage was investigated. This troubled Jacob for a while, but in the absence of any more attacks from pesky magpies, it felt like the menace had gone.

Jacob and Rebekkah returned home with their parents. They were both scarred and changed by their experiences. They were certainly much closer after their adventures, but the real transformation was in Jacob. His strong sense of fairness could not be appeased by his parents who were convinced Robert should pay the price for leading them into the clutches of the Magpie. No amount of arguing would persuade them otherwise. So, Jacob went to visit the vicar whom he had insulted and for whom Robert had worked. He told the man what had happened and why Robert was in custody, the vicar agreed to get the church to support him through the trial. Rebekkah did not ask too many questions, but she gathered from several things Jacob let slip that he had apologised to the vicar for his rudeness at the christening.

Robert was found guilty, but all three young people were present at his trial despite their parent's protests. The press were fascinated by the case and they became known as the eaglets. But as with most stories, once the trial was over, other things nudged their way into the news and gradually their celebrity status faded. Robert was given a suspended sentence with Community Service and had to agree to a tag. He was relieved the sentence wasn't in a prison and he was delighted because he could have his falcons back. He could only see Rebekkah, Tarek and Jacob with another adult present which they all found irritating, but their parents were adamant that this was the only way they could stay in touch.

Rebekkah went back to her old school, where thankfully Miss Cannon had left, and Miss Bates had returned. She and Freda became firm friends; Rebekkah found the girl had a quirky sense of humour and could talk on lots of interesting things. Freda seemed oblivious to Rebekkah's new fame and was genuinely interested in what Rebekkah had been through. After her experiences with the Eagle, Rebekkah found some of the conversation with her fellow pupils to be a bit tame, but she liked Freda. Together they went canoeing and Rebekkah continued with her fund raising for human trafficking charities.

Jacob returned to his school where he made a new start and by the end of the year was awarded student of the year for his IT skills which he had used to help a local charity set up a web site. He continued his interest in navigation and joined the school sailing club. He made friends and was happy for the first time in his life. Both he and Rebekkah began attending church; much to the disgust of their father.

Gerald and Susan continued to pursue their careers oblivious to the change in their offspring. Instead, the youngsters had found a community of people at church who cared about them and took an interest in them.

Tarek was awarded his asylum claim and was able to reconnect with his family in Syria, although the news was depressing as the war continued to make food and medical supplies difficult to get hold of. The publicity of the trial had helped him a great deal. Responding to his story, some kind people had raised money for him and his family. He determined to make the most of the sacrifice they had made to send him to England and enrolled at a college local to Granny and Grandfa. He was soon excelling in his studies.

The friends met frequently and often talked of the Eagle. The wonder and pain of what they had seen and experienced could only really be shared and understood by the three of them, it had created a bond of true friendship that was impossible to break.

Discussion questions to get you thinking about philosophy of religion and theology.

This book can be read in different ways. You can take it at face value - a fast-moving adventure story about two children and the way in which they are caught up in a battle between two creatures: the Eagle and the Magpie.

Or, you can also read it for hidden meanings. By this I mean the books are an allegory for the spiritual journey that takes place in all human beings as they seek to connect with God. In a loose sense the books trace the fall from that relationship, as shown by the behaviour of Jacob and Rebekkah in the nest; the battle for hearts and minds between the Eagle and the Magpie; this is most clearly seen in Jacob, to the mending of that relationship by the Eagle's sacrifice. More specifically:

Book 1 explores the nature of God and miracles.

Book 2 explores the nature of suffering and evil.

Book 3 explores forgiveness and sacrificial love.

This is a bit like the way we can read a Holy Book. We can take it at face value and read it literally or we can see it as literature; containing stories with meaning, having much to say about spiritual truth, the nature of human beings and the nature of God. All Holy Books need interpretating otherwise we miss the richness of their stories.

Book 1: What is God like?

1. Draw a picture of what comes to mind when you think of God. Or shout out some words which come to mind when you think of God.

In this book, the Eagle represents God, and the Magpie represents an evil power.

3. What do you not like about representing God in this way?

4. What's good about it?

The nest – a garden of Eden? Chapter 8

This is a rewrite of an ancient story. Some would say that the story as it was first written in Genesis in The Bible should not be rewritten. It should be read as fact and not changed or interpreted in any way. These people are called fundamentalists. They tend to believe that what is written in the Bible is literal truth or factually correct.

Theological interpretation

The story of Adam and Eve in the Garden of Eden is present in the Holy books of all three Abrahamic religions. These are: The Torah, The Bible and The Quran. For each religion it is very important in attempting to explain where evil and suffering came from. For Christian literalists the moment when Adam and Eve disobey God's command not to eat from the Tree of Knowledge of Good and Evil is called the Fall because death enters the world.

Not all religious people take the story as fact some would say it is an allegory, myth or a parable. They would say that all these forms of writing are helpful devices to explain spiritual truths and beliefs. Sometimes these believers are called non-traditional or liberal.

Theological interpretation of texts relating to the temptation of Adam and Eve in The Garden of Eden.

1. It might be helpful to read the original story in The Bible: **Genesis Chapter 3.** You can also read it in the **Quran: Surah 20 Taha, Ayat 116-128 and The Torah: Genesis: Chapter 3**

The Fall in Christian theology.

A very important and influential theologian called St Augustine (AD 354 – 430) said that God created a perfect world with temptation in it because he wanted to give human beings a choice as to whether they would worship Him or not. From the moment of their Fall evil entered the world including death, suffering and pain.

2. How do you think he got this idea from the story of Adam and Eve?

3. If you write, '*The Fall of Man in Christianity, Judaism and Islam*' into a search engine, Wikipedia will give you a brief summary of how each religion interprets this story.

cy4. How are the interpretations different?

5. What do you think?

6. What difference would each interpretation make to the way each believer would practice their faith?

Miracles

In Chapter 2, 'The RE lesson', Jacob challenges his teacher about the nature of miracles and why he cannot believe in them.

In Chapter 5 about the christening, Jacob challenges the vicar about his beliefs and says he is stupid to believe in things which cannot be proved scientifically.

In chapter 12 which takes place in the derelict factory, Robert heals Jacob's broken foot using some cream he has developed to mend bird's wings. This is confirmed by the police psychologist.

1. What do you think about miracles? Do you agree with Jacob?

An 18th century theologian philosopher called David Hume described a miracle as an event that was 'beyond the laws of nature.'

2. If the healing of Jacob's foot can be explained scientifically does it cease to be a miracle?

Book 2 The battle between good and evil

In this book, the battle between the Eagle and the Magpie becomes obvious. The Magpie is running a human trafficking

219

organisation and tries to get Jacob to join him.

The children wonder, is the Eagle powerful? Can she intervene? Does she answer prayer?

The Eagle seems powerless to help until the very end when she attacks the van being driven by one of the Magpie's helpers.

Prayer

Some theists believe that God intervenes directly in their lives in answer to prayer and quite literally 'delivers them from temptation' as set out in the Lord's Prayer. Other theists might believe that God intervenes in a less direct way, perhaps in a dream, or through another human being.

1. Can you identify an occasion when the Eagle helps the children in response to their prayers?

2. What do you think prayer is?

3. Does God answer prayers in your view?

Do we learn through suffering?

Jacob struggles with his conscience as he faces the consequences of his greed when he meets the Eagle in his dream. She says he is learning and growing through his challenges.

This idea is called 'The Vale of Soul making' and is linked to another philosopher called Irenaeus (AD 140 – 203) who said that God created an imperfect world on purpose with challenges in it because he wanted us to grow up as human beings. So,

Iraneus does not accept that the Fall led to human punishment and death. These things already existed.

1. Do you think the children grow up in this book?

2. What do you think of Irenaeus' theory?

3. *You might want to compare it with St Augustine who believed God created a perfect world. Augustine argues that The Fall spoilt God's perfect world and Jesus, the perfect human being had to come to rescue it. By being resurrected He overcame death.*

Which theory fits more with science?

The nature of evil

Evil can be described in this book as the wicked things done by the Magpie and his attempts to drag Jacob away from following the Eagle. What the Magpie does causes great suffering.

St Augustine described evil as an absence of good.

7. Do you agree or is there more to evil than this?

Augustine also believed in a being called Satan who was a fallen angel. He sees the Devil and God as being in a battle for human souls. Many theists still believe this is the case.

8. Do you see this battle for the children's souls taking place in the books?

9. What do you think about this idea that the Devil and God are in a battle for human obedience?

Book 3 The Atonement

Atonement refers to the forgiving or pardoning of sin (human selfishness) through the suffering, death and resurrection of Jesus. There are different theories put forward by theologians about this.

Here are a few:

1. **The Ransom Theory** *was put forward by Origen in the third century and argues that when Jesus died on the cross he was paying a ransom to the Devil for the lives of all human beings. Basically, Adam and Eve released the power of sin, suffering and evil by their choice in the Garden of Eden. As a result the Devil became more powerful due to their decision. Humanity had made its choice and humans chose not to obey God. Justice required that another human being sacrifice himself to the devil to pay him off. The Devil did not realise that the power of sacrificial love would be so powerful that Jesus would be able to rise from death and take all human beings with him to heaven.*

2. **The Christus Victor theory** *was believed by the Christian church until the 12th century. In this theory, Jesus Christ died in order to defeat the powers of evil (such as sin, death, and the devil) in order to free mankind from their bondage. This is related to the Ransom view with the difference being that there is no payment to the devil or to God. Within the Christus*

Victor framework, the cross did not pay off anyone but defeated evil thereby setting the human race free if it wanted to be.

3. **The Satisfaction Theory** *this was put forward by St Anselm in the 12th century. He was bothered by the Ransom theory because in his mind God owes the Devil nothing. Instead he believed human beings stole justice from God in the Garden of Eden and therefore human beings had to pay God back for what they stole. None could be found who was worthy to do this and so Jesus, the sinless one, had to die to appease God.*

4. **Penal Substitution Theory** *this was a development of the satisfaction theory and was developed by the protestant reformers during the 16th century, namely Calvin and Luther. They argued that not only did God require justice but he also required punishment. A human needed to be punished for the first act of disobedience in the Garden and then all subsequent acts of disobedience. Jesus therefore took the punishment that every human deserved and so the wrath of God was satisfied.*

5. **The Moral Influence Theory** *was an idea developed by St Abelard (AD 1079 – 1142). Abelard focused on changing man's perception of God as being offended, harsh, and judgmental towards the human race, to being loving, kind, forgiving and merciful. According to Abelard, "Jesus died as the*

demonstration of God's love, a demonstration which can change the hearts and minds of the sinners, turning them back to God." In this way, the Moral Influence theory emphasizes Jesus Christ as our teacher, our example, our founder and leader. It says that a true Christian will follow in His example and seek to be forgiving and selfless. In this theory there is nothing magical or supernatural about Jesus' death on the cross.

There are other theories too but there's enough here to make you think.

1.When the Eagle gives her life for Jacob and Tarek, which of the theories do you think it is similar to?

2.Might her sacrificial act demonstrate a mixture of theories?

3.What does the fact that there are different theories written over time suggest about theological ideas?

4.What impact does the Eagle's sacrifice have on Robert, Jacob, Rebekkah and Tarek?

5.Do you think the main characters deserve to be forgiven in the end for what they had done? Why?

6.Do human beings deserve forgiveness from God if such a being exists?

7.Do some research on The Atonement and Islam.
a/What would a traditional Muslim think about

representing The Eagle as God?

b/What would a traditional Muslim think about The Atonement?

The Eagle and The Magpie

ABOUT THE AUTHOR

Vicki is a retired teacher and lives in Wokingham, Berkshire with her husband Allan. She has two daughters and four grandchildren. Her passion is getting children and adults to engage with the big questions of life in a fun and accessible way and she believes that stories are a great medium to do this. Latterly she taught Ethics and Philosophy of Religion at one of Britain's top independent schools where she also served as School Chaplain. Her mantra was that she sought not so much to tell young people what to think but to get them to think. Her books are designed to do just that. Happy thinking!

The Eagle and The Magpie

Printed in Great Britain
by Amazon

24594789R00327